Romancing the Bride

ALSO BY MELISSA JAGEARS

UNEXPECTED BRIDES

Love by the Letter: A Novella

A Bride for Keeps

A Bride in Store

A Bride at Last

Blinded by Love: A Novella

TEAVILLE MORAL SOCIETY

Engaging the Competition: A Novella

A Heart Most Certain

A Love So True

Tied and True: A Novella

A Chance at Forever

NON-FICTION

Strengthen Your Fiction by Understanding Weasel Words

ROMANCING THE BRIDE

MELISSA JAGEARS

UTMOST
PUBLISHING
www.utmostpublishing.com

To Lynn and Harrison, the two I had to leave behind

Momma misses you

CHAPTER ONE

Wyoming Territory ~ Spring 1884

Annie Gephart pressed her lips together to keep from begging Tom Passey—the greasiest, most foul-mouthed cowpuncher she'd ever met—to stay on.

"I'll take my wages now." Tom held out his filthy palm. His pristine sombrero contrasted with his scraggly mustache, tobacco-stained teeth, shabby woolies, and worn boots.

She'd rather cuddle up with a rattlesnake than keep this man inside her cabin any longer, but she sorely needed him to stay.

She crossed over to the roll-top desk and opened the upper drawer. There was just enough money to satisfy his demands, but she hadn't intended to pay him until he sold some of her beeves in Cheyenne. She turned to Tom, who couldn't be taller than five-foot-two, and looked down at him. "I'll give you an extra five percent if you stay until you drive the cattle to market."

"No, I'll take what you owe me now." He spit on her well-scrubbed puncheon floor.

She couldn't keep from staring at the dark spittle and clenching her fists. "But why?"

He rolled his chew from one side of his jowl to the other. "I have my business, and you have yours. Besides, you don't make for the best boss, being a citified woman." He tilted his head. "Do you even know how many head I ought to sell in Cheyenne? How many to hold back to strengthen your herd?"

Though they both knew the answers, Annie only raised her chin farther. "Are you certain you want your wages now?"

"Unless you can give me a sweeter deal than what I've been offered."

"What percentage do you want?"

"Not a percentage. I've been promised better wages, with a boss man who knows what he's doing. And when the boss man makes better money, I make better money." He shrugged. "But if you want me to stay, the deed to the ranch would be enough."

She narrowed her eyes at him. "I'm not selling."

He cocked his hip. "Oh, you don't need to sell, darlin'." He gave her a look that made her breath clog in her chest. "I'll take you too."

Annie whirled around and grabbed the stack of bills from the drawer. "Seems you've made my decision easy, Mr. Passey." She counted out his wages.

"Suit yourself." Tom reached for the money, but instead, cupped her fingers and caressed her palm with his thumb.

A slimy shiver bored through her fingers, crept up her arm, and skittered down her spine.

How dare he?

She shoved the cash into his hand and stepped out of his reach.

He folded the bills and eyed her for several long seconds.

Hugging her arms across her thin chest, she returned the glare.

He shrugged and strutted out the front door, letting it slam behind him.

His sweaty stench lingered, so she reopened the door and

leaned against it, letting the cool spring breeze waft in to expel every trace of him.

Tom mounted his black mare, doffed his hat, and rode past her children busy in the nearby pasture.

Every shred of hope disappeared with him, tangled up in his knowledge and experience—the only worthy things the man possessed.

Spencer's exuberant holler sounded at the pasture's edge when his thrown lariat ringed a cow skull mounted on a barrel, and Annie's heart lightened a fraction. At least she wasn't completely alone. Mud spattered her eight-year-old son's freckled face, and his windblown hair reminded her of his father. Where else could she raise the boy but here?

Nearby, Celia worked her cow pony, circling several calves. Annie's mother would drop in a fit of apoplexy at the sight of Celia astride, wearing a worn split skirt, and her two long braids swinging without the constraint of a bonnet. Mother always said if you're not a lady, then you aren't anything. Annie hugged herself. She was definitely nothing now.

Though just fifteen, Celia knew more about cattle than both her brother and mother put together, but not enough to run the place. Thankfully the girl was willing to work with the cattle, but she wouldn't do much beyond that without a fight. Annie heaved a sigh and stared out over her ranch. The cattle boom indicated this was the year to make money, but thirteen years of her late husband's hard work here in Wyoming mattered not if all she knew how to do was clean and garden.

On the far edge of her land, a sheepherder pushed his flock over the top of the ridge and headed north. If her husband were alive, she'd have set off to tell the lonely herder to move back across the valley, but she wouldn't bother now. Her animosity for sheep had died with her husband.

She strode back into the house, cleaned up after Tom, and then paced her little parlor crammed with the furniture they'd brought from Virginia in hopes of making this simple house feel more like home.

She couldn't run a ranch without a handful of gunslick men, and now she no longer had the unsettling Mr. Passey to depend upon. Annie licked her dry lips. If only she'd listened to the men talking cattle prices or animal husbandry. But no, she'd been content to keep care of hearth and home.

Could she have done anything more foolish?

She stopped at Gregory's favorite chair. The indentation in the headrest would probably still smell of him if she pressed her face into the recess. The cushions beckoned her to curl up in the seat and sob, but she thumped the headrest with her fist instead. How dare Gregory leave her to provide for their children alone?

And why had every one of her cowboys left when she needed them most?

Annie dropped onto a hard kitchen chair and stared at the desk overflowing with ledgers and receipts she'd yet to make sense of. Tom had surmised the truth—a widow who'd done nothing but cook and clean for a rancher would not magically turn into one.

But he was wrong about her being citified. Her work-roughened hands indicated she was no longer the sophisticated woman she'd been raised to be.

She belonged in neither world.

A change in the wind forced Annie to leave off staring at her hands. Though Tom's odoriferous presence still clung to her nostrils, the cool breeze cut into her oil stove's efficiency. She stepped onto her squat cabin's porch, shut the door against the cleansing air, and trudged through mud toward the corral. Each squishy patch grabbed her boot heels and slurped when she took a step. Not even halfway across the yard, the hem of her black skirt grew heavy with muck. If only her mother could see her now. She would have covered her pert nose with a lace embroidered hanky and declared that this was exactly why she hadn't given her blessing at the wedding. Ladies didn't go west; they died there.

Annie had always thought Mother meant literally, but now she knew there was more than one way for a lady to die.

At the fence, she leaned against the top rail. "Celia!"

The girl wound up her lariat and trotted her horse over.

"Have you taken care of the chickens yet?" At her daughter's suddenly defiant posture, Annie sighed. "I shouldn't have to ask."

With a huff, Celia redirected her mount and headed to the barn.

"And see to supper," Annie called.

Her daughter didn't answer, but her empty stomach should urge her to comply.

"Mama." Spencer's shaggy brown head slipped into the crook of her arm. "I finished all my chores before I came out."

She smiled down at him as she pulled him in tighter, his bright blue eyes sparkling with his desire to please. "I wouldn't have expected anything less from you." She wiped the mud from his cheek.

A far-off whicker caused her to turn. A lone horse and rider trotted on the rut that served as a road from Armelle, and a lawman's badge glinted in the sun.

The marshal's horse—a beautiful brown and white splotched pinto—nearly blended in with the tiny bogs and melting snowdrifts covering the land. Perhaps he had information on her stolen cattle. She rumpled Spencer's unruly locks. "Why don't you go inside and work in your primer?"

"But I want to talk to the marshal."

She gave him a stern look, and he let out an exaggerated sigh. "Yes, ma'am." Heading toward the house, he couldn't keep up his pouty, trudging pace long before he started to skip. If only Celia obeyed that easily.

Pushing off the fence, Annie turned to wave at her visitor as his horse trotted toward the fence line.

If the marshal had come to tell her Celia had been trying his nerves in Sunday school as much she was trying hers today, she wasn't sure how she'd keep her temper.

She'd heard from enough people about her daughter's poor behavior. When was it her turn to gripe?

To ease the tension pulsing behind her eyes, she rubbed against her temples. She couldn't burden the marshal with her cantankerous daughter every Sunday, and make him listen to her break down today. The confirmed bachelor could probably only handle one ill-humored female a week.

Marshal Jacob Hendrix tipped his hat and slid off his saddle. "Good afternoon, ma'am."

Not much good about it really.

She crossed her arms to defend herself from the wind and hide her worn coat, which reeked of animals. She blew a tendril of straight limp hair from her face. She hadn't cared that Mr. Passey had interrupted her while mucking the barn, but looking disheveled in front of this fine-looking gentleman made her squirm.

The marshal patted his horse's neck, taking his time before turning his tall, lean frame in her direction. Though likely a few years older than her, he seemed younger. Probably because his job didn't require as much back-breaking work as she'd endured for well over a decade.

From his jacket's inside pocket, he pulled out a white envelope and tapped the letter in his open palm.

Annie smoothed back the loose hair tickling her face. The words *Armelle County Clerk* grabbed her attention, and she suppressed a moan. Taxes.

But why would he bother to bring her notice all the way out here? "Have you caught the rustlers?"

His features remained smooth and striking, though his brown eyes glinted, then narrowed. "No, but it can't be long before I do." Looking over at the corral, he brought up his hand and rubbed his thumb along his square jaw, shadowed with the beginnings of a dark beard. "Any more of your cattle missing?"

She pursed her lips and shook her head. "Just the twenty I reported last week." But since she now had zero cowboys under her employ, more would likely be missing within days.

"Make sure your hands keep a lookout."

She pressed her lips together tighter, lest she spill her woes and end up a sodden heap on the ground.

Besides, no advice the marshal could give her would make up for her ranch's lack of manpower.

"This is for you." Marshal Hendrix handed her the envelope.

With trembling fingers, she plucked it from his hand. "Has the mayor made you postman as well?"

He grabbed his saddle horn and hoisted himself back upon his mount. "Don't give McGill any ideas. He has me busy enough." A tired smile graced his rugged face. "No, I just figured that while I was out checking if anyone had run-ins with the rustlers, I could hand out tax notices since it's that time of year." He tipped his hat. "Good day, Mrs. Gephart."

The marshal turned his horse, and his pinto kicked up mud.

Annie sniffed and tore open the envelope, hoping the numbers hadn't gone up, though they did almost every year. They'd been in danger of having their name printed in the *Daily Ricochet* last year with the other delinquent taxpayers. But Gregory's meager reserves had saved them from prematurely selling the cattle needed to strengthen the herd.

... This year's taxes on the aforementioned property are $82.17. Due 30 April 1884. Payable to the Armelle County Treasurer.

She crumpled the paper in her hand. Could today get any worse? She stuffed the notice in her pocket and trudged over to the white picket fence.

Her heart dropped lower in her chest with each step, as it always did when she visited this section of the property. She flipped open the narrow gate and headed to the solitary cottonwood tree, under which dead daffodils slumped in front of a line of wooden markers.

She knelt beside Gregory's cross, dampness soaking through to her knees, and traced Spencer's poor attempt to etch his father's name into the wood. "Do you know what a predicament we're in?"

Only the wind responded.

She stared at the three smaller crosses aligned with his larger one. Only one of these babies had taken a breath—the eldest, who'd passed away before her third birthday. Annie ran her finger along Catherine's name and pressed her trembling lips together to ward off the tears. She scooted away and brushed the dirt off Gregory's marker. "This was your dream, not mine."

Unbidden, the image of his body stiff across his wild-eyed mare and the large bloody hole bursting from his chest, wrenched her insides.

At the church service after his death, she'd overheard one of the mayor's ranch hands saying he'd seen her husband sending an encroaching sheepherder to his Maker that fateful night.

But the worst part was everyone hailed Gregory as a martyr. The populace cared more for their bovine than the life of an innocent herder.

What had possessed her husband to go against his faith and abandon his family over an animosity for sheep? She leaned forward and rested her head against his marker. "God forgive you," she whispered. "I'm not sure I have."

She'd never dreamed Gregory would get mixed up in the feuding. Sure, he had enforced the local deadlines set by the ranchers to keep cattle-grazing land unspoiled by ground-ruining sheep, but to kill a shepherd and shoot a quarter of his flock?

Gregory might have been one to keep his emotions tucked inside so long he was wont to burst when things set him off, but murder?

She didn't want to believe it.

Couldn't.

She brushed the dead leaves off his grave. If she sold the ranch, would the new owner tend the cemetery and plant more flowers? Could she leave these children behind, buried in Gregory's precious land, to be attended by someone who had not loved them?

Even if she sold cattle to pay the taxes, that wouldn't change the fact she couldn't run this ranch.

No hired hand would take on the work of a ranch for a cowboy's salary, and only an owner would have the drive to force her spread to flourish.

Which gave her two options—marry or sell.

CHAPTER TWO

Steady rain dripped off Annie's bonnet as she guided her team forward. Ahead of them, Armelle swam into view in puddles of blue, gray, and brown. She tugged her wool coat tight around her slender frame, wishing she'd noticed the storm clouds rolling in before they'd left. The wind whipped cold, threatening to transform the rain into a late spring snow. What she wouldn't give for her oilskin right now.

Celia hunched on the wagon seat beside her. "I told you we shouldn't have come. Now I'm wet through."

If the day wasn't miserable enough, Celia would make it so.

"Darling, it's the Lord's Day. If we can't drive through a simple rainstorm to worship Him, then we don't deserve His provision." Yet why hadn't God provided for her taxes after He'd taken her husband into His arms? God knew she had children to care for.

"You always say we can pray and worship wherever we are." Celia's shaking legs made the wagon seat vibrate beneath them. "I'm sure He'd rather hear my voice warm and happy, than wet and miserable."

Annie scrunched her eyes tight. "Thank you, Celia, for

reminding me of my own lesson. If only you'd remember the others I give." As eager to be under the church's roof as her grumpy daughter, Annie flicked the reins. "So, here's a new one to memorize: Be happy or don't speak."

Celia huffed and flopped against the seat back. The frigid air swept the white puff of her breath over her shoulder.

Spencer's cowboy hat brushed Annie's arm as he wiggled his way between her and Celia from where he'd sat in the back. "Does that mean I can talk? I'm happy."

The water collecting in his brim ran off into Annie's lap. She grimaced as the rivulet trickled in through her coat.

Celia grunted. "You're always happy."

"Hey, you ain't supposed to talk!"

Celia stuck her tongue out at her brother.

Despite wanting to growl, swing the wagon around, and speed home, Annie put on a calm, stern face. "Spencer, it's 'you aren't supposed to talk.' And Celia, what did I say?"

Celia rolled her eyes. How Annie hated that gesture.

Lord, help me. I'm losing control.... No. I've lost control—of everything.

Spencer tapped her shoulder. "So can I talk then?"

Annie tried to give him a smile. "Of course, son."

"As long as I'm happy, right?"

"Yes." If that was the only rule in regard to talking, her youngest would rarely have to be quiet. "Why don't you sing? Cheer us all up?"

> *"Come in, you naughty bird, the rain is pouring down.*
> *What will your mother do, if you sit there and drown?*
> *You are a very thoughtless—"*

"Something else, son." Only a boy would think a song about a drowning bird would cheer people up.

By the time Spencer started the second verse of "Oh, Susanna," Annie could no longer concentrate on the lyrics. The church on the outskirts of town was but a few minutes away. She pulled at her wet and clingy clothing. What would the marshal think when he saw her in such a state?

She looked up to the heavy gray clouds obscuring the heavens. If only God would make this decision for her. Two weeks until taxes were due, and if marriage was the right solution, she had even less time to decide.

On Main Street, a straight shot between brick and wood storefronts, Annie steered around a few pedestrians darting from one side to the other. And cows. A beautiful black heifer with a muddy white face loped alongside Annie's wagon for a block before turning into an alley. The council had published a warning in the paper a few months ago that the marshal would impound wandering livestock, but they surely wouldn't enforce the statute. The cattlemen around here would rise up in arms if it cost them to regain their cattle—and their money kept the city afloat.

The marshal had actually delivered Mayor McGill's steer to him during a board session last month and threatened to take the beef to the jailhouse if the mayor didn't pay the fine immediately. Picturing portly McGill steaming over paying the fine to enforce his own law made Annie chuckle.

The vision of the marshal with the mayor's steer turned her thoughts to her own precarious situation. The bubbled-up mirth returned to her belly and curdled. The marshal was the only person who could help her with the path she'd chosen. And how could she convince him her plan was worthwhile?

God, please reveal some other way during the church service, or I'll likely end up embarrassing myself more than I ever thought possible.

The little white church, nestled between two evergreens, appeared through the drizzle. Annie pulled into the soggy side lot alongside the wagons of the few families who'd ventured out in this weather. Skirting the church building, the three rushed to the marshal's neighboring house where the children attended Sunday school.

Under his porch overhang, Annie squeezed the water out of her skirt as best she could. Spencer shook like a dog, and Celia stood dripping.

Annie grabbed the darkened hem of Celia's skirt and squished the wetness out onto the wood planks. "Help me wring out this water. You don't want to create a mess for the marshal."

"He don't care." Celia crossed her arms over her chest. She was too big to spank, and correcting her grammar would only fuel her attitude.

Spencer opened the door and ran inside, joining his high, squeaky voice with the laughter behind the doors.

Annie shot out her arm to keep Celia from stomping in after Spencer since she was still dripping.

Was there anything she could do to get this girl to obey? Celia's hurt over losing her father was so deep, Annie wasn't sure anything would make a difference right now. "If you aren't willing to make yourself presentable enough to go into Sunday school, you can come with me instead."

"He won't care, Ma. Really."

Sure he wouldn't. He owned one of the nicest homes in Armelle. A two-story house he'd purchased after a family of eight left for Oregon. How one person could feel comfortable living alone in a house so large stymied Annie. But she wouldn't let her daughter drag in enough water to ruin his floors either. "It's your choice: Sunday school or the adult class."

Celia's teeth rocked on her lower lip.

Perhaps her daughter felt too old for the children's class. "You'd be welcome with the adults. You're a young lady now." If she'd only act like one.

Bending over, Celia gathered handfuls of fabric and twisted. "I'll stay here." She glanced up. "You can go. I promise I'll go in."

"I know you will, but I thought I might peek in and check on things."

She'd never paid much attention to the children's class.

What if the marshal had a helper already? Or what if he was fond of one of the young ladies in town? If so, he wouldn't accept Annie's plan.

Celia shrugged and crossed the threshold into the warm air wafting out the front door.

Annie peered into the house. The large parlor contained only one chair at the end of the carpet on which the children sat cross-legged in an oblong circle. No sofa. No end table. Not even a vase for flowers. How did the marshal entertain guests?

"Hello, Mrs. Gephart!" A chorus of children's voices greeted her.

She waved to them while standing in the doorway. "Good morning, children."

A redheaded boy with huge brown eyes ran to her. "Are you going to help with class?"

"Do I have an assistant today?" A deep bass voice followed the child's treble.

The marshal's frame filled the doorway that led into the kitchen. His suit jacket stretched to fit his wide shoulders, and his crisp white button-up shirt was open at the throat, void of the long, thin bow tie he usually wore. Catching herself staring at his disheveled collar, she averted her eyes over his shoulder. A stack of messy bowls covered the table behind him. His kitchen appeared bigger than her kitchen and parlor combined.

The marshal stepped forward and grinned. She swallowed the lump in her throat. No wonder so many of the town's eligible ladies flocked to him at gatherings. A simple smile turned his countenance into perfection. She struggled to find an answer to his question. "Uh, no. I just thought I might ... check on things." A sudden gust of wind sent rain through the open door and soaked her back.

And she'd been worried about Celia making a mess.

She stepped inside and shut the door. The standing water at her feet would mar his high-glossed floor, fancier than the natural planks and packed dirt of her place. "Do you need a helper? If so, I could talk to the adult class about getting you one."

He cocked his head to the side, his dark eyes assessing.

Her heart flipped. "Or well, I mean, I could help. Maybe you'd like a break? You've taught this class for so many—"

"I've got things handled, but thanks for thinking of me." He crossed the room in a few strides, carrying a baking sheet full of little cookies, too brown around the edges. "Do you want a cookie?"

"I do!" An eager voice yelped behind his back.

"If you don't take one now, there won't be any for you later." The marshal's mouth tipped up into a charming smile.

"Thanks." She plucked one from the tray, hoping to cover the tremor affecting her hand by taking a bite. The burnt sugar cookie stuck in her mouth. "I'll just head over to church if you're all right?"

He nodded. "Thanks for dropping by, Mrs. Gephart."

"Nothing to speak of, Marshal."

Balancing the pan of cookies in one hand, he opened the front door for her.

She had no choice but to go now. She avoided looking into his eyes as she passed under his arm.

The sound of giggles, begging, and more giggles erupted once the door closed behind her.

She ran along the sidewalk, but a wave of heavy rain caught her before she gained the church entrance. The cookie had disintegrated into a soggy mess in her hand. She dropped the wet lump into the foyer's wastebasket.

Leah Whitsett, a petite brunette, turned from the coat closet. "Oh, Annie, you're soaked!" Annie gave Leah's husband, Bryant, the thinnest of smiles before he ducked into the sanctuary. Her predicament wasn't his fault, but his signature at the bottom of her tax notice made it hard to muster a genuine smile.

Annie glanced at the puddle her dripping skirts left on the

floor. "I am indeed. I should have listened to Celia." The rat-tat-tatting on the roof increased. "I was insane to come in an open wagon, but..." Her other reasons for coming had pressed her.

Leah turned Annie around and tugged at the shoulders of her coat. "Let me help you out of this and hang it on the hall tree. Maybe it will dry before you leave."

Annie tugged her arms from the clingy sleeves and shut her eyes against the reflection in the opposite wall's mirror. Opening her eyelids showed her the same dismal image she wished had disappeared—a bedraggled hat sat limp atop her wet auburn hair, loose tendrils plastered her splotchy cheeks. With the coat off, her lack of curves was even more defined. She crossed her arms over her chest and shivered.

Why worry about the bad impression Celia was making on the marshal when she could do that well enough herself?

"Here's my shawl. You look dreadfully cold." Leah smiled and, with a strong grip on Annie's shoulder, led her into the sanctuary. "Please sit with us."

After taking a seat, Annie tried to follow along with the words in her Bible, but instead, summoned up the faces of every man in the county. Married men, elderly men, boys whose voices had yet to change, a few vagrants she'd seen in town, men she'd glimpsed exiting the houses of ill repute and gambling dens, and the marshal. His wavy brown hair and strong clean-shaven jaw above his perfectly pressed, open collar popped up every time her mind lost momentum. She squeezed his image from her mind and scanned the men sitting near her in case she'd forgotten someone of quality.

Were there no other God-fearing bachelors in this county?

She'd have to sell the farm. The marshal would never agree.

While prodding Spencer along in line, Annie tried to moisten her suddenly dry mouth. Marshal Hendrix stood at the church exit as usual. She'd never done anything but wish him a good day and shake his hand.

Years ago, Gregory had invited the marshal over to show him his firearm collection. They'd talked politics, and she'd scooted gun paraphernalia out of the way to set down a plate of cookies. That's all she remembered. Having him in the house had been quite insignificant then.

Two more steps until she stood in front of the marshal. She needed to rehearse what she'd planned to say, but her brain refused to work. Perhaps that was a good thing. Thinking too much about what she was about to do would only convince her this plan was ludicrous and freeze her mouth shut.

His collar was buttoned up tight now, and he'd put on his crisp black tie, tucked appropriately beneath his vest. He smiled down at her as he thrust out his hand. "Have a good day, Mrs. Gephart."

"You, too, Marshal Hendrix." She failed to release his hand.

His eyebrows rose.

She pumped his hand again, pretending she'd meant not to let go. "How were my children today? Celia's been a handful lately."

"Ma," Celia grumbled behind her.

His eyes twinkled. "She was fine." He withdrew his hand. "Thank you for your earlier thoughtfulness in seeing if I needed help. If I ever do, I'll let you know."

There, a lead in, take it! Her lips wouldn't unglue.

"C'mon, Mama." Spencer tugged on her damp coat sleeve.

She made her lips move. "I ... I hope you do take me up on that favor if you ever need me, and I hope I might ask one in return?"

His eyebrows descended.

People most likely pestered him for political favors all the time. She cleared her throat. "Nothing—"

Goodness, she'd about said "nothing big." What was bigger than pledging your life to another?

"Nothing that should be discussed here. But I thought you might come over for supper tomorrow. I need ... help on a matter." She evened out her breathing and checked to see how her nervous burst of words had affected him.

His face was serene as he tipped his head. "I'd be happy to advise you in exchange for a home-cooked meal. I hope I can help." He touched her lightly on the shoulder and crisscrossed his other arm behind her to shake someone's hand. "Mr. Ivens, good to see you this morning. Miss Ivens."

Barely acknowledging the other "howdy do's" from the rest of the parishioners, Annie rushed to her wagon.

She had a little over twenty-four hours to form a sound argument to convince the marshal to marry her.

CHAPTER THREE

About a quarter mile before he reached the Gepharts', Jacob Hendrix spurred his horse, Duchess, into a trot.

A home-cooked supper would be the best thing about this day.

Despite the other problems facing the county—rustling, gambling, and vagrants, to name a few—his boss had insisted he spend all afternoon enforcing the city's sidewalk code.

While nailing down boards, he'd overheard a few ranchers wanting to declare war on the rustlers.

Vigilante justice made him cringe, and yet, if the town's only marshal was strapped with jobs unrelated to law enforcement, there was little chance he could do much to stop organized rustlers, though he tried every spare chance he got.

Up ahead, the Gepharts' wooden cabin, tiny in comparison to his monstrosity of a house, sat snug within a dip on the austere plains.

Sheets flopped on a clothesline in the breeze, the chimney puffed cheerily, and chickens scratched the muddy ground. What he wouldn't give for a little cozy domesticity. His house was bare and cold, even in summer. He could barely stand to live in the silent, still place. If only he'd never bought it. He patted Duchess's neck. "At least, you don't mind how often we roam about, do ya?"

Duchess whickered and he prodded her to pick up the pace, letting her stretch her legs.

Once he reined her in next to the little cabin made from the stout pines off the mountain ridges and the reddish-brown sandstone from the river, he breathed in the smell of what would hopefully be a sugary pie. He slipped off Duchess and tied her reins to the porch railing before heading to the front door.

Jacob fidgeted as he awaited the answer to his knock, staring down at his scuffed cowboy boots. He'd never seen Annie look anything but prim and proper when the Gephart family came in for church and an occasional trip to the mercantile. Her bedraggled appearance yesterday, along with the uncertainty in her wide, warm amber eyes and the trembling in her handshake, had pulled at his heartstrings.

He'd heard her cowboys had deserted her for McGill's ranch. How McGill slept at night after bribing the widow's cowpunchers to work for him instead, he didn't know. The man held enough power—owning the most profitable ranch in the county as well as being mayor—so why take from a grieving woman?

From somewhere inside, he heard a pair of voices, but no one called out to him, so he knocked again.

The property tax hike had likely hit Annie hard. Had she asked him out here in hopes he could help her avoid the bill? He could offer a listening ear, but Armelle's citizens were never thrilled when he reminded them he only had the authority to enforce laws, not change them.

But Annie's late husband had quite the arsenal of firearms. Maybe she wanted to sell one to pay taxes? He wouldn't mind owning the Henry Repeater Gregory had once shown him. His new Colt Single Action Army Revolver used the same cartridge.

Scuffling sounded from behind the door.

Jacob loosened his shoulders. No reason to stand rigid as if he were a fourteen-year-old boy getting ready to ask his first girl to take a twirl around the dance floor.

The door creaked open, and Spencer's beaming smile appeared. "Marshal Hendrix!"

"Hi, squirt." He ruffled Spencer's tousled hair. "You going to let me in?"

"Sure." The boy swung the door open wide. "I didn't know you were coming. You wanna see the horntoad I caught this afternoon? Or..." his eyes grew wide and his voice descended into a whisper as he scanned the horizon behind Jacob, "...are you here to arrest somebody?"

Jacob let out a chuckle. "Does someone need arresting?"

The boy shrugged. "Mama's been onto Celia all afternoon. Can you get scolded so much you have to answer to the law?"

Jacob laughed, turned the boy around, pushed him inside, and shut the door behind them. Though the Gepharts didn't make it into town every Sunday, he'd always enjoyed having Spencer in his class before church service. "Haven't heard of a case like it yet."

Celia stood by the table in the cramped dining area, her hands on her hips, her right foot tapping. "Spencer, mind your own business."

Jacob patted her arm, full of tight muscles. "No harm done, now."

Annie backed in through a side door. "This creature cannot be roaming free in my pantry." She turned around, gingerly holding out a fat horned lizard. "Come get—" She dropped the reptile and blinked as she met Jacob's gaze.

The lizard hit the floor with a soft smack.

Jacob cringed.

"Mama!" Spencer rushed over to capture the horned lizard that had scrambled between a couple of crates.

She squatted beside him and hugged his head. "I'm sorry."

The boy cupped the spiny reptile and flipped him over to rub his soft, round belly. The lizard relaxed as if he were enjoying the rubdown. "Aw, he's all right."

She straightened with lightning speed. "Marshal Hendrix. I apologize. I should have been out here to greet you."

"No apology needed, ma'am."

Annie wiped her hands across her apron more times than necessary. Her mouth was so pinched her lips were paler than normal. If she'd just relax, her features would probably transform into something more pleasant, but she'd always sported the look of a prim schoolteacher.

"Please have a seat, Marshal." Annie gestured toward a flowered sofa in the adjoining parlor-like room. "Supper will be ready shortly." She beckoned to Celia. "Get him something to drink, darling."

Spencer brought the well-fed lizard over. "Want to see him?"

"Take the reptile outside, son." Annie clinked a lid on a pan.

Spencer poked out his lower lip. "I don't understand why she doesn't like him."

Jacob mirrored the child's pouty face and shrugged.

Spencer cuddled the horntoad against his chest, and pivoting, crashed into his sister directly behind him.

Celia gave him a slight shove toward the door. "Tea or water, Marshal?" She stared at him with one eye half-closed, as if daring him to choose wisely.

He kept the grin off his face. Celia'd been testing his Biblical assertions and values in Sunday school for the last several months. Last week, she'd asked how he could believe in a loving God when bad things happened to good people. Though she often bordered on rude, he never refused to answer her, no matter the question. His father had always encouraged him to give a kind answer to people attacking their faith, for one never knew when God might use their words to soften a heart. "Water would be fine, ma'am."

She trudged to the cupboard, leaving him alone in the

corner to listen to Annie slide cast iron pans around the cook stove.

He settled back and relaxed. Strange how such a small place seemed less confining than his, even with all the furniture and doodads filling up every tiny corner. The cabin looked much the same as the last time he'd been here, decorated as if it were one of the big houses he'd visited in Texas as a boy. One would think Annie entertained society ladies every afternoon, what with the piano in the corner, patterned wallpapered walls, and a crystal light fixture casting a warm glow on the parlor trinkets arranged in corner hutches.

He assessed the value of the furnishings. Gregory Gephart must have had a lot of money before settling here. Why would a man leave wealth behind for the sparseness of Wyoming?

And why would a woman need such a fancy room when she wasn't involved in the social circle of Armelle? He scratched his head, left his fingers tangled in his hair, and leaned back against the sofa.

"Here you are." Celia handed him a glass of water. "Remember to keep it off the wood."

He straightened to take the glass. "Sure thing." He took a sip before placing his drink on the lacy doily on the side table. She flounced away, and he settled back into the cushions. He ought to get a soft seat like this for his own front room.

A few minutes later, Annie stood before him, her cheeks flushed. "Supper's ready."

He grabbed his glass and walked to the kitchen table set with candlesticks and fancy napkins squeezed through napkin rings. Had he even sat at his table this week? He stopped himself from rubbing his gurgling stomach. Tomorrow he'd go back to eating beans straight out of the can on his back porch, but tonight, he'd be sopping up every last smear of gravy with that heavenly smelling bread arranged in a fancy pyramid on the table's center platter.

Annie motioned to the head of the table. "If you would have a seat, we'll start."

As much as he wanted to swipe a roll and grab his chair, he pulled hers out first, earning a pleased look that lit up her plain features. Had he ever seen her smile? He seated himself and waited to observe their routine.

"Shall I pray, Mama?" Spencer flopped into the chair next to his mother.

"Um, actually..." Annie's fingers rubbed, or maybe quivered, on the table top. "If the marshal wouldn't mind?" Her teeth creased her lower lip.

"Not at all." He bowed his head. "Heavenly Father, I thank you for the food we are about to eat, the hands that made it, and the land which provided it. May you help me be of assistance to this family. Help these children respect their mother for the hard decisions she makes and the work she does. Would that you lead us in paths of righteousness. Amen."

Jacob looked up.

Celia eyed him, Spencer grabbed a roll, and Annie's head remained bowed. He didn't know if it would be appropriate to pass around plates before she finished her attitude of prayer, so he waited.

She cleared her throat, but she didn't look up. "Thank you." Her words seemed thick.

He shrugged as his stomach rumbled.

Spencer cried, "Let's eat."

Annie set coffee in front of the marshal and grimaced when the hot liquid sloshed into his saucer, but he didn't seem to notice.

She'd sent the kids to milk the cow and had stayed the marshal with dessert, but hadn't yet found enough courage to say what she needed to. And considering she hadn't wrangled out more than a few words during supper, how was she ever going to speak aloud the words she'd practiced over and over this afternoon?

The sun would soon disappear behind the sky's long edge. Now had to be the time.

She shivered though she stood right next to the cook stove.

"Cold?" The marshal pushed his chair away from the table.

"No." She wrung her hands, wondering where to start.

"Seeing as the sun is about to set, you'd best ask me for that favor." His china clinked as he set his drink down. "I enjoyed supper, but I know you didn't have me over to feed me."

She couldn't make herself sit. Couldn't make herself look at him. This was all so ... improper. A lady didn't ask a man to marry her. Let alone a marriage of convenience for her and one of inconvenience for him. Her mother would be appalled.

Peeking at him, she forced in a breath.

He cocked his eyebrow.

She had no qualms about his being an upstanding man who could fill the role of husband and father adequately. But did she want to look into his eyes when she asked? Would they be filled with pity, revulsion, hilarity, indifference? She stood transfixed by his concerned expression, but the words wouldn't come.

"I know people are having a tough time paying taxes this year." The marshal leaned back in her kitchen chair as if it were a chaise lounge. "If you need help, there's no shame in asking."

She couldn't keep from widening her eyes. Did he already know what she planned to ask and was encouraging her? Impossible. Unless—

Letting the legs of his chair thump forward, he propped his elbows on the table. "I'm supposing your firearms would bring in a nice chunk of money. I know they might be difficult to let go of, but I could advise you on what you should ask for them."

She blinked.

"I wouldn't be the best person to ask about the farm implements or the livestock, but I could ask Bryant—"

She shook her head violently. She could've asked Mr. Whitsett about her personal property when she'd gone into town to plead for more time to pay taxes. He hadn't budged on the due date. "The guns, um..." Gregory's firearms had been his pride and joy. "I guess whether or not I sell them depends on you."

He smiled and rubbed his hands together. "I'd hoped you might sell me the Henry. I have—"

"Actually, that's not it, but I guess if you agree to what I'm asking, the Henry would be yours by default." Surely he'd not keep Spencer from inheriting his father's guns later.

"How's that?" His face contorted.

Her left hand clenched the fingers of her right. "Difficult times often call for unusual solutions." She gazed out the window toward the pasture. "I have no cowhands and am woefully ill-prepared to run a ranch." She avoided glancing at him and stared at her desk instead. "No one seems willing to work for me, and I can't pay my taxes."

She couldn't help but squirm, but the man needed to know what he could be getting into. "All I have is a husband and three children buried on the property Celia and Spencer's father dreamed they'd grow up on. I won't leave it if I have another option." She took a breath and peeked at him.

His hand rubbed his jaw. "I'm guessing the purchase price on the Henry wouldn't be enough, but I'm assuming you still have the Sharps. I could give you money for that, which I'm willing to return whenever you have enough to pay me back. Would that help?"

She dropped into her chair and traced the wood grain in the table with a fingernail. "No." She squared her shoulders and looked straight at him. "I appreciate the thought, but at some later date I'd be in the same financial straits I'm in now since I don't know how to run the place." She pulled in a steadying breath. "What I'm asking for would put you out of more than just money."

Oh how could she ask him to give up his life, his job, everything?

He leaned in, his fingers steepled in front of his nose.

"If—" Her voice squeaked to a halt. She swallowed to loosen her vocal chords. "If you might consider becoming owner of this land—the head of this household—we could stay."

He sat up stiffly, his jaw working in a nervous fashion.

Heat radiated up her torso and into her face. "I know this seems strange, being I don't really know you, and you don't know me well either. But I'd feel wrong selling this place without giving remarrying a chance."

His stony expression wasn't encouraging.

She cleared her throat. "Of course, I would only marry an upright man of the same faith who could raise my children well. You may not know much about ranching, but I bet it's more than I know about it, and since no other man around here seems to fit the description, I figured I'd ask you."

He sat back and did nothing more than stare at her.

She tried not to fidget, but nervous tremblings shook her skirt's fabric anyway.

He turned to stare out the window and moved his thumb along his jawline.

The quiet thickened. Why didn't he say something? "I know that you're..." *too handsome, more than I deserve, dedicated to Armelle and shouldn't quit to take on my broken family,* "...little more than an acquaintance at the moment, but I felt led to ask."

Maybe not really led. I'm simply humiliating myself out of desperation. At least when you say "no," my other option is to sell and move far away from here, never to face you again.

She fiddled with the handle of her coffee cup and waited for him to frame his reply. Hopefully it wouldn't begin with hollow praise for her, or pity.

The door blew open and slammed against the opposite wall. Spencer stomped in, his boots thick with mud. Celia followed, spun around, and pushed the door closed against the strong wind.

Why hadn't she told them to stay in the barn? She bit her lip and heat scampered up her neck. Because that would have sounded inappropriate.

The marshal's eyes traveled up and down Annie's frame.

She wanted to scoot around the corner of the table and wrap her arms about herself.

How dumb of her. Several single ladies in town were sweet on him. Especially the young Miss McGill. Not only was the twenty-something the prettiest thing around, but her father was the wealthiest man in the area. Annie's mousiness and failing ranch would not tempt the marshal even if she was closer to him in age. She grabbed her coffee and drank until she hit dregs. She should have gone along with his assumption and sold him the guns.

Spencer's red nose rubbed against her warm cheek. "Can I have some crumb cake?"

"Sure, honey," she whispered.

Celia pulled the curtain farther aside. "Marshal, if you stay much longer, it'll be dark before you get home."

He jerked straight in his chair. "Right." His dark brown eyes assessed Annie's for a few seconds before he stood and shrugged on his coat. "Might I come back Wednesday night to discuss this further?"

Annie's heart pounded itself toward oblivion. He was considering her proposal? Or did he not want to embarrass her in front of the children right now? "Yes." She forced the word out. "For supper?"

His lips slanted into a small smile. "I'd be obliged. See you Wednesday." He crammed on his hat. "Good night."

He chucked Celia on the jaw before striding out the door.

Her daughter glared after him, slammed the door, and then served herself cake.

Annie skirted the table and pulled back the curtain. The marshal's mare was galloping toward town, their silhouettes quickly dissolving into the shadows the setting sun was throwing across the plains.

She forced herself to continue breathing.

What if he said yes?

CHAPTER FOUR

Duchess hated pulling a carriage, but Jacob didn't want the sun dictating the end of his upcoming visit with the Gepharts. There would be a new moon tonight, so he needed the carriage lanterns in case he stayed as long as he suspected he'd need to.

The steady clip-clop of his horse's hooves seemed like a funeral cadence in comparison to his erratic heartbeat. He breathed slowly and deliberately in hopes of lowering his pulse. He didn't have to come out here—it was his decision, and yet, his insides were intent on panicking.

Strange how the mealtime prayer he'd uttered over the Gepharts' supper table Monday had set him up for a marriage request that had come out of nowhere.

He'd been interested in guns. She'd been interested in him.

He'd had several ladies throughout his life hang on his arm, bat their eyelashes, and whisper flirtatious nonsense in his ear, yet none had ever wriggled into his heart enough that he'd decided he couldn't live without them. So why did a virtually unknown woman, marginally attractive, spark an interest he'd never felt before?

Perhaps it had to do with Celia and Spencer.

Since their father had passed away, he'd spent a lot of time praying for Annie's children. And now he was being offered to personally give them what he'd asked God to provide—the soul-nourishing love his father had lavished upon him.

Not that all men had to be like his pa to be a good father, and Gregory Gephart couldn't have been less like Wallace Hendrix if the man had tried.

A few weeks ago, after a particularly difficult Sunday, Spencer had confided that Celia had argued on the ride in that their father couldn't have loved them, not with how he'd done something so stupid to orphan them. Celia was beginning to doubt their father had ever loved them at all.

Though he hadn't really known Gregory, he'd met him enough times to know Annie's husband hadn't been a man to wear his heart on his sleeve. But at the same time, Gregory had let his daughter spend enough hours beside him that she was practically his most trusted cowhand. No man who did that could be accused of not loving his girl.

And though Jacob couldn't bring Celia's father back to prove that her father had loved her deeply, could stepping into Gregory's place help Celia become the girl her father had believed he could depend upon?

Up ahead, vultures rode the air currents in lazy circles above the bright spring green earth.

And there was no use pretending that owning six hundred and twenty acres of land with all its improvements and livestock didn't tempt his soul. Like the Gepharts, he'd once faced the same shocking realization that the land he'd expected to live on forever could be gone in a snap.

He'd always assumed his family's ranch would be his since his older siblings had chosen more citified occupations and residences. But the year he'd gone off to fight the last few months of the war, his parents had sold their land for triple their purchase price to support themselves as missionaries in Central America.

How could he have argued against that?

Adjusting to the loss of his projected future along with his parents moving out of the country had been difficult. He couldn't imagine how he would've coped if he'd doubted his father's love.

Duchess slowed as she pulled in front of the Gepharts' home, and Jacob got down to scratch behind her ears and look out over the land. Sturdy outbuildings and several rows of cold frames surrounded the cabin. The naked branches of a line of short willows created the beginnings of a northern wind break. He sighed and let a small smile tweak his lips. Annie's family didn't have to obey the city code requiring tree planting this far from town, and yet, they had. Her ranch's location along the cold, trout-teeming water of the wide Laramie River, plus its proximity to town while still abutted to acres upon acres of public rangeland, made it choice property. Someone would snatch this place up in a heartbeat if put up for sale.

The front door swung open under the power of Spencer's little arm. His bright smile caused Jacob's own lips to turn up.

"Ho there, Spencer!"

"Ho there!" The boy skipped to his vehicle. "You have a nice carriage." He caressed the black leather cushion. "We sold ours."

"I'm borrowing this one." Jacob untethered Duchess and led her to green grass. "Bet your mother had to part with lots of things she wanted to keep."

Spencer frowned and nodded. "She cried about it."

"I bet." Spencer was always asking for prayer on behalf of others, but not once could Jacob recall the lad complaining about his own life. Jacob ruffled Spencer's hair. "Have you been helping your mother with supper?"

"Yes." He ducked out from under Jacob's reach. "And she made cake again. Twice in one week!" Spencer licked his lips and rolled his eyes as if he were sampling the pastry. "She's always telling us she has to save the sugar, but she must be having a real hankerin' for sweets." He ran to the front door and tugged on the latch with all his might.

"A good thing, right?" Jacob chuckled.

"Yes, sir."

Jacob used the boot scraper on the porch before following the boy inside where the smell of warm cinnamon apples filled the room. "Smells good, Mrs. Gephart."

A shy smile perched on her lips as she pulled a golden cake out of the oven, yet her gaze didn't quite make it up to his. "Applesauce cake. Celia's favorite." She set the hot pan on a trivet. "And you can, uh, should probably ... call me Annie."

Her face reddened, and she glanced at him before busying herself with a pot. When she lifted the lid, the aroma of peppercorns escaped. "I'm sorry supper's not ready yet."

"Not a problem." How would it feel to call her Annie? He preferred the sound of Anne, but he couldn't call her that yet, or maybe never. He swallowed against the pulsing in his throat and grabbed the pile of silverware on the counter. Following Celia around the table, he placed the utensils next to where she set plates. Celia eyed him a couple of times, but kept her thoughts to herself.

How quickly did Annie need him to make a decision? "Your taxes are due in two weeks, right?"

"Yes." Her voice came out raspy.

If he agreed to the marriage, he didn't have to marry her before he paid the taxes, but what would they gain by drawing out an engagement—if you could call it that—when a ranch needed to be run?

Celia shot him a questioning glance.

Maybe they ought to enlighten the kids about what they were contemplating. "Do you mind if I tell the children what we're considering?"

Annie slowly wiped her hands on her apron, her face a mixture of hope and fear. Celia and Spencer both stopped their progress around the table to stare at him.

Receiving no answer from Annie except a shrug, Jacob sent up a prayer for his words to be blessed. "Your mother and I talked on Monday about your family's financial needs. About how to keep from losing your ranch. Your mother's afraid she'll have to sell if there isn't someone to help her."

Annie gave him a blank stare, and Celia set glasses next to the plates, trying without success to act uninterested.

"Are you going to help us?" Spencer stepped in front of him, a handful of napkins hugged against his scrawny chest.

"Possibly." He turned to Annie, her face still frozen. "Your mother's asked me if I'd be willing to become your stepfather."

Celia fumbled the glass she was setting on the table, but grabbed it before it rolled off.

"That'd be swell!" Spencer dropped his napkins and squeezed Jacob's waist.

His heart melted onto the floor with the table linens. "Hold on, buddy." He rubbed Spencer's back. "I'd like to see how things work around here and talk with your mother more before we decide."

Celia stirred the turnips around in her bowl, less from the fact she didn't like turnips, and more because her mother and the marshal discussed marriage like a business deal.

Daddy should've known fighting with the sheepherders would've landed them in this mess.

She glanced up from her stew. The marshal was using his fingers to keep track of the assets Ma was listing. They didn't act any different than they did at church when they all shook his hand on their way out, except maybe Ma was stiffer than normal.

This was a mistake. Though if Ma sold Daddy's land, that'd be even more so.

The marshal turned to her. "So, Celia, what're your jobs

around here?" He leaned in his chair, a long leg casually flipped to the side, poking out from under the tablecloth like he already owned the place.

She leaned back in her own chair and gave him the side-eye.

She did what she wanted, but considering the lawman didn't let her get away with nothing on Sundays, he'd likely have a conniption over that. "I help with the cattle."

"What else? You do more in the summer, I assume."

Ma lifted her eyebrows and turned toward Celia.

If she mentioned any more chores, would Ma hold her responsible for them? Even if she didn't marry the marshal? "Considering there's no one else to work the cattle right now, I'd say that's plenty."

"May I have another slice of cake?" Spencer held up his crumbless plate.

Ma shook her head. "No, son. Time for bed."

Good, if Ma was going to deny her a slice of her favorite cake just because she wasn't about to finish her mushy turnips, he shouldn't get seconds. She stood, and her chair's legs scraped across the floor. "I'm going to bed, too. I'll help, Spencer."

Ma's brows rose again. "Thank you, darling."

Leading Spencer by the shoulders, Celia pushed him across the parlor. "Get in your pajamas." She then stalked into her room, the attached lean-to her parents had converted for her, and shut the door. She didn't want to hear the adults deciding her future without so much as a care for her. Sure, the marshal had put on a good show asking what she thought, but how could she answer truthfully?

How could you think I'd be happy about this?

But with Daddy dead, I have no choice.

She fumbled with her buttons and searched her mind for an alternative Ma had to be overlooking. They were certainly having difficulty caring for the place with no cowboys. The well-being of the cattle had been placed all on her shoulders since Tom had left. She didn't mind not having to go to school so she could take care of their small herd, but she did miss her friends—when they bothered to attend school themselves.

And though Daddy had treated her as if she were a ranch hand—stealing her away to help with the men's work more than any girl she knew—she couldn't run things on her own for long. She definitely didn't know what to do on a cattle drive or how to deal with stockyards. Daddy had told her this was the year she could ride along...

She slumped and dropped onto the bed to pull off her shoes.

The chilly spring air seeped more easily through the chink in her lean-to bedroom than the rest of the house, so she hurriedly changed from dress to nightgown and grabbed her quilted robe. She and Spencer still needed to brush their teeth and say goodnight, not that she wanted to go back into the living area in her nightdress considering the marshal was still there. But if he chose to marry Ma for their ranch, she'd have to deal with it or be stuck in her room every night.

Peeking out her door, Celia saw the marshal leaning forward in intense conversation. His thick hair curled over his forehead, and his hand rubbed his face, which was more attractive than usual with the slight shadow of whiskers on his jaw. Many of her friends practically swooned while whispering about the marshal, hoping he'd stay single until they were old enough to catch his eye. Silly girls. The man was older than Ma though he didn't look it.

The shawl Ma wore tonight hung on her shoulders, and the few wisps of limp rusty hair that had escaped her bun only highlighted the thinness of her bones. The worn black mourning dress she wore made her skin look pasty.

Why was the handsomest man in Armelle interested in Ma? Would she love him more than Daddy, who'd also been plain and had given Celia his frizzy hair and freckles?

No matter how attractive the marshal might be, she'd never forgive him if he came in and changed up all of Daddy's plans for the land.

Quickly padding to her brother's door, she let herself in. Spencer was struggling with his shirt, the yoke stuck around his big ol' head because he hadn't unbuttoned it. But instead of helping, she walked past him toward the window to stare at the calves bawling across the fence.

What if Ma sold the place?

Could people cry after they died? Daddy surely would if his land ended up in the hands of some stranger who didn't love the smell of wet sage and sand after the rain, or riding through the larkspur when the long blue spikes were tall enough to tickle a rider's legs, or rounding up the cattle as numerous as the sagebrush.

Cattle.

She ground her teeth. If Daddy had really loved anything, it was cattle, always singing to them until their big vacuous eyes rolled and they mooed in inconsistent harmony.

Though the sheep might've killed off the grass, they wouldn't have destroyed their family's life.

Spencer tapped her shoulder. "I'm ready."

Celia directed him into the kitchen.

He climbed onto the stool in front of the washbasin's mirror to watch himself brush his teeth while Ma and the marshal continued discussing the ranch in soft tones. After Spencer spit more than ten times, Celia tweaked his ear, but not hard enough for him to yelp. "Get done, Spence. It's my turn."

"All right, sis." He spit again and wiped his face.

Pushing him around when he was nothing but bubbles and sunshine never made her feel good, but there was no reason for his constant cheerfulness. He'd invite a monster to sleep in his bed if he thought it would please someone.

And with a face-splitting grin, he'd welcome any man into the house who promised him attention.

She pushed him out of the way. "Go tell Ma good night."

Brushing her teeth, she watched the marshal in the mirror.

When Spencer tapped on his knee, the marshal stopped talking and turned to her brother. "Are you headed to bed?"

"Yes. Will you read to us?"

The marshal ruffled Spencer's hair and faced Ma, his right eyebrow raised.

"You don't have to, but maybe talking to them without me around would be a good idea."

"Why don't you get a book, Spencer?" The marshal met Celia's eyes in the mirror. "Do you join him for stories?"

"We read the Bible." She garbled her words around the baking soda grit in her mouth.

His smile gleamed. "Even better."

Yes, her friends would be jealous. How she would hate to listen to their questions and surmises if Ma really did hook him.

She'd keep this whole mess to herself until the in-town girls found out on their own—if anything came of it. She'd have to tell Spencer to keep his yap shut.

She followed Spencer into his room, took a seat in the rocking chair, and handed the marshal the Bible. "We were going to read Jonah next. Ma reads the whole book if it's short."

He settled back against Spencer's headboard as if he read to them every night. Tracking the words with his index finger, the marshal used lots of silly character voices as he read, which Spencer ate up. Celia rolled her eyes despite no one paying attention to her.

"So." He shut the book, put his arm around Spencer, and looked toward her. "I know the thought of my joining this family probably shocked you, and you may be afraid of what that might mean, but I want you to know, no decision's been made yet. If you have any feelings or thoughts you'd like me to know, you can share them now. But whatever happens, know that I've enjoyed every minute I've spent with you two—"

Celia snorted, but instead of giving her a glare, the marshal's eyes twinkled.

"—and no matter what, I hope you know I love you. As I do all my students."

"I'd love it if you were my pa." Spencer snuggled against him.

"And being your pa would be a wonderful thing, but..." He pulled Spencer in front of him. "If that were the only thing I had to think about, I wouldn't hesitate a moment. But there are many things adults have to consider. So if I don't choose to marry your ma, I want you to know it isn't because I didn't want to be your father, because that sounds like the best job in the world. Do you understand?"

"Yes, Marshal Hendrix."

Celia eyed the lawman. He sounded good, but the cattle would take most of his time just like they took Daddy's. Ranchers didn't have time to play with their kids. Daddy had explained that often enough. She didn't dare hope the marshal would give Spencer the attention he was promising. There wasn't time for such foolishness on a Wyoming ranch.

And if the marshal thought he'd send her inside to work with Ma, he'd have another think coming. Nothing would stop her from doing the work she wanted to do when she wanted to do it.

The marshal looked deep into her little brother's eyes. "And until we make our decision, you shouldn't tell anybody about our discussions. All right, buddy?"

Spencer nodded and tried to look serious.

Good. The marshal's request for silence would hold more weight than her ordering Spencer not to blab it about church and town.

"What about you, Celia?" His kind expression ruffled her.

She shrugged. "Adults do what they have to do."

His mouth twisted a bit. She squirmed under his gaze, the same look he often gave her on Sundays when she got to arguing with him.

The marshal scooted to the edge of the bed. "Do we pray now, or something else?"

Spencer bounced onto his knees. "Mama always asks us what we want her to pray for, and then she prays."

"All right then, what would you like me to pray for?"

Spencer bit his lip and looked up at the ceiling.

Celia sighed. No telling how long his list was going to be tonight.

"Well," the boy drawled. "Whenever I ask Mama to pray for Mama, she always gets sad, so I'll have you pray for her." He snuggled close to the marshal.

Celia clenched her teeth.

Spencer looked at the marshal, eyes filled with admiration. Wouldn't take Spencer long to forget about Daddy. "Maybe you can pray that Mama will have someone else to talk to instead of our pa?"

"What do you mean?" The marshal shot Celia a confused look.

"Well, she talks to him all the time." Spencer shrugged. "Even though he's not here anymore."

Celia picked at her fingernails. "He means she still talks out loud to Daddy. She thinks we don't hear her, but we do."

"She cries sometimes too. You think God can help her not cry anymore?" Spencer's lower lip stuck out.

"Sounds like a good thing to pray for." The marshal tipped his head toward Celia. "Anything you want to add?"

"No." She twisted her body around to gaze out the window, the rocking chair squeaking with the movement. She wasn't sure what she wanted in regard to her mother marrying the marshal. And nothing could bring Daddy back, which was the only thing worth wishing for.

She brushed away the tears lining her eyelashes, hoping the marshal hadn't seen them.

CHAPTER FIVE

Jacob shook his head at the Smiths' lush lawn—complete with no sidewalk.

At the end of the month, he'd have to report them to the city council for not having one built according to the new city ordinance, and then next year, he'd have to endure their griping over how much the council had charged them to pay him to do it.

Though maybe he wouldn't be here next month to serve the Smiths their notice or build their sidewalk for them.

Annie had offered him what no single woman trying to hogtie him into matrimony had ever offered—a ticket out of this job and a hardworking woman to help him ranch.

Besides, he wasn't doing that well at being marshal anyhow. The only reason he was checking sidewalks was because he'd lost the rustlers' trail this morning. North of Annie's land, the tracks had forded a stream but hadn't reappeared on the other side.

A few men this week had accused him of being lily-livered for not joining the lynch mob riding off every night in search of the rustlers, but he wasn't about to be responsible for hanging a man without a trial like the self-declared posse had just a year ago.

He'd catch them the right way if he could catch them at all.

He stepped foot onto Main Street just as a girl's high-pitched scream made the hair on the back of his neck prickle. He pulled his hands from his pockets and scanned the street, hoping to catch the sound again.

"Help!" A little girl ran out of the alley straight for him. The child, not more than four or five, ran with her blond braids flying behind her.

He caught her and shoved her behind him. When nothing barreled out of the alleyway after her, he looked back at the little girl. "What's wrong, young lady?"

"Monster's scary." She clung to his leg.

"Is there a monster around the corner?" At her nod, he squeezed her shoulder. "Stay here and I'll have a look-see." Probably just some street rascal pestering her. He untangled the girl's fingers from his pant leg and deposited her beside the hitching post.

Ever since the Denver police started cracking down on vagrants and ne'er-do-wells, many had migrated north in Armelle's direction. This monster could be something serious.

Taking quick strides, Jacob made the shadowed alleyway, and the moment he turned, his heart kicked up at the sight of a gigantic black monstrosity lumbering toward him, its hairy snout spasming. The five-hundred-pound sow plodded through the dirt, knocking over a haphazard stack of crates.

He waved to the creature, making sure she saw him before she bowled him over. "Stop, Lullabelle!"

The sow slowed and kicked back her head, her snort resonating in the alleyway.

"How many times do I have to take you home, pig?" He forged into the alley and grabbed a mop off a backdoor stoop. Using its handle, he encouraged the old sow to turn. "Maybe I ought to fine your owner the same day I serve a notice to the Smiths."

Once Lullabelle started back the way she'd come, he moved back toward Main Street to check on the girl. The mercantile owner's wife had stooped down to talk to the little blonde. Seemed he was free to corral the pig. "Come on, pig. Get movin'."

Outside of town, Lullabelle meandered through the overgrown grass surrounding her owner's ramshackle house. Jacob herded her into her pen, and then left a warning for Mr. Sullivan to keep his livestock secured.

Why even bother pretending he was a marshal rather than the town's errand boy? Other than the rustlers he couldn't catch, the worst crime in Armelle this month had been clothesline thievery. And the culprit was likely one of the students who often played hooky.

After returning to town, he slogged toward city hall.

Marrying Annie meant someone else could hold old women's smelling salts, lock up pigs, and pester people until they built sidewalks.

The clank of the tin bell above the collector's office door announced his arrival.

Bryant startled behind the hip-high counter and slammed the ledger shut in front of him. The man's dirty blond hair was mussed, as if he'd been working in the wind instead of inside. "Hey, Jake. Didn't expect you to drop in. Thought you'd had a lead."

"'Had' is about right." Jacob stepped to the counter separating them and held up his hands, making a gesture like he was strangling air. "Those rustlers like to frustrate me. My tipper knew what he was talking about though. I was out at dawn, and sure enough, on the Laramie under that clump of chestnuts, I found signs of a fresh camp. But the tracks disappeared into the river as they always do. Looked like they stole about thirty head this time. I know of some cattle missing from the Crawfords', but not that many." He didn't want to think of how close he'd been to nabbing them. He picked up a shred of paper from the counter and rolled it between his fingers. "However, I came here to see if you had time to talk about something else."

Bryant wiped at the sweat on his forehead despite the cool spring breeze coming through the windows. "I'm expecting someone." He glanced at his timepiece.

Jacob held in a sigh. Why did he feel as if Bryant would only talk to him if cornered lately?

Bryant wet his lips and then nodded. "But I can squeeze you in."

After looking about the office to make sure no one would overhear, Jacob leaned forward. "What would you say to me getting hitched?"

Bryant's eyebrows hit his hairline. "I'd ask which young lady was blackmailing you." He laughed, and then, tickled, seemingly couldn't stop.

Jacob's lips tightened into a thinner line as Bryant's laughter turned into amused tears.

After a few attempts to control himself, Bryant abruptly sobered. "You ... you mean you're seriously interested in one? Surely every single woman in this county has made a bid for you at least once already. Has Miss McGill finally won you over?"

Picturing himself taking tea at the mayor's mansion of a house with its gingerbread ornamentation and its pastel paint job made him shudder. McGill's daughter was all frills and lace and fluttering eyelashes. Whoever married her would probably have to tiptoe across pink rugs and dry his hands on his pants so he wouldn't dirty the embroidered towels. Perhaps McGill was always so irritable because he had to sleep in a room painted lavender and could never put his feet up on his doily-covered furniture.

Having McGill as a father-in-law would surely land success in Jacob's lap, though. The crotchety man possessed several places of business, the large ranch north of Annie's with forty cowhands, the mayoral position, and men falling all over themselves to solicit his good will.

Yet, if being the self-righteous McGill's employee chafed, then being his son-in-law would be intolerable.

And Miss McGill would probably dress him up in silk cravats and top hats.

"Not her. Considering I've been single this long, if I choose to marry someone that young, she'd have to be unusually mature—which is not an adjective I'd use for Miss McGill." She might be able to make a man sweat with a simple sweep of her hazy blue eyes, but she had no substance. A man didn't marry a pile of fluff and lace just because forty loomed closer every year. Better to be alone the rest of one's life than regret every last year of it. Perhaps he'd been too picky, but he'd seen too many unhappy couples result from careless matchmaking.

Besides, there just hadn't ever been anyone for him.

Bryant tapped his pen. "Who are you asking then?"

"Actually, she asked me."

"Really?" Bryant cocked his head and smirked. "Didn't think you'd go for a bold one. Though with the way you drag your feet..." Bryant forced a laugh. "That's probably the only way a woman could snag you with the matrimonial noose."

Jacob shook his head. "Don't you give me any 'ball and chain' talk. No man would think twice about settling down if he could get a wife who champions him like yours does."

Bryant tugged at his shirt buttons. "Yes, she does think I'm something." He cleared his throat. "But I'm curious to know who's turned your head."

Jacob leaned across the counter, but stopped, pressing his lips together. He hadn't decided on how to answer Annie's offer yet, and she'd be embarrassed if people knew he'd refused her—if that ended up being his decision.

Pulling back, he tapped his knuckles on the counter. "I best not say. It is a rather abnormal way to go about this, considering it'd be a marriage of convenience and all."

"What convenience do you need?" Stepping back, Bryant held up his fingers and ticked them off. "You own one of the best houses in town. You have a job that commands respect. You have girls vying for you, pretty ones I might add. You're good looking, have no real demands on your time outside of work, and shoot better than most in the county." Bryant clamped his hands on his hips. "What haven't you got?"

Stepping back to the wall behind him, Jacob seated himself in a chair. "I'd rather not live in town, my job is meaningless, and the girls you've seen following me around like puppies can't offer me more than an attractive face."

Bryant scoffed. "But this other girl can?"

Jacob put his hands behind his head and listened to the clock tick. Annie's ranch would give his time meaning. And though she wasn't the prettiest woman he'd ever seen, she sported a personality he admired—dedicated to the Lord, giving, hard working—and had children in need. He glanced at his friend, who waited with his elbows propped against the counter. "I believe so."

Bryant came around to take a seat a few feet away. "Don't tell me she'd be able to get you a ranch."

Jacob couldn't keep the smile off his face.

A groan emitted from Bryant's lips. "You'd be giving up one of the best jobs in the area. Your job as lawman is secure. But just one bad winter—"

"Nothing I've done since my parents sold the ranch has satisfied me, and you know that. I've yet to have enough money to buy property I'd be happy with since I waited too long and all the prices have shot up. But with her, I could have what I came up here for." Jacob leaned back in his chair. "I might be daft to pass on the offer."

Bryant leaned forward, his elbows denting his knees. "Unless the woman would make you miserable."

Jacob pictured Annie. Quiet, unassuming, and something behind her eyes that made his guts knot up. "I don't think so.

The girls in town can't compare, and bachelorhood doesn't hold much charm when you're living it."

The clatter of the bell made Bryant shoot up. Conrad McGill eyed the two of them, his nostrils flared like usual, as if his white walrus mustache constantly tickled his nose. "Gentlemen."

Jacob touched the brim of his hat but refused to jump out of his chair despite the censure he saw behind his boss's eyes. "Mayor."

McGill turned to Bryant, leveling an intense glare at the man. After receiving a slight nod from Bryant, the mayor walked behind the counter. "I'll be in my office if you need me."

As soon as McGill's door closed behind him, Jacob turned to his friend, who was standing straighter than a fence post. "McGill has the personality of a mule."

Bryant shrugged and sank back into his chair.

"He isn't making your work difficult, is he?"

"Why—" Bryant's voice cracked. "Why, not really." He stood again and smoothed his pants. "Just, you know, bosses are bosses. They're never happy."

"He's my boss too, but he seems more hands off with me." Jacob mentally shook his head at Bryant, who kept his gaze averted. What had happened to their carefree friendship? Any time he inquired into his friend's life lately, Bryant answered with clipped, careful sentences and changed the subject. Maybe he was facing hardship at home with Leah, though the thought of anyone having a hard time getting along with that sweet lady was almost impossible to believe.

"Ah, but you're free to walk around town, out from under his thumb. I'm under it all day." Bryant walked back behind the treasury counter. "So, I ought to at least act like I'm working." He flashed a smile that reached no deeper than his lips. "But as to your marriage plans, follow your gut. You generally make well thought-out decisions." The ledger's cover thumped onto the counter as Bryant flipped open pages. "Certainly, you make wiser decisions than I."

Jacob crossed his arms. "If any man in this territory chose a better wife for himself than you did, introduce me to him."

Ducking his head, Bryant twiddled a pen. "I can't take credit for Leah. She's a gift from above I don't deserve."

Was Annie and her land a blessing from God?

He'd never been so nervous to accept a gift.

After Jacob's long stride took him from the office, Bryant heard his boss's hefty plodding behind him.

"So Jacob didn't find the rustlers, I take it?" A wheeze whistled through McGill's vocal chords with every word.

"No." Bryant shook his head. Why did he even bother asking?

"You got the papers?"

Bryant slipped out the document he'd slid between the ledger's pages when Jacob walked in. He shoved it toward his boss. "Yeah."

"And the books?"

Footsteps in the hallway made Bryant look up. Once they passed, he turned to McGill. "They'll be done this afternoon, as long as I'm not interrupted again."

"Good. I need to take them to Robert on Monday for his approval. I want everything done by next week." His fingers drummed on the counter next to the ledger. "Remember, this is for their own good."

Right. Taking land from people was always for their own good. His heart thumped in a pathetic rhythm.

If only he had won a few more hands of poker. "Whatever you say."

McGill leaned on the counter and got in Bryant's face. "You're not backing out." He wasn't asking a question.

"No." If he revealed their boss's crimes to Jacob, McGill would end up in prison, but so would he. And then his sweet Leah would discover he was not what she thought him to be, and his daughter, Jennie, would no longer be able to attend the blind school.

He had a few small debts left, but he'd not stoop to ask McGill to cover for him ever again.

Using his pen, Bryant jabbed the air between him and McGill. "But this is the last time. I think I've more than paid for the debts I owe you."

Steepling his hands in front of his face, McGill stared Bryant down.

Bryant refused to lower his gaze.

"That's if you don't rack up any more debt."

"I won't, and even if I did, I won't be asking anything more from you."

"If that's so, get this one done right, and it's over. Probably a good thing. Don't want the marshal to start catching on. Four's probably pushing our luck anyway."

Bryant nodded. He knew how easily one could push his luck, because that's how he ended up in this mess.

McGill thumped the ledger. "Make it good and clean."

After his boss left, Bryant glanced through the hallway door window and listened for anyone heading toward the office. Once the quiet lasted a couple minutes, Bryant flipped open the ledger and found his place. He'd already fixed the critical lines, but he'd have to make sure there were no more entries needing doctoring.

He rubbed his temples. Would Leah forgive him if she discovered his involvement with McGill's underhanded dealings? At a minimum, she'd never think highly of him again.

He flipped over another page.

Thank you for keeping her from having any idea about what I'm doing.

But that prayer brought him no comfort.

CHAPTER SIX

"Wanna race?" Spencer poised himself to charge up and over the pond's bank.

"Not fair." Jacob waved the fishing gear in his hands. "You'll win for certain."

"I can carry something." Spencer extended his empty arms. "Then we'll both have to run with stuff."

Laughing, Jacob shifted everything into his right hand and ruffled Spencer's reddish-brown hair. "I think your mother would have a problem with me letting you run with pointy things." At Spencer's pouting lower lip, he added, "We'll race another day. Why don't we catch up with your sister?"

Off like a shot, Spencer ran after Celia. The girl had been indignant over him pulling her away from working the cattle earlier. Spencer would welcome a new father into his life, but Celia? Jacob quickened his pace to catch up.

Ahead on the bare plains, Spencer giggled as he circled his sister through the swishing grasses, darting in close to tickle her, ducking her attempts to smack him on his way out.

A Saturday morning of playing with the children had lightened the boy's spirits if not Celia's, though he'd caught her smiling at least once. Ranch children worked hard at chores, and rightfully so, but sometimes kids needed to play. He cherished the memories of his father occasionally dropping everything to romp around with him and his siblings for an afternoon.

He glanced at the Gepharts' little cemetery, a line of markers under a tree, a common sight in the west. Families were often quickly torn apart by life, but they had a bond stronger than any other.

Jacob plodded through the quick growing grass.

I hardly know her, Lord. These children aren't mine, and I haven't ranched in years. Shouldn't I be losing sleep over this decision? Am I imagining your peace, or am I smothering my jitters because I want this ranch so badly?

Last night, thinking perhaps he'd lost the sense to be nervous, Jacob had envisioned wedding Gwen McGill instead.

A shiver ran down his spine. Now that had worked him into a cold sweat.

If God disagreed with the decision Jacob had made last night, the Lord would have to warn him away before the wedding.

In the distance, Annie scurried from the barn to the house, her skirt caked in mud and decorated with stray straw. He didn't deserve a ranch, a wife, and children with so little effort.

Thank you, Lord, for your blessings.

With long strides, he caught up to the children and surveyed the land that would soon be his. Cows lowed in the distance and birds soared lazily in the blue haze embracing the mountains. Each whiff of air drifting from their peaks brought the spicy scent of cedars, pine, and sage. He sucked in that smell and held it for a minute before releasing his breath.

Before today, only his parents' Texas ranch had stirred him so.

At the porch steps, he dropped the tackle and poles.

"Spencer, why don't you put these away and bring in more wood? Celia, finish lunch for your mother, please."

Spencer darted off, but Celia cocked her head, a question written across her face, yet she kept her peace and finally turned to climb the steps.

He followed her in and walked over to where Annie was washing up. "Would you mind going on a walk with me? Celia will take over lunch."

After throwing a surprised glance toward her daughter, Annie nodded but didn't meet his eyes. "I'll just need to give her some directions first."

"Sure. I'll wait on the porch." He gave Celia a look, hoping she understood he expected her to follow through.

Outside, Jacob scanned the stubbly land. Green sprouted amidst the dead brown grasses covering the ground, and the cottonwood, standing guard over the gravesite, waved in the wind. He pulled on his tightening collar. How did a man offer his hand to a woman after she'd already proposed to him? A woman he'd be spending every day with—and every night. He squelched the heat radiating throughout his body with a deep breath. Her husband's death was too recent and her grief too raw for them to move forward with their relationship quickly, so he'd have to follow Annie's lead. How long until she'd decide her second marriage was no longer convenient but desirable?

No time for courting before the wedding though. The county required her tax payment next month—and two weeks was barely enough time to work in a wedding and a move.

The front door creaked open.

Annie's hands twisted in her apron with every step she took.

Jacob straightened and almost offered his arm, but she passed him and stepped off the porch, as if drifting in a daydream. Following, he placed one hand on her back and pointed toward the spring. "Why don't we head that way?"

The few times he'd talked to Annie in the past, she'd struck him as a decisive, confident woman, so her present shyness plucked at his heartstrings. He wished he could pull her into an embrace and smooth away her fears. "Thought we should talk."

She nodded. "Thank you for getting Celia to cook."

"No problem." How long had Celia been slacking on her chores? Hopefully she'd not be too much trouble. Enough young people in town bandied about defiant attitudes which often got them into scrapes with the law. But soon, worrying over the townspeople's foibles would no longer be his battle to fight.

After walking stiffly next to each other for a few paces, Jacob decided on a safe topic. "So, I've looked over your books, and you're right. You need help to keep this place running, but at the same time, I commend you for how well you've done."

Her eyebrows crinkled. "I've lost more cattle than we ever have before."

Jacob laid a hand on her shoulder. "You're not responsible for what rustlers do." He swallowed hard. Just because he couldn't catch them, didn't mean he was at fault for every new missing calf either.

Annie's head hung low, and her chest expanded with a huge sigh.

She sorely needed a hug, but he held off. She might not welcome an embrace yet. "You've got remarkable property here, and I have to say your garden arrangement is the neatest I've ever seen. I can't wait to see how well it produces this summer."

Her head snapped up, and she halted mid-stride.

His tongue turned into cotton as he looked into her wide eyes. Yes, he intended to be with her when the bean trellis flowered and the tomatoes fell off the vine.

She swallowed multiple times.

He pulled on his shirt collar, wishing he could unbutton it without looking uncouth. How did one propose when love wasn't part of the equation, yet make the moment something they'd treasure in the future?

Annie wrung her hands. Was the marshal saying what she thought he was saying? She'd been grateful when he hadn't turned her down flat the night she brought up this crazy idea, but truly, nothing about her would attract a man like him.

Well, besides the property. She shook her head at the ungracious thought, for that was exactly why she'd proposed to a stranger—to save Gregory's ranch. So if that's the reason Jacob chose to accept her unconventional proposal, she would never blame him for it.

Searching his dark brown eyes, she saw no pity or greedy anticipation. He'd proven himself this last week to be a sensible, caring man. She couldn't have made a wiser choice. If he didn't say yes, she'd sell. No other suitor could measure up.

His firm jawline indicated maturity and honor. His muscled arms hinted at hard work and strength. How would they feel wrapped around her? Her cheeks burned, and she looked away. No recent widow should think such things.

This is a business deal, Annie.

"I ... well—" Jacob exhaled, grabbed her shoulders, and looked her square in the eye. "That is to say, I would be honored if you would do me the favor of accepting me as your husband."

She wound a stray thread around her finger and tried to focus on him, but the word she needed to utter stalled on her lips. She should say yes—no question, no hesitation. She'd asked him for this, but now, a sudden need to know more ached in her chest. "Why?"

His eyebrows furrowed.

"I mean, I know you're offering because I asked, but how did you come to your decision?"

Nodding, he laced her arm through his and walked toward the natural spring. "Lots of reasons. I've wanted to ranch since my parents sold their cattle farm in Texas, but I've never had enough money for a piece of property I thought worthy of the attempt—I'm not a gambler. You and your husband chose your land wisely, and your improvements are sound."

Her chest filled with the pride Gregory would've felt from such a compliment. His inheritance had easily purchased the land, but he had run ahead of his expertise, making so many costly errors the money had disappeared. Jacob's exercise of caution before jumping into a profession, a commitment, boded well.

And she hadn't known about his prior experience with cattle, which made one of her fears melt away. She didn't want to relive the many ranching mistakes she and Gregory had made if she could help it. They'd been young, and with Gregory's unexpected inheritance from the early deaths of his parents, he'd come out to tame the West, hopping from one territory to another before they'd settled here. She'd never thought the money would run out, that she'd have to be responsible for more than hearth and home. But this time, she needed to be more involved, in case something happened to—

She shook her head. She'd not continue that thought.

"Also, I love your children. I know how it is to go years without a father's wisdom and a mother's love. With Mr. Gephart's death, Celia and Spencer are without a father and that hurts my heart." His hand slid across her back, and his arm settled across her shoulders.

Her skin tingled from his touch, and she looked up.

"And you, Annie Gephart, are an admirable woman whom I'd like to help."

Her heart pounded in her ears as her body focused on the warm arm wrapped around her. If God could help her future husband not get so tangled up in the land that he ignored his family, perhaps life could be better. Nothing wrong with wishing for the future to be better, right?

"And what about your ... expectations?" She shook her head and looked at the dirt at their feet. What was she thinking to lead a man on when she wasn't ready for—

"We're practically strangers, Annie." He tilted her chin up to gaze into her eyes. "We'll have plenty of time to get to those expectations."

She filled her lungs with pine-scented air until her chest nearly burst and glanced at the grave markers a handful of paces away. "Then I'll assist you in any way that I can if you'll help me keep this ranch for my children."

Thankfully, she'd not have to leave her three little ones behind. It was hard enough to think about them buried in the icy ground at night while she slept in a warm cabin, but it had been even harder to think of abandoning them forever. An irrational thought, yes, but one that had made her unable to sleep comfortably these past several days.

May you bless what I'm committing to for the sake of my family.

She squared her shoulders. "I suppose all we have left to do is set a date?"

"It'd be nice to hear you say 'yes' first." His sly grin caused her to blush.

She wrapped her arms about herself. "Yes," she whispered.

At his brightened smile, goose bumps traveled up her arms.

"When should we marry, Marshal Hendrix?"

His tongue darted out to wet his lips. "I think at this point you should call me Jacob." He took her cold hands and enfolded them into his warm ones. "And as for the date—tomorrow."

She blinked. Once. Several times. "Tomorrow?"

CHAPTER SEVEN

No matter how many times Annie wiped her sweaty palms on her skirt, they refused to remain dry. Unable to take her focus off the little white church they were heading toward, Annie couldn't keep the wagon from bouncing over every rut and hitting every hole in Main Street.

She passed Celia the reins. "Take these. I can't keep hold of them."

Her mouth grew drier the closer they got—the closer she was to being married again. All the time she had left as a widow was the time it took to sit through a service, shake people's hands, and walk an aisle. She pressed her eyes shut, wishing Spencer wasn't whistling so loudly she couldn't fully process the second thoughts swirling inside her.

Marrying really ought to be for more than material security, shouldn't it? Was this right for Spencer and Celia? Could Jacob ever—

Ploomp. Annie slid across the bench almost falling into Celia's lap. She smashed a hand against her hat to keep it from flying off.

"Sorry." Celia tugged the reins to the right.

Regardless, the wagon's back wheel followed the front's lead and thunked down into a hole the size of Mr. Sullivan's prize sow. Why did the council bother having Jacob insist on everyone building sidewalks when the road was in such need of repair?

Of course, in a matter of hours, he'd no longer need to deal with the city council at all.

Celia halted the team in the churchyard and said nothing. She'd held her tongue ever since Jacob had told the children they'd decided to marry.

Could she hope that under all her daughter's gruff defiance, a glimmer of maturity sparked? She could only pray it was so. She'd never had much problem with her daughter until after Gregory died, so perhaps a male adult's influence was what she needed to curb her rebellion.

Spencer scrambled out of the back of the wagon and ran straight for Jacob's house.

Celia remained in her seat, smoothing the folds of her nicest dress. "Are you all right, Ma?"

She wasn't. But her daughter wasn't who she needed to talk to about the swirling unease that made her want to jump off the wagon and run far, far away.

Annie's eyes grew hot, and she shrugged while staring down at the grime outlining her fingernails. What kind of woman got married with dirt embedded in the cracks of her hands? She'd been too busy keeping up with the garden to prepare properly for a wedding.

Celia leaned back against the hard wagon seat, but hadn't huffed in aggravation or impatience.

Annie looked up to see concern in her daughter's eyes. Was Celia truly thinking about someone other than herself today? "I'm nervous, I guess."

In front of them, couples and families walked through the churchyard. Some tipped their hats or gave them a friendly smile.

How would they look at her tomorrow once they learned of her quick nuptials? How many would shake their heads at her for marrying again so soon?

Celia climbed down, took a step toward the church, but then turned back and offered her hand to help her mother down. "Everyone's likely nervous on their wedding day, Ma. And you have more reason than most, I'd reckon."

Once Annie had alighted, Celia backed away and shrugged. "But I think Daddy would be happy you're saving his land. So if marrying the marshal's the best way to do it, then don't worry about it anymore."

The girl hadn't been this thoughtful in ages. Annie sighed. "Thank you, Celia, I—"

"Hey, Daniel!" Celia waved at a group of boys loitering across the street and ran straight for their neighbors' youngest.

"Celia! Sunday school's about to start." At Annie's call, the girl turned just enough to throw her a scowl before changing direction to stomp toward the marshal's place.

Now that was the Celia she knew.

But oh, how she preferred the daughter she'd glimpsed a few seconds ago.

Celia disappeared into Jacob's house, and Annie's heart beat hard against her chest. She had no reason to visit Jacob right now, but it felt odd to avoid the man she was about to marry.

She tried to brush the road dust off her best navy skirt and the carefully pressed rose-colored shirtwaist she'd pulled out of storage, but her damp palms acted more like magnets.

Walking over to one of Jacob's curtained windows, she used her reflection to adjust the flat-topped straw hat she'd purchased late yesterday. She couldn't afford a new dress, but she'd wanted something to mark the day and to appear as if she weren't in mourning anymore, though it was technically too early for that.

She frowned at her face beneath the ribbons and silk roses and stopped fiddling. No amount of fine-tuning could make her appear more beautiful. The wide pink and white striped ribbon around the hat's brim did make her eyes seem a little brighter though.

She looked up at the line of windows that spanned the second story of Jacob's house. Would he feel cramped in her cabin? Would she, once he moved in?

Nothing could be done about it now unless they called off the wedding.

And if he was having as many second thoughts as she was, he very well could.

Maybe popping her head into his Sunday school to ask if everything was set wasn't a good idea after all. If his handsome face was marred with a frown of displeasure or his eyes flashed pity when he saw her, how would she keep herself together during service?

"Jacob, you are so funny!"

A tinkling feminine giggle seized Annie's anxiously beating heart.

"Well, thank you. And thanks for the cookies as well." Jacob's low timbre dripped of solicitude.

Annie tried to swallow but couldn't.

However, her feet propelled her to the corner of the house just close enough to see who was talking to Jacob on his front porch.

The backside of a tall curvaceous blonde hid most of the marshal from view.

Gwendolyn McGill.

The young lady was never seen without a dainty hat atop her perfectly coifed hair and white gloves secured by dozens of pearl buttons. No woman out West should be able to keep such gloves as pristine as Miss McGill did, but then, the socialite never had reason to dirty them, considering her father was the richest man in Armelle and she the ultimate woman of leisure.

"After hearing how you burnt the cookies last week, I told Papa you'd welcome me taking care of that for you." Gwen placed her hand on Jacob's arm quite longer than necessary.

Annie slid back into the shadows and fingered a loose tendril of her own hair. She'd been so happy to coax it into thick waves this morning, but it was nothing like Miss McGill's perfect ringlets.

Miss McGill had never hidden her favor for the marshal, but Annie hadn't thought to think about their relationship before accepting Jacob's proposal. Did he have feelings for the young woman?

"I'll bring treats every week if you'd like." Miss McGill's voice quieted, her tone nearly a purr now. "Why! How about we just make this official and have little ol' me help you with Sunday school each week? Goodness knows a man ought to have a woman helping him with so many kids."

"Thanks for the offer, but I have it under control." Strolling footsteps sounded against the porch's planks. "I'll let you know if that changes."

Annie nearly took off to hide behind the house, but that would certainly look foolish. She forced herself forward to meet them at the stairs.

The pair noticed her at the same time as they stepped onto the ground together. Miss McGill stepped closer to Jacob, tightening her arm around his, and gave Annie a dazzling smile. Jacob stiffened.

"Good morning, Mrs. Gephart!" The blonde's blue eyes sparkled. "I just told Jacob he ought to get himself an assistant with so many children here on Sunday mornings. Don't you think he ought to take my advice and let me help out?"

Absolutely not.

Jacob's eyes widened like a deer's alerted to a human's presence, and he slid his arm from Miss McGill's grasp.

"Perhaps he does need a helpmate." Annie's voice came out flat, but the twinkle in Jacob's eye relaxed the tension in her jaw.

She let out a breath. "Good morning, Jacob."

"Good morning, Annie." A tilt of his lips made her feel

warm inside, but the warmth turned to heat when his gaze cascaded down the rest of her.

Miss McGill's smile twitched as she eyed the two of them. "Well, I think we're a tad late for our class, Mrs. Gephart. Why don't we let Jacob here get back to the children? If he needs help, he knows where to find me." She flashed her straight white teeth at him and then sashayed toward Annie. Her mouth was still curved, though downward now. "We are quite late, are we not?" She linked her arm through Annie's rigid one and pulled her in the opposite direction.

Annie looked over her shoulder as Miss McGill dragged her away.

"I'll see you after church." Jacob winked.

Annie gave him a timid smile.

Miss McGill dropped her arm and pivoted back, sporting her bright smile again. "Yes, after church."

Jacob's mouth skewed to the side, his eyes glittering more than usual. He tipped his head and walked back onto his porch.

When he disappeared inside, Miss McGill started them back toward the church.

Looming over town, at the far end of Main Street, the McGills' large house sat nestled against a small rise. Its twin turrets ascended toward the thin clouds wafting overhead, the pristine lawn full of flowering bushes.

Annie's smile faded. Why had Jacob chosen her over Miss McGill? Though Gwendolyn had no land of her own, her father surely had more than enough money to buy her and any future son-in-law five ranches twice the size of Annie's.

And Miss McGill was prettier, younger, and without the burden of children.

The young lady leaned to half-whisper in Annie's ear, keeping tight hold of her arm as she marched them toward the church doors. "I say, Jacob's downright good looking, isn't he?"

Miss McGill looked away to snag the attention of the town

lawyer, who tipped his hat at them as he passed. She reached out to clasp his coat sleeve and pouted becomingly. "Where're you going, Mr. Grayson? Don't tell me you aren't coming to church this morning."

He swept his hat off, revealing a glistening high forehead stretching toward his receding hairline. He gave her a slight bow. "Oh, no, Miss McGill. I'll be back shortly."

She pushed his shoulder with a playful flick of her hand. "Good. Wouldn't want to miss having your handsome self in there."

Annie switched her weight from one foot to the other and tried to put some space between her and Miss McGill. The woman always did flash smiles and flutter eyelashes at every man who walked past. Annie didn't want any man thinking she was as much of a flirt as Gwendolyn.

And why was Miss McGill latched so tightly onto her arm now anyhow? The young lady had never acknowledged her before, not beyond the normal exchange of pleasantries anyway.

Scowling, Annie tried to quicken the pace of Miss McGill's gliding walk.

A stride or two away from the entrance, Miss McGill whispered into Annie's ear again. "I think I've decided it's time to limit my charms for the enjoyment of just one man. Don't you think that's a good decision?" She waved her fan at a young man tethering his horse in the church's side yard.

Annie fought not to roll her eyes. It was a most unbecoming gesture, and she already looked dowdy enough attached to Miss McGill's fashionable arm. "Yes, I'd say that's wise."

She forced herself to take a slow breath. Could the town flirt be in want of motherly advice? After Gwendolyn's mother died, the mayor had become taciturn and difficult. Perhaps the young lady just needed someone to talk to. "Once a man shows you interest, it's best that—"

"Oh, I've got plenty of interest. Bored with it actually. So

I'm going to let the one I've chosen know I've decided on him. Don't you think the marshal and I would make an adorable couple?"

CHAPTER EIGHT

Upon spotting his wife trying to peer through a City Hall window, Bryant sped up. The blister forming on his heel stung, but he forged on. If only he hadn't needed to wear his dress shoes for this morning's unexpected "errand." But he'd known he'd be unable to swing back home and make it to church on time.

Which is where his wife should be already.

Leah backed away from the darkened window and tried the main door's knob, then turned with a frown.

He closed his eyes for a second as he crossed the last few feet to City Hall. What reason had he given her this morning about leaving early? He couldn't afford to mix up his stories.

"Oh, there you are!" Leah's beautiful face practically shone when she caught sight of him.

He returned the smile as best he could and held out his arms. She rushed to his side and snuggled in.

He leaned down to kiss her brow. Hopefully, he could keep her from asking where he'd been. "I told you I'd be at church before you finished your scales." He brought up her hand to kiss the long graceful fingers that played the piano so well she transformed an entire congregation's inability to sing into a pretty sound every Sunday.

"I know, but after overhearing the pastor talking to Jacob, I couldn't contain myself." She shimmied her shoulders, the movement making her seem younger than forty-two. "I thought you told me he was only thinking about getting married. I didn't realize the wedding would be today!"

He stiffened, but she didn't seem to notice since she was practically floating.

"I figured you were getting the license ready, so I came over to find out who the lucky bride is."

He repressed a sigh. Yesterday, Jake had dropped in to ask about getting a marriage license, but he'd come in right before one of McGill's lackeys was supposed to arrive.

He'd told Jake it would be easy enough to take care of before church and had practically pushed his friend out the door.

It was just as well. McGill had been particularly difficult yesterday. How long until Jake grew suspicious at the escalating tension between them—if he wasn't already?

But it would all be over in a matter of weeks, and then life could return to normal, for him anyway. He wasn't the one marrying a stranger. "Uh, if Jake didn't mention who he's marrying, maybe he wants to keep it a secret."

He'd have to slip out of church during the sermon and fill in the license as best he could to keep Jake from asking why he'd not met with him this morning. He hadn't expected some lowlife to accost him on his way to the privy last night, demanding he pay something on what he owed unless he wanted his bookmaker's henchman to break every bone in his body.

As long as Leah didn't dig through their youngest daughter's hope chest any time soon, he'd be all right. Her great-grandmother's opal ring was acting as collateral, but he'd have it back within the week.

"Oh, pooh, it'll only be an hour and a half before everyone

knows who she is, though I bet I can figure it out beforehand. Since we don't have many visitors, a new woman would likely be the one, but if it's someone we already know..." Her eyes lit up. "Do we already know her?"

Considering he was the worst of friends and hadn't been able to talk to Jake about this wedding—or rather talk him out of it—he didn't even have to bluff. "I can't tell you, but I'm sure you'll have fun guessing."

"I'm not supposed to be having fun guessing. I'm supposed to be paying attention to the sermon."

He smiled stiffly. He'd been pretending to pay attention to the pastor for about a year now. Some days he could've sworn the man knew what he was up to and had fashioned his sermon especially for him. But Pastor Lawrence didn't know a thing, so he'd tuned him out to keep from feeling worse than he already did. "Admit it, if I told you who she was, you'd still have a hard time paying attention."

"Yes." She heaved a sigh. "Isn't it romantic?" Her eyes turned dreamy.

Though they'd been married nineteen years, that look always took his breath away. He leaned down to kiss her well, savoring her sweetness.

When they'd first married, he'd thought he'd deserved such bliss, but now he knew how unworthy he was of it.

He broke away and kissed her forehead instead.

She laced her fingers into his and pulled him toward church again. "Come. If you refuse to tell me, I'll want to figure it out before service starts or I'll flub up every hymn."

He chuckled as if enjoying the thought of the game and sped up to match her happy pace. "If you figure out who she is before the service starts, help me get Jake to reconsider by convincing this woman that they need to think this through for longer than a second."

She slowed and furrowed her brow. "Why would I do that?"

"Because Jake's got some notion that she's the one, though

you and I both know he'd attempt to ranch a rock-strewn desert if it meant he'd be out from under McGill's thumb."

She just gave him a silly shake of her head and went back to tugging him forward. "Jake's not that foolhardy; otherwise, he'd have bought a place already. Besides, I knew you and I would end up together the day we met."

"Yes, but you had the sense to wait more than a week to get hitched."

She twirled her arm around his and laid her head against his shoulder for a brief hug. "But we hadn't any pressing business to attend to once the war was over. We had no reason to skip the fun of courting."

He sighed and pulled her closer. If only adult matters weren't weighing so heavily upon him now, he'd be carefree enough to recreate some of that courting fun.

Just a few more months and all would return to normal. She'd been a peach while he'd been stressed lately, leaving him alone when asked, treating him as if everything was fine though he was gone more than usual and testier than he ought to be. She deserved a few nights out lying under the stars, or a fancy supper at the hotel, or—

"So where were you this morning?" Her voice stayed light, but sounded breathless against his side. "I saw you coming from Second Street ... and I can't come up with a reason you'd be coming from that direction."

He forced his hand to keep rubbing her arm as if the question hadn't just catapulted his heartbeat up into his throat. He should have encouraged her to keep guessing about Jacob's bride. "Oh, I ... heard of someone who needed money. Lots of people are facing higher taxes this year."

Both sentences true, though they had little to do with each other. "I figured I could help the man out."

"You're so good." She looked up at him, wearing the grin that meant she was waiting for him to kiss her breathless.

He pretended to stumble instead, then nodded toward the

church. "Let's get you to the piano before Sister Elspeth decides to take your place. If the congregation is glaring at you all through service because you allowed Elspeth to murder their ears, you won't have much fun trying to figure out who Jake's bride is."

He glanced up at the sky.

I know you're likely not listening to me at the moment, but if Jake's going to do this fool thing, bless him with a good woman. He deserves one more than I do.

The sermon was halfway over when Annie tucked her trembling arm around Spencer. The boy had dozed off against her side, so he was oblivious to how tightly she was squeezing.

But each bump and jostle from her other side, where Jacob's warm arm kept rubbing against her as he took notes, was sending sizzling rivulets of awareness through her skin.

Miss McGill, across the aisle and two pews up, was doing her best to douse that fire with the cold glare she kept sending their way.

The young blonde wasn't the only congregant interested in Jacob's new choice of seating. Leah Whitsett smiled at them from behind the piano between each new hymn, and an older woman up front kept looking between the three women as if trying to discern what Annie had done to earn such opposite reactions from the other two.

Jacob's attention never wandered from his Bible or the preacher.

Despite the evil thoughts Miss McGill surely directed her way, Annie couldn't help but smile a little.

The self-assured, young lady would soon learn that Jacob was in no danger of being trapped by her daintily-gloved, feminine hands, but Mr. Grayson or the other bachelors in town?

Heaven help them.

Annie shook her head and tried to focus on what Pastor Lawrence was saying, but it hardly did any good.

Soon, the first chord of the final hymn sounded. The congregation rose, and Annie had to extricate herself from Spencer, who was limp as a dishrag. Celia didn't bother to stand, just continued writing in the journal she'd brought along.

Annie held her breath and forced herself to face forward instead of glaring at her daughter. She'd not get into a tussle on her wedding day.

Jacob held his hymnal between them and his rumbly bass voice, which she'd only ever heard from afar, reverberated in her chest. The last verse brought her shudders back in full force.

Once the building was empty, the pastor would hold the ceremony.

Jacob had requested that Pastor Lawrence not invite the church members to stay, though they did need witnesses. But Jacob was sure the Whitsetts would agree, and she was too. It was well-known that Jacob could be found at their place if not at his office. Would they still invite him over with a full-formed family in his wake?

Hopefully. Annie closed her eyes to stanch the warmth behind them. She hadn't enjoyed friendship with another woman in a long while. She was going to need someone to talk to as she navigated the choppy waters of being married to a man she hardly knew.

The song's last notes faded and the congregation came to life as they shuffled out of pews and called to friends.

"I'll be out front." Jacob squeezed her hand and left for the foyer where he usually stood with the pastor on Sundays, exchanging small talk with those exiting and helping elderly widows down the steps.

After pretending not to see the frown Miss McGill directed at her and exchanging pleasantries with the women who engaged her in small talk, Annie sat down to wait, smoothing her son's hair against his furrowed forehead. Surely he wasn't having a bad dream; he'd been so happy with her decision to marry Jacob.

Celia drew in her journal, sighing every few minutes.

Annie worked to keep her legs still.

The noise in the sanctuary lessened, and Spencer's head jerked forward. He blinked with exaggeration. "Mama, why didn't you wake me up?"

He rubbed the side of his jaw where the imprint of the curve of the pew's seat dented his cheek. "My face hurts."

Smiling, Annie pulled him close. "We weren't ready yet, so I decided to let you sleep."

Miss McGill's tinkling laughter caught her attention. Shouldn't the young lady have left already?

Turning, Annie craned her neck to see into the foyer. Gwendolyn was tapping Jacob with a gloved finger, but his face remained blank.

Twisting back around to stare at the Bible in her lap, Annie fiddled with the worn ribbon marker. If she had set her cap for Jacob when she was nineteen or twenty—as Miss McGill obviously had—only to find out someone of lesser means and beauty had captured him, the heartache wouldn't have been small.

Lord, help her get over her disappointment quickly. Help me to stay humble, for nothing I did won him over.

The foyer emptied save for Jacob, Bryant, Leah, and the pastor. Annie swallowed a deep gulp of air and stood up. "It's time, children."

Spencer popped up from his seat like a disturbed sage chicken flying from the brush, and Annie grabbed his hand before he flew pell-mell down the aisle.

Celia sighed before rising to shuffle after them.

She'd intended for the children to stand up with her during the wedding, but until this moment, she'd not thought about the ceremonial kiss. How would they react to that? Her insides quivered. How would she? Surely Jacob would give her nothing more than a peck on the lips—if the pastor even included it in the ceremony.

Moving toward her intended, she took in his heavy brow and smooth-shaven jaw. Even a small kiss from such a handsome man would likely make a woman fall to pieces.

Leah smiled brightly at Annie and the children as they moved toward the foyer.

She put on a matching smile and straightened her shoulders.

Everything would be all right, kiss or no.

Bryant grabbed a fistful of Jacob's suit coat and shook his head. "Not her, Jake." His voice was a low, quiet growl, but still loud enough that she could hear it. "You can't marry her."

Annie stopped mid-step and forced herself not to run for the back exit.

Seemed as if worrying about whether or not Jacob would kiss her was all for naught.

Not marry her? Jacob frowned at Bryant's furrowed brow and erratic jaw movements.

Behind Bryant and a frozen Leah, Annie had jerked to a stop in the church aisle and pulled Spencer to her side.

What did Bryant have against her? Jacob's lips twitched at the fierce glare Celia was directing at his best friend. The look he'd given Bryant a second ago probably hadn't been much nicer.

Whatever Bryant's reasons, he didn't have to speak so vehemently against Annie within her hearing.

Jacob tipped his head toward the exit. "Let's go outside."

He gave Annie a reassuring smile, but it didn't seem to work. She looked away, her bottom lip tucked under her top teeth.

After stepping out onto the sunny church steps, Jacob waited for the door to shut behind Bryant before gobbling up the sidewalk with long strides, heading straight for his house next door.

He clomped up the porch steps, leaned against the railing, and set his jaw.

Bryant took his time, waving at church-goers on the street driving home.

McGill's carriage horse bolted out from around the corner of the church. Unfortunately, Gwen winked at him from where she sat on the other side of her father, and Jacob looked away.

Bryant had often asked if he intended to marry Gwen, a flirtatious, spoiled rich girl nearly half his age, yet Bryant insulted a woman of real depth and character? Practically to her face?

Jacob heaved a sigh to calm himself. Over the years, Bryant had said he trusted Jacob's instincts, so the man must have something heavy against Annie to have said what he had.

Shaking his head, he ran his fingers through his hair. He should've gone to Bryant's house early this morning or waited longer for him to show up at City Hall, but Bryant had said there'd be no problem drawing up the license quick and he'd not stayed around to question him since Bryant had been swamped.

If he hadn't dropped in while the man was so busy yesterday, this wouldn't have happened.

His friend's gaze darted up and down the street before he finally walked up the porch steps.

For a man so adamant that he call off this wedding, Bryant sure didn't seem eager to tell him why.

Bryant stopped several feet in front of him and strangled his hat. "You can't marry her, Jake."

"You've already said that. In front of Annie." His voice rang out loud enough he needed to rein in his temper lest the whole town hear them. He swallowed and tried again. "But your say-so doesn't mean I'll call things off. I need reasons."

His friend's Adam's apple moved slowly with a big swallow. "Well, you hardly know the woman."

Jacob uncrossed his arms and put his hands on the railing, squeezing the rough wood. That was it? "Do you have something personal against Annie?"

"It's more that..." He twirled his hat in his hands. "Would you be happy with her if she didn't have all that land?" Bryant sniffed and scratched his head. "I mean, you are just marrying her for the land, right?"

Had Bryant not listened to him the other day? Did he think him so desperate as to marry for land alone? Sure, Annie's ranch was the initial enticement, but the woman and her family pulled at his heart too.

During the last few months, his and Bryant's relationship had been strained, but not so much he'd believe Bryant would think so badly of him. "Of course her property figured into my decision, but I'm confident the marriage will be satisfying ... in time."

"You want Annie for herself?" The disbelief in Bryant's voice stung.

He tensed his jaw. "She may not be as attractive as your wife, but she displays the same worthy characteristics—strength, maturity, respectability."

Bryant's face reddened, his lips as tight as a steel-jawed bear trap.

Jacob wanted to whack the tension from the man's face and give it a flush of a different sort. Instead, he glanced toward the church, then closed his eyes and envisioned his intended. The only woman in town who wasn't shorter than his chest pocket. A lady who took on a man's job without complaining during the worst time of her life. The quiet but assured demeanor that stirred something more than compassion in his chest. Life with her should be enjoyable once they got to know each other.

Jacob rolled his neck and turned to fasten his gaze on Bryant. "You said days ago I should only consider marrying for land if the woman attached to it wouldn't make me miserable. Can you speak ill of her?"

Frowning, Bryant stared at their feet.

"Maybe we can't speak of love at the moment, but I can't fathom why there wouldn't be that in our future."

"But I'm concerned." Bryant pulled so hard on his hat Jacob feared he'd rip it in two. "For you."

Jacob sighed. "If you have no concrete reasons, you're going to have to trust me. If you have a problem standing up as witness, I can find someone else. Annie's waiting, and with your ill-timed advice, who knows how much she's panicking." He jerked his head toward the church. "Are you coming?"

Bryant's breath shuddered, but his gaze remained pinned to the ground.

"Yes or no?"

CHAPTER NINE

From her pew, Annie stared at the pulpit—where no one stood. The pastor had told her to fetch him from his office when they were ready to proceed.

With slumped shoulders, Leah slid onto the pew beside Spencer, who was snuggled up against Annie's side.

She hadn't seen Leah this subdued except once—at a funeral. Annie hung her head. Her chance at keeping the ranch and having another adult help rear her children had left before it came.

"Will he come back, Mama?"

She pulled Spencer to her side and squeezed. Would her son bounce back after yet another tragedy? When did the boy's God-given talent to keep his joy in the midst of trials run dry? She nuzzled her chin into his soft hair and felt him sigh. "I don't know."

Celia hadn't yet said a word since they'd returned to sit in the pew, but evidently she was worried enough to cease drawing in her journal.

"I'm sure this is nothing, but prayer never hurts." Leah bowed her head.

Colored light, shining through the stained glass window of Christ praying in the garden, flickered behind the pulpit. The clouds racing across the sun made the splotchy light flicker from shadows to bright spots as quickly as Leah's whispered petitions changed from one request to another.

Minutes ago, Leah had seemed certain the men would settle their differences and return for a wedding. Perhaps she didn't think so any longer.

Was Bryant's reluctance God's way of stopping Annie from making a mistake? She'd prayed God would stop her if things weren't right, but her heart must have gotten more attached to Jacob than she'd thought, or at least the idea of Jacob, since she didn't really know him.

Though she wanted to watch for his return—to know immediately what his decision was by the look on his face—she didn't. The faint ticking of the foyer clock filled the room, and her heartbeat grew louder with each slow-going minute.

Did Bryant truly have that much against her?

She hadn't faulted him for his signature at the bottom of her tax notice or his refusal to extend her deadline—not much anyway. Yet now, when she'd found a way to comply with the county's demands, he stood in her way. That felt vindictive.

Annie exhaled hard. She shouldn't be making judgments.

Well, maybe she would later, but not before she knew the outcome of the men's conversation.

She lifted her gaze to the Gethsemane glass. *All right, not even then. He's yours to judge. But you're going to have to help me not think ill of that man if I end up at home alone tonight.*

Leah reached over and pried Annie's fingers off the wooden seat and held on tight.

The screech of the front doors' hinges broke the silence.

A sudden shiver of hot then cold raced down her arms, and Annie fixed her eyes on the angular drops of blood marring Christ's forehead. No matter what happened, there were worse things in this world to face. If she could survive the day her husband's murdered body had been found draped across a horse, she could live through this.

Spencer squirmed in his seat like an anxious puppy. Leah's hand was clamped so tightly around hers, one might think Leah's life was hanging in the balance.

Annie couldn't keep herself from turning around any longer.

Bryant walked up the aisle, a false smile marring his lips.

No Jacob.

"I think everything's fine. He's smiling," Leah said and released Annie's hand.

Annie's muscles refused to relax though, and she rubbed her tingling fingers. Why hadn't Jacob returned?

Bryant's gaze caught hers, and his half smile twisted into a grimace.

Could he not even stand to be in the same room with her?

"Bryant, dear." Leah sidled up close to him as he neared the cluster of Gepharts. He slid his hand across Leah's shoulders and visibly relaxed.

But Annie couldn't. Not until she knew if she was leaving this church with or without a husband.

"What was wrong?" Leah's whisper traveled across the sanctuary as if it were a ringing tower bell.

Annie watched every muscle in Bryant's face.

He rubbed his wife's shoulder. "Nothing. A misunderstanding."

"Good, I'm glad." Leah nestled into his side.

This saint of a woman obviously loved her husband, and here Annie was thinking ill of him. Maybe she'd read too much into his hesitation. Perhaps his rudeness hadn't been on purpose.

She forced herself to speak. "Where's Jacob?" The rasp in her voice hurt her throat.

"He forgot something." Bryant wouldn't look her in the eye. "Said he wouldn't be long."

Celia melted back into her seat, and Spencer hugged Annie's waist.

Leah threw Annie a dazzling smile. "Since the day Bryant told me Jacob was thinking of marrying someone, I've been praying it was you. Isn't God good?"

"If anyone knows, dear, it'd be you." Bryant patted her arm, though his gaze seemed unfocused.

Lord, help me to give over my fears. Let me have Leah's faith that you won't hand me a snake when I request a fish. Let me—

The groan of the foyer door halted both her prayer and the beating of her heart. She pulled in a deep breath to restart her pulse and turned.

Jacob walked in, shut the door, and hung his hat on the hall tree—all without taking his eyes off her.

"Come on, you two." Leah beckoned to the children. "Let's get Pastor Lawrence." She pulled Bryant toward the front as if she'd been looking forward to this wedding for ages, and Spencer and Celia dutifully fell in line.

Strolling through the foyer doorway leading into the sanctuary, Jacob gave her a lazy smile that made her insides soften into slow-dripping molasses. His eyes drilled into hers, as he walked toward her, palms open in front of him. "You still willing to be my wife?"

The corners of her eyes grew moist, and the breath she'd been holding escaped. She rose unsteadily. "I think so, if you think so."

He chucked her chin. "I think so." He pulled her arm through the crook of his and led her to the front where the pastor now flipped through pages, his spectacles balanced on the end of his nose.

The Whitsetts and the children gathered around them and Pastor Lawrence looked up from his book. "Shall we begin?"

Annie nodded. Though the pastor started reciting the familiar ceremonial passages, all she saw was the pastor's bald spot as he read from the Bible in his hands.

And all she felt was the warmth of Jacob—close beside her, fingers betwixt hers.

Not so long ago, Gregory had stood at her side before a similar pulpit, his tenor voice spitting out the repeated phrases as if the faster he spoke them, the sooner they could kiss. His bold gaze had made her thankful to be wearing her grandmother's veil.

Her breathing sped up. It was too soon to be in front of an altar again. The room seemed to close in, as if she were a chicken cornered by a fox in the coop.

She placed her clammy hand against her temple.

Jacob started rubbing the back of her other hand, the rhythmic motions sending a fresh calm sweeping through her.

"Do you have rings?"

Annie glanced down at her left hand. The wedding band she'd worn for the last sixteen years was still there, pitted and dull. The ring never came off without a liberal application of olive oil soap and lots of twisting. How had she forgotten?

Jacob grabbed her hand and quickly covered the plain gold band with his large thumb. He shook his head slightly. "Just one for Annie."

"Very well, repeat after me."

The pastor's words faded as she stared at Jacob's thumb. Would he pretend the ring on her finger was from him?

"With this ring, I thee wed." A bright multi-colored stone on a silver band appeared. Jacob slid it on top of her wedding band, the jewelry piece so large it covered the smaller ring with room to spare.

"My grandmother's," he whispered.

She stared at the large square stone offset by four tiny bluish ones. She'd never seen anything so exquisite.

The pastor cleared his throat. "Since you don't have a ring, Annie, simply hold Jacob's hand and repeat after me."

She clenched her fingers so Jacob's ring wouldn't slide off and reached for his hand.

"I thee wed," the pastor said.

She took a steadying breath and looked up at Jacob. "I thee —" His fetching brown eyes grew softer at her words. "—wed."

"You may kiss the bride."

Her breathing escalated and heat warmed her cheeks. While she'd waited for Jacob and Bryant to return, she should've told the pastor to adjust the ceremony's end—but then, she'd been certain there wasn't going to be one.

Jacob's hands traveled up the length of her arms and took hold of her shoulders. Her hands traveled up his in a similar fashion, and she held on as if dangling from a precipice.

She braced herself for a quick, cold press of the lips, but his warm, soft ones met hers. And stayed. A sweet soft pressure. She peeked through her eyelashes at him, but his eyes were closed. Then his image blurred, and nothing but the light weight of his kiss existed.

She'd never kissed anyone but Gregory. How would he feel if he could see the race of heat rushing from her lips and into her cheeks right now?

Jacob's mouth left hers, and a tear slid from her right eye.

"I now pronounce you Mr. and Mrs. Hendrix." The pastor's words echoed in the nearly empty sanctuary. Jacob's thumb smudged the wetness from her cheek, and she opened her eyes.

Jacob smiled, Bryant groaned, and Spencer gave a celebratory yip.

Annie loosened her hold on Jacob's shoulders, leaving his suit fabric mangled from her tight grip, and took a step back.

The pastor gestured to the best man. "Let's sign the license."

Bryant gave a start and pulled a folded paper out from under his suit coat. Striding quickly across the room, he nearly tripped on his way to the communion table.

They all followed, but with how Bryant hunched over the paper like a coyote guarding his lifeless prey, did he intend to keep them from signing it?

Leah stepped beside him with a hand to his back. "Dearest," Leah whispered. "Careful. Don't tear the paper."

Jacob moved to Bryant's other side, his mouth scrunched, gaze guarded.

Bryant had said they'd only had a misunderstanding, but Jacob's every visible muscle was taut as he watched his best friend seemingly hesitate to sign his name.

Once Bryant handed the pen to Leah, Annie moved to the drafty window.

The long-lasting blizzard snow that had swirled around her dead husband's body still dotted the shadowy places against the foundation of Jacob's house across the yard. Yet here she stood, married to another.

Leah came over to clasp Annie's arm. "Please have lunch with us. I would've whipped up something fancier if I'd known what a special day this was. Regardless, there's enough for everyone."

Annie looked to Jacob, who nodded.

Just because Bryant didn't seem to think today was something to celebrate, that didn't mean she needed to act likewise. "That sounds wonderful. I hadn't thought of food."

"Of course you didn't." Leah pulled on her arm, and Annie followed her through the sanctuary and outside to where her children had disappeared.

Celia sat on the church railing near Spencer, who was balancing atop it as if standing on a tightrope.

Annie tugged on his pant leg. Hopefully the pastor hadn't followed them out to see her son's misuse of church property. "Come down. The Whitsetts are going to feed us lunch."

"Woohoo!" Spencer jumped from the rail with a thud.

Bryant stepped off the porch, squinting against the sun. "I can't stay to eat. I've got work to do."

Leah's eyebrows descended. "Since when do you work on Sundays?"

"If I'm able to write up a marriage license on Sunday, I can surely record it the same day. Plus there are other things I have to attend to." Bryant turned to Annie and gave her an awkward bow. "I'm sorry I can't stay." He shuffled off without a glance at Jacob.

Leah clamped her hands onto her hips. "I don't know what's gotten into that man." She cast Annie a sympathetic expression. "He's been out of sorts lately. Please don't think it's just you."

Jacob's hand slid to the middle of Annie's back. "Don't let him trouble you."

Oh, but he did. She spun the rings on her finger and looked back at the church. "Celia, go with Spencer to the Whitsetts', would you? I'll be along in a moment."

Leah gave her a worried glance before following after the children, and Jacob looked toward the church doors.

His lips skewed to the side. "If you're planning to go back in there and ask for an annulment, you'd discuss it with me first, yes?"

Annie couldn't help but melt a little at his unease, even if he was just marrying her for the land. "I promise I'll return with this ring still on my hand." She wriggled her fingers, the sunlight catching the stone.

"Good." He grabbed her hand, brought the ring to his lips, and kissed it. "Hurry back, Mrs. Hendrix." He gave her a dimpled grin and then strode off to catch up with the children.

The warmth on her hand from his kiss matched the warmth he'd left on her lips earlier. This man was going to do right by her.

So she had to do right by him.

She climbed the stairs and quietly entered the church. Stopping next to the first pew, she pulled off her giant ring, holding it up to the light. Her mother would be impressed. She put it in her pocket and walked to the lamp in the corner. After disassembling it, she dipped her finger into the oil and twisted Gregory's ring off.

The red velvet offering bag lay limp on the front row, the collected money most likely in a deacon's possession for depositing in the bank tomorrow. She dropped the tarnished gold band inside and messed with the fabric folds so no one would notice anything had been left in the pouch. It'd probably be smarter to wait until next week, but she'd married Jacob today. For him, she needed to put Gregory behind her.

However, she couldn't tear her gaze away from the plush bag. How could she throw such a big part of her life away in seconds? Forget a man in a matter of months?

She fished the ring back out and looked out the side window where she could see her family about to cross the street in front of Jacob's house. He laughed at something Celia said and ruffled Spencer's hair. The scowl on Celia's face indicated she hadn't said anything she thought was funny.

Jacob hadn't asked her to give up this ring. One of the children might want it, dull as it was.

With a quick inhale, she dropped it into her skirt pocket.

She slipped the wide silver ring Jacob had given her back on and held it in place with her thumb. The stone caught the light and added minuscule rainbows to the stained glass highlights splashed across the walls.

Dear Lord, help me find peace amid the war raging within me. I can't be faithful to two men, and yet I feel as if I've just betrayed both.

CHAPTER TEN

Bryant's heart beat so fast and his breaths came so shallow, it was as if he'd run the entire way to City Hall. With shaky hands, he managed to unlock his office door on the second try. After crossing the dim room, he reached for the curtains, but stopped. He couldn't chance anyone alerting McGill that he was rummaging around, at least not until he was done saving Jacob's land.

At the front counter, Bryant fumbled around the shelves for the barely used lamp.

"Please let there be oil in it." He swished the base, and liquid sloshed. He patted around for the box of matches. Once his vision adjusted, the sunlight creeping in around the curtains was adequate for walking around, but finding the correct paper in McGill's office would require more light since he'd not risk pulling up the shades.

The hinges on his boss's door groaned. Bryant clicked the door shut and set the lantern down. Then he cranked the wick high.

Flickering shadows filled the room.

Scurrying behind his boss's desk, Bryant jimmied the lock in the top drawer. Thankfully McGill had never taken the time to fix the cockeyed compartment.

His boss had intended to evict the Gepharts two days ago, which would've kept Jacob from marrying Annie, and Bryant from adding to his pile of sins. But McGill had been called out of town last Wednesday, delaying his plans.

How had he been so wrapped up in his own problems he'd not bothered to ask Jacob anything more about the woman he intended to marry? Of course Jacob would fall for the most desperate of women.

After the ceremony, he'd nearly spilled his whole list of crimes right then and there to keep from filling in the license and sealing Jacob's fate, but then he'd remembered McGill driving off with Gwen after church—which meant he'd not be in the office.

Please Lord, I know I don't deserve any kindness from you, but Jake does. I don't know if I'll escape with my life if I succeed, but at least if McGill murders me, Leah won't find out why since he won't incriminate himself. Anything you could do for me to keep her from knowing, anything…

If he could just destroy the loan document he'd forged, redo all the doctored entries, and whatever else he could think of to ruin his boss's ability to steal Annie's land, Jacob could own that ranch and not be stuck with a destitute wife.

Bryant licked his fingers and whipped through another stack of pages.

The pendulum clock ticked relentlessly behind him as he thumbed through useless information and old bills.

Thump.

A door slam.

Bryant froze.

Light spilled in through the edges of the closed office door.

Bryant lowered his handful of papers back into the drawer and slid it shut as noiselessly as possible.

How likely was it that McGill wouldn't visit his office?

The doorknob turned.

Not likely at all.

Bryant turned down the lamp wick, though the effort was futile.

The office plunged into darkness for a second before the outer light spilled in.

Bryant pushed the heels of his hands into his eye sockets and groaned.

"What are you doing in my office, Whitsett?" McGill's low grumble made Bryant shiver. The mayor's footsteps thumped toward the window, and he pulled open the curtains. "And why are you in the dark? I doubt you have a good explanation for this."

Bryant slapped his palms against the desktop. If he didn't defect now, the mayor would own his soul. He yanked the stack of papers back out from the drawer and glared at the man for a second before thumbing through them. "I do." Paging through the documents, Bryant tried to will his body to cease trembling. "You told me the first forgery would cover the debt I owed. It wasn't my fault it didn't profit you as much as you'd projected." He tapped the pile of papers he'd shuffled halfway through. "I'm not taking part in this anymore."

McGill's casual stance told Bryant he had the wrong stack.

He threw the papers back into the drawer and shut it.

"You agreed to this one. You aren't backing out."

"Who says I'm not?" Bryant pulled open the next drawer.

"I'm sure your wife would thank you if you didn't."

He narrowed his eyes at his rotund boss and wrenched out a folder crammed in the back. "What's that supposed to mean?"

Without moving from his leisurely position against the wall, McGill grabbed a toothpick from his chest pocket and took his time picking his teeth.

The man believed he had Bryant right where he wanted him.

And he most likely did.

Bryant set his jaw and urged his stomach to settle.

"I doubt she'd like to hear what sort of things her hero of a husband's been doing lately." McGill used his toothpick to mimic a bird in flight. "If some little birdy flew by a'singing, she just might be devastated to hear the lyrics."

"You won't tell her." Bryant's hands trembled, but thankfully they were hidden from view behind the desk. "You'd implicate yourself."

McGill's mouth scrunched back and forth. The clock's ticking grew louder. "True. But she'd not share what she'd learn with anyone else lest you end up in jail. But you, however, would suffer the consequences of a woman scorned."

"She's too good. She'd turn me in along with you." Bryant wouldn't ask her to cover for him, not when he deserved punishment. "She'd be consumed with guilt if she didn't."

McGill pushed off the wall. "So why's your conscience plaguing you now? We've already discussed how this would be good for the widow."

"In your opinion."

"Yes." McGill snapped his toothpick. "So what's panicked you so much you're sneaking around in my office?" He grinned, slow and wide. "Looking for papers that aren't even here?"

Bryant fought to keep the defeated groan inside. He pushed his chair back and stood. "Because this one will hurt a friend. A friend I didn't know would be involved."

McGill's face went blank for a moment, but then he smiled large enough to contort his mustache, making Bryant want to vomit. "I'd overheard something about the marshal getting married." He huffed a semi-laugh. "Chose her, did he?" When Bryant didn't respond, he walked around the desk and shoved the open drawers closed. "That does put you in an awkward position. But then, he'll never know."

"Correct. He'll never know his land was in jeopardy if we stop this now."

"Too late." McGill set down his satchel and unhooked its straps. "I had Mr. Grayson draw up the papers last Friday. Judge

Macrow has been informed, and my boys have taken care of the evidence." McGill licked the tips of two fingers and snatched some pages from inside his case. "And since Macrow is completely oblivious, it wouldn't be wise to turn yourself in to the man who'll be sentencing you, considering how often you've duped him."

Mr. Grayson was a paid accomplice, but Macrow was known for being just, and harsh.

McGill handed the papers to Bryant. "Now don't be tearing these up since it'll do you no good and will only make me angry."

Bryant took the papers, the pages seeming to sear into his flesh. He dropped them onto the desk.

"I want you to deliver those to Mr. and Mrs. Hendrix." McGill's satisfied smile pushed his cheeks up, the wrinkles about his eyes growing more pronounced.

Bryant shook his head despite the pressure pulsing behind his ears. "Jake will see right through me if I hand this to him. And if he gets suspicious, you won't be able to keep this up, let alone get away with what we've done."

"He didn't catch on the last two times we had him evict people we were *helping*."

"I can't do it." Bryant swallowed hard. "Not after I just signed his marriage license."

"Then you'd better brush up on your stage skills quickly." McGill leaned down, his nose only inches away from Bryant's. "Understand?"

Bryant scooted back. "You've already stolen two properties. Abandon this one. It's too risky. Jake's the law. He'd have means to investigate."

"You mean meddle," McGill bellowed. "The man should do what he's assigned to do without all his fussing."

How many times had Jacob stood up before the council and argued against McGill's frivolous codes? His sound logic always made McGill look like a fool, and the man hated anyone who made him look like a fool. But as mayor, he had the power, and Jacob, though often opposed, always did his job. Even when those jobs were assigned as punishment for not keeping his mouth shut.

McGill's mustache twisted up on one side above his smirk, and he leaned against a cabinet. "Besides, he ain't that good at his job now, is he? How long has he been chasing after those rustlers?"

Bryant shrugged.

"The town ought to get rid of a lawman who can't protect our county's most precious commodities." McGill snorted. "Perhaps it's a good thing to have him ranching."

The tension in Bryant's shoulders melted. "So we'll reverse this?"

McGill rolled his eyes. "Don't be daft."

How Bryant ached to strangle McGill's fleshy throat.

"How about this?" McGill laid his meaty hand on Bryant's shoulder. "Keeping a sniveling, cowardly man like yourself on board will not help me in the long run, so I'll agree to this being the last one."

So he'd intended to keep him fixing books indefinitely? His fists clenched, but he kept them at his sides. He should've come clean to Leah about the gambling from the beginning, even if it meant his daughter had to wait a year to return to the blind school. "I don't see how you expect that to make me happy."

"Seeing as how doggone worried you are about the marshal, I'm letting you know it's to my advantage to let the man have a ranch at some point." McGill sat on the desk corner. "If he's got land, he'll quit, and I can get someone better into his office."

"Better" meaning a paid-for pushover.

"But, unbeknownst to Mrs. Gephart—"

"Mrs. Hendrix." Sadness along with a twinge of happiness for his friend mixed together at the sound of her name.

"Whatever." McGill pulled out another toothpick and rolled it between his fingers. "She's got a rich placer up on a bend of her part of the Laramie. My boys have already brought me in a bag of gold." From his breast pocket, he pulled out a small shiny nugget, no bigger than a lady's pinky nail. With a flick of his wrist, he tossed it at Bryant. "So how's this? We go through with taking the land as planned. My boys strip the gold, and then I'll sell it to Jacob at a price he can afford."

"He's going to want to buy it the second I hand him eviction papers." Bryant shook his head. They were going to get caught. But what could he do to thwart McGill without landing himself in Wyoming's Territorial Prison? He fingered the little rock.

"Tell him we've already got a buyer, and we're obligated to give the man first bid." McGill shrugged. "Of course, this unidentified man will win the bid, not take residence, and after a few months, decide he no longer wants it." McGill tsked, shaking his head dramatically. "Rich men have more money than they know what to do with."

Bryant rubbed his eyes, then stared out the window. Would that work? Could he get out of this mess without landing himself in jail and get Jacob land too? "Fine. But I'm not doing this anymore."

"As you've said, you've paid your debt. I'll give you a share of the gold, sell the marshal back the land, and everyone's happy."

Bryant shoved away from the desk and scooped up his hat.

McGill grabbed his sleeve. "Where're you going, sonny?"

The demeaning nickname heightened Bryant's hatred of the man. "Home. Wedding lunch."

"Is that where the marshal is this afternoon?" At Bryant's nod, McGill snatched the eviction notice off the desk. "Give the happy couple this."

"It's Sunday," he hissed.

McGill walked past him and opened the office door. "You were awful eager to be working on Sunday when I came in." With a wave of his hand, he indicated Bryant should vacate the office. "I want her off the property by Tuesday."

CHAPTER ELEVEN

Jacob stretched in the wooden chair at the Whitsetts' kitchen table. The room still smelled of ham and beans despite Spencer leaving no leftovers, and the ladies were taking care of the dishes.

He closed his eyes and took a deep inhale of the smell of domestication. Soon, home would be a big beautiful ranch he'd run with a hardworking woman at his side. In the space of a week, his life had become exactly what he'd always wanted. Only God would gift Jacob the desires of his heart without any effort of his own.

Thank you, Lord, for the family you've given me. Help me be a balm to their heartache but not crowd out Gregory's memory. Let me honor his desire to provide for his family by giving me the wisdom to work his ranch to the best of my abilities.

When thumping sounded on the front porch, Leah, juggling bowls and plates, turned pleading eyes toward him. He started to push back his chair, but stopped when Annie bent in front of the oven to pull a pie from the lower rack. He looked away to keep from lingering on her slender form, but then allowed himself to look. They were married now. He could look as long as he wished. Though she'd not have caught his eye only weeks ago, he couldn't say there wasn't something attractive about a lithe, willowy woman.

"Jacob, could you please get the door?" Leah's question startled him.

He caught her tickled smile and responded with a sly grin. "Sure."

Who would be the first person he'd get to introduce to his new wife? Strangely feeling like skipping, Jacob sauntered through the Whitsetts' modest parlor and opened the door.

Bryant stood on the porch, his hands behind his back.

Jacob glanced behind his friend, then up and down the street.

Bryant's eyes didn't quite meet his.

"You may come in?" Jacob let his question ring with amusement. However, Bryant didn't budge or look amused, so he crossed his arms and dropped the lightheartedness. "Why are you knocking on your own door?"

Bryant cleared his throat. Twice. "I don't rightly know."

Jacob moved to the side, and Bryant took one step through the door and stopped, staring at the women bustling about in the kitchen.

Celia came into the parlor and flopped down. If Bryant wasn't acting so strange, he'd have ordered her back into the kitchen to help with cleanup.

Jacob nudged Bryant out of the way so he could shut the door. What was wrong with the man now? He'd agreed to witness their wedding, but still acted as if he couldn't reconcile himself with Jacob's choice of bride.

If he said anything against Annie now, Jacob would pound him flat. Friend or not.

The shuffling in the kitchen ceased and the women moved out of view.

Bryant cleared his throat again. "I'm afraid I have bad

news." His attempted whisper sounded louder than a coyote's howl.

"Get to it, then." How long was he going to parade his misgivings about?

Bryant pulled some papers from behind his back. He took a quick glance over Jacob's shoulder toward the kitchen before thrusting out the documents. "This is a notice that Annie Gephart, now Annie Hendrix, is to vacate her property by noon on Tuesday. She's defaulted on her loan, and the city has begun actions to repossess."

Celia gasped, and something clattered in the kitchen, sounding just like his heart might if it was spasming against wood instead of flesh and bone.

"What?" Annie darted into the parlor and grabbed the paper from Bryant's hand. She pulled the notice so taut, she about ripped it.

Jacob watched Bryant's face. The timing of this news was wrong, and it wasn't the only thing. "Why," he spoke through gritted teeth, "did you not mention this before?"

Leah came up to peer around Annie's shoulder before giving her husband a cold glare. "*This* is what you needed to do on a Sunday?"

The paper in Annie's hands fluttered so much there was no way she could be reading it. "What loan?"

His lungs relaxed a little. At least she hadn't hidden the loan from him since this was the first he'd heard of it. If she had kept such a thing from him—

"I—I drew that up a week ago, but I ... forgot about it. It's not like your name at the time stood out to me." Bright red crept up Bryant's neck. But he took in a long breath and met Jacob's eyes. "But when you said her name after church this morning, I thought it sounded familiar, and something in my gut warned me she was ... trouble."

Jacob glared at him and Bryant ducked his head.

"I mean, her name was what troubled me. So on my way to

City Hall, I prayed all the way there that it wasn't because she was on the eviction list. I didn't mention that's what I was thinking, because if she wasn't, well, I didn't want to throw a wet blanket on your day."

Celia harrumphed. "You thought you weren't already being a wet blanket?"

"Hush." Annie whispered with just enough force to be heard.

How she remained standing despite trembling so, Jacob wasn't sure. He reached over to steady her.

Bryant pulled on his collar. "McGill walked in while I was in the office checking, and since he'd finished proceedings, he wanted me to deliver the notice directly." He stared at the floor. "Not my choice," he mumbled.

Annie shook her head. "This can't be. Gregory wouldn't have put our land up as collateral for some loan."

"I think—" Bryant's voice cut out and he cleared his throat for the hundredth time. "Or rather, I seem to recall Gregory came in a few years ago to talk to McGill."

"But I never saw any money or..." Annie's voice faded off.

Bryant shrugged. "Perhaps he might have been gambling? You wouldn't have seen money if he was paying off a debt."

"Gregory didn't gamble." Annie grabbed Jacob's arm and dug her fingers in. She looked up at him as if willing him to believe her.

Whether he did or not, the eviction notice was proof something hadn't been as she'd assumed. And with how the man had likely been killed while taking another man's life...

Bryant licked his lips, glanced toward the children, then at Jacob. "I haven't yet recorded the marriage. An annulment could be—"

"Bryant Whitsett," Leah hissed. "Spencer. Celia. Why don't you head into the kitchen and get some pie?"

Annie had frozen so completely, Jacob had to take a second look at her to confirm she was still breathing.

With a backward glance, Celia ushered Spencer through the door.

Jacob tightened his grip on Annie and pinned Bryant with a glare. "I've said vows before God. No law permits me to abandon a marriage just because it happened minutes before—"

"The law doesn't take into account something like this, surely—"

"No." Jacob let his voice end on a sharp, final note though his gut roiled over how completely his future had just changed. "I told you. I wouldn't marry a woman just for her land." Jacob coaxed Annie closer, but her body lost none of its tension.

Bryant turned to Annie. "I'm sorry, ma'am. I was only trying—"

Leah cleared her throat and Bryant straightened and swallowed. "I know it's hard to think ill of the dead, but I know for a fact, that gambling can overtake many a man, making him go to extremes to pay his debts and hide it from his family. You wouldn't be the first woman unaware of her husband's activities."

"No," Annie whispered, but seemed to have no more to say.

Months ago, Jacob had been involved with another eviction where a woman had refused to believe her late husband had taken out a loan. When the papers to back McGill's assertions were handed to her, she'd been devastated. She'd asked for an extension, but McGill had wanted her property. Jacob's stomach churned. The Laramie River and the Gepharts' improvements would make anyone looking for a ranch salivate—it's why he'd chosen to consider Annie's unexpected proposal rather than dismiss it out of hand.

McGill was no fool. He knew what he had.

Bryant faced Jacob. "Maybe you could try to talk with McGill on Monday. Pay it off?"

"That's exactly what they'll do." Leah grabbed Annie's

other arm and rubbed it. "I don't suppose you feel up to having pie?"

Annie's mouth formed the word "no," but there was no sound as tears bubbled onto her lower lashes.

Leah gave her a quick hug. "I'll see to the children."

Jacob handed Annie his handkerchief, wrapped his arm around her shoulders, and listened to her uneven breathing. His stomach felt as ragged as her breath.

He was afraid to inquire after the amount, but waiting wouldn't change the answer. "How much is the loan?" Annie's property was worth more than he'd saved to purchase a ranch, but surely God—

"If I remember correctly, eight thousand dollars." Bryant's gaze fastened onto something immaterial in front of him.

"That's more than it's worth!" Annie's fingers bit into Jacob's flesh, and she dropped the papers.

Bryant picked the sheets up, folded a page over, and ran his finger down to the bottom. "I believe I assessed your property for a little under seven thousand five hundred." He tapped his finger on a line and handed the document to Jacob. "The loan was for eight."

Jacob grabbed the paper. The huge number stared back at him.

"Do you have enough?" Bryant's voice was rough and breathy.

Bryant knew the answer as well as he did.

Annie tensed beside him, and her fingers dug deeper into his arm.

He broke the silence with a single whispered, "No."

CHAPTER TWELVE

Standing next to Gregory's desk in the cabin she'd thought she'd saved by remarrying, Annie took the loan paper back from Jacob and stared at it again.

How had she not known?

She slumped onto the desk's chair.

No use fighting the city. She'd found proof of the loan tucked into the back of one of the ranch's ledgers. Gregory had signed away their land without her knowledge.

Jacob moved to lean against the front room's window. His head rested against the pane as he stared out at the grazing cattle.

What should they do with the cattle while they looked for another place? Could they afford to keep them? Oh, what were they to do?

Jacob heaved a sigh, and Annie dropped her head into her hands. He probably mourned the ranch's loss more than she, for he'd ended up marrying her for nothing.

"Don't cry, Mama." Spencer's little hand patted her thigh. "We've got the marshal."

And the marshal sure had them. Poor Jacob.

She sniffed and tried to smile at her son as if life hadn't just imploded. "Go gather some crates. I think there are some baskets in the barn loft. We can use them to pack."

Spencer shuffled out the door, letting in a breeze that snaked its cool tendrils into every gap in her clothing. At least they had somewhere warm to go.

Annie forced herself up and crossed over to Jacob. "Do you think there's a way to get this place back?"

"I've been thinking, but…" His voice was husky. "I'm not knowledgeable enough on property law." His hand clenched against the window's ledge. "I'm not a marshal because I know what I'm doing, I took this job because..." He inhaled sharply through his nose, and his lips flattened in a small, tense line. "Because I hadn't enough money for a ranch, and Bryant put in a good word for me. I hadn't intended to be marshal this long."

How he must rue marrying her as well.

"Since I know so little, we'd have to hire a lawyer, but Mr. Grayson's a good friend of McGill's. Too good a friend."

A meadowlark hopped outside in the new grass, chirping a string of high notes, unaware that its cheery melody clashed with the minor chords of distress filling the cabin.

"And by the time we find another lawyer, this property will be sold." Jacob hung his head. "And that's if anything can be done anyway. The city should've told you, should've given you a chance, but McGill's middle name isn't 'fairness' and if the deed and loan aren't in your name..."

The tears clogging his voice made it hard to keep looking at him. Gregory had never cried, and right now, she was barely keeping her own emotions in check.

"I'm so busy following orders and doing the same never-ending tasks that I've never studied the law beyond what I needed to know. Not that I ever wanted to know more." Jacob struck the wall with the side of his fist.

Annie licked her lips, but couldn't think of anything to say. No words would fix this.

Spencer opened the door, wearing a wicker basket on his head while dragging in a dusty crate. If Annie's ears weren't reverberating with the sound of Jacob punching the wall, she might've been tempted to chuckle. But the chains of hopelessness tightening around her chest made it difficult enough to breathe.

Could Jacob really do nothing?

"It seems a lawman I remain." Jacob's whisper grew in intensity. "So you bet I'm going to start digging. I've always thought McGill was shady, but with Bryant there, I figured he'd warn me if anything needed investigating. But I'm not so sure now." He shook his head. "McGill must be pressuring Bryant or something. He isn't acting right and has clammed up every time I've asked him about what's worrying him."

"What should we do then?" Annie scanned the room. "We have to be out by Tuesday, and I'm not certain I can…" The knot in her throat choked out any further words. How could she leave this place where the last of her children had been born and her late husband's dreams lay?

How could he have signed it away without telling her? This ranch was the inheritance he'd worked so hard to give their children.

"Pack enough for you to be comfortable tonight. We'll take the rest home tomorrow."

Home. Jacob's home. Inside the city limits. Surrounded by dusty roads, city clatter, and people.

The back bedroom door slammed. Celia forged into the room and stomped her foot, her expression as fiery as her hair. "*This* is home. I'm not living anywhere else."

As much as Annie wanted to throw her hands in the air and scream the same thing, she also wanted to throttle her daughter. Now was not the time for tantrums. "Unfortunately, that's not possible." Her voice cracked.

Celia pointed at Jacob and marched toward him. "You were invited into this family to save Daddy's land. So save it." She stopped and put her hands on her hips. "You're the marshal, and I say we don't leave. If you don't force us off, who will?"

"I'm sorry, honey, but I can't defy the law, because I am the law." Jacob pushed off from the wall and reached for her shoulder.

She took a step back. "Don't 'honey' me," her voice warbled.

"Only her father called her 'honey.'" Annie shot Jacob a look to warn him to tread lightly.

"That's right, and you're not half the man he was considering he would've fought for this place." Celia waved her arms about with vehemence. "Don't you believe Ma? Daddy *wasn't* a gambler." Celia drew her brows down so far Annie couldn't see her daughter's eyes behind her fine lashes.

Jacob drew a breath, filling his chest with air, and Annie braced herself for him to shout back, but his voice came out quiet and steady. "I do believe your mother didn't know about this. I wouldn't have married her if she wasn't trustworthy. But as you said, I'm the marshal. I'm not a—" Jacob's voice disappeared. He swallowed. "I'm not a rancher, so we have to return to town. If I try to fight this without any legal standing, I'll end up fired. And then how will I feed us?"

The sheen of wetness in his eyes caused Annie's heart to squeeze. Celia had to stop. "Darling, you should be thankful for the marshal. If he hadn't married me this morning, we'd have nowhere to live." She placed a hand on Celia's tense forearm. "He'll do what he can. But for now, I think you best talk to God about your anger and ungratefulness, for He has been good enough to provide."

Celia huffed and stomped back to her room. Her daughter deserved heavenly discipline for the way she was acting.

Annie likely did too with how often she'd grumbled this past year over the hand God had dealt her. And yet, He'd saved her in the nick of time.

Lord, I am grateful for your provision, even if I may not feel so at the moment. Help me not to dwell on what I've lost.

But poor Jacob. Why had God dragged him into this mess?

CHAPTER THIRTEEN

With Spencer and Annie slumped beside him on the wagon fast asleep and Celia pouting in the back, twilight was all that welcomed Jacob home. The windows of his house were void of light, but soon this monstrosity for one would have more than enough residents to chase away the emptiness.

"Whoa!" His call slowed Annie's team and startled her awake. Her fingers clamped around his arm as she scrambled for something to keep herself upright.

Though the land he'd hoped to gain would never be his, he wasn't completely cheated—though the ache in his chest begged to differ. With his free hand, he cupped the warm, delicate hand clenching his bicep. He had a wife to honor and children to protect. Though right now it didn't feel real, and maybe even slightly unfair in light of the circumstances, many a man considered that a privilege. So he would choose to see it that way until he no longer had to remind himself of the truth of it.

Annie released her hold as soon as she righted herself. "Must'a fallen asleep." She yawned then shook Spencer's shoulders. "Wake up, son."

His head lolled to the side, and Annie smiled. "He's always slept like the dead." Her smile quickly reverted into a frown.

Jacob grimaced. Perhaps that hadn't been the best way to put it, but if not for his little chest moving, he sure did look as if he'd left this world. "Don't wake him. I'll carry him upstairs."

Celia jumped off the back and trudged onto the porch. With a huff, she sat on the lone outdoor chair, her arms tucked about her waist.

Jacob assisted Annie to the ground. She plodded toward the porch without even glancing up at him. Her dragging feet and drooping shoulders put a twist in his gut.

He grabbed one of the crates off the wagon. Though the loss of land had taken the spring from his step too, thanks be to God he'd not married Annie solely for her ranch.

He placed the crate on the steps and walked over to his wife, who'd slumped against the siding. "Annie, look at me."

She raised her head just enough for him to catch a glint of moonlight in her amber eyes.

"Don't feel bad about this. I wish we were at the ranch instead of here, yes, but I'm still glad to have you." He turned toward Celia. "All three of you."

Celia humphed.

He squeezed Annie's upper arm. "Why don't you get your things, and I'll get Spencer." Heading back to the wagon, Jacob raised his voice, "Help your mother, Celia."

The girl stomped over to the crate he'd left on the porch and hefted it with an exaggerated groan. Her overall attitude needed adjustment, but he'd ease into that slowly. First, he needed a better idea of how Annie felt about her eldest's grouchy outlook and what she'd already tried discipline-wise.

Once inside, Jacob lit the lamp in his empty parlor while supporting Spencer's sleeping frame. The boy hung heavy over his shoulder. If only that kind of sleep would visit them all tonight—they'd need good rest to face the upcoming days of adjustment and broken dreams. He'd known this evening wouldn't be anything like a honeymoon, but he'd not thought it would feel like a nightmare.

Annie set her trunk inside the entryway and rubbed her arms. Celia headed back outside, letting the door slam behind her. Spencer didn't even flinch.

"So, this is home." Tonight was the first time he was thankful he'd purchased such a large house, which had been the only place available when he'd agreed to take the marshal position. He'd been too impatient to sleep in a jail cell until something smaller could be built or came up for sale. How he'd lamented his impatience every night since. The house's creaks and groans had magnified the emptiness.

But it seemed God had planned for this *disaster* all along. If the Almighty knew years ago he'd need this house tonight, then why worry about tomorrow?

Annie hadn't moved from where she'd dropped her things, her eyes wide open despite looking heavy with sleep. "I had, um, back at the cabin, figured I'd put the kids together in Spencer's room, so that we'd be able to well, have separate ... rooms."

He cleared his throat, hoping to sound unaffected. "That would've worked just fine."

Sleeping together would be difficult right now. And not just because they didn't really know each other. He could only imagine what a woman next to him in bed would do to his mind and body, and he wouldn't force his attentions on Annie. He'd wait until she was ready.

Celia barged back inside, skirted her mother, and dropped another crate. Jacob cringed at the loud echo, but Spencer still didn't flinch.

Jacob pointed toward the stairwell. "There are four bedrooms upstairs. No one will have to share."

He didn't have furnishings for each room, but he'd packed the kids' blankets and pillows. He'd get their beds tomorrow. "There's not much in them since I don't have many visitors. Most of my overnight guests are drunks."

Annie's eyes widened.

He twisted his hand in the air as if turning a key. "And locked behind bars."

She relaxed and nodded, but didn't return his smile.

Time to settle in and hope things looked brighter in the morning. "Celia, follow me with Spencer's bedding. I'll show you the rooms."

He led them up the squeaky staircase.

Though the house looked spacious from the street, upstairs, one entire side was taken up by one bedroom and the stairs while the other side was split into four, making the three bedrooms and storage room all quite small. He chose the first room for Spencer as it was hardly wider than the hallway. "Lay his things in the corner there."

"It's so sma—"

Annie's elbow stopped Celia from finishing the thought. "Thank you, Jacob."

He passed through the door and settled Spencer onto the bedding Celia had dropped, and Annie stooped to unlace the boy's shoes.

"We'll go down and get the rest while you make him comfortable. Celia, you'll sleep in the next room." Jacob gave her a look, warning her not to protest, and was happy to hear her clomp downstairs behind him.

Once outside, Jacob gathered Celia's blankets and handed them to her. "I'll grab your mother's things."

But where should Annie sleep? Celia was right, the guest rooms were small, though the two others were bigger than Spencer's. But Annie would likely protest taking over his room since she'd done nothing but repeatedly apologize for inconveniencing him.

Then again, if she found her tiny quarters uncomfortable, she might be tempted to move to his room faster—

He tripped on a stair and nearly lost the trunk before he caught the railing, keeping himself mostly upright. Celia looked at him over her shoulder as if he were an annoying little brother before continuing to climb.

He shook his head to toss out every thought of Annie leaving her room for his so he could get up the stairs without busting his nose.

After waiting for Celia to disappear into her room, Jacob walked to the next one, certain he'd find Annie there since she was no longer with Spencer.

She sat on the cot he'd placed here for the times he'd housed friends passing through. With the moonlight behind her, she was nothing more than a silhouette.

He placed her trunk by the window. "Can I get you anything?"

"You've done enough, thank you." She stared out the window. "I just want to lie down."

"Of course." He nodded and turned for the door.

"And never wake up."

Surely she hadn't meant for him to hear those whispered words, but they stabbed his heart nonetheless.

He hesitated for a second before stepping toward her. He laid a hand on her soft hair and placed a light kiss on the top of her head. "Sleep, Annie. Things will look better in the morning."

When she didn't answer, he backed out of the room, crossed the hall, and slumped into the chair next to his washstand. What Annie had said simply reflected her fatigue and upset. He shouldn't let the careless whisper affect him.

He leaned over to take his boots off. Just days ago, she'd said she wouldn't have been willing to marry anyone else in town, so there had to be something other than his able back and ability to ride that she'd looked forward to having in her life.

But since she seemed so despondent, maybe not.

Though she'd told the children to be thankful he was here for them, she seemed less than encouraged herself.

He studied his reflection in the nearby mirror. Had she

mentioned anything other than his being morally upright for why she'd chosen him? He closed his eyes and tried to think of what else she'd said—other than he'd been her choice over any other.

But what if she'd only said that so he'd agree to save her land?

The last crate. Annie swiped her brow, then packed the remainder of her belongings into a box the mercantile had loaned her.

In the corners of her empty cabin, cobwebs waved goodbye in the drafts.

She ran her hand atop the cook stove, a present from Gregory's parents. There was no reason to force Jacob into hauling the heavy appliance into town when he already had one.

She pulled the loan paper out again and reread every word for the third time that morning. Gregory's signature looked a little shaky. Had he been a drunkard as well? Had everything she'd known about him been a lie? She let the paper fall to the floor so she could massage her temples.

Could the man she'd lived with for sixteen years be nothing like she'd believed him to be? They'd married at the tender age of seventeen and eighteen, so he hadn't been old enough to hide a shady past from her.

Though he'd never been one to talk much, she'd never thought he'd hide something as life-changing as this. Had he truly been a murderer, a gambler, and possibly a drunk? Was she that gullible? Had she no discernment?

Before she'd proposed to Jacob, she'd convinced herself he would do right by them, but without a ranch, would he? Her beliefs in regard to Jacob's character would now be tested by fire. Would they prove any better than her assumptions about her husband?

Her *late* husband.

When would she get used to thinking of Jacob as husband first?

She scooped the loan paper off the floor and crammed the horrible thing into the crate next to the ledgers. She marched outside and shoved the last of her stuff onto the farm wagon.

Only one more thing to do.

Her feet crunched atop the old clumps of dry grass as she walked across her ranch for the last time.

After passing through the picket gate, Annie sat on the ground near Gregory's rock-outlined grave and hugged her legs against her chest. She perched her chin on her knees and gazed at the graves, trying to memorize the details of each one. The dull ache in her chest these last two days gave way to full agony. How could she leave them? Why must her heart throb more now than when she'd placed these three children in the ground?

Should she take their markers? No. Years of wind and rain would obliterate the slight mounds, and she'd never find them again—if she'd ever be allowed upon the property in the future.

Scooting to the most recent little grave, she put her hand upon the sun-warmed earth. Born dead a little over a year and a half ago. She hadn't even gotten to see his eyes. Leaning over, she rested her head on the hardened pillow of earth covering him. She hadn't had much time to mourn his death before her husband had made his bed beside their tiny son.

Tears trickled down her cheeks, wetting the earth. Could anything make leaving behind this small tract of land bearable?

Perhaps naming her two stillborn sons.

Gregory and Catherine's names were etched into their wooden crosses, but she hadn't named the boys.

She drew in a shuddering breath and closed her eyes, envisioning her relations back home, recalling Gregory's stories of family members, searching for names.

She crawled over and touched each cross, whispering their

newly chosen names: Jack and Augustus. That's who she had to leave behind. Forever.

"Annie!"

Jacob's holler broke through the sound of the ragged gulps filling her ears.

Life went on.

It had gone on four times before. It would go on when she left those same four behind.

Knowing Jacob couldn't see where she was, she wiped at her eyes and stood to flag him.

He caught her signal and started her way.

Scanning the cemetery one last time, she said goodbye to the family that had gone on before her as she finished drying her face. She couldn't still be standing here when Jacob arrived. He was her life now; her old family had to be left behind.

She threw an apologetic glance to the loved ones who'd gone before her. They weren't old, not at all. And they'd be missed. She tried to walk away, but Catherine's grave pulled her forward. She could still remember the feel of her daughter's damp curly hair plastered against her fevered brow that long, heartbreaking last day. Annie sank to the ground, but kept her lips pressed together to keep the streams of sadness from flowing again. She'd never been so far away she couldn't come and kneel beside these children when she thought of them. Leaning heavily upon Catherine's worn cross, she put her forehead against her engraved name. "Mama loves you," she whispered. "You have to believe me. I'd not leave unless I had to."

The sound of Jacob's strides through the new grass grew louder.

She pushed herself up, wiped her face with her sleeve as she crossed over to the fence, then fumbled with the gate's latch, desperate to get out before Jacob came in.

He stood but a few feet away and she stopped right outside the gate, her hand clenched tightly to its top. She couldn't take another step, couldn't move, couldn't answer the question in his eyes. Her throat was too clogged to say anything anyway, not that she had something to say.

"You don't have to leave now." He crossed the remaining distance between them and wiped a tear off her cheek with his thumb. "We have until evening for you to ... do whatever you feel needs doing."

"I'd never be done." She fixed her gaze on the distant ridge behind him, not wanting to see the compassion in his eyes. She couldn't renew the flow of mourning she'd just stanched. Taking deep breaths, she started for the wagon. "We should go."

He walked beside her, his hand at the small of her back, saying nothing.

But the more steps she took, the more difficult it was to keep moving. Jacob's arm slid farther around her waist as she nearly slowed to a stop, inviting her into a hug without saying a word.

Unable to move forward another inch, she turned into his arms and let her tears drench his shirt. His unfamiliar, yet soothing masculine scent permeated the starched fabric.

The rumble of his voice in his hard chest and his hand rubbing circles on her back couldn't fix the hurt, but they tempered her weeping after a time.

Was it wrong to find comfort in one man's embrace, aware of his every muscle wrapped around her, when she wept for another lover and the children she'd borne him?

CHAPTER FOURTEEN

Jacob opened his desk drawer and took out his badge. Morning sunlight glinted off its five points as he ran a finger around the star's inner circle and then swiped his thumb across his last name. Just days ago, he'd been practically giddy about handing this star over to McGill and never looking back.

But now, he needed this job more than ever, especially if he wanted a chance at unearthing what had happened with Gregory.

Jacob pinned the badge onto his left lapel, leaned back in his chair, and stared at the cell bars that lined the wall across from him. Unfortunately, today his most dreaded task demanded attention—mucking streets and filling holes while keeping a lookout for busted street lamps.

Some prankster had been targeting the new lights. Probably the same kid who'd stolen undergarments off clotheslines last week.

Maybe he should ask the council to offer a reward for information leading to the perpetrator.

Jacob let the front legs of his chair hit the floor and jotted himself a reminder to ask at the next meeting. Surely for a few dollars, someone would snitch on the troublemaker.

A soft rat-a-tat-tat sounded at his door. The morning sun glowed bright and furious behind the figure on the other side of the window. Who expected him to still be here? He rarely lingered this long before starting work. He took a sip of coffee and rubbed his eyes before hollering, "Come in."

Bryant's blond head poked in through the doorway. "Didn't think you'd still be here."

Jacob frowned at his friend. Leah had helped Annie unpack yesterday, but Bryant had come up with one excuse after another for not helping carry the larger items upstairs.

He rubbed at the back of his neck. Why did this uneasy hitch lodge in his chest any time Bryant showed up?

"I have papers to give you." Bryant slipped farther into the room, then placed some documents on the desk's edge. "Uh—" He cleared his throat and shoved them forward. "Another eviction notice and a few fines to deliver." The man's eyes didn't quite rise high enough to meet Jacob's. "McGill wants you to give them out today."

Jacob itched to flick the papers onto the floor and grind them into the rough planks with the heel of his muddy boot. No wonder Bryant had hoped to drop these off while he was out. "What? You're not up to handing out the eviction yourself this time?"

Bryant took a small step back toward the door.

Jacob brought his right ankle up to rest on his left knee. He wasn't going to evict anyone today.

A cold shiver ran up his neck, and he rubbed the sensation away. He'd never before been intentionally insubordinate, but then, that was before the mayor had stolen his dream out from under his nose.

Though an anonymous buyer was supposed to be purchasing Annie's land for the required eight thousand dollars, he was certain anonymous was synonymous with McGill.

Pressing Bryant for the name of the interested party had gotten him nowhere.

Somehow, he got the feeling that pestering those two much more would get him into hot water, and he needed to keep this job, for the time being anyway.

Jacob dropped his foot back onto the floor. If only he knew more of the law. Was there a way widows could hold off eviction?

McGill had hired him despite his inexperience, and he'd thought himself fortunate, but perhaps McGill had been the lucky one since Jacob had never questioned the legality of McGill's actions.

He'd always figured his boss hadn't cared about his lack of qualifications because he was more custodian than marshal, but what if there was more to it?

"I understand if you don't want to hand them out today." Bryant's voice squeaked but smoothed out. "I tried to talk McGill out of it, but…" He shrugged. "You know him."

Jacob rubbed his temples, tired of trying to understand his best friend's behavior. "What's wrong with you?"

"Me?" Bryant's cheeks reddened. "What do you mean?"

"Something awry at home?" Jacob tried to read his friend's face. "Why are you so evasive lately? You worried McGill's going to fire you for something?"

Bryant took another step back toward the door, his gaze actually meeting Jacob's for once this week. "McGill isn't the easiest to work for." He put a hand on the doorknob and shrugged. "And that's probably all I should say."

Jacob pushed himself out of his chair and grabbed his hat. Bryant's answer cleared up nothing. "Right, thanks for the insight." He snatched the rake from the corner and twirled it in his hand, letting the handle's end pivot in the knot on the plank floor. "When you decide to talk to me about why you're acting as if I've lifted up a rock and exposed you to sunlight, you can find me filling in potholes."

Bryant didn't so much as utter a grunt of protest.

Jacob shook his head. "Don't expect the eviction or the fines to go out today. I'll be too busy catching up."

"I'm sorry, Jake." Bryant looked like he was biting his cheek. Or had the man taken up chewing?

"I know. You're just doing your job." Jacob strangled the rake handle in his hands. If only he'd mentioned Annie's name to Bryant earlier, perhaps they could've stopped the repossession process and he'd not be twirling a rake right now. Or at least not this rake. With a squeeze, he stopped the spinning handle and a splinter broke off in his flesh. Just what he needed, a splinter.

"Perhaps I could make it up to you." Bryant jiggled the knob behind him. "I can keep my eye out for cheap land. Maybe suggest to someone behind on their taxes that you could make them an offer? Something's bound to turn up." His jaw clenched so tight, every muscle surrounding his mouth stood out.

"But you're not going to tell me what's wrong with you?"

"No." Bryant's mouth flattened into a thinner line. Then he turned the knob and spun to step out the door only to stumble forward.

"Ow!"

Spencer had evidently been about to knock, but had become a stumbling block instead.

Bryant quickly righted them both before stalking off down the porch steps.

"What'd he do that for?" Spencer rubbed his head, eyes wide and dewy.

"He didn't trip over you on purpose." Jacob pulled him inside and took a quick look at the boy's head. No hint of a bump. "But something's eating at him, and he wasn't paying attention."

Was Bryant beating himself up over not being able to warn them about Annie's eviction? Or was there more to it?

Likely more. But how was he supposed to figure that out when Bryant refused to talk?

He roughed up Spencer's hair, and the boy winced, though he still sported a slight grin.

His chest puffed up at the eight-year-old's cheery pluck. At least someone wasn't hard to read. "Why aren't you in school? Thought your ma said you'd be going again."

Spencer thrust a paper sack into Jacob's hands. "She told me to give you this first and let you know to come home for lunch." The boy stared at Jacob's middle for a second before launching his arms around Jacob's hips. "Thanks for helping us. You're the greatest."

For the first time today, his heart didn't feel constricted. "No problem, kid."

Spencer ran off, leaving the scent of cinnamon buns wafting up from the bag. Annie hadn't left her room early enough this morning to make him breakfast. When she'd finally come downstairs, right before he'd had to leave, her red-rimmed eyes had indicated she'd once again cried more than slept.

But at least today she'd bucked up enough to make him something other than toast.

What would his wife make him for lunch?

His wife. He liked the sound of that.

The squeak of the marshal's front door opening made Celia slump down in her kitchen chair. She popped the last piece of her cinnamon bun into her mouth, readying herself to remain seated no matter what. There was no reason to go to school. As soon as the marshal got their land back, she'd be needed to help with the cattle.

Ma walked in carrying a crate of groceries and dropped it onto the sideboard with a sigh.

Celia didn't look at her, just scraped up the last of the icing from her plate.

"If you feel well enough to come down for breakfast…" Ma picked up the empty baking pan from the table and transferred it into the sink. "You're well enough to clean up after yourself."

Ma was trying to make her expression steely, but she was twisting her new wedding band something fierce.

She never enforced anything when she was regretting her decisions.

"I don't see why." Celia relaxed in her chair. "We aren't going to be here very long."

"We can't eat off dirty dishes."

Celia shrugged. "I'll wash them after lunch."

"If you can do chores, you can go to school."

"Don't want to."

The kitchen's back door swung open, and the marshal's tall frame blocked the sun for a second.

Celia scowled. He was supposed to be working. He'd likely not give in to her as easily as Ma did.

He frowned at her then hung up his hat. "Why aren't you in school?"

"I don't feel up to it." She slumped some more and tried to look pitiful.

He took a long look at her face. "Unless you have a fever, get yourself ready."

Ma cleared her throat. "It's about lunch time. Perhaps she can eat before going? Then I wouldn't have to fix her something to take."

"That'd be fine." The marshal nodded, but he didn't look pleased.

He might respect Ma, might like Spencer, but nothing about her would ever make such a tight-laced man happy.

Well, she hadn't been born to make him happy. And he was already too comfortable with being in charge. Ma should be the only one making decisions about her and Spencer.

She folded her arms atop the table. “What are we having?” If lunch wasn’t anything good, she’d just go without.

“Scrambled eggs, ham, and biscuits with this apricot jam I found at the mercantile. Hopefully it tastes as good as it looks.”

Apricot jam would be worth sticking around for, even if the marshal was staying.

Ma winced as she turned toward him. “I hope you don’t mind I bought things to refill your pantry.”

“No, buy whatever you need.” The marshal busied himself with taking off his gun belt.

Why did he even wear it? Her friend, Daniel, said the marshal was too busy cleaning up after horses to deal with real criminals.

“Why don’t you help your mother?” The marshal’s glare pinned her as if he was trying to get some sort of message across. But she’d only help if she wanted to.

Of course, there was the apricot jam to consider.

She shoved away from the table and got down a bowl to scramble eggs in.

After a quarter hour of doing just enough to keep from getting sent straight to school, Celia sat at the table, and the marshal bowed his head to give the blessing.

She tapped her foot as his prayer went on and on thanking God for his new family.

The man was daft. There was nothing to be thankful for in this situation. The only thing that would make this new arrangement tolerable was for him to get to work figuring out how to take back their ranch so she could disappear for hours on end on a horse, riding along the ridge.

Now that they were in town, Ma seemed to think she needed an account of every second of her daughter’s day.

“Pass the jam to Jacob, darling.” Ma’s voice cooed out of nowhere.

Celia pulled the jar closer, slapped more jam onto the last of her biscuit, then slid it across the table to her stepfather. She cringed. No, she wouldn't call him a father of any kind. She was too old to need a father anyway. "So, Marshal. How's the plan for getting us back home going?"

His eyebrow raised, but he simply continued spooning out jam.

Ma cleared her throat. "Celia, I already told you an investigation will take time. This is our home for now." She took a side glance at the marshal. "We'll trust Jacob to do what he can, but we can't expect miracles."

Celia frowned at the marshal. "You're the law. You should see something ain't right."

He coughed, but not because he was choking on his biscuit. No, it was one of those adult coughs meant as a warning. She scowled right back into his intense glare.

"I agree something doesn't feel right. And as your mother said, I'll do what I can. But things may not end up as you'd like, and you'll have to deal with it."

Celia shoveled in the last of her eggs. She never got what she wanted. If she did, she'd be on Daddy's ranch right now, talking to him about his day, getting a hug from him every chance she got.

But even when he was alive, she'd only gotten a hug every once in a while. The closest she'd ever felt to him was when he'd let her ride with him on rounds. Which is what she should be doing now, not hanging around in town.

"So, Jacob." Ma wrung a napkin in her hands. "What have you been doing this morning?"

"Raking alleys and filling potholes." With a sigh, the marshal sopped up a stray glop of jam. "That'll probably keep me busy for the rest of the day and maybe even tomorrow."

Celia pushed her plate away. That was all she needed to hear. "I best be going." She leaned over to kiss Ma's cheek and then gave a nod in the marshal's direction.

There was no reason to sit in a stuffy school room, especially on a sunny day like today. Daniel definitely wouldn't be. No, he'd be down by the river. She'd look for him there.

The door slammed behind Celia, making Jacob startle in his chair. How much of her hardness was grief, and how much was willfulness? After her father's death, she'd become quite stubborn and mouthy whenever she'd come to Sunday school, but that didn't mean her disobedience had started then.

He didn't relish taking over as disciplinarian so soon after the wedding, but he wouldn't tolerate the way Celia treated his wife much longer. "Did her attitude need work before Gregory died?"

"She was a handful before, but not this much." Annie pushed a slice of ham around her plate. "Gregory was the one who took care of the discipline, and I haven't been able to make myself reprimand her. I know how it is to feel lost, abandoned ... hopeless." Her voice cracked on the last word.

Hopeless?

He took in a deep breath. He wasn't Gregory, and his house sat on a city block. But did Annie and Celia still feel such things? Hadn't Annie told the children he'd been God's provision?

Perhaps Annie was referring to how she felt in the past, but if she was feeling that way now...

Time. He'd have to be patient while they adjusted and try not to let their talk in the midst of grief wound him. But if life were to continue smoothly, some things could not be tolerated. "No matter how she's feeling, I won't abide Celia disrespecting you. After supper tonight, we should discuss how we'll correct her."

Annie's meek nod made his heart go *ka-thunk*. They were virtually strangers, yet every muscle in his arms begged him to scoot around to the other side of the table and embrace her.

He wiped his mouth with a napkin and went to her.

Stooping down, he waited until she lifted her dark-honey eyes to meet his gaze. “Thanks for lunch, Anne.” He took her hand and kissed her knuckles before going to retrieve his gun belt.

Her wide-eyed stare followed him to the door. He winked at her before slipping outside. Maybe he’d leave work a little early today. Give her a thorough tour of his house so she’d not feel so lost, show her she hadn’t been abandoned.

That there was hope.

CHAPTER FIFTEEN

Annie handed Jacob the last soapy dish and watched as he rinsed and dried it. Gregory had never helped with dishes. Of course, he'd never had to. He'd lived with his folks until they'd married and she'd never asked him to pitch in. Didn't even expect it.

But even if Gregory had washed his own dishes for years, as Jacob had, he'd have abdicated the chore the first chance he got.

And here she was comparing the two—she'd vowed not to do that.

She picked up the dish pan and headed outside to toss the dirty water off the back porch.

Of course, if she compared herself to Jacob, she'd likely not measure up either. He was certainly more agreeable to people taking over his house than she would've been. He'd not complained once while she rearranged his furniture, reorganized his pantry, and delegated his chores over the last several days.

Why, when she and Gregory had married, it had taken nearly a year before they'd agreed on where the boot scraper ought to be placed.

Jacob's easy manner in accepting this catastrophic turn of events made her feel even worse for the first prayer she'd uttered under his roof, asking God to wake her up from this nightmare.

Somehow, she was certain Jacob hadn't had such a thought, let alone prayed it. She leaned against the railing and stared out across the small yard.

"All right now, go upstairs and get ready for bed." Jacob's voice sounded kind but firm despite being loud enough to travel through the walls of the house.

Annie looked up at the moon in the nearly darkened sky. It was still early. She'd been allowing the children to stay up later than usual since time seemed so empty now that they weren't working sun up to sun down. Celia had yet to bring home any schoolwork and Spencer always did his as soon as he came home. School hadn't been enough to keep them busy.

And if she and Jacob weren't busy, and the children were off to bed...

Well, what was wrong with her? Having time to get to know Jacob should be something to look forward to.

But what if he realized he didn't like her? If they'd had the ranch, it wouldn't have mattered so much. He could've done what Gregory had the last couple years, spend most of his time with the herd and come home for little beyond food and sleep.

Jacob hadn't had but a few days to convince himself he was willing to marry her for the ranch, and what if all the nice things he'd imagined about her turned out false? What if she didn't measure up?

The door whined open behind her.

"Do you need help?"

She shook her head as she passed by him on the way back into the kitchen. "No, I was just lost in thought."

"Anything you'd like to share?"

"Oh, no, just rambling thoughts." She wouldn't force him into assuring her of things that might not be true.

After closing the door, he took the empty dishpan from her. "If you need someone to listen to those thoughts, I'm willing."

"Thanks, but, there's a table to—" She frowned at the clean table and counters. The floor sported nary a crumb. "I guess you've already cleaned up."

He took her hand in his, not as big and calloused as Gregory's, yet just as warm. "I know you said I don't have to help, but I'm used to it, plus we have some talking to do if you remember."

Her heart sunk as she followed him into the parlor.

Disciplining Celia.

If only he'd forgotten.

As much as her daughter needed to be taken to task, it just felt wrong to worry about that now. She had let Celia grieve her father for a few months before trying to fix her attitude. Shouldn't the girl have some time to grieve the ranch as well?

Jacob kept hold of her hand as they moved through the house until they stood in front of the sofa, and without letting go of her hand, he sat.

She lowered herself beside him, willing her heart to stop its crazy rhythm. There was nothing wrong with holding his hand. Nor was there anything intimate about sitting beside him.

Until his arm came around her shoulders and she nearly jumped from her seat.

With a frown, he took his arm away, and she started playing with the folds of her skirt.

Could she have made that any more awkward?

Though she'd held hands with several people throughout her life, no one but Gregory had wrapped his arm around her.

She drew in a shuddery breath and traced the swirly pattern in her skirt. Jacob was well within his rights to put his arm around her, well within his rights to more.

And now she couldn't breathe at all.

"What are you thinking?" Jacob tucked a strand of her hair behind her ear, an amused tone coloring his voice.

She untucked that same strand of hair in a sorry attempt to cover the redness that was likely aflame on her cheeks. "I'd rather not say."

He sat quietly long enough she ventured to look at him again, and with the way his eyebrows were raised and his grin was half-cocked, she had a feeling he'd guessed where her thoughts had wandered all on his own.

He took her hand and tugged her closer.

She forced herself not to resist. How was Jacob better at acting as if they were husband and wife than she was? She was the one who knew what it was like to be married. Though it wasn't as if she and Gregory had been getting along well before he'd died. After they'd lost Jack, they'd both struggled to cope, and after Augustus had arrived stillborn, they'd pulled apart even more.

Yet, even back when they'd been heady with new love, she'd not let Gregory get this close this quick.

Not that she'd married him within a week either—she hadn't even been sure she liked him in that amount of time.

Jacob was still quiet, so she peeked over, and the lazy smile on his face made it hard to breathe. If she let herself, she could really like a man who looked at her like that.

And she was allowed to let herself.

She cleared her throat. "So, Celia." As much as she'd rather not talk about disciplining her daughter, it seemed doing so would be a good thing at the moment.

"Yes?"

"Don't you think we should let things settle down before we worry about making her—"

"No."

And now his face was stern enough she could look at him without worrying her whole body would flush.

"My parents never let us get away with being disrespectful, even when we were hurting."

She sighed and looked away. Since she and the children had

taken over his house, he'd not asked for anything but this. And he was right. She'd had to fight harder and harder to get Celia to behave these last several months. "All right."

"Good." He sighed and picked up her hand again, inching closer.

She stopped herself from scooting away.

She'd prided herself on being a good wife and mother, but maybe she hadn't been if she couldn't simply sit still next to the man who'd given up his life for them, or keep her daughter from back talking him.

Had her inability to be a good wife and mother been what had really pushed Gregory away these last several years? Would Jacob end up pushing her away too? She sniffled, and out of nowhere, tears took over her face and she dashed them away.

Jacob stayed her hand. "It's all right to cry."

She shook her head, extricating her hand to swipe at her cheeks. She would not cry about Gregory in front of Jacob. Surely no man wanted to watch his wife cry over how she wished she could redo the last couple of years with her previous husband.

She sniffed one last time and made herself place her hand on Jacob's knee and look at his face, which was clearly more handsome than hers would be at the moment. Crying did not become her. "I'm sorry."

"Don't be." He put his hand atop hers.

"Mother?"

Stiffening at the harshness in Celia's voice, Annie quickly pulled her hand from Jacob's and stood to face her daughter.

Celia was staring at Jacob, and Annie turned to see his expression had hardened.

She sucked in a deep breath. "To bed, Celia, as Jacob told you. Save your questions for morning."

Celia's face flashed defiance, but after a glance at Jacob, she headed back up the stairs.

That had been easier than expected. Annie turned to smile

at Jacob, but he didn't look any happier than when he'd first spied Celia.

He stood and gave her a weak smile. "Good night, Anne." He let his hand travel down her arm a little before following Celia up.

Had she not handled that well enough? And had he called her Anne?

Though she'd rather lower herself onto the sofa and let the tears flow and fall straight to sleep, she put the afghan back on the chair and turned down the lamp.

While everyone was gone tomorrow, she'd let herself cry until she could cry no more. Hopefully come evening, she'd be able to put one man behind her and focus on the other.

CHAPTER SIXTEEN

The haze of night had disappeared, ushering in dawn's crisp scent as Jacob walked toward his office, and yet, he might as well be walking in a fog.

He'd gotten nowhere in regard to Annie's ranch this past week. Mr. Grayson had been no help, though he'd expected that. Even if the town's lawyer wasn't deep in McGill's pocket, he always talked in circles.

He'd yet to hear from his father's old lawyer in Texas. And the sheriff he trusted in Cheyenne hadn't been able to recommend a lawyer that practiced anywhere near Armelle.

Plus, Annie was completely mystifying him, skittish, quiet, rarely speaking to him unless spoken to. But then, he'd never had to figure out a woman before, so it was even more irksome Bryant had closed himself off. His friend should've been available to help him understand what was going on in his wife's head.

Perhaps he needed to find himself another friend—

"Jacob!"

He stopped in the middle of the road and searched for Leah.

Several feet in front of him, Leah stepped off the sidewalk with an amused tilt to her head. "You need to watch where you're stepping."

Then the smell hit him. He glanced down and groaned. He stomped to the side of the road and scraped his boot in a clean patch of dirt. "That's what I get for being awful at my job." He couldn't afford to be awful at it. If the city council asked him to resign…

"You work plenty hard, but that was quite fresh." She wrinkled her nose and gestured for him to join her. The ease with which she hooked her arm around his made him wonder why Annie jumped at the slightest touch.

Perhaps Leah had spoiled him into thinking women were easy to be around. "I'm surprised you can stand so close to me, considering the stench." He scraped his boot one last time for good measure.

She chuckled. "It's not as if the street doesn't always smell like this."

His chest relaxed with her easy conversation. "So where're you headed?"

"To see you actually."

"Me?" He looked down at her, quite far down, since she was nearly half a foot shorter than Annie. Leah's face seemed tense. "I hope you don't need a marshal."

"Just this marshal." She grinned as she squeezed his arm, but it quickly faded away. "I was wondering." She swallowed hard. "I mean, did Bryant stop by your house last night?"

"No, was he wanting to talk to me?" Hopefully—

"No, it's just that..." Her expression contorted for a second, but then with a shrug, her face went back to glowing. "Well, I wanted to invite your family to supper tomorrow."

And here he'd been thinking Leah had been easy to read. "I'll have to ask Annie, but I doubt she'll refuse."

"Great." She smiled up at him. "And how are you two doing?"

He turned his attention forward as if needing to concentrate on navigating the boardwalk—the empty boardwalk. How truthful should he be? If Bryant wasn't available to help him, perhaps Leah could. Considering she was a woman, maybe she'd be better at advising him anyway. "I'm afraid my ability to understand women is woefully lacking."

Leah broke out in a full guffaw.

When Mrs. Tate sent her a censuring glance as she passed them on the boardwalk, Leah covered her mouth with her hand, but laughter still shook her petite frame.

She sucked in a deep breath as soon as Mrs. Tate passed and gave Jacob a beatific smile. "Only you and a thousand other men suffer from such affliction."

He tried to give her a menacing glare, but her dancing eyes kept him from pulling it off. "Well, yes. Plenty of men are confused by the fairer sex, but I've never had trouble communicating with you. Annie's much more quiet, painfully so."

Leah's features sobered. "I don't know her well enough to tell you what's going on in her head, but I think any woman, or man for that matter, would have trouble grappling with the circumstances she's been thrown into."

"But I thought women liked to talk. She's not telling me anything. I can't help if—"

"Not all women like to talk. I've never known Annie to be chatty."

"No, but I'd thought as her husband..." That certainly felt weird to declare aloud. "That I'd be the one she'd talk to. But maybe it's a woman thing. Maybe you could get her to open up. She looks about ready to burst, or well, she actually does. Randomly. The tears appear with no rhyme or reason, but I can't help her stop unless I understand why."

Leah patted his arm, her smile growing bigger. "Now, there's a good husband, wanting to fix everything. But only she can find herself."

"'Find herself'?"

"Who she thought she was and where she'd thought she'd be was suddenly yanked away from her. It'll take time to adjust to her new role."

"I'd thought Annie was tough. But right now, she seems anything but."

"Give her time." She patted his arm again, and this time he frowned at the patronizing gesture. How long would it take Annie to find herself?

With a sigh, he stopped in front of his office and Leah looked toward the horizon where the mountains created a dusky blue ridge around the northern half of Armelle.

She shook her head a little and looked back at him. "When Bryant's sick, he's flat out cranky. But I love him anyway because I know who he is when he's well. Unfortunately, you don't know who Annie is beneath the turmoil. But if you can focus on the woman waiting for you on the other side, things will come out right before you know it." She turned to smile up at him, but her smile didn't look as joyful as the ones she'd given him earlier. "What I've learned after nineteen years of marriage is that the breakthrough always comes. It might take longer than you wish, it might not be the breakthrough you want, but the confusion always clears up at some point."

He squeezed Leah's arm. "I suppose all I can do is make sure she knows I'm willing to listen when she's ready."

"A good plan, I'd say." She gave him a wink and then headed back the way they'd come.

He blew out a noisy exhale as he pulled out his keys. He'd prepared himself to wait for Annie to learn to love him, but he'd not realized how hard it would be to wait for her to trust him—not just for protection and provision, she'd chosen him for that—but with her thoughts, her worries, her heart.

Even if love took a long time to develop, he'd at least hoped for a friend and confidante. And considering how Bryant was shutting him out—

Jacob opened the door and something white floated up with the gust of air.

He stomped on the paper with his foot and bent to retrieve it.

Three rustlers are encamped with cattle south of the county line, about a quarter mile north of the hollow tree adjacent to the Quincee property on the north side of the Laramie.

No signature.

The words were written with a stiff hand, likely to keep anyone from recognizing the handwriting—just like the last two he'd found.

He'd at first wondered if these were actual tips or a criminal's attempt to get the marshal out of town, but considering the last one panned out, they were likely real.

After stuffing the note in his pocket, he crossed the room to grab extra ammunition. Then he locked up the office and jogged back down Main Street.

Nolan Key could watch over the town while he was away. Though Nolan's amputated leg kept him from serving as deputy, he trusted the man to stop any mischief if these notes suddenly proved themselves to be an elaborate distraction.

Before he retrieved Duchess from the livery and rode out to the Keys' ranch, he'd have to let Annie know where he was headed.

Within minutes he let himself into his kitchen, but the house was quiet and dark. No bread was in the oven, no fire in the cook stove. "Annie?"

No answer. She'd not mentioned she was going anywhere this morning, but then, she'd been reticent as usual.

Time was too precious to run about town when the rustlers could already be half a day away from the spot the note described.

He swiped paper from Annie's desk but halted. Was someone crying? The clock ticked out three seconds and all was still. Evidently, he'd heard nothing. He searched for a pencil.

Thankfully he'd already informed Annie his job could call him away unexpectedly. He would let her know he'd be gone a couple days, longer if he caught the rustlers. His hands shook as he wrote. Could he indeed bring in three rustlers on his own? He couldn't ask Nolan to come along, and Bryant, well ... maybe Frank was in town, but if not...

He paused only a second before signing, "Love, Jacob," to the bottom of his note.

Though he wasn't in love yet, if the worst happened, she'd know he'd pledged his heart to her. Hopefully it would bring her some comfort.

Please bring me home safe so that the hope for love isn't all there ever was between us.

CHAPTER SEVENTEEN

"Not much farther, girl." Jacob patted Duchess's neck, but didn't bother prodding her to speed up since he was enjoying the sun's slow but colorful ascent over the ridge. Its fiery glow transfigured the gently rolling plains from a frosty-looking greenish blue to a cheery orange.

Besides, he'd ridden Duchess hard yesterday and she deserved to take her time getting home. He'd received the anonymous tip nearly twenty-four hours ago and had ridden her halfway across the plains that morning. The site hadn't been as fresh as he'd hoped, but he'd found tracks indicating a small herd of cattle and a couple of horses heading north. He'd followed those tracks for hours, but come nightfall, near a creek, he'd lost all sign of them.

He'd bedded down on the ground under an endless expanse of twinkling stars, waiting for first light so he could continue tracking, but his mind hadn't let him sleep.

And then the rainstorm had rolled in, obliterating any chance of success.

Since the moment he'd left town, he'd prayed God would put obstacles in front of the rustlers and give his horse light feet so he could bring them in. But instead, he'd seen no one and was headed home empty-handed again.

Did God not want to use him to bring about justice?

Or was he simply that poor of a marshal? If so, why had God allowed Annie's ranch to be taken away if God wasn't going to use him in this job?

He rubbed his bleary eyes and forced himself to hum a lively tune.

At the sight of several men galloping on horseback in Jacob's direction, he pulled Duchess to a halt.

Mr. Sullivan, several Crawfords, and a handful of other men who made up the county's self-proclaimed posse trotted up.

Jacob straightened his shoulders and held back a sigh. How many times would he have to tell them nobody would be swinging from a tree without a hearing in this county, rustler or no? Years ago, his oldest brother had lost a good friend that way. The posse had hung first, proved innocence later. As long as Jacob was marshal, he'd never sanction such vigilante justice.

Levi Crawford, Annie's former neighbor, held up his fist, calling the group to a stop. The men circled their mounts like a pack of coyotes ready to pounce upon poor tired Duchess. She tossed her head at the fence of horses closing in around her.

"Heard tell the rustlers took thirty head from the O'Conners' place." Levi leaned slightly in his saddle to spit. "Thought you were tracking them?"

"I lost them in the Laramie."

Levi grunted, and his mount pranced. "Lost them?"

"Yes." Jacob kept his gaze steady.

"Of course, he lost them." Sullivan slapped his horse's reins and crowded Duchess with his mustang. "He don't know how to track."

Jacob let Duchess back away. "I beg your pardon, Mr. Sullivan." He eyed the pock-faced ne'er-do-well who couldn't manage to keep his prize sow penned. "I can track."

"Why didn't you ask us to come along?" Sullivan leaned

atop his saddle horn, his ever-present alcoholic fumes mucking up the air. "Deputize some of us. You obviously need the help."

Jacob scanned the crowd of men, none he trusted. "Perhaps I do need a deputy, but I don't want a posse." Maybe it was time to ask the council to pay for a tracker who could spend every day scouring the land.

"Every county around here has a posse." The other men's mumblings affirmed Levi's statement. "Why you're the only one who despises them, I don't know. Wanting to hoard the glory for their takedown yourself?" He spit again. "But when we catch the rustlers—since you cain't—the county'll be thanking us. When they replace you, then you'll wish you'd let us help."

Jacob gritted his teeth and jerked his head in the direction he'd come from. "You can search if you please, but you'll be wasting your time." He glared at Sullivan. "Even a skilled tracker would lose them in the storm I endured last night."

A younger Crawford pulled forward from the circle. "You ain't been able to bring them in for over a year now. Next time you should hand your tips to us. With no cattle of your own, you ain't taking a hit to the money box, so maybe you don't have enough incentive."

"If you keep letting them get away, you'll pay for it with your job." An older Crawford pulled at his straggly beard. "We can't afford to keep a useless marshal." He pointed behind him toward Armelle. "I heard you can't even catch the kid vandalizing city property."

Jacob steeled his jaw and his right eyelid twitched. He forced himself not to snap at the man.

For how could he? The man spoke truth.

Sullivan cocked his head. "Or maybe you're too soft to string up a thief?"

"I think he's gone and gotten himself distracted by his homely wife."

"Enough," Jacob barked. "Gentlemen, if I need you, I'll call for you." Nudging Duchess, he pushed through the ring of horses and didn't look back. After putting a fair bit of distance between them, he rolled his shoulders yet maintained his broomstick posture. He couldn't afford to let them see they'd hit a nerve, even from afar.

What if they were right? What if he didn't have enough guts or drive? Annie distracted him all right, but even before she came along, he'd not been able to catch the rustlers.

Within a mile of town, a fine black carriage raced toward him. Only three people from town owned such a vehicle: McGill, Mr. Ivens, and the banker. But none of them should be in such a rush. After reining Duchess to the side of the road, Jacob shielded his eyes and tried to make out the driver.

Gwen—not the McGill's family coachman—was whipping the horses. Her face was as pale as the white feathers dancing about in her hat. Her father hung onto his seat's edge with both hands.

Why were they in such a hurry? He waved an arm to snag their attention.

Gwen yanked the horse to a stop with one hand, while squashing her precariously perched hat against her head with the other. Her golden curls whipped forward with the momentum.

Once she'd righted herself and checked that her hat was in place, Gwen rested a hand on her heaving bosom. "Oh, I'm so glad you're all right, Jacob."

He cocked his brow. Even if she'd thought he'd met his doom, what had made her think racing to his aid would've done any good?

"Those men said they were coming out to teach you a lesson." Her breathless voice and concerned pucker made him want to flog each and every man in his would-be posse.

"Confound it, Gwendolyn." McGill stumbled out of the carriage as if he'd just tumbled off a bucking bull. "Remind me to never let you drive again, no matter how much of a hurry you're in." He jerked on his lapels and scanned the area.

Had his boss thought he'd have been able to stop the men? Without a gun, McGill would've been as effective as spit in a dust storm. He had influence, sure, but not that much. If they'd been intent on a hanging, they probably would've strung up the roly-poly mayor as well.

A man didn't monopolize choice grass land, water access, and political clout without making lots of enemies.

Jacob ran his reins through his hands. "Perhaps you misunderstood. I just spoke with them, and they mean to show me up by out-tracking me—which they won't." At least he hoped not. If they could find the remnants of a trail in all that mud, he might as well quit.

He noted the flush in Gwen's cheeks which only served to enhance her fair skin. What would she have tried to do if those men were bent on lynching him? Neither of the McGills could've stopped that riffraff with stern words or logic—which was exactly why he had no use for a posse. "How'd you hear of their plans?"

Her cheeks bloomed brighter. "In town."

"Where in—"

"I hurried to Papa straightaway. I couldn't bear to think of you being accosted when I could stop it."

Jacob frowned at her father. This girl got her way more than she ought. "Thank you both for your concern. Though next time, you might want to gather more men before attempting a rescue."

"So you didn't catch the rustlers?" McGill wiped perspiration off his forehead and floppy jowls.

Jacob sighed, and then took a long look to his left and his right. Where did the man think he'd stashed the rustlers he would've trussed up if he'd caught them? "Not a single one, sir."

McGill's eyes narrowed into menacing slits.

Jacob simply shrugged.

"But he will, Papa." Gwen flashed him a smile. "He will."

"Your time would be better spent clearing the roads, Hendrix."

Jacob blinked. Did McGill not care about the rustlers? Then again, of all the cattlemen in the area, he had the most ranch hands, all armed to the teeth. He'd yet to lose a good amount of cattle. Many couldn't afford such protection.

"Now trade me places, Gwendolyn. I'm driving." McGill gestured for her to switch seats. "I want to get home in one piece."

Gwen scooted over and winked at Jacob while her father's back was turned. "I know you'll catch them."

Her infatuation must be strong for her to believe that.

Jacob gave the McGills a good lead before following them into town.

When the livery came into view, Duchess quickened her pace all on her own. The big girl must want oats something fierce.

His own stomach rumbled. Hopefully Annie had something good on the menu, along with some words to soothe his ego. Gwen's unmerited belief in him hadn't helped whatsoever, but Annie was sensible. Whatever she chose to tell him in regard to his failed mission had a much better chance of encouraging him.

Thank you, Lord, for giving me a wife. I certainly need her today.

CHAPTER EIGHTEEN

The tiny bell rang above the mercantile's front door, and Annie looked up to see who'd come in, but the crowded shelving made it impossible to see past the stacks of cans.

Could it be Jacob?

She'd instructed Celia to inform him she'd gone shopping if he returned.

If he returned.

She shook her head at herself for thinking the worst again. She set down a pickle jar and attempted to swallow down the butterfly wedged in her throat.

God's plan for her couldn't be to lose two husbands in less than a year.

Jacob had been kind enough to leave a note, but wearing a rut in the glossy planks of his parlor had done nothing to dispel the worry-laden clouds hanging over her as one day had rolled into two.

Holding her breath, she moved to the end of the aisle and peeked around the corner.

Just Mrs. Tate.

Annie let out a noisy, unladylike sigh.

The old woman's gaze caught hers and grew intense and ... sour?

Annie glanced behind her, but no one else was in this part of the store. She turned back to Mrs. Tate, but the woman had already walked away.

Had she imagined Mrs. Tate glaring at her?

Annie shrugged and went back to perusing the canned goods. Jacob's pantry was practically empty. Was he so picky he only ate crackers and canned beans or had he eaten at the Whitsetts' so often he needn't much food on hand? She'd meant to ask him about foods he liked and disliked, but he'd left before she'd gotten around to doing so.

Would he turn his nose up at oysters?

She spun the tin cylinder around, leaving fingertip trails on its dusty lid. She picked up the can and squinted at the image of the round gray shellfish, imagining how they might taste. She'd only learned the basics of cooking as a girl since Mother thought them above kitchen work. The ranch cook Gregory had hired their first two years in Wyoming had only shown her how to cook meat, beans, potatoes, eggs, and cake. The only thing she'd bothered to learn beyond that was fruit pies.

Learning to cook more than four basic meals might help soften Jacob's disappointment over ending up with three extra mouths to feed instead of a ranch. Oysters wouldn't be enough to make up for that, but what else could she do?

Though with the way he looked at her, one might think he didn't mind ending up with her much at all.

Annie plunked the can into her basket and tried not to read too much into the looks he'd given her since their wedding.

He'd not looked at her as if she was a woman he knew he was in his rights to fully possess, but as if he esteemed her.

As if he truly cared.

But if anyone deserved to be appreciated in this marriage, it was him, not her.

So she'd purchased a cookbook yesterday in hopes of finding

something special to make him for supper once he returned. She'd found several oyster dishes, and if nothing else, attempting such a daring recipe might get her mind off worrying about Jacob's whereabouts.

Funny how she'd felt crowded this past week with all of his asking about whether she was all right, but now she was positively jittery wondering whether he'd ever come back to pester her with questions again.

She grabbed a can of baking soda, the last thing on her list, and headed to the counter, where Mrs. Tate was digging through her coin purse to pay for two spools of thread.

"Good morning, Mrs. Tate." Annie gave her a small smile. She'd have to get used to seeing people so frequently now that she lived in town. Maybe she could gain some friends. Without all the chores and animals to care for, there was more time to fill up than she'd ever thought existed, or at least had forgot existed. Being a young woman of leisure was now more than a decade behind her. She emptied her basket onto the counter. "A beautiful day for shopping."

Mr. Owens, the shopkeeper, handed Mrs. Tate her receipt but looked to Annie. "It sure has been pleasant lately, Mrs. Hendrix."

Annie nodded at the rail-thin man with the meager mustache. "And I'm enjoying being able to patronize your store any time I feel the need."

Mrs. Tate adjusted her spectacles and raised her eyebrows. "You have a *need* for oysters?"

"Well, no, but I bought a new cookbook yesterday and thought I'd try some new recipes."

Mrs. Tate's pointed gaze took in Annie's green work dress, from collar to hem.

She glanced down to make sure she hadn't a tear or a stain causing such censure.

"Perhaps you ought to consider purchasing another dress before you purchase oysters."

Annie's chest tightened. "I'm sorry?"

"Seems to me mourning colors would be more appropriate. You are still mourning, aren't you, Mrs. Hendrix?" She humphed. "Or at least you should be." Mrs. Tate pivoted and barreled out the exit.

Mr. Owen gave Annie a worried look, and she dropped her gaze to examine her dress. She'd put on the spring colored garment because it was wash day. Her three black dresses were presently hanging on the line. They'd been dyed many times over since she'd lost her daughter, Catherine, to brain fever, and they'd been worn more often than anything else in her wardrobe.

But after wearing her navy and rose outfit for her wedding...

Annie ran her hand along the pleats in her faded, flower-sprigged dress. If she'd still been living on the ranch, she'd not have come to town on wash day.

Mr. Owens coughed and she forced herself to look up.

His dark brown eyes looked like a puppy's—sad and questioning. He'd already stacked her items back into her basket, except for the oysters in her hand.

Annie shoved the can across the counter. "I won't be getting this."

"Are you sure, Mrs. Hendrix? Just because—"

Annie sucked in a loud breath. "No, thank you. Maybe another time."

He nodded, but he must know she was lying. She'd never be able to pick up another can of oysters without thinking of being accused of not properly mourning Gregory.

You are still in mourning, aren't you? At least you should be.

How many years had she been in mourning for one loved one or another?

More than she could count. More years than she had children, that was for certain.

Yet she'd never once thought of cooking something fancy for

Gregory, and here she was about to purchase an expensive, unnecessary ingredient to impress Jacob.

What had she been thinking?

Without looking at Mr. Owens, she paid for her groceries and left.

A trickle of wind played in her hair on the sidewalk in front of the mercantile, and the sun gently warmed her face, but she no longer had the desire to stroll down Main Street and stop in the shops she'd been hoping to browse this afternoon.

She marched down the road and within minutes slipped into Jacob's house. Once the door closed behind her, she let her shoulders droop. How many people thought as Mrs. Tate did?

Gwendolyn probably.

Leah? Her expression during the wedding had been practically aglow. She likely didn't think too badly of her. And yet, how would anyone know if Leah thought badly of them? She seemed too kind to hurt anyone's feelings, whether they deserved censure or not.

Upstairs, it seemed Celia and Spencer were having a tiff, but since their argument sounded less than serious, Annie trudged into the pantry. The dim room closed in upon her as she set her purchases on the shelves. Despite going to the mercantile more this past week than she had the last two months, the shelves still appeared bare. Of course, this pantry had been originally built for a family of eight. She'd have to fight the urge to keep buying foodstuffs simply to fill in spaces.

Once she'd unloaded her basket, she flipped a crate upside down in the dark corner, sat on it and cupped her chin in her hands.

Despite no window in the pantry, the air smelled of loam and impending rain. If she'd been home, she'd be weeding and tending seedlings already. Her gardens would've produced enough to fill this pantry two times over, but not this summer.

Without a ranch's endless needs to take care of, how was she supposed to fill her days? Go visiting, throw tea parties?

Mrs. Tate wouldn't come to chat considering she looked down her nose at Annie for throwing off society's expectations in order to save her ranch and had failed to do even that.

If she found the gumption to host a party, how many townswomen would decline the invitation?

Annie rubbed her eyes, but she had no more tears. She'd shed enough these past two weeks, that if she'd collected them, Mrs. Tate would've been satisfied with how thoroughly she'd mourned. She'd not had time to cry when Gregory died at the beginning of November. She'd had livestock to feed, ice to melt for drinking water, wood to haul, and her children's grief to attend.

Annie wiped at her very warm but dry eyes and hung her head.

The night after she'd married Jacob, the dammed up tears had burst forth and awakened Celia, so for the last two weeks, she'd cried silently to make sure no one heard, not Celia, not Spencer, not Jacob.

No, Mrs. Tate. I know how to mourn.

Life hadn't given her the time to grieve a year and a day like a proper woman should.

Asking Jacob to marry her had been the only thing she'd gotten right this past month, for if she hadn't, her children would be homeless. And yet, every day since the wedding, she'd fought the desire to hole up in Jacob's tiny third bedroom and never come out.

Just when she'd cried herself out and was ready to move on, Mrs. Tate judged her for it.

Spencer's squeal as he thumped down the stairs, followed by the door slamming and Celia's muttering, made Annie suck in a deep draught of air.

She was supposed to be working on becoming a better wife and mother. Neither of which she could do in a dark pantry corner hiding from Mrs. Tate's censure.

Annie grabbed two cans of beans Jacob stocked by the

dozens. If they were good enough for him before she came, they'd be good enough now if he showed up.

After preparing cornbread and placing it in the oven, Annie poured the beans into a pot.

She peeked outside to make sure Celia was still watching Spencer—she wasn't, but at least she was reading on the porch swing near where he was twirling a rope above the neighbor's playful kitten.

An urge to tell them to get to their chores bubbled up, though there were none to be done on a Saturday in town.

She dropped the curtains back into place and went to read Jacob's note again. He'd hoped to be gone quite a while if it meant he'd catch the rustlers.

But if he went alone...

She'd not heard anyone mention he'd taken along any men. What if he was outnumbered?

She ran her finger over his last two words. *Love, Jacob.*

Of course, that was the proper way to end a letter, but the thought of being loved again when she'd figured all hope of that was gone...

Which it would be if he never returned.

How many days needed to pass before she should round up men to go looking for him? Should she have gone around town and asked some to follow after him the moment she'd found his note?

Pushing herself away from Jacob's desk, she went back to preparing lunch.

The beans had started to burn on the bottom. Probably a good thing she hadn't bought the oysters. She'd likely have blackened them into a crisp with how well she was paying attention.

No sooner had the cornbread browned than Jacob walked through the door with a handful of flowers he immediately stuck in her grandmother's empty vase. "I'm home."

His deflated tone made her stiffen.

Was he not happy to be home?

Of course, this house was no longer a place of sanctuary for him. Not with Spencer's hooting and hollering and Celia's stormy temper. "I'm glad you've come back."

The corner of his mouth twitched into a fleeting smile, but his shoulders stayed slumped as he pulled off his coat and hung his hat.

"Would you call in the children?"

"Lunch ready, then?" He crossed over to the oven but frowned at the contents of the pot. "Canned beans?"

"Yes." She banged the lid onto the pot. "You didn't expect something fancy, did you?" Her hand stilled on the handle. She shouldn't have snapped. It wasn't his fault oyster soup wasn't boiling on the stove.

He searched her eyes, his breath whispering across her cheek. "No." The corners of his mouth drooped. "It's just that I'd looked forward to ... well, it doesn't matter, now does it?" His voice dropped and strangled into silence. The dark circles under his eyes indicated he wasn't ungrateful, just weary.

She reached for his sleeve, but missed as he turned to head out the door.

"I'll call in the kids."

"Jacob, I—" The whine of the door's hinges was followed by its subsequent slam. She lowered her hand.

Outside the window, Jacob ruffled her son's hair.

How dare she be prickly when he'd done nothing but give, give, give?

Spencer ran inside and hugged her leg.

Jacob walked in behind him and grabbed Spencer around his middle. "Boy, let's get you out of those muddy pants."

Her son giggled as Jacob flipped him upside down over his shoulder. They ascended the staircase, and Annie frowned as she watched them leave.

He was already on his way to being a better father than she was a mother. She needed to get herself together and—

"Beans?" Celia slammed the lid back on the pot and wrinkled her nose. "That's all?"

Now, if anyone deserved being snapped at for their unappreciative tone it was Celia, yet she hadn't the desire to fight with her girl today. She rubbed her face. "There's cornbread too. Sit please." She grabbed the bowls and divided the meager meal.

Jacob and Spencer tromped down the stairs, and Annie forced herself to slide Jacob's bowl of beans in front of him instead of throwing the contents out for slop and announcing she needed more time to make lunch.

While they ate, Jacob kept up a steady banter with the children about their studies, Celia grudgingly giving vague answers, Spencer bubbling over with unnecessary detail.

But Jacob asked her nothing as she choked down the beans to which she hadn't even added seasoning.

"If you will excuse me." Jacob stood before the rest of them finished and folded his napkin. "I'm going to take a nap." Without waiting for an answer, he strode toward the stairs and disappeared.

Celia cocked an eyebrow at her mother.

Annie looked away to stare out the window. Her daughter was right to assume Jacob's leaving the table early was her fault.

She'd never been in the dark on what Gregory had thought of her, for he told her straight, often bluntly, but Jacob was always asking after her feelings rather than venting his. Always trying to put her at ease when she was the one who'd messed up his world.

She'd not even gotten around to asking him how his trip had gone so focused was she on grumbling to herself about the awful food she'd welcomed him home with.

This self-sacrificing man needed a better wife.

Tonight, supper would be better.

CHAPTER NINETEEN

Jacob slogged up to his back door after a week of degrading work and getting nowhere with his inquiries about Annie's property, but today had been the worst. What chance did he have of a conflict-free evening tonight? He stretched a few kinks from his shoulders and rubbed his face before entering.

Inside, he wasn't surprised to find the kitchen empty despite something smelling of onions and garlic simmering on the stove. "Anne?"

Since he'd lost the rustlers' tracks two weeks ago, she'd been intent on cleaning every nook and cranny of the house, polishing everything to a high luster, finding things in crevices and under furniture he'd not even realized he owned.

Surely she was about out of rooms to tidy. He'd told her such meticulous housekeeping wasn't necessary, but she'd insisted it was the least she could do while he worked.

He groaned as he lowered himself into a kitchen chair to pull off his boots. Since he was home early, perhaps he could convince her to take a break and talk to him a bit. With the children always about and the in-depth cleaning she was doing, getting her to open up seemed impossible.

At least she fed him well. He'd apologized for complaining about the beans, but she'd not cooked the same thing twice since.

Annie peeked out from the pantry, her hair falling about her face in a rather adorable way. "Jacob?" She glanced at the clock and then back at him. Her hands stilled in the towel she was wiping her hands with. "What happened to you?"

He examined his mud-caked pants and figured telling her the truth might ruin her appetite. But if he wanted her to open up to him, keeping things to himself—even the not so nice things—wouldn't do.

"I had to dig up the—" His mouth went dry, so he swallowed. "I had to relocate the, um, residents of Hillview Cemetery today."

"Cemetery? You mean corpses?" At his nod, her face contorted, and she placed a hand against her throat. "Whatever for?"

He wiped his palms against his denim trousers, trying to erase the sensation of the coffinless he'd dealt with this afternoon. "Creek water won't stop encroaching on the graves. So the council voted to move the cemetery to higher ground."

She walked into the kitchen, but stopped several feet shy of him and put a hand against her cheek. "And they made you do it? They made you disturb the..." Her voice disappeared on a whisper.

He cringed, strangely feeling as if he needed to apologize. "I'm afraid so." Though he knew other marshals raked alleys and corralled livestock, and maybe even some had to worry about terrible sidewalks, digging up corpses was beyond the pale. He stripped off his gun belt and tossed it onto the table. Why bother wearing it? He'd never used his Colt and probably never would, not here in Armelle anyway. Not when he was expected to do all the dirty jobs no one wanted. "What else would the mayor have me do? Arrest rustlers, shut down gambling halls, breakup brothels? No, not when sidewalks need fixed and flooded cemeteries rearranged."

He still couldn't believe McGill had reprimanded him for not repairing the broken street lamps before charging off after the rustlers.

"You are washing up before supper, yes?"

The stink emitting from his clothing was more than just his own body odor. He shivered. "I plan on taking a scalding bath if I can manage it."

"Good." She gave him a small smile and then disappeared back into the pantry.

The muscle in his upper lip twitched. Would it kill her to sit and talk a little? But then, with how he smelled, now was not the time to insist on getting to know each other better. He grabbed the sun-warmed water off the porch, emptied the hot water reservoir from the stove, and stalked off into the washroom.

After filling the tub and gingerly slipping into the water, he listened to Annie scurrying about in the kitchen and sighed. They should know each other better by now. It was nigh on a month since they'd been married, and not a day went by that she didn't seem to grow a bit more enticing, but it seemed they did little but share a house.

He was going to have to do something about that. But what?

With Spencer vying for his attention the moment he came home, the uneasy dance they all performed to keep Celia from ruining everyone's night, and his inability to stay up much past eight o'clock with all the work McGill was assigning him and his attempts to search for the rustlers until daylight disappeared, he'd had a hard time finding quiet moments to spend with his wife.

And though she likely thought no one heard her occasionally crying in the middle of the night, he had. But what could he do when he was shut out, uninvited? Thankfully, she seemed to have bucked up in the past few weeks, either that or he slept too hard to notice her crying now.

He didn't want to force himself upon her in any fashion. Yet he hadn't known how hard it would be to feel unwanted.

Patience, Jacob. Patience.

Her mourning wouldn't end any sooner if he told her he was lonely. He'd only make her feel guilty. Having her pay attention to him out of guilt wouldn't feel good at all.

How long did it take to court a woman anyway? Most couples were together a year before they married, were they not?

If they had courted first, they still would've had time constraints and children to deal with, so maybe he needed to find time rather than just hope for it.

Besides, being married already gave him quite the advantage. The second Annie could no longer resist his charms, things could be immediately more pleasant around here.

Jacob swiped a bar of soap off the shelf and hummed a happy tune.

Annie tapped the buttermilk bread. Not quite done. Trying new recipes—though nothing with oysters—had kept her busy, but she sorely missed her garden. Through the back window, she eyed the corner of Jacob's small lot. No time for building cold frames, but maybe she could squeeze in a small garden and reap a harvest before the frosts came.

Thumping sounded from the washroom, followed by Jacob's deep masculine growl. A trickle of warmth ran from her neck to her shoulder blades. She'd married Jacob to replace her husband the rancher, not her husband the lover, yet in just a few weeks, Jacob attracted her more than she'd thought possible.

And not just because of his good looks, but he regularly replaced the wilted contents of her grandmother's vase with fresh wildflowers without being asked, took Spencer outside to play catch almost every night despite being ready to fall over with exhaustion, asked about her day as if he cared about laundry and scrubbed floors, turned those liquid brown eyes on her more often than not.

But she wasn't ready to do anything about that attraction.

Shouldn't be, not when she still woke up at night wondering for a second or two where she was and where Gregory had gone.

"Anne!" Jacob's holler made her heart skip a beat.

Had Spencer put that horned toad in the washroom again?

"Anne. Come here, please."

And *Anne*. Only Gregory had called her Anne—'Anne, darling,' actually. And only when he'd been feeling amorous.

She stole to the door and spoke through the crack. "Yes?"

"I forgot a towel." Water swished. "And clothing for that matter. Would you mind running upstairs and grabbing me some?"

"S-sure," she stammered. She stood for a second outside the washroom with her hand upon her chest. Where was Spencer?

She made her way to the parlor to check the clock. Too early for him to be home from school. She'd have to go into the washroom and hand a dripping, undressed Jacob a bundle of clothing. As she climbed the stairs, her breathing grew choppier than a single flight of exercise should've caused.

She opened his door and blinked at the numerous windows letting in light. Her room was only a third of this size and had but one window.

Though she'd cleaned every other room in this house twice, she hadn't so much as swept in here. She'd not felt right invading the last of his space. Though he'd reacted well enough to them taking over the rest of his house, he never complained when she handed him his clothes to put away, in fact, he'd thanked her.

She took a deep breath and barged in.

A simple, but rather large bed covered by a worn quilt took up a quarter of the floor space. A stout wardrobe, a tall dresser with a tiny mirror attached to its top, and a plain washstand along the east wall stood clutter-free. Sparse and basic, yet the room smelled of him—something like cloves and moss and perspiration.

Haphazardly opening drawers, she assembled an outfit and slipped back out of the room as quickly as possible.

The hand on the clock in the parlor had barely moved since she'd gone upstairs, but Spencer might've been let out of school early.

She poked her head out the back door. "Spencer?"

Birds in the nearby trees scolded her for disturbing their peace.

No patter of running feet. No cheery, "Coming, Mama." Just water noises from the washroom to the side of the kitchen. She let the back door click shut and straightened her shoulders.

She'd been a married woman. She *was* a married woman. Hugging his clothing to her chest, she stamped to the washroom. Her fingers felt slippery on the doorknob. "Jacob?"

A quick thump and a splash. "Come in."

Biting her lip, she entered, her hands strangling the clothes in her hands. At the sight of a wet Jacob sitting in the tin tub, she bit her lip even harder. She'd always thought her kids were cuter when wet—their clumped lashes appearing fuller, their hair smooth and glossy, their eyes a'sparkle.

She didn't know what to think of the marshal, with his wildly-mussed hair dripping water onto his shoulders and bare chest.

His eyebrows raised.

She forced herself to quit gawking and dropped her burden onto the solitary chair. Without a backward glance, she left, closed the door, and mumbled, "Hope those will do."

The washroom had been steamy, but not so much as to cause the sweat trickling down her neck. She wiped the droplets away and fanned her face. Supper. Supper needed attention.

In the kitchen, Leah was stirring the pot on the stove. Or rather, scraping the pot, taking into account the burning smell.

"Leah?"

The petite brunette startled and then glanced behind her. "I smelled something burning. When no one answered the door, I thought I'd come in and check." She scraped the spatula against the side of the pan, releasing caramelized onions. "I think it's still edible." She laid down the utensil and looked at Annie. "Where were you?"

Flames of fire leapt into Annie's cheeks. No chance Leah would miss the dark blush that must be covering her entire face.

Leah's mouth puckered and her eyes sparkled. "Never mind."

"It's not what you're thinking," she said in a rush.

At Leah's frown, Annie grabbed her apron and gave it a good twist. "It's not because I—well, I wouldn't be ... not while ... I mean, I'm just embarrassed you caught me being irresponsible."

Leah gave Annie's shoulder a squeeze and winked. "It's all right to be distracted by your husband."

Annie grabbed a towel and moved to open the oven door to check on her bread. Perhaps sticking her head in a hot oven would make her flushed face seem more reasonable. "No, I was, just uh, taking care of laundry."

"Of course you were." A smile played at Leah's lips as she surveyed the room, her hands behind her back. "Goodness, this place is the cleanest I've ever seen it."

"Thanks." Annie rubbed the sore spots on her hands where the excessive amount of time they'd rubbed against each other in soapy water had taken its toll. "I've spent two weeks giving it a thorough scrubbing. A tired body makes for good sleep, you know."

More importantly, dreamless sleep.

Annie returned to her stew to remove anything burnt. "I've got one more room upstairs to do which won't take long." She pictured the small storage room with not much storage in it. "Then I'll start on a garden. I'm hoping to get something growing in every square inch of the backyard."

"No doubt you can. I've seen your gardens." Leah grabbed a kitchen chair and untied her bonnet strings. "Too bad you can't work on mine. I've a talent for turning things brown."

"I'd be happy to help with yours. Would you like something to drink?"

Leah shook her head and ran a bonnet string repeatedly through her hand. "I didn't mean to ask you to give up your free time to work on my garden. It was just wishful thinking."

"But I'd like to. I need to keep busy." Annie grabbed bowls.

"Why?" The tone of Leah's voice was probing.

Annie shrugged before setting the bowls down and grabbing glasses.

Leah remained quiet until Annie glanced toward her.

"You have to invest time *here*, Annie. Busyness won't make the situation you find yourself in go away."

Annie avoided looking at Leah as she arranged Celia's place setting. If Leah could tell she was avoiding Jacob by simply volunteering to help with her garden, what else might she know? Could she trust the woman with her jumbled up emotions? The ones that made her feel bad? The ones that taunted her? "But I shouldn't have gotten into this situation in the first place." Her voice came out raspy. "I thought I'd heard from God and felt His peace, but now I think I was simply trying to fix things on my own." She sniffed. "And landed myself in an even bigger mess."

"How so?" Leah's incredulous tone made Annie shrug.

Taking a quick glance through the dining room door to make sure Jacob wasn't approaching, Annie faced Leah, and whispered, "I'm in a loveless marriage without my ranch. How could my situation be worse?"

Leah snorted and shook her head. "You could be destitute on the street at the mercy of men of lesser caliber."

Annie couldn't look at Leah. It figured she'd not understand. Her life was perfect.

Scooting closer, Leah leaned her head in an attempt to get Annie to look at her. "Have you thought that maybe you did feel God's peace, but His plan wasn't yours, and so the resisting you're doing now is what's making you miserable?" She stood to put an arm around Annie. "Whether this is what you envisioned or not, find out how God wants to bless you here, in this house, with this man." She rubbed at a smudge on Annie's sleeve. "Don't run from His blessings to wallow in dirt."

Annie looked away and swallowed thickly. But what if it felt wrong to accept such blessings?

CHAPTER TWENTY

Jacob tromped down the stairs after retrieving another set of pants. The pair Annie had given him had a torn inseam. Judging by the way she'd looked at him, or rather, tried not to look at him in the washroom, wearing those trousers to the table would've made her extremely uncomfortable.

A smile tugged at his lips.

Shy, awkward, uneasy—all signs of beginning attraction, right? Was she noticing things attractive about him, like he was noticing about her? And not just how hard of a worker she was—as he'd suspected she'd be—but the way she ran her fingers down the side of her long, graceful neck when she was lost in thought, the small, but womanly curves that stood out when she didn't wear all black.

And her tendency to flush just might be his undoing.

If the children weren't soon to return from school, he might've left on those pants she'd brought just to see her color all the way to her hairline again.

He shook that thought from his head and whistled a nonchalant tune. Too early to flirt like a rascal. He'd stick with his smooth and charming plan until he'd successfully lured her into his arms and kissed the daylights out of her at least once, and then he'd tease her mercilessly every chance he got to see that pretty shade of pink on her face.

The smell of burnt food twisted his mouth into a pinched pucker. Maybe one *could* go wrong cooking with onions and garlic. He relaxed his face so she'd not think him ungrateful for her attempt and stepped into the kitchen.

Leah was standing beside Annie with her arm encircled about his wife's waist. The two women were such opposite images. Lean next to curvy, reserved beside vivacious.

But what was Leah saying to make Annie frown so?

"Ho there, Leah." Jacob glanced about the room. "Is Bryant coming for supper?" Though he'd like to see his friend, Annie's mood always soured in his presence. Maybe that's why she looked uneasy.

Leah's lower lip jutted out like a disappointed child's. "No, he's been working late at the office lately. I won't bother starting supper for another hour." Her twinkling eyes overshadowed her pout. "So I came to help Annie with hers. Sorry I burned it."

Annie's head snapped toward the shorter woman, and her eyebrows scrunched in the middle.

What was Leah up to? "Could we convince you to join us? We could send you home with leftovers for Bryant. That is, if Annie made enough." Female chatter at the table would be a good thing. Perhaps Annie would join in. "The children will be here any second."

"No, but thank you." Leah grabbed her bonnet off a nearby chair and sighed. "I miss having children in the house. If you ever decide to have a honeymoon, let me know. We'd be more than happy to accommodate Celia and Spencer for a week or two."

The exposed bit of his wife's neck turned pink.

"Or just a night—whenever you feel like it."

His wife's neck exploded into the color of a fiery sunrise. Even better.

Of course, he wasn't too certain his own face didn't match hers at the moment.

Bustling out the door, Leah flashed one last glittery beam over her shoulder. "See you two Sunday."

Annie grabbed a serving spoon but dropped it. The utensil clattered across the stove before she retrieved it again. "Leah didn't burn supper. I did." She had yet to look at him.

Jacob leaned against the kitchen doorjamb, perusing his wife's figure. Since she seemed determined not to turn around, he was in no danger of getting caught. "Don't worry about it. I've massacred plenty of meals. Can I help with anything?" He surveyed the table and glanced at the clock. They normally didn't eat for another half hour but everything appeared ready. "Where are the kids?"

Annie glanced his direction without quite meeting his gaze. "Good question. It's past time for them to be home."

Barely, by just about five minutes.

She glided out the back door and leaned over the railing as if arching around to see past the church would bring them home quicker. "Spencer! Celia!"

What had the women been talking about that had made his wife so flustered? If it was anything like what Leah had hinted about on the way out, well, maybe he'd ask Leah to drop by more often.

He joined Annie on the porch and laid his hand on the small of her back. His fingers wandered to the curve of her tiny waist, but she tensed, so he let his hand drop.

Slow. He was supposed to go slow.

He settled back against the porch post. "Celia's been coming home later and later. I doubt she's within earshot."

"Yes, but Spencer—he's usually underfoot the minute school lets out."

Yes, and the second the boy bounded in, the less chance he had of keeping Annie's attention. "Has Celia been back in time to help you with supper at all this week?"

Annie played with a thick wooden splinter jutting from the rail. "No." Her shoulders slumped. "And she's no longer responding to me. I think—" She peered up at him with her deep-golden eyes. "Maybe your ... uh, our strictness is driving her away."

He clamped his mouth shut lest he ruin whatever seemed to be starting between them.

He turned to stare past the low backyard fence where the neighbors' children were playing in the alley. Celia didn't like obeying him, true, yet she did so. But if she was ignoring Annie when he wasn't around, the girl was obviously taking advantage of his wife's leniency. How to get Annie to see? He gritted his teeth. Learning to be a father at the same time as a husband was tricky.

A loud whooping noise preceded Spencer running pell-mell across the backyard. The boy grabbed the porch column, swung wide, and barreled around him and into Annie, seizing fistfuls of her skirt. "Save me!" He buried his face in the fabric. "Celia's going to kill me!" Heavy wheezing garbled Spencer's words, but the jolly glint in his eyes told Jacob the boy had enjoyed whatever he'd done to enrage his sister.

Celia stomped into the backyard from the alley, looking as if she were sitting upon a roiling pot but was determined to keep the lid on even if it burned her backside.

Annie crooked a finger at her daughter.

The gangly girl blew out a breath and then traipsed through the yard as if she hadn't a care in the world. She nodded at him and Annie but kept her gaze off Spencer, who shook with mock fright. "I'll help with supper after I wash up, Ma."

Jacob humphed, and Celia faced him, one eyebrow raised as if daring him to state the obvious—she was too late to be of any assistance.

"It's already done," Annie said.

Celia shrugged and strutted toward the door, but a second

before disappearing into the house, she shot a deadly glare at her brother, still hiding in his mother's skirts.

"Spencer." Annie dropped to stoop beside him and smoothed his mussed cowlick. "Why is Celia mad at you?"

Spencer leaned to peer through the open doorway where Celia could be seen at the sink. "I can't tell you."

That so? Jacob pushed off the post. "Spence—"

"Well, then, you get in there with your sister and wash up." Annie turned Spencer by his shoulders and gave him a push toward the door. She followed the boy in, shaking her head.

Jacob sighed. He wasn't sure he wanted to ignore figuring out what was going on between the siblings, but right now, it might be more trouble than it was worth.

After everyone settled around the table, Celia offered a benign prayer before the overcooked food made its rounds. The potatoes were surprisingly underdone despite being burnt, but the seasonings were good.

"I'm sorry about the stew. You can pick the burnt bits out without offending me." Annie was looking down at her bowl, frowning as if the ingredients had come from the compost pile.

"Still tastes good."

She looked over at him for a second, then pulled the butter dish toward her. "Thanks, but I'm sorry that I got ... distracted." The familiar creep of pink climbed above her collar.

So the bathing incident had caused the food's sad state? He couldn't help but smile.

"When are you going to figure out how to get our land back, Marshal?" Celia spoke around a mouthful of food. "We've been here too long already."

He lost his smile and glared at the girl.

Her belligerent expression faded—a little.

Annie cleared her throat and handed a slice of bread to Spencer. "I've been wondering if you've found somewhere else to run our cattle. Crawford expects rent next week, but I think someone else might keep them cheaper. I know you didn't expect to still be uncertain about the status of the ranch, but I don't want to waste money."

Though he wanted the land back too, couldn't she have asked him about other things when she finally decided to talk? "I haven't had time to look into it."

Celia's spoon froze in front of her mouth. "Why not? We need to get the ranch back before whoever bought it gets comfortable."

"Hush, Celia." Annie wiped her mouth. "You're being rude. Besides, we may never be able to set foot on our ranch again." She picked up another slice of bread but did nothing with it but pick it apart.

For the next few minutes, he ate to the sound of silverware clanking and Celia huffing.

After Annie had finished tearing her bread apart and suddenly frowned at the mess she'd made, she turned to Jacob. "So, um, how was work?"

Did she not remember the reason he'd come home early for a bath? "I'm thinking that wouldn't be appropriate table talk."

Her eyelids fluttered. "Oh, yes."

Spencer's chair screeched across the floor, and he leaned across the table, his eyes sparkling. "Why? What did you do? Catch a bad guy? Have a shootout?"

Jacob worked to relax his face, trying not to smile at the boy's animated reaction. "No, nothing that exciting."

Or that worthwhile.

"Running after bad guys might seem exciting." Annie buttered another piece of bread. "But sometimes tedious labor can better reveal a man's true character. Those who work hard and without complaint in the most arduous, demoralizing circumstances are the people who can be trusted to be there for you no matter what." She peeked at Jacob, giving him a slight nod, and then slid the bread to Spencer.

Though she'd turned away, he couldn't help but grin at her.

It had taken a few weeks to get the encouragement he'd

wanted from her the day he'd lost the rustlers' tracks, but he was happy she bestowed it now.

"So you won't complain when I ask you to do dishes tonight, right?"

Spencer frowned before he chomped down on his new piece of bread. "No, Mama."

Though her compliment had puffed his chest a little, did he deserve it?

Jacob stirred his stew, looking for anything burnt he wanted to take out. He certainly tried to keep from complaining about his job, but he did grumble about it often—though mostly to himself.

Annie didn't complain about her lot either—at least not to him. But what if during the night when he'd heard her sobbing, she hadn't been mourning her losses, but crying about having to be here?

He put down his spoon. Seemed burnt onions did ruin the whole pot.

CHAPTER TWENTY-ONE

Jacob threw a stick at the young black and white sow wallowing in the mud on the creek shore. "Get up!"

Bristles grunted and rolled over. Her pudgy body had defied his every attempt to nudge her out of her comfy hole.

He grabbed the largest sandstone he could lift and threw it in the water beside her, drenching them both.

Snorting, Bristles rocked herself onto her feet. Thankfully she didn't seem to want another shower and waddled off. In the wrong direction.

Jacob scratched his unshaven jaw and frowned at the stubborn, mud-speckled pig.

He'd done what he'd set out to do—find Levi Crawford's pig—and she'd definitely not been stolen. Crawford had probably claimed such in hopes of avoiding a fine if she showed up in town.

Jacob scrambled up the muddy bank, wiped his boots clean in the grass clumped along the creek's ravine, then headed toward town. He hadn't time to corral people's ornery livestock. He'd inform Crawford of Bristles's whereabouts and be done with it.

In front of the Joneses' and Hochstatlers' houses, Jacob tripped where the men's sidewalks butted up against each other. He stomped on the upturned bricks next to Hochstatlers's nice boardwalk but they wouldn't budge. He took out a pad of paper and left Jones a notice on his front door.

Forging his way across town to the livery, Jacob tried not to look too closely at anybody else's sidewalks.

Hang sidewalks—dirt and grass were plenty good enough to walk on. Maybe he could rally the citizens into petitioning the council to revoke the sidewalk regulations. He knew every person who'd be in favor of it—he had listened to their grousing every time he handed them a warning or fine.

If only he didn't have to keep his job, he'd...

Jacob gritted his teeth and tried to empty his mind. He had to stop grumbling if he wanted to live up to Annie's opinion of him.

Duchess snorted a greeting the moment Jacob enter the livery.

"Ready for a run, girl?" He saddled her, and they soon sped out of town.

Crawford's ranch came into view over the crest of a small ridge. A wooden fence surrounded the ramshackle structures clustered in the middle of the expansive plains.

Jacob filled his lungs with pure air. Oh, to live in the country free from city rules—to be free from enforcing them. He pulled Duchess to a slow gait and recalled the verse he'd memorized this week.

But as it is written, Eye hath not seen, nor ear heard, neither have entered into the heart of man, the things which God hath prepared for them that love him.

He would have to dig deep to find contentment with the current job God allowed him—but fortunately, better things awaited him in heaven.

Thank you for loving me. May I be worthy of reward.

A heavenly ranch would be nice, seeing as he likely wasn't going to get one here on earth.

About a quarter hour later, he tethered his horse to the Crawfords' porch and then navigated the warped stairs to knock on the door. Two empty buckets of whitewash under a makeshift bench caught his eye. He glanced around. Every wooden structure seemed weathered and neglected.

A high-pitched creak pulled back Jacob's attention. Daniel Crawford's slightly mottled face appeared next to the door jamb. The swarthy juvenile eyed him, opening the door no wider than six inches. "What do you want?"

Jacob returned the boy's glare. "Is your father home?"

"No." His eyes narrowed even more.

"Are you expecting him any time soon?"

The boy shook his head.

Jacob took a long look at the whitewash then looked back at the kid.

Daniel's fierce expression evaporated, and he licked his lips.

"What—" Jacob drew out his words "—have you been whitewashing?"

The boy cocked his head and squinted. "A fence."

Jacob remained silent, waiting. If the boy didn't confess now, he'd nail him later.

The boy's lips flattened, then pursed. "On somebody else's property."

"Whose?"

"Not at liberty to say," the boy huffed. "Any more questions? I got to get to town." The glare returned.

"No." Jacob hooked his thumbs around his gun belt. "If you see your pa, tell him I need to talk to him."

"What for?"

Jacob couldn't keep the smirk off his face. "I'm not at liberty to say." He gave Daniel a razing glance before walking back to Duchess. He'd talk to Levi Crawford about keeping a closer eye on his pig as well as his son.

But at least he'd found his vandal. Now all he had to do was catch him in the act or find some stray whitewash and a witness to prove it.

Annie placed the last supper dish on the table as Celia slid in through the door.

"Where've you been?" Annie's hands found her hips. "I had to cook and set the table alone again."

Celia shrugged. "I was busy."

The urge to shake Celia by her shoulders caught Annie off-guard. She took a calming breath. "Perhaps Jacob needs to have a talk with you." Though his strictness seemed to be turning her daughter against her, Celia at least obeyed him.

"So you're taking his side then?"

"His side? Since we've moved into town, you've done nothing but gallivant around, arrive home late, pout, and stew." School had let out days ago, and she'd expected Celia to help around the house. "It's time you stayed home for a while and assisted me—all day."

Celia growled. "I didn't ask to move into town, but now that I'm here, I have friends I want to see."

The kitchen door swung open, and Jacob walked through, his lips bunched to one side. "Visiting friends is one thing, doing so whenever you please is another." Jacob crossed his arms. "Who are these friends anyway?"

"No one." Celia stared pointedly at her mother.

Annie turned to a mud-splattered Jacob, thankful he had appeared before her daughter won another fight. "I don't know who her friends are either, but I was thinking that Celia needs to stay with me next week." She tried to muster some tenderness into her gaze before looking back at her daughter. "Every day. All day. To make up for the help I've lost."

Jacob grunted. "Sounds fair."

"Fair?" Celia stomped. "All day is too much." She tossed her braid over her shoulder. "I'll help with supper from now on, I promise."

"You can't be trusted to do so." Jacob sidled up next to Annie and put his hand on her shoulder. "Your mother's right, you need to make up for how you've treated her lately."

Annie let out a slow breath. *Father, help her take her punishment without causing a scene.*

"But what about my friends?" Celia scowled.

Annie shook her head. "Maybe if we knew who they—"

Jacob squeezed her arm.

Did he not want to know their names?

Celia huffed. "Daniel Crawford, Harriet Butler, and Timothy O'Conner, all right? They're—"

"Then I'm absolutely certain you should stay home with your mother." Tension radiated off Jacob, almost palpable.

Annie knew Daniel. Celia had grown up with him, being that the Crawfords had been their neighbors. Daniel wasn't a horrible boy, just a challenge—like her own child.

Celia's expression turned pleading, but Annie kept her mouth shut. Did Jacob know something about one of the friends she'd listed that would explain Celia's defiance? She'd met Harriet once, and she'd seemed innocent enough, but Annie didn't even know Timothy.

Her heart thudded.

Her fifteen-year-old daughter was spending several unsupervised hours every day with one girl and *two* boys. "I agree with Jacob. You need to stay home."

Letting out a muffled snarl, Celia pivoted and stomped up the stairs. The sound of a door slam followed.

Annie slumped into a kitchen chair. "I can't believe she's behaving so badly. What must people think of me?"

Beside her, Jacob's chair groaned with his weight. "Some might judge us for Celia's behavior, but we'll not worry about that." His arm slipped around her, the touch comforting. "We'll just do the best we can."

She gazed into his eyes, dark with caring. He'd done nothing to create the disaster Celia had become, yet he didn't expect Annie to deal with it alone.

She looked away from his intense stare. Just months ago, she'd believed herself so destitute she'd had to enter into a loveless marriage.

But destitute and unloved she was not.

Though she couldn't throw herself into loving him yet—not when she still halfway expected Gregory to come through the door in the middle of the day, still thought she heard his voice on occasion.

She stared at her hands clutching the apron in her lap while Jacob rubbed a soft circle above her elbow with his thumb. Gregory had been a good man, a fine provider and protector, even if they had quarreled an awful lot in those last months. But he'd never been this sensitive and caring.

What if she ended up loving Jacob more than she'd ever loved Gregory?

Annie straightened and took a deep breath. Right now, she needed to focus on Celia. "What else would you suggest we do with her? I've obviously failed."

Jacob kissed her temple, causing a shiver to run down her spine. "First, she's going to come down and apologize for how she spoke to you. Then we'll enforce your week of work, and then..." He was quiet for so long, she turned to look at him.

His gaze was fastened on nothing in particular, his thumb absently rubbing the underside of his jaw, which was but a few inches away from her. So close she could lean over and kiss—

She drew in a sharp breath and faced forward, her heart pumping hard enough to leap from her chest. She needed to direct her attention back to safe thoughts, more important thoughts, proper thoughts.

"I'm afraid we'll have to tell her she can't see Daniel and his friends anymore." Jacob's voice was soft with concern.

"Daniel? But they've known each other since they were little." Her voice came out breathless, making her protest sound more vehement than intended.

He sighed. "I think he might be the reason behind her lengthy absences. There've been a string of petty pranks lately—broken lights, stolen undergarments, painted signs. I visited the Crawfords' today and saw some empty paint buckets on their porch but nothing painted. Daniel acted defensive when I questioned him."

Jacob scooted closer.

Could he hear the erratic pulse beating in her ears?

"But even if he isn't the perpetrator, his attitude stinks. So much so, Celia's ill manners won't improve by spending time with him." He looped an arm around her and squeezed. "But I'll check on the other two. Maybe she doesn't have to give up all her friends."

Daniel certainly didn't have the best disposition, but if Celia were allowed at least a few—

"One more thing." Jacob took her shoulders and gently swiveled her to face him. The twinkle in his eyes mirrored the grin tugging at his lips. "The next time you're thinking about doing this—" He lowered his head and nipped a tiny kiss on her jawbone below her ear.

A jolt both cold and hot raised goose bumps from her neck to her elbows.

"—you should."

He stood and threw her a roguish look that caused even more gooseflesh to sweep across her body. He winked before striding from the room, his footsteps beating a steady rhythm up the stairs.

She hugged herself, trying to squelch the feverish chill taking over her.

She couldn't kiss him—not yet.

But he was right, she'd wanted to.

His voice, calm and steady, was muffled by the floor overhead, but she could make out the command to come down and apologize.

How could he expect her to discipline Celia after he'd kissed her like that?

Like a penitent pupil, Annie schooled her features and straightened in her chair.

If he'd been able to figure out she'd wanted to kiss his jaw, she had to get a hold of herself lest Celia also guess her thoughts.

Oh, if only she could lock herself in her room right now.

Footsteps tromped on the stairs.

Annie couldn't bear to look up and watch them enter. What if Jacob entered first? What if he was still smiling the way he had right before he'd gone up? She rubbed the sudden gooseflesh that popped up on her arms again as she stared at her lap. If simply thinking about his smile caused such a reaction—

Celia's feet appeared in front of her. The girl knelt down beside the chair, her face no longer impudent. "Ma, please don't let him do this. Daniel's been my friend since I was five." She grabbed her hands. "Daddy liked him well enough."

Annie swallowed hard. Her daughter's eyes, round with pleading, made her want to cave. "Jacob feels you shouldn't—" Celia squeezed her fingers hard "—associate with him for the time being, and I agree. You need to understand that how you're acting is unacceptable. If this is how we have to prove it, then so be it." She extricated her hands and put them on each side of Celia's face. "Prove to me you're the lady I taught you to be, and we won't have to put restrictions on you."

"But—"

"I told you not to badger your mother." Both ladies jumped at Jacob's voice. He stood in the stairwell doorway, but he might as well be filling the whole room. "Have you apologized?"

"No." Celia's voice squeaked. She turned to face her mother,

her chin quivering. "Sorry." She stood and pushed past Jacob, her footfalls whisper fast as she ran upstairs. Then her door closed—but no slam. An answering bang of the kitchen door behind Annie made her jump.

"Whew!" Spencer swiped the bangs from his forehead, revealing a streak of white flesh amidst the dirt covering him from head to toe. "All done."

"What have you been doing, rolling in a barn somewhere?" Jacob smiled as Spencer ran over and hugged his waist.

"No. Mama made me pull the grass and weeds out of the garden."

"We turned dirt over this afternoon." Annie stood and walked to the window, not sure she trusted herself to look at Jacob. The dirt patch seemed virtually free of plants. "Good job, Spencer. You may have an extra slice of pie tonight."

"Yes!"

"If you eat all your supper." Annie wiped at the dirt on his cheek with her thumb. "Though you'll need to change your clothes before you sit at the table."

He pivoted and raced for the stairs.

"Tell Celia it's time for supper after you're done," Annie called after him.

"I'll set the table." Jacob walked past her, his hand flitting across the small of her back as he passed, and grabbed the plates from the hutch. Would this man ever cease anticipating her needs?

She busied herself with setting out the food. The children would be down any minute, and she needed to be doing something.

Spencer's feet scuffed across the floorboards. "Celia said she ain't coming."

"*Isn't* coming. But don't worry about it." Jacob patted the boy's shoulder, but she was certain his words were meant for her. "Everything will be all right."

Annie looked up, where shuffling sounds scraped above the ceiling. "You're not going to make her come down?"

He shook his head and pulled out the seat next to Spencer. "We'll let her stew if she wants. It won't hurt her to go to bed hungry."

Annie took the plate of bread and settled herself in the chair he held out for her. His hand ran lightly across her upper arm, bringing back the gooseflesh that had only receded a few minutes ago. He took a seat and said the evening prayer, but she didn't close her eyes. They remained transfixed on his lips forming the words. When he asked the Lord to bless the hands that prepared the food, she dropped her gaze and bowed her head in time to whisper *amen*.

The second she looked up, Jacob was looking at her.

She quickly turned to serve Spencer some beans.

Surely Jacob had been too busy praying to have realized where her thoughts had returned. Because she didn't know what she'd do if he kissed her like that again.

CHAPTER TWENTY-TWO

Celia yanked her dress fabric loose from where it was hung up on the window frame, then clamped her fingers onto the windowsill. She lowered her body over the edge until her arms stretched full length. Dangling, she searched for a foothold, but the climbing vines clinging to the north side of the house thwarted her. She stretched her leg farther out toward the trellis and finally poked a toe into the latticework. With a daring lunge, she grabbed onto a wooden crosspiece and pulled her body over.

A popping sound above her made her heart jump. She tightened her grip and plastered herself against the wall. After the pulsing in her eardrums quieted, she tested her weight on the next hole down and then slowly descended, trying not to pull the lattice off the siding.

About three feet above the ground, she slipped, and with a thud, hit the dirt. She scurried up against the kitchen's exterior wall and held her breath.

Ma's laughter floated out through the propped-open window. How could Ma be so happy this quick? She'd apparently given up on getting the ranch back. She didn't even ask the marshal about it anymore.

And Spencer already called him Pa.

She'd never call him that.

"What do you think Daniel did with the paint?"

They were talking about Daniel? Celia inched closer to the window.

"Our town sign now proudly welcomes our visitors to Hades."

Celia slapped a hand over her mouth to suppress a giggle.

"What's 'Hades,' Pa?"

"Oh my, Jacob. What're you going to do?"

"Fix the sign." Jacob sighed. "Then talk to Levi. I'm not sure Daniel did it since no one seems to have seen him around that area, but if his father doesn't know what the whitewash was used for, then I'll keep an eye on the boy. Catch him on his next prank."

Since everyone's voices were accounted for, Celia hunched over and scurried from the yard. She didn't have much time. Ma would surely come to her room to lecture her before going to bed.

After darting through alleyways and slinking across streets, Celia crept up behind Harriet's house. On tiptoe, she peeked over the south bedroom windowsill.

Dark and empty.

She crept to the parlor window and took in Harriet's parents and three siblings all busy with one pursuit or another.

Good. Harriet had already escaped.

At the edge of town, Celia left stealth behind and flat out ran, pulling mighty draughts of country air into her taxed lungs. The sun hovered above the horizon, so she pumped her arms faster. She had to get there and back before dark.

Between two thin willows, she veered onto the hidden path near the river obscured by shrubbery and slowed to avoid getting scratched by overeager thorn bushes.

In the clearing, sitting at the river's edge, Harriet threw a large rock into the water, and the splash hit Timothy in the face. He growled and swiped at his forehead with a red neckerchief, and Celia sputtered a laugh.

Daniel hoisted himself up from where he'd been sitting on the bank, hitched up his patched pants, and moseyed toward her. "How'd you get here so early?"

Celia sucked in air until the stitch in her side abated, but she wouldn't double over and pant. Couldn't let Daniel know a simple run to the river had winded her this much.

"Chased by a wolf or something?" Timothy looked at her with slanted eyebrows. He was the eldest of the group, but with his thick facial hair, he seemed even older. "You're crazy if you ran the whole way from town."

"Shut up, Timothy." Harriet back-handed his shoulder and pushed off the ground. Though she was a couple months younger than Celia, she'd filled out much quicker and could talk to boys like that.

Harriet walked up the embankment to put her arm around Celia's shoulders. "Come sit with me and catch your breath."

Celia shook her head. "Don't have time." She blotted her hairline with her shirtwaist's sleeve. Hopefully her face wasn't too red. "Just wanted you to know." She sucked in air. "That the marshal and my ma have decided to lock me up in the house for a week."

"Yet here you are." Daniel's lips formed into something that resembled a smile and a sneer at the same time. "Knew you were my kind of girl."

Celia's fast pumping heart stumbled at his words.

Harriet's posture stiffened and her arm tensed against Celia's back.

Though Timothy was older, Daniel was the one whose eyes could make a girl swoon—a girl weaker than her, anyway.

Celia straightened and tilted her chin up, trying to appear as put together as her lungs would allow. "That's right. No marshal is going to tell me what to do."

Daniel faced Timothy. "She'd come in handy, for—"

"She's too young." Timothy's gaze swept her from head to toe.

Harriet took a step away from Celia and frowned at the boys.

"I'm not." Celia threw back her shoulders. "I just turned fifteen. Ma married at seventeen. If I can marry in two years, then I'm not too young for anything."

Timothy shrugged and returned to throwing things in the water.

"I just came to tell you why I might not see you for a few days. No telling how many times I can sneak out before getting caught."

Ma marrying the marshal had been good for one thing: the group needed her now. She knew his whereabouts and suspicions.

"Don't get caught." Daniel twirled a knife handle between his fingers. "I don't want anything happening to you." He winked.

Her lungs filled up as if they had not just tried to collapse from lack of air. She attempted to give Daniel the smile Miss McGill flashed around that made men stumble over their words. "It's you I'm worried about."

Ignoring Harriet's glare, Celia walked toward Daniel in the way Ma said proper ladies walked, instead of how she normally clomped around. She sat down beside him. "Were you the one who changed the town's name to Hades?"

"Yep." An amused twinkle lit his eyes, those beautiful dark blue eyes.

She swallowed and made herself stop staring at them. If anybody found out she liked him enough to practice signing her name as Celia Margaret Crawford, she'd lose her reputation for being tough.

She threw a stick into the water. "What else did you paint?"

Daniel picked up a twig and sliced off a long wooden curl with his knife. "Nothing. Didn't have much paint."

"The marshal saw the empty buckets on your porch. He's on to you. Plans on asking your daddy about them."

Timothy squinted against the dying sun. "You could tell your pa you whitewashed my fence yesterday."

Celia sneered at Timothy. "And did he whitewash your fence yesterday?"

He sneered back. "No."

"Then how would that work if the marshal checks on it?"

Timothy glared at her before picking up a rock to throw into the rapids.

Harriet sighed. "Do I have to do all the thinking around here?"

"And what would you do?" Daniel dropped what was left of his stick onto the ground and grabbed another. "We can't go whitewash his fence now. His pa won't lie about when we did it."

Harriet put her hands on her hips. "Tell your pa you finished painting your fort last night."

"I don't have a fort."

Harriet shrugged. "So? You think your daddy's going to go tromping around to find it? Even if he did, not finding your fort doesn't mean it doesn't exist."

Daniel snapped his fingers then pointed at her and winked. "I knew there was a reason I liked you."

Harriet's heart-shaped face lit up.

Celia glowered at the two of them, but they didn't seem to notice. Stepping between them, she picked up a rock and chucked it clear out past the two boulders in the middle of the river. "So what fun am I going to miss this week?"

"We should steal clothes off Mrs. Tate's line this time." Harriet dropped onto a tree stump and fluffed her skirts about her. "I bet they're big enough to fit Sullivan's pig. Then we let her loose wearing fancy drawers. Now wouldn't that be a hoot."

Daniel smirked and turned to Celia. "Is the marshal in for the night?"

Celia nodded.

Timothy grunted. "Daniel and I got better things to do than dress up pigs."

"Like what?" Celia cocked her head.

"I'm not telling you."

Harriet sat up straight. "Why not?"

"Men stuff."

Harriet rolled her eyes.

Daniel placed his hand on Celia's shoulder and an ooey-gooey feeling crept up her neck. "Listen. You come whenever you can, but don't get into any more trouble with the marshal. We can't get away with much if we don't know where he is."

The thought of groveling to the marshal made her stomach churn, but if Daniel wanted her to do it, she'd do it.

CHAPTER TWENTY-THREE

Jacob handed Annie the last dish to dry, then leaned his hip against the counter to watch her. Without Celia at the table this evening, Annie had seemed more inclined to talk. Was it Celia's presence that caused her to freeze around him?

The night she'd purposely placed her hand on his leg had made him think their relationship was finally going somewhere, but the moment her daughter had shown up she'd pulled away. He'd tried to hide his disappointment, but hadn't succeeded.

She'd yet to purposely touch him again.

"Think Celia's all right?" She put the bowl away and wiped her hands on the towel, bunching the fabric in her hands.

Jacob loosened the towel from her white-knuckled grasp and tossed it aside. "What trouble can she get into in her room? Don't worry so much." Taking Annie's hand, he pulled her toward the parlor doorway and peeked in.

Spencer's forehead was puckered in concentration as he stared at a paper on the writing desk.

"You still writing your story?"

Spencer turned to smile and waved his pencil at him. "Yes, sir."

"I can't wait to read it. You keep working on it until we come get you. All right, son?"

"Sure, Pa."

He'd never thought being called *Pa* would feel so good. He stepped back and tugged on Annie's hand. Without protest, his wife followed him onto the back porch.

"Wait here."

He reentered the kitchen, grabbed two chairs, and returned. "Have a seat."

He placed his chair next to hers and inhaled the loamy, fresh-turned earth smell drifting on the cool night breeze.

A frog under the porch croaked a lullaby for the setting sun.

Hunched over and hugging herself as if cold, Annie stared up at the full moon glimmering in the bright yellow and rose sky. "Pretty sunset."

He fixed her shawl to cover her exposed neck, left his arm around her, and then settled back against his seat. A few seconds passed before Annie's muscles relaxed under his arm. Then he pulled her in tight.

As much as he'd like to just sit and hold her while watching the dying sunset, he needed to tell her about Bryant's offer. "How would you feel if I started looking into purchasing another tract of land?"

Her face contorted a bit one way and then another, but she said nothing.

"I can't afford anything as good as yours was, but it would be something."

An owl's screech echoed about in the silence.

Did she not like the idea of starting over again? "Or what about me looking for a new job? I'm not meant to be a lawman. I could herd sheep."

"No, we'd never see you." She shook her head adamantly, turning to stare at him, the horizon's red and orange flickers dancing in her eyes.

If the thought of him working the long, lonely hours of a

shepherd made her protest, perhaps he'd captured more of her heart than he'd thought. He studied her delicate profile surrounded by stray strands of auburn hair blowing in the breeze. "Then we'll hold out for ranch land. Bryant offered to keep his eye open for a good deal."

"A deal like mine?"

"Not that good of a deal." He cleared his throat. "We'd have to settle for less."

"But where would we get the money?" Annie's voice trembled.

"I have savings. It just wasn't enough to pay for your land. But if Bryant learns of a distressed property, I might be able to haggle with the owner before he loses his land to auction."

The neighbors' upper story shutters opened and their youngest boy's violin bow screeched across strings. Jacob braced himself for the nightly torture.

Over the past year, he'd thought Joe would improve, but he'd clearly been wrong. Why the boy's parents hadn't yet talked themselves out of paying for music lessons, he didn't know.

The boy's screeching stopped for a second. "I think I have enough to buy a small plot I could fence. We'd never be able to compete with the big operations, so maybe I'd try my hand at breeding fine horses."

"But what would you—" Annie grimaced so forcefully at Joe hitting a particularly atrocious note that if she didn't already have a headache, she'd probably just given herself one. "What will we do with my cattle?"

Surely she had to know this was coming. "Unless I hear of something promising soon, I think we should sell them."

A musical screech split the air, and a shudder took over her body. "I don't know enough about land to help you make decisions."

"Bryant could advise me on the land's worth." He tried not to grit his teeth as Joe started playing something that sort of sounded like *Twinkle Twinkle Little Star*. "As long as I don't try negotiating directly after an evening of listening to Joe murder his fiddle, I should be able to keep myself from paying three times its worth for some country silence."

She chuckled. "I trust you. However you decide."

Had he earned her trust for anything other than putting a roof over her head yet?

He could find out.

Sucking in a fortifying breath, he leaned across their chairs and placed a kiss on the soft spot below her ear.

The same look that had crossed her face earlier when he'd kissed her temple scurried across her features. He forced himself not to run a finger against the gooseflesh that had popped up on her arm and reached for her hands instead. "Come."

"Where're we going?" She looked over her shoulder as he tugged her to stand. "Spencer might—"

"Not far." He walked her out to the strip of hard-packed earth she'd left between her gardens. "Just out here to enjoy the music."

She screwed her face up at him. "You call what Joe's doing 'music'?"

"Can't let a few bad notes fool you." He threaded her stiff arm around his waist and clasped her free hand. On the next note, an oddly recognizable one, Jacob started a waltz pattern. Annie tripped a little as he struggled to find a triple beat to dance to.

After a few box steps, she blew the hair from her face. "Coyotes sound better than this."

He chuckled. "Much better, I'm afraid. We need to buy the kid more rosin or tell him to lighten up on his pressure."

"You play?"

"Not anymore. Couldn't keep from screeching." He smiled and twirled her around. "But we have to practice dancing together before the church fundraiser next Sunday. So, why not take advantage of the serenade under the lover's moon?"

Surprisingly, she didn't stiffen at his silly attempt at romantic words and shook her head at him. "I'm pretty sure the lover's moon is in June."

He slipped his arm completely around her waist and pulled her in tight. "Hush," he whispered against her ear. "Don't stop me with technicalities."

Humming, he moved back into a closed position and tried anew to find a triple beat.

She stepped on his toe, and he tripped on a dirt embankment. Then a terribly harsh note caused a shiver to run down his spine.

She huffed after tripping over him yet again. "How can you pretend to keep any sort of time when there isn't a melody to be had?"

"Don't ruin my fun, woman." He changed to dancing in common time and moved her into a two step. Once he got her into a consistent, albeit repetitious pattern, he fought to sing lyrics against Joe's successful attempt to play anything but music.

> *"Then we all would eat our supper, after that we'd clear*
> *the kitchen,*
> *That's only time we had to spare, to have a little fun,*
> *Neighbor Joe would take the fiddle down..."*

She chuckled at his forcing Joe's name into the song.

> *"...that hung upon the wall,*
> *While the silv'ry moon was shining clear and bright—"*

"I'm impressed."

He reeled Annie out and twisted her back in. "With my singing or my dancing?"

"That you can do either while Joe's playing." She stepped under his arm.

He twirled her back against him. "Sing with me."

She stepped away and laughed. "I can't. I think you've changed keys no less than three times in the last line alone."

He pulled her closer and nearly lost his ability to stay on his feet when she laid her head on his shoulder. "Just following our talented neighbor's lead," he murmured.

Now where was he?

> *"How the old folks would enjoy it, they would sit all night*
> *and listen,*
> *As we sang in the evening by the moonlight."*

The boy's practice ended abruptly on a flat note, but Jacob dared to place his hand against Annie's head to keep her against him, humming a second time through the song—staying in *one* key this time.

She exhaled and wrapped her arms about him, joining in with a pleasant soft soprano for the last chorus.

> *"Neighbor Joe has laid the fiddle down, that hung upon*
> *the wall,*
> *While the silv'ry moon was shining clear and bright,*
> *How us old folks would enjoy it, while we danced all*
> *night and listened,*
> *As we sang in the evening by the moonlight."*

In the silence that followed, her warm breath against his neck sent chills through his body.

He no longer worried about fancy dance moves, just swayed to a nonexistent beat.

When she didn't bother to pull away, he unlaced his fingers from her waist and tilted her chin up, letting his thumb trace her upturned jaw.

She lifted her eyes to meet his, the brown specks in her irises nearly drowning in the golden vestiges of sunset. She swallowed hard but didn't look away.

He let his fingertips trail down along her neck, and she closed her eyes.

His pulse thundered like a thousand stampeding hooves, and beneath his fingers, her accelerated heartbeat matched his beat per beat.

He did rouse her senses. What a lovely thing.

He lowered his mouth within a hair's-breadth from her lips.

Her breathing quickened, but she didn't retreat. And like a butterfly alighting on a sprig of new spring grass, he touched his lips lightly upon hers. A hint of sugar and vanilla pulled him in, but this evening's apple dumpling wasn't the reason she tasted so sweet.

She voiced a tiny moan and pressed against him.

With his pulse pounding in his ears, he continued to kiss her, drawing her in as if she were bracing nectar.

Though only the space of a few heartbeats had passed, if he didn't break away soon, he wouldn't stop. He pulled away, struggling to catch his breath.

Her cheeks were warm beneath his palms, and she seemed intent on not looking up.

"How should we end tonight, Anne?" He choked on the words he hadn't meant to voice.

"Not the way you want it to." Her emotionally wrought whisper mashed his heart. Her gaze finally traveled up to his, and her breathing grew frantic. "Not yet."

Though he tried not to, he couldn't help but stare into her eyes with all the longing that kiss had created.

Her gaze dropped back down to his chest. "Sometime soon. I just don't know when."

He wrapped his arms around her, pulling her close, and kissed her forehead with a shuddery sigh. "I'll wait, Mrs. Hendrix. I can wait."

CHAPTER TWENTY-FOUR

The deep furrows of cottonwood bark gouged into Annie's back. She rocked her head against the tree to peer through the slats of the fence that surrounded her family's little cemetery.

Why had McGill evicted her the second the loan was past due if the city didn't plan to sell the property immediately? Hadn't Bryant said they'd had a buyer? Were they holding out for more money?

When Leah had informed her this morning that no one yet owned the property, she'd begged Jacob to ask the city to allow her to tend the graves. Later that afternoon, Bryant had come by to tell her she was free to visit as long as he was informed.

Tears had welled up with the knowledge that she could come back, and Leah had volunteered to go with her. Bryant hadn't been keen on them going without him or Jacob who'd gone off in search of the rustlers again, but had been appeased when they'd promised to return before supper.

Annie stared out across the vacant pastures that used to be filled with the endless bawling of calves in the spring.

Why wasn't the city at least leasing her land to graze cattle? Why couldn't she have left hers here?

In the south field, Leah was picking handfuls of feathery-leaved bloodwort and placing them in the flat basket she'd brought along.

Annie brushed her palms atop the marigolds she'd planted on Jack's grave, loath to leave. After Jack's birth, she hadn't wanted to be pregnant ever again, but God had other ideas and she'd lost Augustus a year later.

And here she was, married to a man who likely hoped for children of his own.

He didn't know how badly bringing them into this world could hurt.

She looked across the small earthen mounds toward the six-foot-long one. "You don't fault me for marrying him, do you?"

Gregory wouldn't blame her for trying to save his land, but if he knew how quickly she'd become attracted to another...

She wrapped her arms around herself and closed her eyes. She could still feel Jacob's warm hands cupping her cheeks as he'd kissed her.

His arms had felt good and safe. But his lips against hers had made her feel vulnerable and defenseless, and yet, called like a siren's song.

When he'd asked her about her desires for the remainder of the evening, she could have told him yes, had even wanted to.

"Don't you look pensive."

Annie jumped at Leah's voice. "I didn't hear you open the gate."

"I could tell." Leah put down her full basket and gracefully lowered herself beside Annie. "Want to talk?"

Yes. No. Annie blew out a breath.

Leah laid a hand on Annie's knee. "Why didn't you want to see if we could find Jacob before coming here?"

"He might've been too far away, and we would've wasted daylight." She grabbed a blade of grass and twisted it around her fingers. "Besides, I doubt he'd be thrilled with my reason for coming."

Leah's brow furrowed. "To tend graves?"

"No, to talk to Gregory." She glanced at his marker and tried to summon up his image. His likeness swam before her mind—clear except for the contour of his jaw. The profile was wrong somehow. Too much like Jacob's.

"Ah. Because you know you should be talking to Jacob."

Annie squirmed, the sticks and pebbles beneath her only part of her discomfort. "I can't talk to him about this."

"Why not?"

"He wouldn't understand." Annie stood and brushed the dirt off her hands. "Besides, he wouldn't want to hear." Walking to the fence line, she countered the swirling in her stomach by wrapping her arms around her middle.

Leah's footsteps whispered over the grasses and stopped beside her.

Meadowlarks hopped amidst the grasses on the other side of the fence, their bright yellow bellies scattered about like dandelions.

Annie inhaled deeply and plunged in before she thought better of it. "I'm talking to Gregory because I know I can't hurt his feelings." She turned and looked at his grave. "Because I can't tell the husband I'm falling for that I'm still stuck on a man buried beneath a tree." She clenched the wooden railing behind her. "That's simply something that shouldn't be discussed—it isn't proper, loving two men like that. If Gregory were still alive and walked into the same room as Jacob, I'm not sure who'd call to my heart more. It's wrong. Terribly wrong. But it's how I feel."

Leah placed a hand against Annie's arm. "Not proper, maybe, but understandable. I bet he'd—"

"No. It's wrong somehow." Annie swallowed hard. "Like adultery—loving two men at once."

Leah pushed back her slat bonnet and peered up at Annie. "It's not adultery when one of them is dead, honey."

She winced. Why couldn't Leah have said, "passed on" or

"gone to the Lord" or some other euphemism? Though her voice had been gentle, the word "dead" just couldn't be softened. "Call it emotional adultery then."

Leah huffed and Annie braced for a lecture.

"Give yourself some leeway for what comes naturally—"

"Sin is sin."

"It's not a sin, and even if it was, I'd be more of a sinner than you." Leah shook her head like an exasperated mother. "You're too hard on yourself. Stop it."

Annie's harsh laughter ripped through her vocal chords. "That's like telling me to be someone else's daughter. Impossible."

Mother would definitely be on her side about this.

"Forgive me." Annie shrugged. "Please, don't allow my gloominess to ruin your joyful disposition."

"Oh, Annie. I'm not joy-filled because I've never gone through trials." She leaned against the fence. "When I said I'd be a bigger sinner than you if measured with your measure, I wasn't being disingenuous."

"How's that?"

Leah's mouth flexed in amusement. "I had a life before Wyoming."

"And you've been in a situation like mine?"

She lost her smile quicker than a rabbit disappearing down its hole. "Before I married Bryant."

Annie quickly tallied Leah's age and years of marriage. "That would've made you—"

"Young, yes." Leah's eyes twinkled. "Though I don't feel much older than my twenty-year-old self."

"Nor I." Annie grinned. "Not *much*."

Leah tilted her head toward the gate, snatched up her basket, and waited for Annie to follow.

The cottonwood's shadow had fallen over Gregory's resting place, covering him in darkness. They had to head home, whether she was ready or not. Annie gathered her gardening tools and after one last look at them all, followed after Leah.

Once Annie clicked the gate closed, Leah slipped her hand through the crook of Annie's arm and set a leisurely pace toward the wagon. "Your love for Gregory will grow fainter in time, but it will always be there."

Perhaps, but that didn't help her now.

"I, too, am guilty of loving two men. However, both are still alive."

Annie stopped and cocked her head.

Leah tugged her back to walking. "Deep-rooted feelings don't change quickly. Whether your relationship is torn apart by an act of God or men. You can't simply discard love because you've been forced to let a beloved go."

"So you had a beau back East who didn't feel the same for you as you did him?"

"No." A faint smile lit her eyes. "He definitely felt the same for me. His proposal couldn't have been more romantic."

She wrapped her arm tighter around Annie's. "William and I planned on marrying in 1862, but he was shot in the head in 1861, during the Battle of Bethel Church. My William was in the 3rd New York Infantry, shot upon by Bendix's 7th New York Regiment during the wee hours of the morning."

"I remember that story." Annie recalled reading about the Northern troops firing in confusion upon their own. At the time, she'd believed, like most, the war wouldn't last much longer.

How wrong they were.

"William came home with a ghastly gash." Leah stopped walking and touched a hand to her forehead, as if outlining a memorized scar. "More of a divot. Right here."

She let her hand drop. "Strangely, William refused to believe he was no longer under a commanding officer, or hurt for that matter. If you reasoned with him, he became violent. Very violent." Leah shuddered, gingerly touching her neck with a trembling hand. "And sometimes violent for no reason at all."

Annie squeezed Leah's hand to reassure her. How often had William's irrational rage been turned on this sweet woman?

"He was not the William I knew." Leah started forward again. "The doctor diagnosed chronic mania. His mother wanted to assume his care, but in his manic states, he was too powerful. She had to put him in a soldier's home and I visited him every Saturday." She smiled. "And every Saturday, I saw Bryant. He kept the home's books until he joined the army the following spring."

"So he knows about William?"

"Yes. If it hadn't been for my devotion to William, I never would've made an impression on Bryant. Before he left for the war, he stopped me in the home's hallway to ask if I'd consider waiting for him with the same faithfulness I gave a man who no longer remembered me."

Annie imagined herself in the same situation and shivered. Even without a war, Jacob could die as unexpectedly as Gregory.

"Those were the longest days of my life, visiting the shell of a man I loved while waiting for another to return from the war that had stolen my first love away."

At the wagon, Leah placed her basket in the back, pulled out a pungent flower, and twirled it between her fingers. "I married Bryant a few months after he returned." Her lips formed a smile, but the furrow in her brow made the expression wistful. "But I still loved William."

Annie chewed on a fingernail. "So how did you deal with loving two men at once?"

"Like I do now. Time helps, of course." She gestured toward the cemetery. "Do you still love those children buried beneath that cottonwood?"

"Of course."

"Did your love for Celia or Spencer diminish with every grave you added?"

Annie's throat grew tight. She'd never forget a single burial.

Waiting for Gregory to dig each tiny, cavernous hole. Trying to soothe Spencer or Celia with what little assurance she could muster from the emptiness inside her. "No."

Leah put her hands on her hips. "If you could toss away the love you felt for Gregory in a few short months, that would be the tragedy. Jacob doesn't want a woman who could love so fickly." She placed her flower back in the basket and emptied Annie's arms of her tools. "You give Jacob as much of your heart as you can, and time will grow his portion. Then one day, Gregory will be a pleasant, heartbreaking memory."

Annie swallowed and looked away from Leah's penetrating gaze. The woman believed her to be better than she was—for how could a man she'd known but two months have turned her head so quickly from her husband of sixteen years?

Had her love for Gregory been that shallow?

"Does that help?"

Oh, how it didn't.

As sad as Leah's story was, their situations were different. Leah had not married William and borne his children. But that wasn't what her friend wanted to hear, so Annie nodded.

Leah climbed up onto the wagon seat. "As with Gregory, your life with Jacob will have its ups and downs. You'll love your husband when life is good." Leah settled in her seat and looked toward Armelle. Her expression so gloomy, it was almost like that of another woman's. "And you'll love your husband when it's not."

CHAPTER TWENTY-FIVE

Crack.

Jacob dropped back down as the simultaneous report of yet another bullet echoed off the river rocks.

For three hours, a hidden marksman up on the ridge had kept him pinned behind this infernal boulder. Whoever was shooting at him had shot at Duchess first, scaring her off into the overgrowth far from the rocky riverside that offered him no cover.

"Arrrrrrah!" Jacob picked up some rocks and flung them. He'd sat quiet for an entire hour before lifting his hat above the boulder, only to find the marksman still there.

He slumped but kept his pistol ready, in case whoever was shooting was circling around to confront him.

While scouting this morning, he'd found a print that looked identical to ones he'd seen at the rustlers' campsite weeks ago. The boot was narrow with a gouge in its leather sole, and the tracks disappeared into the river as the rustlers' often did. He'd ridden the riverbank for hours, praying this time he'd find where the prints exited the water.

Not far from where he was now, he'd gotten down to inspect

a fresh print when the crack and echo of a bullet came out of nowhere. But there'd been no mistaking what the marksman was aiming at when a second bullet kicked up rocks near Duchess's hooves.

She'd hightailed it to higher ground, and he'd scrambled for cover.

And now he was stuck. The rustlers had to be on the other side of that ridge, and a lookout was buying them time to move out whatever cattle they'd swiped, or else, why keep shooting at him?

He was so close, and yet, so useless.

Closing his eyes, he visualized where he was on the Laramie from memory. There wasn't enough cover for him to approach the ridge or get away. The shooter either had to leave, come for him, or Jacob would have to wait until nightfall.

And he'd not go home without tracking this scoundrel down. Come evening, he'd have to travel a fair piece upstream to cross the river safely in the dark so he could circle back and apprehend the man whose gun-sight was set on him.

These criminals needed to be hauled in, but he had to do it in the wisest way possible. Going down in a firefight would do nothing but leave his wife and children abandoned once again, and the county's cattle even riper for the picking.

With a shiver, Jacob stepped out of the cold river water hours later, his boots squelching. If only the nearly full moon weren't so bright.

Moonlight might keep him from falling flat on his face, but he stood out like a sunbathing lizard. He hunched over and stole across the rocky riverbed. Though he believed he hadn't been shot at while crossing the Laramie, the loud rushing of the river might've drowned out such noises, so he didn't stop until he was shrouded in trees.

Quieting his breathing, he listened to the night sounds. He had about a half-mile to backtrack to the ridge.

Though he really wanted to bag the shooter who'd kept him pinned for hours, the fact that he'd stolen away from that boulder so easily in such bright moonlight meant the marksman had likely moved on.

Had he joined back in with the rustlers or was he coming after Jacob?

He had to find him first.

From one stand of trees to another, Jacob moved as quickly and silently as he could to the bend of the Laramie where he'd spent all day ducking and covering. At the ridge, he crept along its perimeter until he came to a section he thought he could climb without using his hands since they were busy holding his gun ready.

The roar of the river he'd listened to all day faded as he ascended one rock after another and started traversing the backside of the ridge. The sounds of night continued with not a single low of a steer or bawl of a calf echoing faintly across the plains.

No sounds of men. No smoke rising for miles around.

Had he spent all day behind that rock, frozen his toes in the Laramie, and nearly beat the heart out of his chest for nothing?

Once a half hour passed without the sound of a bullet fired, Jacob eased up on his crouch and climbed the ridge faster. Where had his marksman camped out all afternoon?

Halfway across the top, between two massive rocks that would make an excellent lookout, spent casings glinted in the moonlight.

Jacob picked one up and scanned the area. Seeing no movement below, he descended back down the ridge and then crept around the clearing toward the river where it bent behind a stand of rocks. The muddy areas between the shore and grasses didn't seem disturbed by cattle. There was indication of recent activity along the riverbank, but nothing worth trying to kill a marshal over.

With a huge sigh, he dropped down to squint at a barely illuminated print, but it was larger than the one he'd been tracking.

Too dark to see much, seemed it'd be best to return to Duchess, depart for Armelle, and squeeze in a few hours of sleep before returning to see if he could track down his shooter.

And if he couldn't bring Frank along, he'd have to see who of his would-be posse was available to come back with him. A hothead or two might actually be an asset in a stand-off.

Bryant filed the paperwork Jacob had brought in yesterday before he'd gone out tracking. His friend's probing gaze as he'd handed him the papers had unnerved him. Did Jacob suspect something?

It didn't matter though. Nothing would make him tell now.

He'd refrained from visiting the gambling hall for an entire month. If he lost no more money and his past forgeries remained undetected, Jacob would never know of his involvement.

Neither would Leah.

The hallway door opened, and his boss lumbered across the room toward his office.

Bryant slowly stopped moving. Hopefully McGill wouldn't—

"What have you got on the schedule today, Whitsett?"

Seemed invisibility was not a skill he possessed. He shrugged. "Paperwork, mostly."

McGill dropped a map onto the counter, unrolled it, and placed a thick index finger on a spot near the southwest corner. "Look up the property surrounding the river here."

Bryant's eyes narrowed. "Why?"

"Just do as I tell you."

Every muscle tensed. "I'm not fixing any more books or—"

"I only asked you to look up the property." McGill pushed the map toward him. "Don't get up on your high horse. You don't deserve to be atop a noble steed any more than I do."

Bryant looked at the place where McGill had pointed. The land was on a bend of the Laramie near some acreage McGill owned, or rather, had stolen the first time he'd gotten mixed up in his boss's messes.

A likely spot to find an alluvial deposit.

He turned to face his file cabinets but only stared at them.

"I'm waiting."

McGill had nothing new to blackmail him with, so why did his insides tremble so? It wasn't as if he didn't look up properties every day.

With quick movements born of filing paperwork since he was thirteen, he searched through the books for the owner, shutting out any worrisome thoughts on why he was doing so.

CHAPTER TWENTY-SIX

Surrounded by children, Annie sat across the parlor listening to Jacob's Sunday school lesson, her eyes closed, listening to the calm timbre of his voice.

After he'd been unexpectedly gone for an entire day and night, she'd nearly worn out the parlor's lone rocking chair, waiting at the window for a glimpse of him.

That chair hadn't begun to see how many miles she could rock in it until the next day when he'd gone back out to the ridge in search of whoever had shot at him, accompanied by two impulsive Crawford men, no less.

Though the three men had been upset that after a full day of searching they'd found no tracks worth following, she wasn't.

She hadn't forgotten how much a person's livelihood could be chipped away by rustlers just because her cattle were munching away on someone else's property, but the potential loss of Jacob had nearly frozen her heart in place.

What would she do without him?

Though this parlor felt homey now with her chairs, tables, knickknacks, and lanterns lining the walls, without Jacob sitting on the rug, reading a Bible story with character voices and silly sounds to enliven the story, the place would be lifeless.

Right now, half a dozen children sat cross-legged on the floor while others were piled upon the chairs and sofa, eating the cookies she'd baked that morning.

Three-year-old Rebecca left her place on the rug to curl up in Jacob's lap. Her new seat had to be more comfortable than the chair Annie sat on with her back ramrod straight like Mother had made sure she'd done ever since she was little. Or was it because she'd yet to fully relax since Jacob had informed her that someone had intentionally tried to take his life?

Jacob reached around Rebecca to turn the page as he finished reading David and Goliath's story. His long legs were folded beneath him as he sat on the floor, his back against an end table, Rebecca sunk into his chest as if she belonged there.

Mother would be appalled at how these children sprawled about the room, and yet, Annie was a bit jealous of Rebecca's seating situation, no matter how unladylike.

Jacob shut his Bible and laid it on the rug. "We never know when a big ol' giant is going to challenge us, whether it's a bully of a giant or a giant of a problem. But, like David, if we pray to God, believing he can help us do anything, we can be as brave as David was."

"And if God chooses not to help?" Celia stood slouched in the corner. She'd wanted to stay in her room this morning, but Jacob had given her two choices: attend the adults' class or the children's. Celia had slunk down the stairs as if he'd asked her to sit in boiling water.

Please, Lord, help her hold her tongue or choose her words wisely.

Celia leaned forward, arms crossed. "My daddy didn't deserve getting shot, but God didn't stop him from dying. And Jennie is as good a Christian as her ma, and after her accident, she'll never see again."

Annie dug her fingers into her chair's armrests. Next week, Celia was definitely attending the adult class.

"I didn't say God helps you by giving you what you want." Jacob shifted the curly blond toddler in his lap as if Celia's question was nothing out of the ordinary.

Had her daughter been badgering him every week?

"What I said was, you can ask God for courage to face your problems. There are days when being a marshal is a dangerous thing, but God helps me face it. When Jennie feels overwhelmed or discouraged—"

"But it's not fair." Celia's words came out so forcefully, she'd almost spit on the carpet.

Several kids kept their gazes fastened to the rug at their feet, while others glanced between stepfather and stepdaughter. Would Jacob discipline Celia for her disrespectful tone or let it slide? Celia had been unusually well-behaved the last few days, but this morning, she seemed intent on antagonizing him.

"Not many things in life are fair, and I'm sorry," he finally answered.

"You got that right." Celia's response was but a whisper.

"Life isn't fair, but that doesn't mean God has abandoned us." Jacob looked at each child in the room. "He won't always get us out of trouble, especially if we make the trouble ourselves."

He turned back to Celia. "When we do wrong, we can't be surprised if we get disciplined. But even if you're not responsible for the things that happen to you, God can help you be brave and strong."

The clock chimed the half hour, and Jacob prayed.

Once he said 'amen,' Annie gestured to the two boys who'd fidgeted the most. "Mark and Isaiah, why don't you start our line?"

The children scrambled up and out the door, and Annie let Celia pass without a word.

As much as she wanted to chastise Celia about her apparent need to make a scene wherever she went, she'd hold her tongue for now. After lunch, however, she'd inform her daughter that she'd be joining the adult class next Sunday. Perhaps being the youngest in the group might rein in her tongue.

Upon entering the sanctuary, every child scurried to sit with family, and Annie followed hers to their usual pew.

Jacob slid in beside her and draped his arm around her shoulder as if he'd done so every Sunday. She refused to look around at who might be glaring at them for sitting so close, because today, his arm around her was a blessing.

She looked up and his smile caused her neck to prickle with heat, and she couldn't look away.

She forced herself not to squirm. It wasn't as if his arm tucked behind her was inappropriate. Now, if he'd leaned down for a kiss, that would be...

His lips twitched and she looked up.

He winked.

Her body flushed, and she quickly faced the front where the pastor was flipping through his hymnal.

Imagine that.

Winking in church with a look like that on his face.

But then, she'd been the one who'd been thinking about kissing in church.

The flutter of pages all around her made her flush again. Had the pastor called the song number already?

She snatched up her hymnal and tried to peek over the pew to see what song they were about to sing, but Mrs. Tate held her hymnal too close for Annie to see a thing.

Leah started playing, but it wasn't an opening she recognized.

She looked to Jacob who was still smiling, seemingly not at all inclined to save her by taking over the hymnal.

She handed the songbook across Jacob's lap to Spencer. "Why don't you be in charge of the hymnal?"

Thankfully, Spencer took the book and started flipping pages without asking for the number.

Jacob caught her eye and winked again.

In front of them, Mrs. Tate belted out the first words of the song. Luckily, the old woman was all about formalities and wouldn't dare turn around during service to catch her sitting snug against Jacob.

How much of a stir would she cause if her family moved to the empty pew at the back of the church? Ever since the day Mrs. Tate had chastised her about those oysters, sitting behind her every Sunday felt as if Mother were once again beside her, ready to rap her daughter's knees any time her legs jiggled.

Perhaps Mrs. Tate's censure was affecting her as much as it was because she'd yet to write Mother about Jacob. The reply would inevitably contain an echo of Mrs. Tate's lecture on the indecency of marrying before her mourning period was over, and she'd not wanted to endure that twice.

But keeping her marriage a secret only legitimized Mrs. Tate's opinion that she'd done wrong. Would facing her mother's indignation help wipe away the guilt Leah insisted she needn't feel and allow her to move on with life? With this man who might not be here as long as she needed him to be?

The congregation began verse two, and Celia was giving her the side-eye, clearly wondering why she hadn't started singing yet.

Annie scooted closer to Jacob since Spencer wasn't holding the hymnal out far enough to see and joined in with the third verse.

For the joy of human love,
Brother, sister, parent, child,
Friend on earth, and friends above,
For all gentle thoughts and mild;
Christ our God, to thee we raise
This our hymn of grateful praise.

She bowed her head. Was this merely coincidence or was

God telling her she could revel in the feelings she was shying away from and simply praise Him for them?

Of course, the song was describing familial love, not those of attraction. Though a husband and wife's bond created family.

Annie gave up singing and concentrated on not thinking about that any further.

God might be absolutely fine with her thinking about all the ways she could rejoice in her groom.

But surely not this very minute.

"Annie."

Leah caught her just as she stepped across the sanctuary's threshold into the church foyer. The older woman's face was shining brighter than the afternoon sun streaming through the stained glass.

Annie's lips curved up to match Leah's. "What can I do for you?"

"Eat lunch with us. Where's your basket for the auction?"

Annie frowned. She'd rarely been able to stay for after-church fundraisers. "Why would I make a basket? Isn't that for the single ladies?"

"Why should they have all the fun?" Leah raised her basket and jiggled it a bit. "We know exactly who'll buy ours!"

She shook her head at Leah's exuberance. "And if Bryant gets outbid?"

"Won't happen. He knows which is mine, and if someone has a hankering for my pie enough to run up the bids, it just makes him more charitable."

Annie laughed. "Why not simply hand your money over to the schoolmaster?"

"That's no fun." Leah's eyes twinkled. "Besides, Bryant

needs a little competition. Keeps him from taking me for granted."

"I'll consider that next time." However, this was not the year to make a scene out of Jacob bidding on her basket. "Though surely once Bryant starts bidding, everyone realizes it's yours."

"I don't let him start bidding until it reaches five dollars." Leah looped her arm around Annie's as they took a few steps forward in line. "But you're right. They usually stop bidding, but not always. My meringue's the best in the county, you know. Two years ago, Jacob decided he wanted the pie for himself. When Bryant bid six, he bid fifty." Leah chuckled. "We couldn't afford it, and Bryant groused the rest of the afternoon because Jacob refused to share. But then, when you single-handedly pay for all of next year's school books, you deserve to eat the whole pie in a sitting if you so desire."

Up ahead, Jacob was helping the widow Morris down the front steps.

Fifty dollars for a pie? When was the man not doing something good for someone in the community?

"I see you're giving in."

Annie turned back to Leah. "Giving in to what?"

"Him. And there's no mistaking how he looks at you." Leah pulled her arm away when she spotted Bryant weaving through the line toward them. "Bryant, darling."

Annie schooled her features. She didn't know how she'd looked at Jacob to make Leah say that, but whatever the expression, she didn't want Mrs. Tate to see it. And since that woman was just now shaking hands with Jacob, she didn't want him to look at her and earn himself a lecture on how he should or shouldn't look at his wife in the house of God.

And yet, why worry about that anyway? She'd been looking forward to spending the day with him without the demand of jobs and chores, but if she was constantly worrying about what her face looked like, how would she have any fun at the picnic, let alone relax?

Her husband had come back alive and intact. What was there not to celebrate about that?

Bryant put an arm around Leah's shoulder and kissed the top of her head. "You're much too eager to watch me empty my pockets on something that's mine by rights."

He smiled over the top of Leah's head at Annie. Though he was still rather distant, he'd eased up on the cold stares he'd given her weeks ago. "Has my wife convinced you to eat with us yet? Considering I won't have to compete with your husband for my pie this year, I think I can stand to share our lunch with him."

"Actually, Annie didn't make a basket for auction, so you might still have competition."

Bryant groaned.

After shaking hands with Mrs. Tate's son, Jacob walked back their way, giving several people a pat on the back before joining them. He pulled Annie into a side embrace, though she couldn't quite melt into her husband's side like Leah was doing.

She smiled up at him. "Would you mind if we joined Leah and Bryant for lunch?"

"I think I can find at least one reason to force myself to sit next to them for an hour."

Bryant rolled his eyes. "Don't count on me sharing. I didn't eat breakfast, so I have a hole that needs to be patched with meringue."

Jacob grinned. "Who said you're going to win the pie?"

The front door banged open and Spencer raced in. "I can't find Celia anywhere!"

CHAPTER TWENTY-SEVEN

Shielding her eyes, Annie searched the gathering crowd for a splash of Celia's orange print dress. She'd evidently agreed to run the three-legged race with Spencer, and now he was upset she'd run off after church.

Their afternoon of relaxation and fun wasn't starting off too well.

Spencer plopped down onto the picnic blanket Annie had laid out while Leah helped her eldest daughter unload her wagon. "She promised me," he grumbled.

"Then she will." Annie sighed and dropped her hand from her face. Celia had been less than trustworthy lately, but she'd done nothing to purposely disappoint her brother—yet. "The race doesn't start until after lunch anyway."

"What if she doesn't come back?"

Annie frowned at the crowd, not seeing a single hint of her daughter's long auburn hair. "Why not ask a schoolmate to run with you?"

"All the kids in my class are girls." Spencer ripped up a handful of grass.

"What about Joe?" The neighbor kid was sitting on a bench

near the band. Was he holding his violin case or someone else's? Surely his parents wouldn't allow him to play in public. "He's only a few years ahead of you."

"He can't run with his glasses on."

"He could take them off." If Spencer kept Joe busy running races, the young man couldn't play his violin.

"He can't. Don't know why though. I can't see anything when I try them on."

Perhaps blindness explained Joe's terrible fiddling.

The band members started tuning their instruments, and unfortunately, Joe joined right in. Hopefully he'd be drowned out.

Jacob had told her he looked forward to twirling her about the dance floor to the accompaniment of a well-played violin, but if Joe screeched through the songs and Mrs. Tate sat by glowering at her and Jacob, how could she possibly enjoy herself?

And if he kissed her at the end like last time? She held her breath. Gregory would've never kissed her in public, but Jacob...

She'd always been at ease with Gregory, no surprises, no lavish compliments, no worries about whether or not he'd kiss her in front of anyone and everyone.

And yet, whenever Jacob was around, he made her jittery in a way she'd never been before. Maybe a relationship of a different sort wouldn't be so bad after all.

Spencer threw a wad of grass at his shoes, stood, and brushed himself off. "Do you think Pa would run with me?"

Gregory?

Oh, Jacob.

A spot inside her chest both froze and melted.

It hurt a little knowing Spencer had already moved on to calling Jacob "Pa," and yet, hadn't she just been miffed that Mrs. Tate would make it hard for her to enjoy dancing with her new husband?

If it wasn't for all these people, she'd be wondering when

their next kiss might be instead of worrying about it.

"Mama? I said, 'do you think he'll run with me?'"

"What? Oh." She needed to keep her head out of the clouds. "Can't hurt to ask."

Annie scanned the grounds again, this time for Jacob. He'd gone off looking for Celia, and if he'd found her, Spencer wouldn't be disappointed if Jacob said no.

Leah, carrying a quilt and a basket bedecked with curly green ribbon, wove her way through the crowd toward the auctioneer's table.

Annie pulled a roll from her basket and tossed it to Spencer. Maybe filling her son's stomach might cheer him up. A good thing she'd not added their picnic basket to the line of lunches. Auctioning them off would likely take half an hour.

Leah made her way toward them and unfolded her quilt to place it next to theirs. "I'm glad you snagged this spot; it'll make Ava happy. Her ankles are so swollen; she's second-guessing whether she should've come. At least there's shade." She waved at Bryant, who'd just joined the crowd near the auctioneer. "She says she's quite anxious to have that baby in her arms, but she can't nearly be as excited as I am about my first grandbaby."

The schoolmaster, Mr. Hucket, who seemed too young and short to teach Armelle's oldest students, waved his arms from where he stood behind the baskets.

Whistles and commands to shush popped up sporadically until the crowd quieted.

"Since we're all hungry—" He pulled on his bowtie while clearing his throat, probably in attempt to eradicate the warble that had cracked his voice. "—let's get to the auction."

A shout of hoorahs started another round of shushing.

How did this man control a classroom of children when public speaking affected him so? He'd never visited to complain to her about her daughter's behavior in class. What magic had he wrought to keep Celia from running right over him?

"Remember, men, be generous. You reap what you sow, and

it's for a good cause." Mr. Hucket's voice squeaked, but the crowd drowned him out with shouts of agreement.

"We won't get new desks without your help!" Though surely he realized hardly anyone heard his last sentence, he turned to the first basket and tried to catch the tiny paper tag fluttering off its handle.

Poor man, why hadn't someone volunteered to run the auction for him?

"This basket contains fried chicken, turnip greens, stewed apples, and sugar cookies. Let's start the bidding at twenty-five cents."

A group of men, mostly bachelors, crowded in to hear Mr. Hucket's words, leaving Annie able to see Jacob's tall frame appear on the other side of the yard as he strode toward them. Considering the set of his mouth, he'd not found Celia and was none too happy about it.

Evidently days under lock and key hadn't altered her waywardness one bit.

Leah leaned across the quilt and jiggled Annie's arm. "He's auctioning mine now."

After reading the contents, Mr. Hucket wiped his perspiring brow and called for bids. Not a single man in the crowd offered. Mr. Hucket stumbled for words to convince someone—anyone—to start bidding.

Annie fidgeted on the blanket, amused by her friend's exaggerated pout. "They've probably caught on that yours always contains a meringue pie."

Bryant finally lifted his hat from where he stood behind the crowd. "Ten dollars."

A collective gasp and happy mutterings swirled through the crowd.

Leah's face flushed an adorable pink.

"Sold!" Mr. Hucket smiled. "Thank you, Mr. Whitsett."

How much would Jacob have bid on her basket if she'd put one up for auction?

Silly to wonder such a thing when she'd cost him plenty of money already.

A flash of his gold star redrew her attention as he skirted the crowd. The roguish look he sent her made her breath catch.

Mrs. Tate walked past, her ample curves obliterating Annie's view. "Morning, ladies." The old woman dragged a three-legged stool behind her as she moved with a gait indicating her arthritis was flaring up. "I need to use that stump there for my table. I'm too old to eat off the ground."

The sawed off trunk was no more than five feet away. Seemed this nice, shady spot wasn't the best place in the yard after all.

And the hope for relaxation was carried off on the wind.

Leah smiled brightly. "Pleased to have you."

The woman didn't answer, and with a groan, sat her well-endowed posterior over the entirety of her little chair, not bothering to wait for Annie's response. The old woman pulled out a doily from her knitted bag and placed it atop the stump along with two forks, a placemat, and a small vase containing two sprigs of white chokecherry blossoms.

Annie couldn't help but smile at Mrs. Tate's elaborate picnic items. Mother would've likely set up a picnic just the same—if anyone could've convinced her to eat outside in the dirt and wind.

Jacob gave Mrs. Tate a tip of his hat before strolling past her to take a seat between Annie and Spencer.

As Mr. Hucket babbled in an attempt to auction off a basket that didn't appear large enough to hold more than two sandwiches and a napkin, Annie looked surreptitiously to her right, where Jacob sat close enough to stop the cool wind from blowing through her hair.

His hand was only inches from hers, and her fingers itched to creep over and lace through his, but she shouldn't do so in front of Mrs. Tate.

Despite the strong breeze, the older woman's chignon

somehow kept her every hair in place. And though she was not looking at them, her face seemed tense, as if their mere presence behind her caused her consternation.

Annie's heart fluttered at the fleeting vision of her mother being seated there instead of Mrs. Tate, her chin held at that same familiar angle of judgment.

Annie stared down at the scar that trailed across three of the fingers on her left hand.

Mother had cornered her in her father's study only days before her sixteenth birthday. "Annie Lynn Saint, what have you to say for yourself?"

Annie had backed up against a bookshelf. Why was Mother looking at her like that?

"Mrs. Casings told me you were holding hands with that Brubaker boy."

She swallowed. That wasn't such a terrible thing to do, was it? "He likes me."

"Please don't tell me Mrs. Casings was telling the truth about him kissing you." Mother's smoldering glare made Annie's face feel white hot.

"I didn't ask him to." Though Johnny's kiss had been nothing more than a quick peck on her cheek, a warm jolt had traveled all the way down to her toes.

Had Mrs. Casings followed them home after the young people's church gathering? Johnny's cornflower blue eyes had captivated her, so perhaps she'd not noticed her mother's friend.

"How dare you traipse around town like a strumpet!"

A ... a strumpet?

"It wasn't like that!" Though Mother would never consider the livery man's son suitable for either of her girls, he had the sweetest dimples and could always pull Annie out of her low spirits with a random scripture verse—even if it didn't apply to her situation whatsoever. "He might not be from the best family, but he'd never—"

"Hush." Mother snapped her fingers. "You will not mar the

Saint name again with such carelessness. People rise and fall by rumor alone. How dare you give them something to talk about!" Mother's lips pinched together, and her eyes darkened. "You may have already cost your father much with such foolishness. You're far too old for me to have to give you this talk." She snatched the letter opener off Father's desk. "Hold out your hand."

Annie gaped at the blunt, knife-like edge. Surely Mother wouldn't—

"I said hold out your hand."

Jacob's fingers curled through Annie's, and with a gasp, she quickly snatched her hand from his.

His eyebrows descended, confusion crinkling his forehead.

Mr. Hucket's calls barely projected over the crowd of bidders.

"Sorry," she whispered, swallowing against the sudden uptick of her heartbeat. "You just startled me."

A quick glance proved Mrs. Tate hadn't turned to see why she'd gasped. And what did it matter if she did? Mrs. Tate wasn't Mother, no matter how much her demeanor reminded her of the supposed saintliest of the Saints.

With a deep breath, Annie wriggled her hand back under Jacob's and entwined her fingers with his.

He glanced down at their hands before looking up at her, his eyebrows nearly meeting in the middle.

Oh, how cold he must think her for him to look so confused about his wife daring to hold his hand. A hand she'd offered that Brubaker boy without any hesitation—and Johnny's glances had never made her insides churn like Jacob's did.

If it wasn't for her mother, would she have naturally been more demonstrative? Though she likely would've never become as warm as Jacob.

Once he realized she'd never become the doting type of wife Leah was, would Jacob regret marrying her?

Not the time to be thinking such things! She shouldn't think them at all. "I'm sorry."

He still appeared confused.

"I'm trying." She squeezed his hand a little.

His brow relaxed and he nodded slightly, his mouth wriggling up a little as if trying to give her a smile. "It's all I ask."

The voices of the two men bidding against each other on the last basket escalated, so Annie turned to watch. She'd never seen either man before, and the basket, though fancy, wasn't worth such vehement bidding. Were these men trying to prove something to each other? Or perhaps they didn't realize the ladies from the Presbyterian church sold ham and beans for those without baskets.

Though having two men bid above three dollars for the basket was wonderful, Annie cringed on behalf of the basket's owner. Neither man appeared as if he'd bathed in quite some time.

"Anyone else want to bid?" Mr. Hucket patted his damp forehead and scanned the crowd.

The uglier of the two newcomers upped his bid to four dollars.

What if Celia had been old enough to auction off a basket?

Annie leaned toward Jacob. "Why don't you bid? I'd hate to think one day Celia would only have those two men fighting over a chance to eat with her."

Jacob's gaze roved the clearing. "Do you know whose basket it is?"

"Doesn't matter." She squeezed his hand. "We'll just have another guest for lunch."

"Five dollars!" The shorter man near the auction table glared at the uglier, dirtier one.

Leah nudged Jacob's side. "The money will go directly to your own children's benefit."

Bryant, who must have come over while she'd been lost in

thought, held out his palms. "I can't help. I've already shoveled out ten bucks."

"Goodness, I don't need that much prompting." Jacob took off his hat to wave it at Mr. Hucket. "Ten dollars and five cents."

Bryant snorted and rolled his eyes. "Always have to outshine me."

Without giving the men a chance to bid again, the school master pointed to Jacob. "Sold to the marshal."

A smattering of clapping ended the bidding, and a man from across the crowd cried, "Let's eat!"

Bryant and Jacob got up to claim their baskets, and the two unkempt strangers glared at Jacob as he passed, but thankfully they turned away and disappeared into the crowd.

Annie scanned the girls waiting up front and stopped at the smile Miss McGill was flashing at Jacob. Annie tightened her fists as red hot tendrils wrapped themselves around her heart in the same way Gwen's arm slid around the crook of Jacob's.

Of course it had to be Gwen's basket.

The young woman's maroon dress hugged her much younger, curvier figure, and the color enhanced her creamy skin. The way the luxurious fabric moved affirmed her wealth.

And if that wasn't bad enough, she looked as if she belonged on the arm of the most handsome man in Armelle. Voluptuous, attractive, graceful, a woman comfortable with displaying her adoration for all to see.

Gwen was everything Annie wasn't.

Jacob's face offered his escort nothing but politeness, but Gwen's features bespoke more than thankfulness for being rescued from the two less than appealing men.

"Whose is this?" Up at the table, Mr. Grayson held up the basket he'd won, decked out with drooping dandelions.

A questioning murmur snaked around the mass of people, but no girl stepped forward.

An inhuman shriek preceded a young girl's piercing squeal,

and Annie put a hand over her quickened heartbeat. Where had that sound come from?

Near the schoolhouse, a few women screamed and stumbled into each other, while a roar of masculine laughter mixed in with the ladies' shrieks.

Jacob dropped Gwen's arm to race toward the uproar with Bryant.

"What is it, Mama?" Spencer jumped up and stood on tiptoe.

A sudden split in the crowd revealed the black bulk of Lullabelle racing about as fast as a pig her size could run. A woman's large chemise strangled her neck, and a pair of ladies' drawers snugly encapsulated her backside. A garland of dandelions and twine held her floppy ears upright.

"I think we've found the girl who belongs to your basket, Samuel." A man hooted from somewhere in the crowd.

Poor Mr. Grayson's face drained of color.

Mrs. Tate jolted, knocking over her stool, and placed a hand at her heart. "Well, I never!" Her fleshy arms flapped as she pointed at the bewildered pig. "Those are my— Those are my ... my..." Her face turned red, and she clamped a hand over her mouth and sat down heavily.

Spencer cackled, and Annie poked him.

He clamped his hand over his mouth, fell upon the quilt, and rocked in amusement.

At least something had pulled her son from his doldrums, but poor Mrs. Tate! How would she live down having her unmentionables paraded about on a fat, bristly pig for the entire town to see?

"Spencer," she hissed, trying not to let his infectious giggle crack the stern façade she was trying to maintain.

Jacob shooed the pig toward the street with a broken tree limb. "Mr. Sullivan," he yelled.

The pig's owner, carrying a half-eaten drumstick, raced toward Lullabelle.

The barrel-sized pig grunted at Bryant, who was waving his arms in an attempt to redirect her.

Gwen stood with her hands on her hips, watching Jacob, Bryant, and Mr. Sullivan herd off the disgruntled animal. When the men disappeared behind the schoolhouse, she glanced at Annie and then toward her father. After what looked like a moment of indecision, she started toward Annie's blanket.

"Welcome, Gwen." Once the girl was close enough, Annie patted the blanket on the side where Jacob had not sat earlier. Though Gwen's haughty expression rankled, uncertainty showed in her hesitant steps as well. "What lovely things did you pack in your basket?"

The younger woman gathered her skirts and made the fashionably large amount of fabric drape and swirl about her in one smooth transition to the ground. Seated, she looked like a doll atop an intricate cupcake. "I've got cold beef sandwiches, carrot salad, and cherry tarts." She set down her basket. "But that doesn't matter since Jacob didn't buy it because of what's in it."

"Still sounds wonderful." Annie pulled out her rolls and placed one on each plate.

Gwen propped herself up with her hands, leaned back, and stared at the clouds. "I knew Jacob would save me."

Leah's right eyebrow lifted.

Annie shook her head. They could inform the girl they'd prodded Jacob into buying her basket, but there was no need to make a scene—not if today was supposed to be enjoyable.

Behind Annie, a *ploomp* and a grunt made the hair on her neck stand.

Celia blew out a noisy breath and then snickered.

Annie turned and frowned at her daughter's hair, which looked as if a rodent had spent all night tugging strands from her braids. "Where have you been, young lady?"

She shrugged. "Nowhere. But wasn't that the funniest thing you ever saw? Can you believe someone actually got Mrs. Tate's—"

Annie's elbow connected with Celia's ribs, and she used her eyes to indicate Mrs. Tate's location. The woman was sitting on her stool, staring toward the trees, chomping on her sandwich mechanically.

Spencer leaned toward Celia. "How'd you know it was Mrs. Tate's unmentiona—?"

Annie tweaked Spencer's ear. "Hush."

But that was a good question. A question that likely had no good answer.

Her stomach sank like stone.

Celia grabbed a roll and glowered at her brother.

"Stop staring at Spencer as if he's the one who did something wrong," Annie muttered low enough Mrs. Tate wouldn't hear. "What have you been up to?"

Celia grabbed a handful of berries. "Talking with friends."

"I wonder when Jacob will be back." Gwen sighed and pulled a cherry pastry from her basket.

Annie stabbed her roll and crammed butter into the slit. Since Gwen had called Jacob by his given name long before he'd married, she couldn't expect the girl to just stop, though she certainly could've said his name with a lot less wistfulness.

"There he is!" Spencer waved at Jacob, whose long strides ate up the ground. "Did you have to put the pig down, Pa?"

Slightly winded, Jacob lowered himself next to Annie. "No. We just took her back home. Bryant's helping Sullivan de-clothe her."

Celia's short burst of giggles ended with her choking in an attempt not to laugh full out.

Annie thumped her daughter's back as if she were choking instead of dying of laughter until her breathing returned to normal.

"I'm so glad you were here." Gwen batted her eyelashes at Jacob. "Saving us all from that awful ogre of an animal, and me from those nasty men." She handed him a beef sandwich and a small bowl of thinly sliced carrots covered in a white sauce.

How had she whipped those food items out so fast?

"You'll be happy you bought my basket." She held a fork out to him. "It's Grandma McGill's secret recipe."

Jacob took the fork, shoveled in some carrot salad, and nodded. "It's very good." He set Gwen's food down and looked Annie in the eyes. "Now tell me, wife, what did you pack?" He rubbed his hands together. "I'm famished."

Annie kept her smile small despite it wanting to split her face. "Tomato sandwiches, pickles, rolls, applesauce, and snap peas." She handed him a plate. "And butter cake for dessert."

"Excellent." He set the plate in his lap and leaned over to kiss her cheek.

Annie kept her gaze on her lap to keep from looking at Gwen.

Minutes ago, she'd been worrying about what Mrs. Tate would think of her holding Jacob's hand, and here he so easily declared his favor for her in front of a woman who wasn't shy about displaying her affection for him.

Gwen was the kind of girl she'd have expected Jacob to marry.

But he'd not chosen her despite it being obvious Gwen had given him ample opportunity to declare himself.

So why was she letting Gwen outshine her? She could at least do what the brazen young woman did: look at him as if she admired him, sidle up close, compliment him in front of others.

She reached up to brush a crumb off the corner of his mouth with her thumb.

He stopped mid-chew.

She smiled and tilted her head like Gwen might when trying to peek up at a man through her lashes, but then realized she had nothing coquettish to say. Did flirty women like Gwen prepare their flattery beforehand or did such expressions just roll off their tongues? "Uh, do you mind if I offer one of our sandwiches to Miss McGill?"

He only shook his head, and then looked back out into the crowd.

So much for her first attempt at flirting. She turned to Gwen and gestured to her basket. "Would you like anything of ours?"

A muscle in the young lady's cheek twitched, making her look both vulnerable and offended. "No, thank you," she muttered. She grabbed her half-eaten tart and threw the crust at a small songbird hopping and pecking near Mrs. Tate.

Mrs. Tate's steely-blue eyes scanned Annie's family, stopping on how little space there was between her and Jacob before moving to stare at Celia's mussed hair.

The old woman harrumphed, then gathered her things in a basket and left.

CHAPTER TWENTY-EIGHT

The fiddler started a second round of "Turkey in the Straw," and Jacob strode over to the clump of ladies Annie had buried herself in shortly after they'd finished their picnic. He knew it was rude to pull her out of a conversation, but he'd been bombarded with so many questions about the pig and the rustlers that he'd had no chance to dance with her yet.

He clasped her by the elbow. "Excuse us, ladies."

Annie blinked up at him. "Is something wrong?"

He pointed to the slow-moving thunderhead a few miles away. "They called the last dance. Rain's coming."

"So soon?" She frowned at the storm clouds, then glanced around. "Where's Celia?"

He shook his head. The girl had disappeared twice without permission after the pig incident. "We'll have to put our foot down harder tonight. But after we dance."

Annie sighed and her shoulders drooped. "I'm afraid she was involved with the pig incident."

"I know."

Her brows knit together. "Then why didn't you insist we leave right away?"

He'd debated doing so on the walk back from corralling the pig, but hadn't wanted to ruin Spencer and Annie's fun.

Or his.

"Because I practiced dancing with my wife a few nights ago," He gave her his most persuasive grin and walked backward toward the dancers. "So I'm not letting my chance to swing her around accompanied by a good fiddle player get away."

At the edge of the dance floor, he wrapped his arms around her and pressed his lips against her ear so she could hear him despite the music and the foot stamping. "We can't let that practice go to waste."

"However." Annie stepped back and held out stiff dance arms, though a smile seemed to be trying to overturn her lips. "Swaying won't work for 'Turkey in the Straw.'"

"Rather unfortunate." He winked and was rewarded with the blush he'd hoped for.

Annie scanned the crowd, whirling about them. "But Celia—"

He jiggled her arms a bit, calling attention to the dance pose they were holding. "She's free to wreak havoc for a few more minutes."

"But—"

Still holding her hand, Jacob silenced her with a finger against her lips. "Dancing. We're dancing." He moved back into position and waited for a twirling couple to fly by before pulling Annie into the fray.

After they got their bearings and took their place in the circle, Jacob hollered back to the caller with the rest of the men. He took care to hold Annie closer than necessary, enjoying the sparkle in her eyes whenever she dared to look at him while they promenaded about.

Catching Mrs. Tate's evil glare from the edge of the dance floor only made him pull Annie closer and wink at the vinegary old woman.

When the elderly caller commanded them to switch partners, Jacob couldn't help but scowl. Couldn't Fritz see how hard it'd been to keep Annie in his arms this long? She didn't need any help getting out of them.

He steered Annie past Mr. Grayson, who was attempting to exchange Gwen for Annie, and stole Mr. Lombard's knee-high granddaughter for his partner instead.

Annie disappeared into the crowd, and Shelby Mae kept him busy bouncing around like popcorn on a greased griddle.

"Allemande left to the corner maid, back to your own, and promenade!"

Finally. His legs were about to give out.

Finding the little brunette's grandfather was easy considering Annie hadn't tried to exhaust the old man by galloping around the entire dance floor. He gave the little girl a small bow before twirling her back into her grandfather's arms and then took his wife back into the line.

While the encroaching thunder lent the band its percussion for the last round, Annie sneaked a glance at him, her eyes warmer than he'd ever seen them.

On a call to swing her around thrice, he twirled her fast enough to lift her feet off the floor.

Her cheeks brightened as she laughed full out.

His heart sped up, and he lost his breath. He slowed his twirl, his feet melting into the well-worn boards. He'd never seen her laugh before.

When he set her down, she quieted, but her lips still clung to mirth.

He'd seen her smile a few times these past several months—which had given character to her plain features—but laughter had made her positively radiant.

"Chain up, ladies, don't be slow. Kiss the caller before you go!"

Annie tried to pull away, but Jacob held on to her.

She frowned at his hand clamped around her dainty wrist. "Didn't you hear?" She tilted her head toward the stage. "I'm supposed to chain up."

The women stomped past in a swirl of colorful skirts, the last one in the chain holding out her hand to Annie.

He narrowed his eyes at his wife. "Don't you dare be kissing Old Fritz."

The lady in yellow hooked arms with Annie and dragged her away. Annie's gaze clung to his until the dancing forced her to pay attention to where she was going.

The men clapped as the ladies high-stepped around the dance floor, but not Jacob. He kept his eyes on his wife. Though she didn't look back at him, the flush coloring her neck likely meant she could feel his steady gaze.

The last bars of the song ended with a flourish.

"Don't forget about that kiss, ladies," Old Fritz hollered above the applause.

Jacob took a few steps to snatch Annie's hand. "Don't you even think about it."

Her lips wriggled with amusement. "Surely you wouldn't begrudge an old man his kiss?"

He arched his eyebrows. "If someone needs kissing..." he stepped closer and tipped up her jaw.

Her sudden stiffness stopped him.

"Best get your lady home." Mr. Ivens thumped him on the back as he escorted his own wife toward the carriages. "That storm cloud's enormous."

Without turning to acknowledge the man or the storm, Jacob kept his hand on the underside of Annie's jaw and let his thumb travel over the soft skin of her cheek.

She didn't move, didn't turn away. And yet, she didn't look like a woman desiring a kiss.

He let his finger slide across her lower lip. "Later," he whispered.

She dropped her gaze to her feet.

Would a kiss have been that bad?

Annie pivoted and hurried toward Leah, who was shaking blankets free of debris.

Despite the storm's quick approach, he couldn't make himself rush after her.

He'd wanted that kiss pretty badly, but not enough to force it.

After their kiss the night they'd danced to Joe's attempts at music, he'd thought they were making progress.

Had he been so enraptured with her that night he'd missed the fear in her eyes?

When she'd told him she'd be his wife in truth soon, had she only said so because she felt pressured?

He ran a hand through his hair. As hard as it would be to refrain from tasting those lips again, he'd not kiss her again until she voluntarily raised her lips to his.

Near the schoolhouse, an angry shout drew his attention.

Harriet Butler and Celia were throwing blueberries at a young towheaded boy. Though the lad was throwing berries back, he didn't appear to be enjoying the game.

Jacob tried to keep the scowl off his face. "Celia!"

She gave a farewell nod to Harriet and started toward him, but only after giving him a look that said she was tired of obeying him.

Which was ridiculous. He'd not asked her to help clean up their picnic or anything else that afternoon because he'd wanted to contain her petulant aftermath to the privacy of their own home.

Annie and Leah had finished packing once they reached them, so he took Annie's baskets.

With how the wind was kicking up and the sky darkening despite it only being ten past three, they needed to get home quickly.

Bryant was having difficulty picking up all of his wife's things along with his daughter's since she and her husband had left early.

Jacob came alongside his friend and took one of his baskets. "Got a favor to ask."

Bryant tensed.

Since when had he ever asked Bryant for something unreasonable? "Annie and I need to have a difficult talk with Celia as soon as we get home. Would you mind taking Spencer to your house for supper?"

Bryant nodded a little too eagerly. "Sure."

Leah shot him a sly wink. "Why don't we keep him until after that meeting Annie plans to go to tomorrow? Then you won't have to worry about the weather passing to come get him. The storm could last all night."

"Mighty obliged." Jacob dipped his head at her thoughtfulness, but he wouldn't let her wink fool him into thinking he'd get far with Annie while Spencer was gone. After the coming fight with Celia, Annie'd be in no mood for courting of any kind.

The wind picked up, and the people disassembling the dance floor scurried about with extra fervor.

Bryant led Leah through the field behind the church as a distant thunderclap shook the first drops of rain from the heavens.

When they met up with the Whitsetts on the sidewalk near his house, Annie stooped in front of Spencer and swiped a damp strand of hair off his forehead. "What do you think about spending the night at the Whitsetts'? I bet they'd let you have leftover pie."

The boy shrugged and then turned to Bryant. "Can you give me a ride? It's a long way to your house."

Despite carrying two quilts and a basket, Bryant went down on one knee and hooked his arms. Spencer hopped on, and Bryant jogged down the street.

"Good evening, you three." Leah took her basket from Jacob then wrapped her other arm around Celia and gave her a big squeeze. "Love you, Celia."

His stepdaughter endured the hug without any smart remarks, though her face couldn't have looked more sour.

Nearly instantly, the rain turned from drizzly to steady and

Leah took off after her husband. Jacob started off after Annie and looked over his shoulder at Celia. "Hurry, lightning's coming."

A sudden downpour caught them before they gained the porch.

Under the awning, he dropped his armful of baskets to dump the rain off his hat. Then he pulled back the shawl Annie had tried to use as a head covering. "That didn't do you much good. You're wet through."

"I'm sure I look a fright." She grimaced.

"Not at all." He smoothed a rogue strand of hair from her face, feeling the damp soft skin at her temples.

Celia stomped onto the porch looking like a drowned scarecrow. "Let me pass, please."

Jacob swung open the door. "After you, ladies."

The clouds had grown thick, making the inside of the house as dark as molasses. He quickly lit a lamp and shivered.

"I'm freezing." Celia's teeth chattered. "I'm going upstairs and curling up under the covers and reading." She headed for the stairs. "Since I ate plenty of pie, no need to make me supper."

Annie's eyes met his in silent question.

"Celia." He wasn't going to let her get away that easily.

She turned on the bottom step.

"You may change into dry clothing, but you will come back down."

She frowned. "Why?"

Annie stepped beside him. "We need to talk."

Celia dropped her shoulders and forced an exaggerated sigh. "Why can't we talk tomo—"

"No."

His voice had boomed enough to startle her, so he clenched his fists and continued with a little less vehemence. "Do as your mother requested. Get dressed—"

"But—"

"Not another word." Jacob eyed her until she turned and stomped up each stair.

He had asked Bryant this afternoon how he'd handled his daughters' insubordination, but as Jacob had suspected, neither of the Whitsett girls had given their parents this much trouble.

He looked back at Annie who was trembling. "Why don't you get out of that wet dress and I'll start a fire." He got her a thick towel from the linen closet and steered her toward the stairs.

He peeled off his wet sack suit coat and hung it by the fireplace. Shivering against the drafts, he arranged his wood and stoked a healthy fire. Celia's plan to curl up under a pile of blankets was tempting, definitely more appealing than going through with the impending conversation, but it had to be done.

Annie returned dressed in a loose-fitting dark purple gown and glided to the couch. "If you don't mind, Jacob, it might be best if I did most of the talking."

He held his tongue. She could at least start the talking.

Celia thumped down the stairs minutes later, her bare ankles showing below her nightgown and the quilt she'd wrapped herself in. Her slippers' cheery red and white pom-poms looked sorely out of place on the feet of someone whose scowl could ward off a starving pack of wolves.

Jacob gestured to the rocking chair, and Celia dropped hard on the seat.

He settled next to his wife as the two ladies eyed each other.

Annie cleared her throat. "Where did you disappear to three times today?"

Celia shrugged.

"That's not an answer, Celia." The thin lines around Annie's mouth deepened, and her eyes flashed.

Celia raised one shoulder. "With friends."

"You can't leave without telling us where you're going."

"I'm sorry, but I didn't want to spend my entire day with you two." Celia's lips curled into a sneer.

Jacob leaned forward. "What about the pig?"

"You think *I* dressed up Lullabelle?" Celia straightened as if offended.

"It's obvious—"

"You don't have any proof." She crossed her arms and leaned forward. "Because I didn't do it."

"Darling—"

"My name's Celia, Ma."

Annie's hands curled in her lap, wringing the doily she'd slipped off the sofa arm. "Celia, you mustn't be so hateful toward Jacob."

"Then he shouldn't accuse me of stuff I didn't do!"

Annie scooted to the edge of her chair. "You were awfully dirty and showed up right after that pig—"

"So you believe him over me?" Celia's nostrils flared.

Annie locked onto her daughter's glare. "None of us can do whatever we wish, whenever we wish. That's not how family works."

"Then maybe I don't want to be a part of this family anymore." Celia puffed out her chest and tilted her chin, squaring off like the underdog challenging the pack leader.

"I'm sorry to hear that, but you have no choice." Jacob stood. He was done watching her spar with her mother with such disrespect. "Go on up to bed. You may come down for breakfast in the morning if you think you can keep a civil tongue in your head. If not, you will stay in your room until you feel like you can handle yourself maturely. We can talk at the next meal where you believe you can control of yourself."

Celia turned her reddening face toward Annie. "You can't let him stuff me back into that room again for days on end."

"He said you could come down whenever you could behave—"

"Why are you taking his side?" Celia pointed at Jacob, the quilt sliding off her arm. "He's not my father."

Annie stood, though she appeared ready to wilt. "Whether or not you like it, Jacob is indeed your father now, and you will honor him in that capacity."

Snatching her fallen quilt, Celia stood with a jerk and stomped for the stairs.

Jacob caught Annie around her middle before she slumped. He gave her a squeeze, rubbing her arm. "I'm proud of you."

"Thanks." She fished out a handkerchief and wadded it against her eyes. "But I'm afraid I have a headache now." She lowered herself back onto the sofa and stared at the empty stairwell.

"A quiet evening we shall have, then." He grabbed her patchwork quilt off the rocking chair.

She stood abruptly. "But I can't. I have to make supper."

"There's no need. I ate more pie than Celia. And if you want something, I can make you a sandwich." He handed her the book she'd been reading over the last several days and slipped the quilt around her shoulders. "Don't worry about us more than necessary."

She sat, frowning at her book, but it looked as if she'd stay put.

He went upstairs, and after listening to the grumbling and shuffling behind Celia's door for a moment or two, he moved to his bedroom to change into something dry. He might not have a nightshirt he felt capable of walking around the house in, but his work clothes sure were an improvement over soggy ones.

After coming back downstairs, he smiled to see Annie reading.

He settled across from her with the newspaper while intermittent thunderclaps filtered through the walls, echoing the unrest in the house, though everyone held their peace.

When the clock struck eight, he folded his paper and leaned over to pat Annie's knee.

She startled and clasped onto the book now steepled across her chest. "I must have fallen asleep."

He reached over to take her book. "About twenty minutes ago. Why don't we head upstairs?"

She placed her hand in his, and his palms grew sticky.

With no Spencer to tuck in and Celia already cloistered away, it was just the two of them heading upstairs ... to separate rooms.

He suppressed a sigh.

In the upstairs hallway, Annie glanced at Celia's door.

"Want to talk about it?"

"It's hard to know what to do." She looked down at where she was running her thumb along a scar that cut across her knuckles. "I'm not my mother—which might be just as bad as it is good."

"How's that?"

"I never dared to talk to Mother like Celia does me. Her grandmother would be appalled."

Jacob nodded. He didn't have to meet his mother-in-law to know that was true. Though far away, in both distance and time, she seemed to be in Annie's head, calling into question her every decision.

"Though I was a good girl, Mother found fault with most everything I did." She stopped twisting her hands by clamping them together. "I'd always thought if I were more lenient with Celia, the self-doubt that fills me wouldn't cripple her. But Gregory must have disciplined her more than I was aware." She turned to face Celia's door, the contours of her countenance stark in the flashing light of the resurging storm. "Perhaps I've been too lax with her since his death. She's far more conceited than is good for a fifteen-year-old."

He wouldn't argue that.

"What do you think?"

He took a deep breath and weighed the value of saying anything. What did she need to hear at this moment?

Cupping her crestfallen face, he gazed into her eyes, trying to drill down to that inner part of her where his words might take root. "You're a good mother, that's what I think."

She gave him a weak smile, and he leaned down to kiss her temple.

Her breath left with an exaggerated shudder, and his lips seemed unable to leave the soft skin they'd landed on.

When she didn't move away, he let himself press another kiss against her warm cheek, then another to the soft skin below her ear. And one atop the beauty mark on her jawline. And then—

She tensed, and he halted just a breath shy from her lips.

What was he doing?

Had he not just vowed hours ago to wait for her to initiate the next kiss?

He took a step back, and when she didn't even try to hang on to him, his heart slowed and sank.

The feel of her skin was still impressed upon each of his fingertips, so he jammed his hands into his pockets in hopes of erasing the sensation.

Words of apology formed in his mind, but he didn't voice them.

For he wasn't sorry.

Her hand fluttered up to her face, her fingers trailing along the path he'd kissed.

He closed his eyes to keep himself from pulling her back and continuing where he'd left off.

He was ready. Oh, so ready. But she wasn't. And he would do nothing to hurt her.

The rattling of a knob made him open his eyes again.

Annie was pressed up against her door, her hand behind her back. "Goodnight, Jacob." She backed into her room, her eyes locked on his until the door closed between them.

He exhaled loudly. What had he been thinking?

The mood had been all wrong for kissing her like that, and

yet, before she'd disappeared into her room, something in her dark hazel eyes had seemed to be inviting him to—

He lifted his hand to knock, but let it drop.

No, if she'd actually been inviting him to partake of more, there'd be no door between them.

He still had to wait.

CHAPTER TWENTY-NINE

After Jacob's footsteps shuffled away from her closed door, Annie stopped leaning against it. She'd half hoped he'd knock, but...

But what?

She could've reopened the door, knock or not. What was she hoping for that she couldn't have if she wanted it?

With a slow step forward, she headed toward her cot while taking off her wrapper. She slipped her legs under her blankets and stared out her lone window. The rain droplets, refracting the light of the fancy street lamp, slowly trickled down the pane.

She placed a hand on her jaw where Jacob's lips had applied the gentlest of pressure.

When would she stop lying to herself?

All her hesitations, all her excuses, all her worries about what people would think were only vain attempts to stave off her worst fear.

The sooner she had a real marriage, the sooner heartbreak might come. She could just as easily lose Jacob as she did Gregory, maybe even more so, considering his job. Plus, what if she lost a child, or two? Would Jacob pull away from her as Gregory had?

Being widowed twice over would be bad enough, but losing a second husband's affections over something she couldn't control and would almost rather die than face again?

A tear slipped down her cheek.

If she ever gathered up enough courage to write home about the marriage she'd rushed into only to lose her land anyway, Mother would be sure to point out that following the rules of propriety would've kept her from all these worries.

Yet, would she have laughed as deeply as she had this afternoon on the dance floor? She'd not laughed once since being widowed.

And though God hadn't saved her from hardships and heartbreak, He'd still provided her with a roof, security, laughter, and a husband she was shutting out.

Not just with a door, but from her affections as well.

Because if he knew what she was feeling...

She stared at herself in the mirror she'd hung behind the door and rubbed her hands up and down her skinny arms.

With no lantern, she couldn't see much, but nothing magical would have transfigured her in one day's time—she was still a gaunt woman with muddy eyes and freckles.

And yet, Jacob, a man whose face would shame a fairy tale prince's, had just looked at her with a look she knew well enough.

How had he become attracted so quickly?

She'd hoped a mutual admiration would evolve after months of living together, but she'd never expected that hungry, painful look of suppressed desire—at least not so soon. Not for someone like her.

But she'd seen it twice. The first time, she'd figured she'd misread him. But now she could no longer pretend she was seeing things. He really did want his plain wife.

Her fingers returned to the curve of her neck where his

thumb had so lightly caressed her throat as his kisses had turned into something more than a peck on the cheek.

When she'd proposed to Jacob, she'd thought she'd have time. Lots of time.

Now it seemed she wasn't the only one who wished this marriage wasn't so ... inconvenient.

She wrapped her arms around herself. How was she already yearning for the intimate hold of a man when Gregory's memory still haunted her?

Annie flopped onto the bed and stared at the ceiling as a bout of thunder rolled over Armelle. Sleep. She should sleep. Things would be clearer come morning once the stresses of the day had been forgotten.

She curled up into a ball and counted to one thousand.

The downstairs clock chimed eleven.

Twelve.

She kicked off her blankets and paced, though not much pacing could be done in a room the size of a pantry. But if she left her tiny cell, where would she go?

His room or downstairs?

She stopped at the window and placed her clammy forehead against the window pane, the condensation cool and soothing against her heated cheek. The few trees in the yard thrashed in rhythm with the storm's bluster, her heart and head commiserating with the wind-whipped branches.

She closed her eyes and with an exhale, pushed away.

She took one step, then another, and cracked open the door.

Nothing stirred.

Her heart beat hard against her ribcage as she padded into the hallway.

Both Spencer's and Celia's door were closed. If her son had been home, she'd have diverted herself in that direction. Staring at his angelic, slumbering face would have taken her mind off things.

Celia's door offered little hope for distraction. She could

watch her daughter sleep, but if Celia awoke, how would she explain herself? And did she really want to get in a tiff at this hour?

Illumination from a bolt of lightning flashed through the windows and lit up the hallway. Jacob's door stood slightly ajar.

A peal of thunder vibrated against her soles, and a sudden downpour pelted the roof. She was in no danger of being heard walking about, so she crossed the hallway. At his door, she rested her hand against it, but didn't push until another roll of thunder rattled the house.

Lightning flashed through his room's four curtainless windows, revealing Jacob sprawled on his back across the bed, as relaxed as a school-aged boy. Though the bed was large, his limbs nearly reached from edge to edge. A sheet was wrapped around his waist and one leg, the rest of him uncovered.

A flash brighter than a lantern filled the room, and an immediate crack of thunder made her gasp.

Jacob sat up halfway, shook his head while rubbing at his eyes, and almost lay back down, but stopped midway. "Annie?"

"I'm sorry I disturbed you." Her voice came out breathless. "Don't bother getting up."

"What's wrong?"

"I thought ... rather, I needed ... or, well I—" She twisted her nightgown in her hands. Oh, what was she doing?

"What time's it, darlin'?" His voice was gravelly and deeper than usual, causing her heart to flutter.

His mattress creaked, and he leaned toward his footboard. His profile was nearly indiscernible with only flickering cloud-to-cloud lightning penetrating the darkness. A shadow slipped over his face—his shirt.

Annie took a step forward, but her other foot refused to follow.

If she didn't push herself over this hill, how long would she stay stuck on the other side? Jacob wasn't the kind of man to command her left foot to take the step it hesitated to take—he'd wait ... and wait and wait. "It's later than it should be."

Another deafening crack of thunder made her jump an inch off the floor.

He looked toward the window and let loose a soft whistle. "That was close." He then pushed off the bed and stepped toward her. "What did you want?"

Want ... Need. "Would you hold me?"

In the darkness, she couldn't see his arm, but after a gentle swipe of his fingers, he found hers and curled his hand around her wrist. "Afraid of storms?"

His sleep-filled, husky voice made it impossible for her to form words, so she shook her head.

He tugged her closer, and her back foot followed.

He wrapped his arms around her. "Better?"

"No." She fumbled for one of his hands and brought it up, placing it against her neck where he'd last kissed her. "But I might be. If you'd start where you left off."

His chest stopped moving and she could hear him swallow.

A glimmer of sheet lightning danced in his dark eyes before his mouth took hers so suddenly she was caught mid-breath.

His hands cupped her neck, his fingers ensconcing themselves in her hair, his thumbs whisper soft against her jaw. His lips pressed against hers with slightly more pressure.

But then he didn't move. His breath held. His hands stilled.

There'd be no turning back if she didn't break away now.

He knew it too.

And he was waiting.

She closed her eyes and brought her own hand up to touch the heightened pulse in his throat and moved her lips against his, pressing, probing, permitting.

He pulled away for a second, his haggard breath caressing her lips.

She couldn't see his eyes in the dark, but she could feel his gaze take her in for a moment before he cupped her face in his hands and reclaimed her mouth just as a crash of thunder echoed through the room.

She easily matched the intensity of his kisses, which only grew with the crescendoing roar of the storm.

And continued, even when the rain was long past.

CHAPTER THIRTY

Annie sat on the cot in her room brushing her hair, staring at her reflection in the mirror. The pink hue of the rising sun slowly softened the shadows on her face.

She'd left Jacob's room while he was yet asleep in case Celia came looking for her, but she couldn't stay closeted away forever. How could she leave this room with a mess of confusion, pleasure, guilt, and anticipation stamped across her face?

He loved her. He hadn't said so, but it was extraordinarily evident after last night.

Did she love him? Perhaps she already did. But did she love him as well as he should be loved?

He deserved a much better wife than the emotional mess he'd married.

Oh, Lord, please let me grow to love him in time. Let me not disappoint him.

Yes, that's all she needed—time.

The knot in her chest loosened. She put her brush on the bedside table, picked up her pins, and set to work on her hair. Her love for Gregory had waxed and waned during different seasons of life, had it not? So too would her love for Jacob.

He'd given up his bachelorhood and rescued her from poverty. When it became clear he'd not get what he'd bargained for, he hadn't uttered a single complaint. How could she not grow to love him?

One day it might feel like the heart-fluttering love she'd had for Gregory during their courtship, but there'd also been times when she'd loved Gregory as the man she knew she could count on, though she was so livid with him she could spit.

She squared her shoulders. Though her emotions wouldn't settle into something she understood, she'd act as if she did. She pinched her cheeks and smiled a little. She did look a touch prettier today.

She grabbed her shawl and forced herself to meet the day. Her door's hinges creaked loudly in the silent hall.

Jacob's door was shut.

She chewed on her lip and took a step in that direction, but the scuffling in Celia's room stopped her. Was it wrong to wish Celia would stay in her room long enough for her and Jacob to breakfast alone?

She sighed and crossed over to her daughter's door and knocked. She needed to know how many flapjacks to make.

"Leave me alone. I don't want to talk."

Annie leaned against Celia's door and tried not to sound happy that her daughter wouldn't be ruining breakfast. "Will you be having lunch with us?"

No response.

A door opened behind her.

Jacob entered the hall, dressed in his usual black trousers and thin tie tucked under his gray vest. "Good morning." His voice rumbled with the vestiges of sleep.

Annie averted her eyes from his overly warm gaze.

Though the sight of him made her heart pound, she hated for anyone to see her blush.

He came up beside her. "I take it she's not coming down?"

At the shake of her head, he pulled her against his side and nuzzled her hair. "She'll come around."

She frowned at Celia's door. If Gregory had been as affectionate with their children as Jacob was with Spencer, would her daughter have turned out so prickly?

Spencer had bloomed under Jacob's attention, and who'd have guessed Spencer had the capacity for even more sparkle?

What if she'd been the one who'd failed her daughter? How many years had she spent mourning lost children and trying to rid the ranch of never-ending dirt instead of sitting down to braid hair or leaving the broom behind to pick wildflowers?

"We'll keep praying." He rubbed her arm and smiled down at her. "Have you started breakfast?"

"No." And how would she manage to cook with him watching her with that mischievous slant to his lips?

"Since I slept late," he wrapped his arms around her, "and neither of the kids are eating, why don't you stop by the bakery and get yourself something on the way to your temperance meeting?"

"The temperance meeting." She smacked her cheek. "How did I forget?"

A sparkle leapt into his eyes. "Perhaps you were distracted by something a lot more fun?"

Her skin grew hot against her hand.

"You're entirely too tempting when you're flustered." His lips met hers in what turned out to be a not-so-quick kiss.

Her heart sang and a moan escaped from deep inside her chest, but she had to push away. "Jacob," she sputtered, stealing a glance at the door beside them. "Celia might hear."

"Then be quieter next time." He winked then kissed her forehead. "See you after work." Whistling, he bounded down the steps.

She rubbed the gooseflesh along her arms but she couldn't erase the raised bumps he'd left behind.

With a deep breath, she knocked on her daughter's door

again. "I'm going to the temperance meeting. Will you be all right?"

"If you consider being imprisoned all right."

Celia's ability to sass didn't seem impaired. "I'll let you know when I return, darling."

Annie rushed back to her room to retrieve her bonnet. At the fundraiser yesterday, she'd learned that the mother of Celia's friend, Harriet, was supposed to be at this meeting. Hopefully Harriet's mother would be willing to discuss what they could do to make sure their girls grew up to be proper young ladies, and how to keep them from running off with those boys.

The second lecture was interminable.

Annie fanned herself with a leaflet entitled "The Power of Temperance Education" that she'd folded accordion style, and slouched down behind the generous width of Mrs. Tate in the row in front of her to hide her inattention. Sitting in the courthouse basement for two hours on this hard chair had made her body beg for the sleep it'd been denied.

Imagining the voice of her mother droning on about the importance of beauty sleep made her grin. If Mother were here to lecture on that topic, Annie could stop her cold by telling her exactly why she'd not been able to sleep last night.

"Would Marshal Hendrix approve of that?"

She dropped her leaflet fan, though her face had suddenly grown warmer than the muggy air.

Had Mrs. Beard just read her thoughts in front of everybody?

"Mrs. Gep—I mean, Mrs. Hendrix? Would he?"

The woman didn't look appalled or censuring, so what was she asking about? Annie pulled at her neckline. "Ah, I think the marshal would likely side with the temperance union?"

"Good." Mrs. Beard's piercing winter-blue eyes shifted to a

heavyset woman in the front row. "Biddy, pass her the remaining leaflets."

Annie sat up straighter. Had she just doomed her husband to hand out their literature, too? "And what would you have the marshal do exactly?"

"Why, just hand prisoners a copy of each leaflet. I suppose he might also call upon us to come deliver speeches on the ills of intemperate living if he hasn't the time to do it himself."

Biddy rose and handed Annie a two-inch stack of paper.

The top leaflet boldly proclaimed, "Sabbath Desecration."

Annie set them down beside the leaflets she'd already been asked to pass out. "I see."

"As long as he doesn't call upon us on a Sunday, of course."

Feeling every eye upon her, Annie fanned herself again. "His work doesn't always make it possible to rest when he pleases, but I'm sure he doesn't expect others to go against their convictions for his convenience."

Mrs. Beard cocked her head. "Good. His profession is one where it would be dangerous to quit on Sunday altogether—but the railroads, the stagecoach?" Mrs. Beard rapped her hand on the lectern and thankfully took her eyes off Annie. "Despite those who claim closing travel on Sunday would be unrealistic—it is, in my opinion, that the stations very well could be closed, except for the apathy of Christian workers—and to our shame, ours as well. If we gave them no business, they would not remain open. Trains on Sundays are not a necessity."

Annie tried hard not to fidget in her seat, but how much longer could she sit in this furnace of a room? When she'd learned Harriet's mother would not be attending after all, she should've slipped out the door and gone back home.

"Too many have said, 'We have tried to schedule Sundays off and failed.' But we must keep to our task, and that brings me to the *Daily Ricochet*." Mrs. Beard held up the newspaper as if it were coated in manure. "Not only does it produce a Monday paper—meaning the purchase of said paper encourages work to be done on Sunday—but Mr. Crandall insists on running ads enticing people to purchase liquor."

Annie made a mental note to hide her newspaper if any of the temperance women came calling.

"At the least, let us all boycott the paper's Monday edition. Now what else shall we be sure to…"

Annie held her tongue while listening to the women generating lists of businesses to boycott and people to confront. The ladies didn't seem to be the kind to listen to differing opinions, but surely trying to shame non-Christians into rigorous Christ-like living wouldn't entice them to seek the Lord, but rather drive them away.

Many of the faces surrounding her were rapt with attention or on fire with indignation. Maybe this wasn't the best place to find new friends—not that she was against the group's goals, but she couldn't imagine joining the militant chorus of approvals as Mrs. Beard condemned many of Armelle's citizens every month.

"Ladies, thank you for your attention, and let us all work diligently on our goals this coming week. Before you leave, feel free to have more cookies and tea."

Annie glanced at the insanely large number of leaflets she and Jacob were supposed to hand out—likely more leaflets than there were citizens in the county—then looked across the aisle to the one woman who'd seemed about as uncomfortable being here as she'd been.

Corinne Stillwater was likely a few years younger than she was, yet a heavy weariness slumped her shoulders, giving her the look of a mother drowning in a sea of children and chores. The woman had yet to rise from her seat, her head bowed. But considering she was rubbing her lye-cracked hands, she hadn't fallen asleep.

Annie slipped across the row and sat beside Corinne. The laundress's clothes were brilliantly white and starched per usual, but they were awfully threadbare. "Would you like to get some cookies with me and chat?"

The younger woman's blond brows rose, then scrunched as if trying to place Annie.

"I know we've never really met, but I'm Annie Hendrix, Celia's mother." Last fall, Corinne had hired Celia to do laundry for a few weeks. "Now that I live in town, I'd like to get to know more people—"

"I'm afraid I don't have time for teas and such. I hardly have time for anything but work." She lifted her right hand and turned it palm up. An angry red welt festered in the crease near her thumb. "I'm only here because this got infected and it makes it difficult to work very long."

She placed her hand back in her lap and gave Annie a smile that was oh, so close to looking real. "But every woman needs a cookie once in a while, right?"

Perhaps Harriet's mother not being here wasn't so terrible after all. If someone could teach Celia a thing or two about persevering without grumbling, this woman could. "Is anyone helping you while your hand heals?"

She looked down. "No, but the doctor says it'll be all right by next week. I just hope I don't lose customers before then."

"Why don't I have my daughter come help you?" She'd hoped to have seen elation on Corinne's face, but instead, her expression tensed.

"I can't afford help, Mrs. Hendrix. I'm already behind paying for what needs to be paid for." Corinne ducked her head and rubbed at her eyes.

Annie gave her shoulder a squeeze. "That's all right. Celia doesn't need to be paid. I was thinking—"

"Oh, but that wouldn't be fair. She knows how hard the work is, and she'd not want to do so for what little I could spare."

Though she wanted to insist that Celia would work for free,

wages might spur her daughter into being the worker Corinne needed. "What if Jacob and I paid her wages? She's been a trial lately, and I'm thinking manual labor might do her some good. Might as well have her help you instead of polishing the floors I've already polished. Of course, if she's more a hindrance than a help, don't feel obligated to keep her for my sake, but if her work earned her a little something, I think she'd do well by you."

"I don't know." Corinne let out a noisy exhale. "But I could ask her. If she says yes, then we can arrange things. If not..."

"Fair enough." If Celia said no, their floors would be that much shinier. "How about you come over tomorrow?"

At the woman's nod, Annie rose. "Let's get some cookies."

"I'm afraid I shouldn't have more. I need to return to the laundry and do what I can." Corinne stood and gathered her things. "But I'll come by your house late tomorrow."

Annie said her goodbyes and started for the snack table.

Mrs. Tate hobbled up beside her with an empty glass. "How are you adjusting to your new husband since it's been such a short time since the last one passed?"

The woman's disapproving glare made Annie fist her hands at her sides. "It's not a situation I ever hoped to find myself in, but I am thankful God provides."

Mrs. Tate simply held her gaze.

The knot in Annie's throat stayed lodged despite repeated swallows. Why couldn't the line for tea move faster?

The elderly woman's mouth twitched. "When I lost my husband, I had five little ones at home." She paused to frown. "I loved Mansferd with a passion nothing and no one could take away, not even his death. Years passed before I could even think about another man raising my children, because no one could measure up to my Mansferd."

Mrs. Tate tilted her head as if in question.

What response did the woman want? "It must be of great comfort to look forward to seeing him again in Heaven."

Mrs. Tate's lips turned into a half smile. "Yes, and I'm sure he'll be comforted by the fact I didn't leave him behind so quickly for the arms of another."

Annie stifled a gasp.

Mrs. Tate's silvery eyebrows rose as she shrugged. "But you do what you must—or so the people around here say. It's what the newspaper owner is saying about Sabbath work, isn't it? Along with the railroad men. Seems to me, if we all had more faith in the Lord, He could bless us at the right time, His way. Good afternoon, Mrs. Hendrix." The old woman leaned more heavily on her cane as she started forward to refill her glass.

Annie shut her eyes and willed herself to think kindly of Mrs. Tate. The whole town knew the real reason no man had ever offered the widow his hand. For who could live with such judgment?

Giving up her spot in line, Annie didn't bother to retrieve her leaflets before heading for the exit.

CHAPTER THIRTY-ONE

Annie stared at the letter she'd started after returning from the temperance meeting.

She'd yet to get past "Dear Mother."

So many things had happened since she'd informed Mother of Gregory's death. And little of what had transpired would be welcomed information.

Loud thumping overhead made Annie frown up at the ceiling. How could Celia make so much noise in such a tiny room? Was she trying to annoy Annie into letting her come down and run about as she pleased?

Annie shook her head and picked up her letter. What should she tell her mother about Celia? That she'd been right? That raising a dignified young lady out West was impossible?

Maybe Celia should deliver this letter personally and stay at her grandmother's Virginian home for an extended visit. No finishing school on this planet could be more rigorous and demanding than Grandmother Saint. If Celia didn't return home a proper young lady, she'd at least be more appreciative of her family.

Annie snatched up her dip pen, re-inked, and set the tip to paper.

I know it's been months since I've written, and you may be surprised at the changes that have occurred in such a short time, for I myself can scarcely believe it. Thank you for writing last winter and offering to pay our way to Virginia to begin anew. I was unfortunately correct in my last letter's assessment. I couldn't run the ranch without—

Gregory.

Annie's pen hovered mid-sentence. It hurt knowing that writing his name was as close as she would get to him now, and yet, she wanted that distance a little more every day. She didn't want to cry anymore, didn't want to hurt.

Her mother had been immensely fond of Gregory—even if he had dragged her daughter off to this "godforsaken land."

Would Mother view her marriage to Jacob as a betrayal, as Mrs. Tate had? Mother still didn't know about Gregory being accused of the sheepherder's death. Annie's outrage at the charges had kept her from penning it last fall, and now she didn't feel right speaking ill of the dead, especially since no one had proven anything. She twirled the pen between her fingers.

How would Mother respond if she divulged the flurry of her mixed-up feelings over the remarriage?

Though Jacob hadn't yet said "I love you" like Gregory had oft repeated in their sixteen years of being man and wife, she felt them more with every second Jacob spent with her.

Above the parlor mantel, Gregory's guns, now Spencer's, glistened like they never had now that Jacob had taught the boy how to give them a thorough cleaning. The broken arm on her rocker had been fixed without her even asking. He'd even set Celia's old rock collection on the parlor windowsill after noticing her daughter had stuffed them under her bed.

Annie's smile slowly drooped into a frown. What had she done for him since moving in? He might thank her every day for cooking and cleaning, but she'd have done so for herself and the children.

She laid down her pen and massaged her forehead.

If Mother wrote back with one unkind word about her marrying Jacob, she'd ignore her every opinion thereafter—Mrs. Tate's, too. For Jacob had chosen to love the family foisted upon him without anything in return.

She picked up her pen. She'd introduce him to Mother with great fanfare and not hide how grateful she was that he'd come into their lives at the exact right time.

The front door flew open, and Spencer crashed through the parlor and fell into her lap. His tiny arms squeezed her torso. "Afternoon, Mama."

She kissed the crown of his head, inhaling the clean scent of him. "Had fun with the Whitsetts, I see. Why don't you go up and ask Celia if she plans to come down for lunch?" The girl had to be hungry.

He gave her a quick peck on the cheek and ran up the stairs as if a bear chased him.

Leah's chuckle sounded from the open doorway. "My girls never had so much energy."

Annie let out a puff of air. "I wish I had a fraction of it. Come in. Thank you for letting him get some of that energy out."

"I'm afraid I actually made it worse. He can stuff more sticky rolls in that lean, little body than I thought." Leah laughed as she stepped in and pulled off her bonnet. "How'd last night go?"

Annie's palm flew up to cover the trail of kisses she could still feel on her neck.

"Hmmm. I take it you didn't waste the entire night lecturing a wayward child?"

Annie popped off her chair and knocked her pen onto the floor. Bending over to retrieve it, she tried to come up with a response to Leah's tease, but nothing seemed appropriate.

Too bad she hadn't a reason to stay under the desk. Her face was so warm, her cheeks were likely a deep crimson. She came up, careful to keep her face turned away from Leah as much as possible, and set the pen down on paper.

Leah's laughter chimed through the room. "Annie, girl, you act as if you've been caught in an indiscretion." She came over and put a hand on her shoulder. "After all that's happened, I'm glad you've found some happiness."

"So you don't fault me for not observing the one year and one day mourning period Mrs. Tate and—?"

"Since when should anyone listen to relationship advice from Mrs. Tate?" She tsked. "If the Lord hands you a blessing, you don't spit on it for the sake of good standing with a bunch of women who'll never be happy no matter how many of their lines you toe."

Annie glanced behind her to make certain Spencer hadn't returned. "But still, in some ways, it feels wrong." She lowered her voice and willed herself not to blush. "I'm not exactly in love—"

"Love comes in many forms." Leah's hand squeezed her shoulder as the now familiar whine of the back door sounded. "Including that of a busy man leaving work to have lunch with his family." Leah backed up a little to wave into the kitchen. "Good afternoon, Jacob," she called through the hallway.

A warm shiver radiated from Annie's chest into her fingers. She hadn't expected him home until this evening. Her feelings were not as collected as she'd wanted them to be upon his return.

"Hello, Leah." He walked purposefully into the room, his gaze pinned on Annie. He stopped in front of her, his brown eyes looking more like fresh brewed coffee than their normal creamy brown. "Anne."

Though Leah was still present, his voice had dipped intimately low.

"I best be going." Leah sounded distant. "Thanks for letting me play mother hen to Spencer."

Annie tore her gaze from Jacob to find Leah backing away. "I hope we didn't put you out too much on such short notice."

"Not at all. Don't hesitate to send Spencer back to me any time you have a need." Her mouth tweaked up into a wicked grin as she snatched up her hat. "I'll let myself out."

Annie stared at her friend's back until it disappeared behind the door.

"Is it time for lunch?" Jacob twirled her around by her shoulders. His gaze lowered to her neck. "I'm hungry."

Oh my, was he in a mood.

She looked toward the empty stairwell. "The children will be down any second. If I'd known you were coming—"

He slid his arms about her waist. "Nothing would've kept me away today."

A door above banged, and footsteps scurried overhead.

Jacob pulled her in closer, his eyes dark and intense.

Wasn't he paying attention to the thumping on the stairs?

"With you in my arms, the weight of the world has slid right off my shoulders." His face nuzzled into the curve of her neck.

She flattened her palms against his chest. "The children," she whispered.

"So?" His breath tickled her skin, and his arms tightened about her.

Her pulse beat erratically against his lips, and she whispered sharply. "It's not proper for them to see us like this."

Jacob shook his head and blinked. Had she just said embracing her wasn't proper? What silly rule was she following now? "A man's allowed to hold his wife in his own home."

"But—"

"Didn't Gregory kiss you in front of the children?"

She stilled. "Occasionally, yes, but that was..." She averted her eyes and her voice dropped. "…different."

He released her.

His fool tongue.

He knew another man had loved her, known her, held her, and he'd sworn he'd never force her to compare. And yet, he just had.

"I see." He swallowed the lump in his throat.

He'd not realized hearing where he didn't measure up would hurt so much.

"I'm not sure you do." Her gaze darted to the stairwell.

His heart clenched. A hug and a kiss in front of the children after last night was nothing indecent.

Unless, she regretted...

He tensed. "Last night—"

"It's not that," she whispered.

"Then what?" He took a step back and crossed his arms. The stress he'd shed last night returned, digging its fingers back into his neck and shoulder muscles.

"I want to make sure Celia's in a good place before…" she whispered as the shuffling of feet sounded on the stairs. "Well, I'm not certain this is the best time for them to see how our relationship has changed. You see, Gregory wasn't—"

"Hey, Pa." Spencer hopped off the last stair, and Jacob cast him a weak smile. He tipped his head in the direction of the kitchen, and the boy obeyed without hesitation.

"I suppose timing is my Achilles' heel." Jacob fixed his eyes on the ceiling where the oil lamp's soot had built up. He shouldn't have come home acting like a love-sick schoolboy. "If I'd visited the Crawfords' northwest section last week instead of this morning, I'd have found rustlers instead of tracks. If I'd married you a week earlier, Bryant could've warned me about the loan defaulting."

If I'd waited until you loved me to show you how much I love you, you'd be counting down the seconds until you were back in my arms rather than worrying about when it would be proper to be so.

A failure all around, that's what he was.

She laid her hand on his arm, and his bicep contracted at her touch. "I just don't want her to think—"

He cut her off with an abrupt shake of the head. "Sometimes I wish you'd worry about what I think."

She snatched her hand back as if burned.

He sighed. She wouldn't be Annie if she wasn't concerned about what Celia and Spencer thought too.

A loose board creaked behind him.

Celia stood with her arms crossed, head hung in defeat. "I'm hungry so I'll talk now."

Spencer's head poked back through the kitchen doorway. "Are you eating with us, Pa?"

"If your mother deems it proper." His bitter words hit their mark judging by the flinch on Annie's face. He rubbed his hand across his eyes. "I'm sorry, Anne, I should've held my tongue." He gritted his teeth to keep from saying anything more until he'd processed her rejection better.

"Great." Spencer nearly bounced back into the kitchen.

Celia gave her mother a probing look before following after her brother.

His first cross word with Annie had been smack in front of the children. Bad timing indeed.

Shaking his head at himself, he followed Annie into the kitchen where she shuffled to the counter and cut into a loaf of fresh bread.

He sank into his chair and propped his head in his hand, elbow on the table. What a fool he'd been this morning while out tracking, unable to concentrate reliving the memories of last night, completely preoccupied with a woman who hadn't been looking forward to his return nearly as much as he'd hoped—if at all.

"Did you know Bryant has two swords?" Spencer leaned across the table. "I got to hold one."

Celia glanced up from her seat with a frown. "Do we have to talk before I eat or can we wait 'til later?"

Annie handed out plates, and Jacob just stared at Celia.

Of all the times for the girl to come down.

The girl's scowl died on her face.

Spencer took a bite of bread the second his mother handed him a slice. "An' den dis morning I saw a fwog on da—"

"Don't speak with your mouth full, son. And we haven't yet prayed." Jacob waited for the boy to swallow then looked at his daughter. "I don't feel like talking right now, Celia."

"So then we don't have to?"

He wanted to swipe off her triumphant grin. "No, we'll talk. When we're both ready. After lunch, you'll return to your room, and perhaps before supper—"

"Unfair!" Celia clanked her fork on her plate.

"Celia." Annie's voice snapped. "Leave him alone. For once, think about someone other than yourself."

"Fine." Celia snatched up her sandwich and milk glass. "I'll go lock myself back into the tower. When the marshal decides to follow his own rules, let me know." She stomped out of the room and up the stairs.

"Celia—" Annie started.

Jacob grabbed her sleeve to hold her back. "Let her go."

Annie hesitated a moment, but then took a seat and bowed her head without looking at him.

He opened his mouth, but clamped it shut. A mealtime prayer was beyond his ability right now. The only things he wanted to ask of the Lord were inappropriate to voice in front of Spencer—especially if simply kissing his wife in front of the children was taboo. He folded his arms across his chest to keep from smashing something.

Annie uttered a quick blessing and turned to Spencer. "Now, tell me about this frog."

Jacob chewed on his sandwich, trying not to look at her. With such an intimate knowledge of her imbedded in his brain, what would he do if she wanted to remain in separate rooms?

He'd noticed she'd left before first light this morning, but he'd only thought she'd needed to visit the necessary.

But she hadn't returned—not that he'd thought much of it since her things were in her room. But what if she hadn't come back to his room because she was ashamed of doing what she thought improper?

Surely, that wasn't it. She'd only said she wasn't ready for him to demonstrate his feelings in front of the children.

But what if she wanted to act in front of anybody and everybody as if nothing at all had happened between them?

His wife straining against his embrace had pained him like no wound ever had.

He wasn't sure he wanted to experience that feeling ever again.

CHAPTER THIRTY-TWO

Jacob fiddled with the lantern's flame in his office, making the shadows of the jail cell bars blur, then sharpen against the walls. Should he extinguish the light or reread the stack of wanted posters that had been delivered this afternoon? He fingered the top poster, but chose the *Daily Ricochet* to flip through instead. He took up his pencil and traced the oval around the tiny blurb he'd already circled a half-dozen times today.

A ranch along the Laramie for auction—horses, cattle, equipment—$5,234.18 owed.

Annie was worried about keeping her cattle if they didn't buy land soon. Celia pined for her father's ranch. He had coveted property ever since his parents had sold the ranch he'd expected to inherit—enough so he'd married a stranger.

But that wasn't what he desired any longer. Not most of all, anyway. He wanted that stranger to be happy he'd married her—to be happy with him alone.

His pencil lead gouged into the paper and broke. He sighed and threw the pencil into the trash. His bank account boasted $4,500. Attending the auction would be a waste of time.

The incessant chirp of a cricket holed up in the wall was

annoying him, now that the summer sun had buried itself below the horizon. No legitimate paperwork held him here. He'd read what law books he had twice over, finding nothing that would help him get back Annie's land, and he'd already written up a letter inquiring after a lawyer in Denver after he'd received the news that his father's old lawyer had passed on and couldn't even give him a hint on whether or not what he was looking for was something he might find. In fact, the work he'd done today would probably have to be redone tomorrow—his mind hadn't stayed focused all evening.

Jacob fingered a drawing of himself atop Duchess. His oddly long stick arm was pointing a gun at ten bad guys in black blindfolds with cut-out holes for their huge eyes. The artist's name was scrawled proudly across Duchess's hooves—Spencer Hendrix.

Surely the boy's opinion of him would plummet if he spent the day watching him rake streets, serve never-ending petty fines, and track rustlers but never catch a one.

He rubbed his temples. Why couldn't he find the rustlers? Did they camp in another county? Were his tracking abilities worse than he'd reckoned? Did a scout watch his every move? Who had shot at him, and why?

Someone was slipping him notes and he'd yet to figure out who that was, so there could be a whole slew of people watching him that he was unaware of.

Jacob grabbed his keys, locked up the office, and plodded home, unable to enjoy the brisk night air. How many prayers could he utter before he stood at his door? He'd need every one to give him the strength to cross the threshold.

Oh Lord, how can I live with a woman who might never love me? I'm certainly not going to win her by being the best marshal this side of the Mississippi—either side actually.

Was I wrong to marry her?

He kicked at a stone glistening in the moonlight.

I thought I was right. I prayed, and you didn't stop me. Did I miss something? It hurts, God, it really does. I know I need to talk to her, but if the conversation goes like it did this afternoon—

He stopped in front of the shadow of the church, crossed his arms, and stared at his enormous house. A dim light burned in the kitchen, but the children's rooms were dark. His shoulders slacked, and a pent-up breath escaped. Regardless of what had occurred earlier with Annie, he should've been home to tuck the children into bed.

They needed a father, even if their mother didn't seem to want a husband.

Opening the back door slowly, he peeped inside. At his place at the table, a plate covered by an upside down one sat next to a sweaty water glass. He walked inside and gently pushed the door closed. He uncovered the dish and touched the potatoes —still warm.

Annie's robed figure walked through the parlor doorway and stopped. Her hair flowed around her shoulders, wispy and soft, like lofty ribbon clouds on a sun-drenched day.

He tugged off his hat.

"Would you like me to stoke the fire and rewarm your supper?" She glided into the room, but came no closer than the other end of the table.

"No, thank you." He set his hat aside and unbelted his holster. "I'll eat it how I found it."

She came around the table and pulled his plate toward her. "It's not a problem."

"Yes, it is." He laid a hand on her arm to halt her progress. A hum buzzed across his palm. He snatched his hand back and took the plate. "A fire would be inconvenient. I've troubled you enough by coming home late." He sat and picked up his fork. "No need to fuss over me."

He sat and bowed his head, more in hopes she'd see his gesture as a signal to retire than because he needed to pray at that very moment. Well, perhaps he did need to pray, considering he wanted to shut her out—Annie had hurt him plenty of times in the past two months when she'd shut him out. He should know better.

She stood beside him for a few seconds, then sat in the chair to his right.

He sighed and prayed aloud. "Father God, help me to never be this late coming home again. Help us both to know how to proceed with the marriage we find ourselves in. Thank you for my wife, who saw to my need for food. Please give me your strength. May you lead us on paths of righteousness. Amen."

"Amen," she whispered.

He glanced at her. "I'm sorry for staying at work so late."

"I understand."

She couldn't. She didn't know him well enough to understand why he'd stayed away. Yet he nodded at her response to keep from having to explain right now. He picked up his fork.

"Can we talk?"

Jacob swallowed his first bite and took his time wiping his mouth. Did she expect dinner talk or deep conversation? He wasn't sure he could handle either at the moment. "Do you mind if I say no?"

Her mouth twitched as she gazed at him. Her amber eyes exuded no malice, but they looked sad.

He bit the inside of his cheeks to keep from giving in. They probably ought to talk, but with how he'd been unable to hold his tongue this afternoon and how he'd not completely worked through his hurt this evening, it was probably best not to. "Not tonight, anyway."

She didn't respond for a moment, but then reached for her knitting basket. Her quilted robe gaped, displaying the hand-worked lace edging of her nightgown's neckline.

He looked away, stabbed his pork steak with his fork, and attacked the meat slab with his knife. "You don't have to sit with me since it's late. I'll wash the dishes."

"All right then." She stopped unwinding her yarn and returned her knitting needles to the basket.

He held his breath as she leaned near. "Good night, Jacob." A light kiss on his cheek stopped his food from continuing its downward path.

He coughed, trying not to choke. "Good night, Anne."

She swept past and headed up the stairs.

He leaned back in his chair and stared at his food.

Within minutes, her footsteps shuffled softly overhead but he couldn't decipher which direction they went.

If she chose her room, he'd feel as if he hadn't measured up. If she chose his, how did she expect him to act?

A marriage of convenience indeed.

All the courting nonsense he'd hoped to skip—the hesitation to display one's feelings, the fear of being rejected, the months, perhaps years, of waiting—hadn't been made any easier by starting off with his grandmother's ring on her finger.

After washing the tableware, he swiped the counters and the stove. He looked around for other things to clean, but more dawdling wouldn't stop tonight from coming. After throwing the dirty dishcloth onto the laundry pile, he drove himself upstairs to his room to discover his fate.

Empty.

He sagged against his bedroom door's frame and looked across the hall. No light seeped out from under her door. Everything quiet. He shuffled to his bed and sat. If only he'd behaved better at lunch, hadn't just now refused to talk to her, she might be curled up beside him.

But did he want to take back anything he'd said?

After working off his boots, he settled himself against his headboard and grabbed his Bible to study the verses he'd read a dozen times at work this evening.

Let the husband render unto the wife due benevolence: and likewise also the wife unto the husband. The wife hath not power over her own body, but the husband: and likewise also the husband hath not power of his own body, but the wife. Defraud ye not one the other, except it be with consent for a time, that ye may give yourselves to fasting and prayer; and come together again, that Satan tempt you not for your incontinency.

Did Paul's words apply to a wife who wasn't in love?

He dropped his Bible onto his chest and stared at the cock-eyed pillow next to him. Its slipped casing exposed the blue and white striped ticking. Last night had changed everything. He desired her even more, yet he wanted her to respond to him out of love—not duty.

He closed his eyes and tilted his head upward.

God, when she comes to me again, give me the grace to accept her without spite.

He fingered the leather binding of his Bible as he stared out the window.

He was a fool. He ought to have asked her to come in.

After the cold shoulder he'd given her this evening, how could he have expected her to choose any differently?

The downstairs clock chimed eleven, and he set his Bible aside. It was too late to talk tonight. Surely sleep would help clear both of their heads, and they could talk come morning.

He stripped to his drawers and rolled back onto the bed.

His door opened.

A light, hesitant step creaked upon his floorboards, and the glow of the moon played in her auburn hair.

Maybe it wasn't too late.

"I wanted to know if you'd want me in here." A tremble marred her whispered words. She took another step, and her thin silhouette disappeared into shadow.

The corner of his lips turned up, and the lightness of his heart surprised him. She was willing to move in?

He'd almost ruined this new step in their relationship by nursing his wounded pride.

"I know you're put out with me, but in light of last night—"

So he hadn't been the only one whose thoughts kept returning to last night.

"Not that I need to be in here, if you, well..."

Her words hit him like a pail of cold water.

"Not that I need to be in here."

Did she feel nothing for him?

He rubbed the heels of his hands against his eyes. If she didn't want to be with him, why had she come? He took a deep, cleansing breath and lowered his hands.

Regardless, he still wanted her here, and the scripture he'd read several times today eradicated any reason to deny her a place beside him. He scooted to the edge of the bed and flipped back the opposite side's covers. She slid in, but he remained upright against the headboard.

"Good night, Jacob."

He grunted an answer.

Good night?

Highly unlikely.

Saying no more, she tucked her pillow beneath her head and curled into a ball.

He laced his fingers atop his chest and stared out his moonlit window. For the past two months, he'd thought living in the same house with a woman was hard. But having her lying next to him in bed, ensconced in layers of clothing as was *proper*?

Far, far worse.

Sunlight pried Annie's eyelids apart, and she moaned. The comfortable bed tick called her back to sleep. Despite the muggy air blanketing her, she snuggled closer to the warmth of her husband. If she got up to open a window, the solace of half-slumber would disappear. She reached across his chest and clamped down.

He could never drag himself out of bed early to attend the animals when she wrapped her arms around him.

The door creaked open, and Annie closed her eyes tight.

No. No children. Spencer's pout could uncurl her firmest

grip. She'd do anything for those bright blues surrounded by long lashes—so she wouldn't look.

All she wanted was ten more minutes. Hopefully Gregory would shoo them out.

"Do you know where Mama is?" Spencer's bright voice invaded her sleepy cocoon.

The firm mattress, the smell of the sheets, the sun spilling in through four windows...

Jacob.

Her eyes snapped wide open. She snatched her hand from Jacob's bare chest and pushed away.

His muscular arm pressed her body back against his side. His chest hairs tickled her nose.

She shallowed her breathing to keep from sneezing.

Shuffling feet sounded at the door. "We can't find—" Celia's voice descended an octave. "Ma."

Celia's tone deflated Annie's lungs. Clamped against Jacob, she glanced over his chest toward her children. Spencer's eyebrows puckered, and Celia's expression was exactly what Annie had feared.

The girl spun on her heel and exited the bedroom.

Spencer took a tentative step forward. "Mama? Are you sleeping in here now?"

"Yes." Jacob's gravelly hum reverberated against her ear. "This is her room now. Just like when she used to share a room with your first pa. But you need to knock before you enter, and that goes for anyone's room." His voice was firm but reassuring. "But since you're already here, what is it you need of your mother?"

Spencer shrugged. "I'm hungry. Celia wouldn't make me flapjacks. Said Mama would."

"She'll be down soon, son. Grab some bread if you're hungry."

"All right, Pa."

The door clicked shut, and Annie pushed against him. "You

shouldn't have kept me flat against you." His arm released her, and she put space between them. She could still feel the warmth of his taut chest muscles against her body.

"Why not?"

He looked as if he really didn't know.

"It's indecent." Her cheeks warmed. "In front of the kids, at least."

He turned to face her and propped himself up on his elbow, his morning vocal chords warmed with friction. "Did you never see your parents kiss? Hug?"

Not that she could recall. Had he seen his parents do so?

Her parents hadn't so much as fought in front of her and her sisters, though they surely had since she could always tell when Mother was put out with Father.

And Gregory had never been one for publicly showing affection. He may have kissed her a few times in front of the children over the years, but they'd been nothing overtly amorous, never had they seen—

"I take your silence to mean no."

"You can't tell me you think children should see ... what belongs in a bedroom."

"Didn't you hear me tell Spencer he should knock?" He flipped off his covers, grabbed his slacks off a chair, and stepped into them.

She sat, dragging the quilt up with her. "Then why did you trap me against you?"

He stopped pulling his pants together in the front and stared at her. A twinge in his cheek gave away his irritation.

She crossed her arms to ward off the chill. What had she said to cause that look?

"If it's proper for you to be in here, then it's proper for them to know where you sleep." He buttoned his pants and reached for a shirt draped over the footboard. "We're husband and wife whether or not you want to be."

She frowned. Did he think she wasn't thankful he'd married her? "I—"

"When Celia and Spencer are older and contemplating their first night with their spouse, I don't want them to recall this moment and believe there should be any shame in the physical side of marriage." He tucked his shirttails in with a stabbing motion.

Her shoulders sagged. Shame? Shame sounded so harsh, yet she couldn't deny the fire still blazing in her cheeks.

He fumbled with his flipped collar. "In the eyes of God, there's nothing wrong with you being in here, but I have to wonder—" He clamped his jaw, and without looking back, left the room.

She pulled her knees up to her chest and hugged herself. She knew there was nothing wrong with her being in here, but Jacob did things so differently, made her reconsider her life so thoroughly, that she wasn't sure she'd ever done anything right at all.

CHAPTER THIRTY-THREE

The minutes-old memory of her family looking at her with disappointment made Annie want to pull Jacob's covers over her head and pretend this morning hadn't happened. Going downstairs and seeing the betrayal in Celia's eyes, the confusion in Spencer's, or the anger in Jacob's again, was the last thing she wanted to do.

Annie dragged herself from under the covers and to the washstand. She smacked her cheeks with the tepid water, then gripped the porcelain basin.

She'd been convinced coming to Jacob last night had been the right thing to do until she was caught in a position she'd never been in before.

Sure, her children had occasionally visited her and Gregory's bedroom, but never when she'd been pressed up against his bare chest.

Jacob's manner of expressing his love for her would look far different than Gregory's ever had, and for Celia's sake she'd hoped to hold off displaying how quickly things were progressing between them until her daughter's animosity toward Jacob had lessened.

How Celia had just looked at her, as if she'd betrayed Gregory, was exactly what she'd hoped to avoid.

And the hurt in Jacob's eyes ... She should've insisted on talking with him last night, but she'd never seen him upset before. She'd figured submitting to his request for time to simmer down wouldn't hurt anything, because if she knew him at all, come morning, he'd have been apologetic, telling her what was bothering him, and asking after her feelings like he so often had.

If only this morning had gone as she'd thought it would.

She returned to sit on Jacob's side of the bed and squeezed her forehead with her hands. What was she to do now? Jacob would likely forgive and forget, but Celia had always responded better to heart-to-heart talks with Gregory than with her.

She flipped through Jacob's Bible toward James, desperate for guidance.

If any of you lack wisdom, let him ask of God, that giveth to all men liberally, and upbraideth not; and it shall be given him. But let him ask in faith, nothing wavering. For he that wavereth is like a wave of the sea driven with the wind and tossed.

If her feelings were anything—sloshed and tossed about would certainly describe them.

Lying on the quilt, she splayed her hand in the oblong indentation on Jacob's side of the mattress. Her dream of Gregory this morning had been all too real. His burly, hairy chest. His riotous red hair cropped short on his head and face.

And though she could still recall how the scents of cattle, mud, and rain had clung to Gregory ever since they'd moved out here, she couldn't remember his underlying aroma.

She bunched Jacob's pillow under her head and rubbed at her eyes.

Jacob smelled of spices, moss, and ... Jacob.

Lord, I loved Gregory, but I need help letting his memory go. I do feel as though I'm betraying him when I love—

She bit her lip and the tears rolled down her face. She rolled over to nuzzle her face into Jacob's pillow and deeply inhale his scent.

She loved Jacob.

Loved.

And so quickly and deeply that she worried her love for Gregory had been but a shallow thing.

The crash of pans and the stench of burning butter wafted up from downstairs.

Jacob shouldn't have to feed the children, especially after how she'd hurt him.

But she couldn't go downstairs yet. Right now, it was more important that she pray for the wisdom she desperately needed for having a talk with her daughter and making amends with her husband.

Jacob scraped the dark brown circles off the skillet and flipped the flapjack. He rushed to throw more butter into the pan before he charred the other side of Spencer's breakfast.

The boy would be disappointed enough that his sister and mother had decided to stay upstairs, so these flapjacks needed to be good to make up for it.

A pool of maple syrup ought to make them palatable.

Spencer finished setting the table, sat in his chair, and picked up the old Jacob's ladder Annie had unearthed in one of her cleaning frenzies.

The toy was one of the few things Jacob had carried with him after leaving Texas and wandering from ranch to ranch until he settled here with his old war buddy, Bryant. Silly thing for a man to cart around, but he couldn't part with the plaything. A cowhand, who'd taken a shine to him years ago, had made it for him, declaring it unconscionable for a boy named Jacob not to own a Jacob's ladder.

The tic-tic-tic of the flat, interconnected blocks climbing down one another soothed his nerves.

Just as God had known Jacob in the Bible, so too did He see into the heart of each person in this household.

Though the inner workings of his wife's heart were hard to understand, if she'd come from a family that hadn't been affectionate, if letting herself love with abandon was a foreign concept, he could understand a little of why she was having such a hard time letting him get close to her.

Yet, it still hurt. Two men vied for room in her heart, and he was currently the one out in the cold. He was obviously nothing like Gregory.

Of course, he'd already known that in a way. He'd met Gregory on a few occasions, a man's man. Tough and strong. Only said what needed to be said and then was done with discussion.

He'd not ventured to think Gregory had treated his wife in the same manner. His parents had been enamored with each other. Countless times he and his brothers had pretended to gag at the long kisses Pa would lay on Ma just to make them squirm.

And come to think of it, though he knew Annie loved her children, she didn't do a lot of touching and hugging with them either. It wasn't just him.

Sliding a well-done flapjack onto a plate, he handed the food across the table to Spencer. "Here you go, son."

The boy wrinkled his nose at the dark circle.

"Just cut off anything too burnt."

Annie padded into the kitchen on bare feet. She smiled at Spencer but wrinkled her nose at his breakfast.

Her gaze found Jacob's, her eyes wide like a doe wary of a hunter's presence.

No matter how completely befuddled he was by her constant pushing him away, he'd not force her to do anything that would make her uncomfortable. Did she not know that?

Sure, he'd voiced some strong words to her earlier, but would she ever stop being so guarded around him?

He stared at the burning butter in the pan for a moment, then held out the spatula in surrender. "I think we'd all appreciate it if you took over."

Nodding, she took the utensil and stiffened when he bent to kiss her on the cheek.

He sighed and walked to the table.

Annie spooned out more batter. "Where's Celia? She ought to eat."

Jacob stopped mid-sit. "I'll get her."

Celia had said she'd be willing to talk this morning. Maybe he could at least fix one thing before he left for work.

Trying to hum as she finished frying the flapjack, Annie lost track of the melody and had to restart.

The fast-paced thumps of her husband's boots on the stairs ended her absent-minded humming. She turned toward the stairs and frowned. Was he running?

He appeared at the bottom of the stairwell and strode across the kitchen, straight for his gun belt. Grabbing it, he slung it around his waist.

"What's wrong?" The acrid smell of burnt cake curled up from the skillet, so she flipped the pancake over while staring at the bleak expression on his face. Her heart raced like a runaway stage. "Where are you going?"

"She's gone." He shrugged into his coat and grabbed his hat.

"Gone?"

He covered the distance between them in two long steps and took one of her hands in his. "Out the window. She evidently climbed down the trellis."

When would Celia's impetuous decisions ever cease to

surprise her? "I suppose we'll have to switch their rooms once she returns. Spencer's window's painted shut."

A quivering smile formed on Jacob's unshaven face. "Thanks for being willing to enforce my disciplinary choices, but I think you were right. I was too strict."

"Even so, she shouldn't have left without permission."

"You don't understand." He looked deep into her eyes. "She took her belongings. All of them."

An unseen hand clamped around her throat. "She ran away?"

The hurt in Celia's eyes this morning had warned her that her daughter was about to throw a fit—but run away?

"Yes." His voice wasn't much more than a whisper.

Annie dropped into the nearby chair. The flowery pattern on her skirt seemed to be moving in dizzying circles.

He clasped her upper arm. "If you wouldn't mind throwing something together for me to eat, I'm heading out to search for her."

What if...?

Jacob crouched in front of her. "Anne?"

"I'm sorry." She stood, but too quickly, for she had to lean against the table to steady herself. "Food. You need food."

He clasped her other arm and leaned down to look at her, his eyes filled with worry.

What was he seeing that made him look like that?

Despair, of course.

Annie let herself fall against him, drawing solace over how quickly his arms wrapped around her. "Please. Please, find her."

If only she could start the morning all over again.

But this morning wouldn't have happened if not for last night—and Celia had obviously not been in favor of how she'd chosen to spend it.

Yet how would continuing to cater to Celia do them any good?

Jacob's embrace tightened. "She couldn't have gotten far."

She burrowed into his chest and let his warmth infuse her for the briefest of seconds before stepping back, wanting to give him a confident smile, but unable to move her lips in the right direction.

He ran a knuckle down the side of her face. "It'll be all right."

She gave him a small nod and began methodically honeying a small stack of flapjacks and folding them in half while he filled his canteen with water.

He quickly kissed both her and Spencer, took a bite of his makeshift breakfast sandwich, and rushed out the door.

She followed him out to the porch's edge, watching him rush down the street until he disappeared into the early morning bustle.

Spencer grabbed her hand. "Will Celia be all right?" His eyes had lost their ever-present gleam.

She forced a bright smile. "Your sister may be foolhardy, but she can take care of herself. When we lived on the ranch, she was gone for hours at a time, remember?"

Taking Spencer by the shoulders, Annie turned him toward the table. "When you finish eating, we'll look about town for her. She's around somewhere."

But if she wasn't?

The plains were vast and the train could take her anywhere.

Annie forced herself not to run back out on the porch and holler for Jacob. If her daughter was rash enough to decide to run away in the space of an hour, she was hot-headed enough to sneak into an empty boxcar.

Surely Jacob had realized that. Probably why he'd rushed from the house.

Spencer ate with a quickness that indicated he knew there was no time to dally, and yet, she couldn't sit still as she picked at the burnt pancakes Jacob had made.

If Celia left town without much money, the brothels and gambling halls lining the tracks from town to town could easily derail a headstrong girl with an empty stomach and the hubris of the prodigal son.

Finding her daughter before she did something irreversibly stupid was completely outside her control.

God alone could protect her girl.

But if He didn't?

What was she supposed to do?

Laying her head in the crook of her arm, she closed her eyes to stanch the threatening tears.

Spencer nudged her elbow. "Mama?"

Swallowing hard, she sniffed and surreptitiously wiped her face across her sleeve before looking up at Spencer.

"Shouldn't we pray?"

"Yes." But though she swallowed again, she couldn't voice more words.

Spencer bowed his head and his little face screwed up in concentration. "God Jesus, bring Celia back. I don't want her gone forever though she picks on me all the time. Thank you for the food even if it's burnt, and help Mama not be so sad. Bring Pa back safe too and ... and lead us through the paths of right stuff and trust you and give you glory forever. Amen."

She couldn't help but smile at Spencer's attempt at imitating the way Jacob often ended his prayers.

And yet, Spencer's garbled words addressed her uncertainties. She needed to focus on doing the "right stuff"—and trust God to do the rest. Choosing her next steps by whatever would glorify God most. No matter the outcome.

How had worrying about Mother's or Mrs. Tate's opinion of her marriage glorify God? She'd told Mrs. Tate she was thankful for His provision, but if she'd been truly grateful, why had she worried about what to do with the gift rather than just enjoy and praise God for it?

How did beating herself up over the choices she'd made—which may or may not have led to Celia's running away—glorify God? Modeling for Spencer how one trusted God by obedience to His Word no matter what happened would've been better.

And how did holding on to her cattle and pining for her lost ranch glorify God? She didn't deserve Jacob, his love, his provision, or this beautiful home, but she'd miraculously been given them all, and she should be investing her time and money here.

Though she seemed to have failed at most everything up until now, her next step only needed to be what would give God the most glory.

Not just because she felt like it. Not only when she was promised success. But because He was worthy of it. Because it was right.

"C'mon, Spencer." She wiped her eyes one last time and took his hand. "Let's go find Celia. And if we don't, we'll pray God keeps her safe."

CHAPTER THIRTY-FOUR

Celia unpacked her belongings onto the floor of a dilapidated covered wagon. Her hands wouldn't stop shaking, so she stopped to take deep breaths and let them out slowly.

Didn't help.

This wagon was a sorry excuse for a shelter.

And though Daniel had sworn nothing bad would happen to her out here, Timothy's expression made her doubt that promise was worth much.

She trusted Daniel well enough, but these strangers? Without another woman around? Daniel would leave at the end of the day, and then it would be just her and two scruffy men, camping out in the middle of nowhere.

She stared at her folded quilt, but decided not to pull anything else out. She got up and pushed back the canvas flap.

Daniel had said this old wagon would be for her use alone, but a rotting wagon bed with a canvas roof was no barricade against a determined intruder, and the next site might not even have a shelter.

If she'd been smart, she would've confiscated one of

Daddy's guns before leaving. She patted her boot, confirming her jackknife was still there.

Knife or no, camping no longer seemed a good idea. She didn't want to go back to the marshal's, but neither did she want to leave one trap to end up in another.

After climbing over the wagon bed, she cupped her hands around her mouth. "Daniel!"

The water rushing around the river bend dampened her holler.

Fifty yards away, a flash of russet hair momentarily appeared above the silvery-gray sagebrush edging the river.

She let out a slow breath. Though he hadn't heard her, he was at least still here.

She headed toward the rocky bank where the small group of men were hunched over, knee deep in the Laramie. Daniel's stocky build and Timothy's dark, stringy hair distinguished her friends from the two older men working with them. The adults were so filthy, it was a shame only their legs and arms sloshed about in the river.

As she approached, the gaunt one with short-cropped black hair, Rufus, stood and sloshed toward the bank, pan in hand. The shorter man, Guy, sputtered when Rufus splashed him as he passed, then hauled off and smacked Rufus with his empty sluicing pan.

Rufus held on tight to his own pan and stomped the rest of the way to shore, before leaning down to grab a rock and lobbing it at Guy, hitting him hard in the lower back.

The two charged at each other, cursing like they had the day they'd fought over Miss McGill's fundraiser basket.

Guy grabbed Rufus and shoved him underwater. Rufus's limbs churning up the river muffled their cursing.

Rounding a boulder close to the bank, she caught Daniel looking her way and glared at him. With a tilt of her head, she gestured toward the two men fighting like children.

He only shrugged and went back to panning, as if an all-out brawl was nothing out of the ordinary.

He couldn't care a whit for her if he left her out here with men as immature as these two.

Even if he was worried about his pa finding her hiding on his property, surely nothing his pa would do to him would be worse than what might befall her here.

She looked east. She'd passed this lonely spot of river before. This bend couldn't be too far from Daddy's old ranch.

But it was far enough away that no one would hear her scream.

She glanced back at the wagon, shreds of the canvas roof flapping in the breeze.

Ignoring the two men wrestling on the riverbank, she strode straight into the freezing water toward Daniel.

He didn't turn, so she thunked him on the back.

He jumped, dropping his wash pan. Lunging into the water, he snatched it back up.

"What were you thinking?" He shoved her away and stumbled out past the newly disturbed riverbed muck clouding the water. "Now I have to start over." He scooped up new sand and swirled the water. "When you start panning, you'll realize how much I want to sock you right now."

She crossed her arms and stepped out of his reach. "I'm going home with you tonight."

"Nuh-uh, my old man's been dogging my every step since your daddy told him to keep a sharp eye—"

"He's not my daddy." She stomped her foot, shooting an icy fountain up under her skirts. "And I'll sleep in an outbuilding. Your pa'll never know."

The two men behind her had stopped fighting, but when she looked over her shoulder, the taller one was watching her. Guy had already returned to his panning.

She gave Rufus a steely glare, but his gaze only dipped down to where her skirts disappeared into the water and then came back up, stopping on her still-flat chest.

She turned away and crossed her arms. "Put me up, or I'll tell."

Daniel straightened, towering over her. "Tell what?"

"You know what. But I'll keep my mouth shut if you hide me on your property." She glanced over her shoulder again.

Rufus still stared at her, the curve to his lips more sinister than friendly.

Her stomach twisted.

Timothy slugged through the water and gave her a slight nod. "Let her go home with you, Daniel." He bent over, pretending to add sand to his pan. "I don't trust them," he whispered.

"Who said I trusted them?" Daniel snarled under his breath.

"Then let her stay with you."

Daniel's mouth turned into a frown. "Fine."

"Thank you." She squeezed his shoulder.

He shrugged out of her grip. "But if Pa catches you, I'll deny everything."

"I wouldn't have expected anything different." She surveyed the strange equipment, stacks of bowls, and wooden boxes. "Now tell me how to go about this gold finding, and I'll get to work."

Timothy shook his head. "No girl should be out here doing this."

What? He thought sloshing water was too hard for a woman?

"Forget staying with Daniel and just go home. Your pa's the marshal. He'll be out looking—"

"He's not my pa," she sputtered. "And you're just worried I'll out-pan ya."

She snatched Timothy's sieve and dunked it under the water as she'd seen Daniel do. "Besides, I got nothing to go home for."

Her heart sank with the words, but they were true enough.

So she needed to get some coins in her pocket. Otherwise she'd never be able to do as she pleased.

When the office cleared, Bryant pulled out the questions McGill had given him on yet another property and scribbled down the last set of details he'd been asked to find.

A bachelor, Arnold Jetts, with few financial assets and no connections, owned land abutting the mayor's property. The parcel contained a good many acres of riverbank along a rocky bend of the Laramie.

Mr. Jetts better have God on his side or the mayor would be propping his feet up on the man's kitchen table by next month.

In the hallway, McGill's familiar heavy footfalls sounded. Bryant's fingers itched to crumple up the list, but handing over this information wasn't illegal—even if he had a hunch on why McGill was asking for it.

The office door swung open and hit the wall with a bounce. McGill strode straight for Bryant. "Got my information?"

He hesitated for a second, then slid the paper toward his boss and retreated for his desk. If he didn't discuss the property with McGill, maybe he'd not feel guilty when he recorded the land's deed changing hands.

McGill leaned against the hip-high counter and lowered his spectacles to read.

Bryant tried to concentrate on his ledgers, but McGill's occasional satisfied humming made the numbers uncooperative.

"Looks good." McGill pushed himself to a vertical position. "Seems I may be needing your help—"

"No." Bryant snapped his pencil. "I will not—"

The door flew open, sending the bell above it clanging.

Leah stumbled into the office, hand to her chest, a frown mangling her pretty face.

Bryant rushed through the short wooden doors separating

his desk from the reception area and placed a hand against one of his wife's flushed cheeks. "What's the matter?" His heart sped up to match the speed of her staggered breathing. "Are you all right?"

"I'm fine." She stepped away and looked between him and McGill. "But Celia Hendrix has run away. Jacob's gone after her, so we need everyone petitioning God for her safe return."

Bryant strode toward the back wall where his suit coat hung on a peg. He wasn't worthy to approach the throne of God anymore, but he could search. "I'll go help Jake."

He cast a glance at McGill as he threw on his coat, daring him to say no.

McGill's eyebrows crested, but he turned to Leah, assuming the air of an engrossed listener. "When did Celia disappear, Mrs. Whitsett?"

"This morning, but I only just now learned of it when Annie came to see me. Their family's already having a difficult time—what with their land and Celia's disobedience." She moved forward to flip down Bryant's lapel, then stood on tiptoe to place a kiss on his cheek. "Thank you for helping. I'm off to get more people on their knees. May the Lord help us see Celia safe in bed tonight."

Leah spun and disappeared into the courthouse hallway so quickly, he hadn't time to tell her goodbye before the door shut.

"Mighty fine woman you got there."

The hairs on Bryant's neck prickled. McGill looking at his wife was something else he could do without. "Yes, she is. I better get—"

"She's right about Mrs. Hendrix's life being no picnic." Something resembling a chuckle mixed with a snarl escaped his boss's lips. "You wouldn't want Leah experiencing that, now would you?"

Bryant glowered at McGill. "I owe you nothing. I'm done."

"I wouldn't be so sure." McGill's unblinking scowl matched

his own. "Seems to me you'll do anything to keep your woman from knowing what I know."

Bryant shook his head without breaking eye contact. "Go ahead and tell her if you want. I won't lie to her anymore. I'll risk her good opinion of me to see you hang."

"I won't hang." He crossed his arms, his legs splayed wide. "But you and I will likely end up as penitentiary roommates."

"Stuck in prison with you can't be much worse than constantly lying to the woman who thinks I outshine the moon. But I'll keep my mouth shut so I can see my youngest marry—that is, unless you keep pushing me." He poked McGill's broad chest. "So unless you want me to confess our sins to Jake, count me out."

McGill's eyes narrowed, and Bryant forced himself not to take a single step back.

A smirk suddenly contorted McGill's fleshy face. "Very well."

His boss snatched the crumpled paper off the counter, plodded into his office, and shut the door.

None of the muscles in Bryant's body relaxed.

McGill's easy capitulation only made the churning in his gut increase.

What hidden snare had he stepped into now?

CHAPTER THIRTY-FIVE

Jacob rubbed his bleary eyes before swinging open the saloon's batwing doors.

The last gambling hall in town—the last place he'd check for Celia before going home.

He'd led the town's search party until supper time and hadn't found a single clue to his stepdaughter's whereabouts.

But as much as he wanted to find her, he hoped she wasn't here.

His boot heels plunked against the plank flooring that shone under the gaudy kerosene chandelier, laughter muffling any sound he made. The smoke curling up from the handful of tables made his eyes itch even more.

To the left, a man with a dingy white beard cascading over his gut grabbed the tankard the barkeep handed him before slogging back to his corner table.

Jacob shook his head. A man that age should be wise enough not to frequent such places.

The barkeep, Big Boyd, leaned against the polished counter, hands spread wide, eyeing Jacob as he approached.

"I have na need of ye, Marshal." The blond barrel of a man cocked his head. "Unless ye're here ta drink. I heard you're a married man now. Better men have been driven ta drink for lesser reasons than that."

Jacob perched his foot on a bar stool's lower rail. "I'm looking for someone."

"The bad'uns have stayed away since I hired Peter." He pointed to a big man hunched in the corner shadows, scanning the crowd. "He's a bit simple, but he knows how ta knock heads together."

Jacob dragged his gaze away from the bouncer and toward the back staircase. A disheveled, but familiar looking man was coming down from the upper rooms.

"If it's a lassie you're looking for, I've got one upstairs right now who might be a tad lonely."

A sour taste filled Jacob's mouth. "I am looking for a girl, but not for that purpose. Thought you had more class than to be turning this place into a—"

"I only said the lassie was lonely." Boyd grabbed a mug and wiped the water spots with a ragged towel.

The tousled stranger stepped off the last stair and finger-combed his hair as he strode toward the bar. "A whiskey, Boyd."

The man's stench made Lullabelle's barnyard odor a pleasant memory.

Jacob flipped through images in his mind trying to place the pungent customer. Black, kinky hair, pencil-thin mustache—

The man turned to Jacob and gave him a curt nod. "Marshal." He snatched his filled glass and strode away.

Jacob closed his eyes. The leering grin, the rotten teeth ... Ah yes, one of the men who'd bid on Gwen's basket at the fundraising picnic.

Cold prickles toyed with the hairs on the back of his neck. Annie had been right—no decent man would've let Gwen or any other woman be forced to endure such company. The woman upstairs might not be considered decent company, but then, how many saloon girls had known what their job would entail ahead of time? Celia's naiveté coupled with desperation might lead her down a similar path.

The thought of any man buying Celia's time, let alone a man such as that, made Jacob want to vomit. "Have you got any new girls up there?"

"I canna say that I have."

"Can't or won't?"

Boyd held his gaze. "I have no new lassies working here."

Jacob put his hat back on. "If a new girl comes in, real young, auburn hair, lots of freckles, send me word immediately."

"And what be in it for me?"

Jacob narrowed his eyes. "Nothing but my gratitude."

Boyd's jaw worked a bit before he picked up another glass to polish. "That be better than your ill will, I suppose."

A shout of exaltation erupted from the middle of the room, followed by a table full of groans.

The bouncer slid from the shadows and inched toward the center table where the stinky, snaggle-toothed man had evidently quickly won his first hand.

The scrawny stranger crowed as he swept the small pile of bets to his side of the table.

Jacob tipped his head toward the victor. "Who's the young, ugly one?"

Boyd barely glanced up from his cleaning. "Name's Rufus. He's been in here flashing gold for a fortnight."

Jacob slid his hand into his pocket and fingered the folded note he'd found under his office door this morning. "Where's his claim?"

The handwriting on the scrap of paper was familiar now, Jacob's anonymous tipster. The clues always panned out, but this note was rather cryptic: *You find gold on a claim.*

What was he supposed to glean from that?

Boyd shrugged. "He'd not tell me, or you, if we were to ask. But he's spending a loot of money, an' that's all I care about."

Two men in fancy vests demanded the barkeep's attention, so Boyd moved down the counter to tend their drinks.

Jacob leaned against the bar, watching the middle table. Rufus's second hand didn't turn out so well—he lost half his winnings—but he only leaned back in his chair as if he didn't care.

The dealer and a redheaded gambler kept looking between Rufus and Jacob.

Did they know something he didn't? He pushed off the counter and headed toward them. Perhaps it'd be best to ask Rufus to join him outside to answer a few questions.

The gamblers quieted as he wended his way through the maze of chairs.

From his peripheral, the front doors opened and a man stepped in, hesitated, then stepped back out.

Jacob pivoted mid-stride and made for the door, a rush of energy quickening his heart. A saloon-goer didn't change his mind about entering so quickly unless, after spotting a lawman, he had reason to run.

Outside, Jacob blinked against the low-lying sun.

No one to the right.

On the left, a man in a suit disappeared into the alley.

With his hand poised beside his gun, Jacob darted down the boardwalk.

In the dim light between the saloon and a neighboring shanty, a cat darted away from the shadowy figure near the wall.

He stopped and gripped his gun. "Who's there?"

The figure straightened. "Jake?"

"Bryant?" Jacob rolled the tension from his shoulders and frowned, releasing his grip on his gun. "What are you doing out here?"

"Looking for Celia."

"In the alleyway?"

Bryant shrugged as he walked closer. "She could be anywhere."

"Why did you leave the saloon as soon as you walked in?"

Bryant's gaze didn't travel higher than Jacob's chin. "You were already in there, so I figured I wouldn't waste my time."

"You didn't tell me you were going to keep looking after the search party broke up."

"I changed my mind." Bryant flicked out his handkerchief and wiped his brow in spite of the cool evening breeze.

How long was Bryant going to keep pretending he was acting normally? "Why don't you just tell me what's wrong with you?"

Bryant looked away. "I probably ought to."

Silence.

Jacob arched his brows. "But you won't?"

"No." Bryant did look up at him then, a mix of guilt and stubbornness swirling in his eyes.

Jacob looked back toward the street where three saloons were jammed across from Boyd's Billiards. "You weren't looking for Celia, were you? You're frequenting saloons."

Bryant's silence confirmed his hunch.

Jacob shook his head. "I can't believe you'd betray Leah like that."

"I don't go upstairs." He crossed his arms over his chest. "Do you really think me capable of such a thing?"

"If you gamble and drink in secret, why wouldn't I assume more?"

Bryant's expression looked as if he could spit fire. "You don't have to worry about that or anything else anymore. I've got everything under control now."

"Now?"

"Yes, now." Bryant straightened and gave him a haughty look, then a nervous tic took over his cheek.

Maybe he should hire Peter the bouncer to knock Bryant's

thoughtless head against Celia's—if they ever found her. "The fact that you haven't told me about this until now means you're either trying very hard to convince yourself or you're flat out lying to me."

Bryant averted his gaze.

Jacob couldn't stifle a jaw-popping yawn, exacerbated by the dim light of the dark alley. He rubbed his forehead, the painful pressure behind his eyes deepening. "I've got to get home and sleep. I can't force you to talk to me, but unless you do, unless you clue me in on what's wrong with you, how can our friendship keep going?"

Bryant shook his head slightly. "I don't deserve your friendship."

"But you have it."

His eyes seemed suddenly heavy. "For now. Thank you."

"Wha—?"

But Bryant had already about-faced, leaving Jacob in the alley.

Despite the urge to pin Bryant to the wall until he confessed every last trip to the saloons, every last dime he'd lost, every last sin that was eating him alive, Jacob only followed after Bryant and watched him walk down the street.

His friend hadn't ducked into any of the saloons, but was that only because he knew he was being watched?

He couldn't stop Bryant from ruining his life if he was bent on doing it, but Celia was a different matter.

He dragged himself back into Boyd's to question Rufus.

The odoriferous man might not know anything about his girl, but he couldn't leave any stone unturned.

Unfortunately, the young man was already gone.

Annie paced in front of the parlor window as the last hint of light from the long-set sun disappeared, leaving nothing but black.

She'd stopped searching to feed Spencer supper, but he'd been too tired to go out again, so they'd stayed home.

Despite how desperately she itched to go back out and knock on every door, prayer was likely the best thing she could do anyway.

Lord, please don't bring Jacob home without her.

Though of course, now that it was dark, did she really want that prayer answered affirmatively? If Jacob stayed out all night, she'd worry about him too.

Pulling her wrapper tighter, she stopped at the window and stared out at the empty street, the lamps barely dispersing the gloom. Why she had bothered to dress for bed, she didn't know. If neither Celia nor Jacob returned—

A man's shadowy form passed through the circle of lamp light.

Annie snatched her shawl and ran outside.

Ignoring the rocks jabbing into her bare feet, she crossed the road toward Jacob. "Did you find her?"

Meeting her in the middle, he put an arm around her and led her back onto the sidewalk. "I'm so sorry, Anne."

She looked behind him anyway as if he might not be aware that Celia was trailing after him.

But the street was just as empty as before he'd shown up, and a cold wind gusted, sweeping away her hope.

What if Celia was gone for good?

She staggered as her breath jammed deep inside her.

How could she go back inside her warm house when her daughter could be in danger somewhere out there? "But if you didn't find Celia, why did you come ba—?"

She smacked a hand against her errant lips. Jacob had done what he could. God was the one who hadn't answered her prayer for her daughter's return.

And she knew exactly how final a "no" from God could be.

A sniffle escaped, and then a big hiccup of a sob. She tried to breathe through her nose, but that only caused her to take random gulps of air in an attempt to suppress a full onslaught of tears.

Jacob pulled her close as they climbed onto the porch. He sank onto the railing, tightening his arms about her, but she didn't want to be held, not when Celia was likely alone in the cold and dark. Not when his holding her would destroy her defenses and allow the sadness to overwhelm her.

She stepped out of his hold and looked back at the street as if she could conjure her daughter up if only she stared hard enough. "I'd prayed that you'd not come home without her."

"I'm sorry to fail you again." Jacob leaned his head against the column. "I've lost your ranch and your daughter. I can't find the rustlers, so I'll likely lose my job, along with this house, and then you'll regret marrying me even more."

She shook her head. "Don't say that."

He threw up his hands. "I'm just stating facts."

"It's not a fact." She swiped at her eyes. She really must've hurt him if he believed that. "I don't expect anything more from you than what you've given."

He slouched as if he was but seconds from sleep. "I'm not sure I can handle what God's putting us through."

"It's my fault. If only I hadn't been thinking about myself so much. If I hadn't let Mrs. Tate's censure get the best of me. If I'd—"

"What's Mrs. Tate have to do with this?"

Keeping this from Jacob wouldn't be right, not when it involved him. "She thinks our hasty marriage is the root of all my troubles. When she learns Celia has run off, she'll probably tell me it serves me right for taking up with a man so soon after—"

"Nonsense." A low growl emitted from Jacob's throat. "If I could strangle a woman—"

"But she's not responsible." The woman might be an old

biddy, but she'd only been one solitary wave in Annie's sea of doubt. "And maybe she's right, maybe Celia's running away is punishment for what I've..." Her throat clogged, and she pressed her hands against her eyes to stop the deluge.

"Shhh." He pulled her against him. "You're not thinking straight. *I'm* not thinking straight. We should get some sleep before we start—"

"But what if..." She tried to speak through her tears, but failed.

If Celia was really gone for forever...

The pressure around the ache in her chest burst into an uncontrolled gasp of a sob.

"Hey, now." He took her arm and guided her toward the front door. "I can't promise sleep will make this look better in the morning, but if you're beginning to think God's endangering Celia in order to punish you, then you need sleep as much as I do. We have important decisions to make and—"

"But what about Celia?" She pulled against his hold and looked back.

"Anne, love." He tightened his grip on her as they entered the dim parlor. "If she isn't bunked in with a friend who's hiding her, she knows how to make a fire. A summer night won't kill her."

A summer night won't kill her.

But what about wolves, fast racing rivers, snakes, jumping off trains, men?

The thoughts of all the ways Celia could die flashed before her. A chest-convulsing cry escaped, and then another.

Jacob's soothing voice was an indistinct murmur above her sobs.

Seconds later, he scooped her up into his arms.

"No." She struggled to breathe enough to say the word a second time, but couldn't. With how his body had dragged with weariness as he'd crossed the road earlier, he shouldn't be carrying a full-grown woman up the stairs.

But with his arms tight around her and his first steps steady, she let the heaving sobs take over and curled up against him, crying into his neck. "Oh, Jacob, I don't know how I'd bear this without you."

"You don't have to, love." He pressed his lips against her forehead and spoke against her hair. "You don't have to."

CHAPTER THIRTY-SIX

Celia groaned while twisting her back in an attempt to alleviate the kink between her shoulder blades. Then she stomped her feet in the icy water to make sure they still worked. Two days of sifting through rock and sand for gold was worse than two months of farm chores.

Going home, curling up under covers, and eating a decent meal didn't sound all that bad anymore, if not for the marshal's rules.

Nobody was going to direct her life from here on out except herself, so she'd stay right here until she made enough money to buy her own goose-down quilt. Even if she did lose all her toes to frostbite.

Besides, it wouldn't be much longer until she could quit for the day. Rufus and Guy had promised they'd all be done once the two of them finished constructing the new sluice box. Said everyone would need to get rested up for the fun they were planning.

Surely whatever they thought sounded fun would be nowhere near as wonderful as sleeping as long as she could. If the festivities were anything like what they found amusing now

—irritating her within an inch of her life and making ribald jokes the whole livelong day—sleeping would definitely be the better choice.

Letting the water slosh back and forth across her pan to remove the finer silt, Celia watched for the telltale shine of precious metal.

Rufus had promised thirty dollars' worth of gold for a month's wage.

Too bad she'd have to exchange the pretty gold for ugly cash, but she would to get out of Armelle. Though if she found a big enough nugget, she might put it on a chain.

She pulled at her wet and clingy oversized shirt. A gold necklace would look silly dressed as she was, not that Rufus would allow her to keep any nugget big enough to string.

This batch had only three flakes anyway.

Hiking her threadbare trousers farther up her slender hips, she sloshed her way toward the river bank. After depositing her find in the collection bucket, she lowered herself onto the loose silt ground and wiggled her stiff toes against hard leather. She ought to take her boots off and let the sun warm her feet.

"You being lazy again?" Rufus walked past her with two boards on his shoulder and a bucket of nails swinging at his side.

"No." She unlaced her boot and dumped its water onto the dirt. "I wouldn't be any good to you if I let my toes fall off, now would I?"

"You were of better use when you were informing us where the marshal was," he muttered as he passed.

Why were they so worried about meeting up with the marshal anyway? Wasn't as if he could arrest them for working their land or being disgusting old men. And gambling wasn't anything that got you thrown into jail.

At least Rufus no longer seemed so fascinated with her after enduring plenty of her sass. Who knew months of back talking her parents would prove a good survival skill? She stifled the urge to rub at the twinge in her chest. Neither Ma nor Jacob had deserved the amount she'd dished out to them—not like these two snakes did, anyway.

Of course, his disinterest could be from the haircut she'd given herself. Rufus had talked a lot about the feminine features of the women he visited in town, so she'd cut her hair like a boy's in hopes he'd lose any interest he might have in her nearly flat body. It seemed to have worked since he didn't leer at her nearly as often.

Daniel sat next to her and pulled a smooshed sandwich from his lunch bucket. He threw half of his sandwich onto her muddy trousers. "Here."

She cringed at the feel of the soggy bread but took a bite anyway. "Do you know what fun they're planning?"

"No, but I doubt you'd want to stick around for it." He talked around a mass of food in his mouth. "I'm surprised you've stuck around as long as you have with how you bicker with Rufus."

"It pays more than laundry." She looked out over the glistening rapids, recalling the nights she'd helped round up cattle with Daddy and camped under the stars next to the Laramie.

"Besides, I love the outdoors." She wiggled her pant-clad legs. "And dressing like a boy."

Though she didn't exactly enjoy the back-breaking work, she'd not complain. Laundry wouldn't have been much better.

"No one will ever consider you respectable in that getup." Daniel kept his eyes on the river. "Don't you want to get married, live in a house, have babies?"

Celia scrunched her face at him. "Children cause more problems than they're worth." She'd certainly been the burr under her mother's saddle for more years than she could count.

Daniel grunted, then shoved the last of his food into his mouth and stomped off.

Celia finished the remains of her mushy meal then dragged her semi-dry legs back into the icy currents to pan. No need to think about the future if she didn't find enough gold to afford one.

Hours later, Rufus and Guy completed their sluice box then showed her, Daniel, and Timothy how the apparatus worked. Maybe working this sluice instead of hunching over all day would gain her a decent night's rest.

Guy rapped his knuckles against the box. "Time to pack up and head out."

She glanced toward the sun. "We still have an hour or two. Why not let us practice with your contraption?"

Ruffling her hair as if she were a kid, Guy shoved her toward the trees. "Tomorrow's work will be a lot more lucrative than panning, and we need to be rested up." He almost looked as if he were excited enough to smile—if he'd possessed enough teeth to do so.

Rubbing his hands together, Rufus circled Daniel and Timothy. "All right now, we've decided to trust you three, and if we cain't..." He eyed them all.

Celia lifted her chin a notch and narrowed her eyes right back at him. She'd not act like some prissy girl who'd balk at whatever brought in money.

Rufus nodded, as if he'd seen what he needed to see in their eyes. "So who's ready for some cattle rustling?"

Celia's chin froze in its uptilted position. Daddy had never been more livid in his life than when he discussed the rustlers plaguing the county.

So that's why they'd wanted to know where the marshal was at all times.

She looked down at her waterlogged hands. Could she do something Daddy would be ashamed of?

But then, she'd never thought Daddy would've been the kind to kill an unarmed shepherd either.

Sometimes, I wonder if I knew you at all.

Timothy stuffed his hands in his pockets. "I can't come tomorrow. My baby brother's birthday is the day after, and my aunt from Cheyenne has probably already arrived. I can't sneak out of the house with her three boys bunked in my room."

His throat worked overtime and he darted a glance at Celia and Daniel.

Timothy had no aunt as far as she knew.

"If this is what you meant by fun, I ain't doing it unless I'm paid more." Daniel puffed out his barrel chest, but being a foot shorter than Rufus, the action only made him look like a banty hen threatening the dominant rooster.

"Of course it pays better," Guy said around the wheatgrass stem in his mouth. He glared at Daniel until her friend took a step back.

Rufus jostled her. "You can ride, cain't ya?"

Daniel shook his head. "She'd just get in the way."

"I've been riding since I could walk." Celia sneered at her so-called friend. How many times had she outraced him over the years? "He's just afraid I'll show him up."

Rufus shrugged. "You'll just be lookout. We aren't expecting you to help with the beeves."

Her fists clenched, and she jutted out her jaw. "I bet I know cattle better than you do."

"Considering he can rarely tell the backside of a cow from the front side, you might be right." Guy rolled his eyes at the murderous glare he received from Rufus. "But, until you know how we do things, you're lookout." He spat out his chewed up wheatgrass.

"But Daniel hasn't been out with you befo—"

"It ain't right bringing a girl along," Daniel interrupted.

"Since when have you ever cared about my being a girl?" Celia shoved him. "No one's ever accused me of being much of a lady anyhow."

Guy stomped over and grabbed them both by the shoulders. He dug his thumb deep into her muscle, but she kept the pain tucked tight inside. She couldn't let him know it hurt.

"Celia's lookout and Daniel's helping with the cattle. If you don't follow orders—"

"I'll persuade ya into doing so." Rufus smacked his fist into his open palm, looking between her and Daniel.

"Now, shut your traps and do as you're told."

Daniel shrugged out from under Guy's hold and stamped off toward the horses.

Guy kept a hold of her and leaned down, his bristly beard scraping against her ear. "You don't want to give Rufus a reason to persuade you into doing anything, you understand?" He squeezed her shoulder so hard, she'd likely find bruises come morning.

"Yes." She yanked away from his grip and shot him a feisty glare. Hopefully, he didn't notice her quaking knees. Cattle rustling wasn't nearly as scary as the thought that Guy might be the only reason Rufus was keeping his distance.

"Good." Guy strode toward Timothy, who quickly assured him he'd not tell a soul.

The older boy took one last glance at her and Daniel before heading out.

Rufus mounted his gelding, then circled to face those left.

He eyed Celia while pushing his tobacco wad around in his cheek. "Get as much sleep as you can."

CHAPTER THIRTY-SEVEN

With an arm around his thin shoulders, Annie escorted Spencer up the Whitsetts' porch steps.

The last two hours he'd hobbled along without complaint, but he was definitely dragging now.

She knocked on the door and shifted her weight. As much as she'd like to sit and rest, the day wasn't over. If Leah could watch Spencer, she'd ride out to the ranch and check Celia's old haunts.

No one answered the door.

Odd. Leah was normally here at this time.

Annie tried the knob. Finding the door open, she pushed it in. "Leah?"

Wood scraped against wood from somewhere inside the house, but no footsteps followed.

Leah almost always called out from wherever she was.

Annie nudged Spencer toward the bookshelf. "Why don't you see if there's something you'd like to borrow while I look for Leah?"

Spencer dragged himself toward the books, and Annie followed the faint sounds of ... sniffling?

Inside the pantry, Leah was dusting shelves and shoving jars around with more force than necessary.

Annie lightly tapped on the wall, causing Leah to jump.

"I'm sorry to startle you."

"No, don't be." Leah turned her back to Annie and pulled up her apron to seemingly wipe at her face.

"Are you crying?"

"No." She sniffed a couple times before turning to give Annie a weak smile.

She narrowed her eyes at her friend's red-rimmed ones. "I never thought you'd lie to me."

Leah batted her eyes excessively and wiped at them with the back of her hand. "Well, I wasn't crying right that second."

She couldn't help but grin at her friend's truth dodge, but then, what reason did Leah have to cry? "What's happened?"

"Nothing."

"Tell me."

Walking past Annie, Leah headed toward the kitchen table. Once there, she pulled out a chair and slowly sat, as if a weight dragged her down.

Something was wrong. "Can I make you some tea?" Annie moved to look at the tins behind the stove.

"No, thank you."

Annie returned to Leah, who was sitting in a dejected slump, then sat in the chair beside her.

"My problems are small compared to yours, and I'm ... fine. You just caught me at a bad time." And all of a sudden, Leah pasted on a happy grin complete with a sparkle in her eye—the expression Annie was used to seeing.

She wouldn't let her off that easy. "Come now, I've burdened you with plenty. You're entitled to have people pray for you too."

Leah's smile faltered and she turned to stare out the back window.

A moment of silence passed. Then two.

Were things worse than she let on? Annie scooted closer. "I promise, even if it's only an ache in your back, I want to hear about it."

"It's Bryant."

Annie tried not to tense at his name. True, there was no reason to dislike him any more than there was reason to dislike Jacob for losing her ranch. But the way he'd acted on her wedding day and how he still held himself aloof made it hard to regard him highly. "What about him?"

"I think..." She stood, grabbed a dishcloth, and started to wipe the table despite it being spotless. "All I have are suspicions, and if I'm wrong, he wouldn't deserve what you'd think of him if I said anything."

Annie had never seen Leah like this. "Have you talked to him about what's bothering you?"

The kitchen door creaked open and Leah stiffened.

Bryant walked in and immediately frowned at Annie. "I'm sorry. I didn't mean to interrupt." He paused and assessed his wife for a moment before moving toward the sideboard. "I'm working late again. Do we have any bread left?"

She smiled prettily and nodded, pointing to the towel-covered lump. "Half a loaf."

He slid into the pantry and reappeared with a jar of fruit and swept up the bread. "Ladies." He tipped his head to Annie and gave Leah a wink before heading back out the door.

Her friend slumped.

"He didn't kiss me," Leah whispered just loud enough for Annie to hear.

Perhaps he hadn't because they'd had company, but then, Leah would know whether or not her presence would've kept him from kissing her.

With a sharp inhale, Leah turned to frown at Annie. "This doesn't go past us."

"Of course not." She shot a glance toward the parlor, but Spencer was quiet and likely asleep in his chair.

"I think he's cheating on me."

Annie blinked a couple of times. Bryant, unfaithful?

What could a man want other than Leah? The woman was a few years into her forties, yes, but she was as trim as a twenty-year-old, her few wrinkles caused by smiling. She kept a pristine house and somehow still found time to help others. Plus the woman absolutely doted on Bryant.

"Why would a man ever cheat on you?" Though she'd not been the best wife to Jacob these past few months, she'd no worries about his faithfulness.

Leah tried to smile. "Thank you for thinking that, but have you not noticed how distant he's been lately?"

She hadn't, considering she didn't know him well at all. Jacob had grumbled a time or two about Bryant's behavior, but she'd assumed Bryant's dislike of her had been the cause.

"He only kisses me now when I kiss him first." Leah continued in a hushed voice, as if she were reciting something she'd repeated over and over in her head. "He's acting as if he's being watched. Normally he tells me right away when something's bothering him, but he's been acting like this for months."

What advice would help? She had no experience with anything like this.

"I can't come up with any other reason, if not for a woman." Leah stopped talking to swallow hard. "I've tried to get him to talk, but he's always too busy or tired. Work, he says. And when I check on him, he really is at work. So maybe I'm just..."

Annie squeezed her hand. "If he's been working a lot lately, maybe he's stressed. Could he take a few days off?"

"He says McGill won't let him. But I'm thinking he just doesn't want to spend time with me."

"Or maybe he's worried about losing his job?"

"He certainly acts that way, but he hasn't told me anything that makes me think so." She shifted in her chair. "I thought to ask him if we could take a holiday to see Jennie. We haven't visited since her birthday, but if he says no, I'll wonder if it's because of me." She looked up at Annie with heavy-lidded eyes. "You haven't heard any whisperings about him being with ... someone else?"

"No. Definitely not. All the whisperings lately have been about me." She tried to conjure up a self-deprecating smile, but her lips wouldn't cooperate. "May I share your worries with Jacob? He could encourage Bryant to talk to you about what's troubling him."

Leah shrugged and opened her mouth to say something, but Spencer entered the room.

"May I borrow this?" He held out a book with a nondescript brown cover.

Leah's usual bright smile covered up her frown. "Of course, honey."

Spencer sat at the table and started reading.

Leah quickly wiped at her face as if she could simply erase her worries.

Annie squeezed Leah's shoulder. "Can we do anything for you before we leave?"

Spencer looked up as if to remind her why they'd come, but she cut him off with a shake of her head.

With a heave of a sigh, Leah wrung her apron. "No, I don't think so. Though I probably ought to go lie down and pray for a while." She got up to leave, but swiveled back. "I'm sorry. I forgot to ask how the search for Celia was going."

"No need to apologize." Annie stood. "But I'm afraid it doesn't look promising."

"I'll pray for her too."

"I'd appreciate that."

As Leah disappeared down the hallway, Annie put her arm around Spencer. "How about we go home and I cook us a good supper?"

His eyes brightened a little, but his frown didn't disappear. "You mean we aren't going back out to search for Celia?"

"No. You're about to fall asleep on your feet, and I didn't feed Jacob last night. I probably shouldn't do that to him two nights in a row." He'd carried her straight up to bed and had held on to her until her tears were spent and she'd fallen asleep. She hadn't realized he'd skipped eating until he wolfed down his breakfast.

Tonight there would be something warm and filling for him to eat.

And hopefully he'd not be too tired to talk.

For as much as she hadn't wanted to worry him with her jumbled up emotions toward him, she didn't want him believing she was keeping something truly worrisome to herself either, as Leah did Bryant.

As much as her insides were twisting up over the thought of not searching for Celia, she couldn't forget that Spencer and Jacob needed her too.

CHAPTER THIRTY-EIGHT

After extinguishing the kitchen lamp, Annie frowned at the light glowing in the parlor. Hopefully Jacob hadn't waited up for her. He'd stumbled in an hour after sunset and had eaten as if he'd not tasted food in days. And yet, he hadn't finished his meal so heavy were his eyelids.

She'd sent him to bed, insisting she could clean up on her own.

In the parlor, she found him slumped against the sofa's arm, his jaw slack, his Bible open on the cushion beside him.

She picked up the Bible so she could sit, and then ran her thumb over his brow.

He didn't even flinch. The furrows crisscrossing his forehead refused to be smoothed away.

"Jacob?" She scooted closer and rubbed his arm, hoping he wasn't the kind to startle awake or she'd end up getting smacked upside the head. "Jacob?"

His brow wrinkled even more, and he groaned as he shifted.

"You'll feel better in the morning if you don't sleep on the sofa."

He shivered and his eyes opened a crack. "What?"

"Let's get you upstairs."

"Right, right." He sat up and shook his head as if trying to awaken his brain. With a jaw-popping yawn, he stood and shuffled toward the stairs.

With a hand over her heart, she watched him go. As much as she'd wanted to talk with him—to start making up for the times she'd chosen not to—the man had clearly exhausted himself by trying to bring her girl back.

After extinguishing the parlor lamps, she felt her way toward the stairs and followed his slow footsteps upward. Though she didn't feel ready for sleep—a problem that would likely plague her until Celia returned—it would be best if she tried. Though if all she ended up doing was praying, that wouldn't be such a terrible thing either.

Oh Lord, how will I live if you don't bring her back? I know I can't neglect these two to search for her, but trusting you is hard right now. I'm still not sure I agree with how you took Gregory from us, but you did provide for us, with a home and a man who loves us, so help me trust you to do the same for Celia as well.

She pushed Spencer's door open and smiled at his slack face illuminated by moonlight. Taking his dangling arm, she tucked it back beside him and kissed his forehead before returning to the hallway.

The door to Jacob's room creaked as she stepped through.

"Anne?" Jacob was seated on his bed, halfway through pulling off his boot.

She'd expected him to have draped himself over the mattress and fallen straight to sleep. "Yes, it's me. Did you need something?"

"Water maybe?"

"It's already there." She pointed to his bedside table though he likely couldn't see her in the shadows.

"Thank you."

She nodded, though he likely couldn't see that either. With

his nightshirt beside him, it seemed he didn't plan to sleep in his clothes as he had last night.

She came over to sit on the bed, and he turned to look at her.

He didn't look sleepy now. Was it wrong of her to want to talk to him about something that might keep him awake?

Though the longer she kept things to herself, the longer he wouldn't know. "Do you mind if I tell you about something that's bothering me?"

A huge yawn overtook him, so he answered with the shake of his head.

"I figured you might want to do something about it tomorrow." She picked up the suspenders he'd taken off and rolled them up. "I talked to Leah today."

Jacob didn't respond or move. Had he fallen asleep sitting up?

But suddenly, he shook himself and started unbuttoning his shirt. "What's worrying you about her?"

"She says Bryant's been acting distant lately and she's thinking he may have another woman." She handed Jacob his nightshirt. "I've never seen Leah so downhearted. Do you think her suspicions have merit?"

He tugged the shirt over his head. "Not about another woman, no. At least I'm pretty sure anyway."

"But you do think there's something wrong?"

"Yes, but..." He stopped pulling off his socks and sat still for a moment. "I've only suspicions, somewhat confirmed by the fact he didn't outright deny them." He rolled his socks into a ball and threw them toward the door.

Another day, she'd ask him to stop doing that.

He put a hand to the back of his neck. "So I think it might be best to keep my suspicions to myself until I talk to Leah." He dropped his hand to the mattress as if he might topple over if he didn't. "I hope you don't mind me waiting to share with you until I know for certain."

"Of course not." She put her head on his shoulder in a sort of hug. His sleeping and peace of mind were more important than her hearing what he only thought he knew.

His shoulders rose and fell on a yawn. "I know you might not want to hear this, but if I want to keep my job, tomorrow's the last day I can spend every hour looking for Celia."

Though her heart sank, she nodded against the soft cotton of his nightshirt. With how McGill seemed peeved with him lately, she'd already figured it wouldn't be wise for him to continue much longer.

This day had to come. If only it hadn't arrived so soon.

"I wish I could—"

"Shhh." She patted his arm and sat up. "I knew it'd happen." Thankfully her voice didn't waver too much. "I understand we can't stop our lives and ruin our health and finances when she might refuse to come back or run away again if we ever do find her. We have Spencer to think about."

He grabbed her hand. "I do intend to look for her every minute I can. After hours, corresponding with other counties—anything I can think of."

"As will I. While Spencer's playing with his friends, I figured I could ride to nearby towns—"

"Don't put yourself in any danger." His handhold tightened. "Don't go into any saloons or—"

"I won't. If anyone points me in that direction, I'll have you check." She blinked against the tears creeping up at the thought of her daughter being found in such a place. "I promise."

"Good." Jacob's body relaxed and he let go of her hand. "Don't give up, though. I'm not. She's my girl, too."

A tear did fall then. If only Celia had realized that running away would likely ruin her more than any of Jacob's attempts to rein in her willfulness.

"Thank you," she whispered. "I'll let you get some sleep."

She pushed herself off the bed and listened to the creak of the mattress as he lay down behind her.

Thankfully the moonlight was just bright enough she wouldn't need a lamp.

She pushed Jacob's door all the way shut, and as quietly as she could, felt her way back to his dresser, pulled the combs and pins from her hair, and laid them in the porcelain dish she'd brought in earlier. Once finished, she moved to the trunk. She opened the lid, thankful to find her white nightgown illuminated in a partial moonbeam. A minute later, she tried to shrug out of her calico top, but she must have missed a button.

"What are you doing?" Jacob's voice sounded gravely, though he couldn't have been asleep more than a handful of minutes.

Evidently she'd made more noise than she'd intended. "Getting ready for bed."

She didn't know why she'd whispered other than she didn't want to keep the poor man up any longer.

He sat up and seemed to be staring at her trunk. "How'd that get in here?"

"Don't worry. Spencer helped me bring it in." It'd been quite the feat for Jacob and Bryant to lug it upstairs, but she and Spencer hadn't needed to pick it up, just shove it across the hallway.

"You had Spencer...?" His voice seemed a bit incredulous.

"We didn't strain ourselves, I promise."

When the room went quiet, she figured he'd fallen back asleep, so she finished undressing, then padded toward the bed, careful not to stub her toes.

Jacob was propped up against the headboard, his eyes only halfway shut and his breathing wasn't the slow rhythm of slumber.

"Why aren't you sleeping?" She nestled down into the covers and let a yawn overtake her.

"I was wondering, uh, what you were doing."

"Going to sleep. Like you should be." He had to be almost delirious with exhaustion. She rolled over and frowned at him, his eyes now completely closed, his arms tightly crossed atop his chest.

"Do you need me to get you something? Perhaps for pain?" She hadn't thought to ask him about that earlier.

"No, but..."

The room quieted enough she could hear the ticks of the grandfather clock downstairs. Had he finally fallen asleep?

"Do you..." his voice had turned rough. "Would you mind if I held you until you fell asleep again?"

If it had been winter, the rush of heat warming her heart would've made a fire unnecessary. "Not at all."

He slid down and wrapped his arms around her, letting out a deep sigh.

Gregory had never liked to cuddle when he was ready to sleep, so she wasn't sure what to do with herself. She stayed as still as she could, hoping she'd not keep Jacob awake any longer.

But the man's breathing never slowed. His muscles never relaxed.

Minutes ticked by. Finally, she let herself scooch around to look at him.

His eyes were closed, but his mouth turned up a little. "Yes?" he whispered.

"If you aren't sleeping, would you mind if I kept talking?"

He shook his head. "I can't promise I won't fall asleep in the middle of a sentence, though."

She rolled over farther to put a hand on his chest, hoping she'd be able to feel when he fell asleep. "It's just, after talking to Leah, I wanted to apologize for how distant I've been."

He hummed, but said nothing.

"Yesterday, I realized I've been anxious about things that don't ultimately matter, that all God requires of me is to do whatever will bring Him glory and to trust Him with what I can't control. And I want you to hold me accountable. All my fretting affects you now, and though I thank you for letting me process things alone when I asked, I'm thinking I've made things worse by doing so. I don't want you to be worried about what's going on inside my head, wondering if I'm keeping terrible secrets."

His breathing was shallow and even.

"Are you asleep?"

"No." His voice barely registered, but he fluttered his eyes open to prove it.

She swallowed and began playing with the frayed edge of his nightshirt's collar. "I've been struggling with how to live with you when I'm still getting over Gregory. I made a vow on our wedding day to put him behind me, but I keep breaking it."

"I don't remember that vow."

"Not a ceremony vow. I made it when I went back into the church." She should've known she wouldn't be able to keep it considering she'd failed to give up her old wedding ring.

"I didn't ask you to do that." He brought up a hand to cup her face. "He was your first love and the father of your children, not someone you should erase from your memory."

"Though I should, shouldn't I? Finding out that he was a..." She still couldn't voice the word *murderer*. It just didn't ring true, though it seemed as if it had to be.

"What you learned of him after he died doesn't change the fact that he was a man you deeply loved, right?"

She shook her head against him, strangely comforted by talking about Gregory aloud, despite Jacob being the last person she'd thought she should be talking to about this.

"Then don't try to forget him, not because of a mistake he made, or for my sake either. I mean..." Jacob shifted and propped himself up to look down at her, his eyes blinking heavily. "If I died tomorrow, I wouldn't want you to forget about me whenever you remarried. If you did..." His voice faded into a whisper. "Well, I wouldn't want you to, even though I know you're not in love with me. So why would I ask you to forget about a man you did love?"

"You're wrong about that."

"You didn't love him?" He rubbed an eye as a yawn overtook him, though he spoke through it. "But if that's the—?"

"No." She put a finger against his mouth as he finished his yawn. "You're wrong about me not being in love with you. I haven't told you yet, because I thought it'd be best if I—"

"You love me?" He held his breath.

"Yes." How could she not?

He snuggled back down against her and placed a kiss against her hairline. "I love you too. If it weren't ... so late..."

He placed a couple more kisses against her temple before his body slowly went limp with sleep.

She ran her hand across his jaw and up to smooth the hair sticking out at a funny angle behind his ear, allowing herself all the time she desired to take in his features, pale in the moonlight, more content in sleep than she'd ever seen him.

Why had she ever cared what anyone thought of her loving such a man?

CHAPTER THIRTY-NINE

Celia rubbed her eyes, but they insisted on staying at half-mast, not that it was bright enough to see much anymore.

Though she'd slept plenty the night before, her body was ready to call it quits. Thankfully her horse didn't need much prodding to follow the group, and she could doze as she rode.

Rufus and Guy better come through with the gold they'd promised, otherwise working all day hunched over the river wasn't worth it.

And this cattle rustling job?

Being lookout for rustlers was bad enough, so she'd not insisted on knowing the pay beforehand. But doing nothing more than staying alert wasn't too terrible, right? Especially since there'd likely be nobody out this late at night.

Ahead of her, the backside of Daniel's horse disappeared into shadow. What was left of the moon barely illuminated the ground around her.

"Wait up." She kicked her buckskin harder, but the nag continued at a lullaby's pace. She hadn't the heart to kick the horse again—the old thing had to be more tired than she was.

Tired enough to die on the spot if she weren't careful how she handled the beast.

"I'm not waiting around for some girl." Daniel's voice echoed against a nearby rock wall.

His horse sped up, leaving her in the dust.

"I don't need you." Celia spit toward Daniel, but most of her spittle clung to her lips. She furiously swiped at her mouth.

Daniel used to want her around. Even claimed she was fun—unlike the prissy girls at school. But ever since she'd started working the river, he'd treated her like a miserable kid tag along.

Just like she treated Spencer.

Biting her lip, Celia concentrated on the clomp and stomp of her swayback horse. The animal walked slowly, unintimidated by their shadowy surroundings.

The small glow of a campfire ahead turned the river's rippling water into a dance of lights. The muffled male voices grew distinctly into Rufus and Guy cussing at each other.

The other day, she'd tried spouting off a few of their forbidden words, but they hadn't sat right. Maybe they'd eventually feel natural.

But did she want to be like them? How could she live like Rufus—sporting near rags for clothing, an ugly fighting scar on his left cheek, matted hair growing out in scraggly swaths, and a stench only bathing with something stronger than soap could rectify? She'd be unfit for anybody's company except scoundrels like these.

She pressed a hand to her stomach, which rolled with the sway of her horse's slow gait. Weeks ago, she'd overheard the marshal talking of a gal named Belle Starr in Arkansas, a rough woman who'd been sent to prison for horse thieving.

Celia glanced down at her oversized shirt, her body odor imbuing the fabric covered in stains large enough to see in the dim firelight. Did Ms. Starr look and smell like this?

At the camp, the silhouettes of Rufus and Guy stood next to

a very short man, whose sombrero seemed as wide as he was tall.

A lump wriggled near the visitor's feet.

Celia sat straighter in her saddle and squinted at the blurry shape—it wasn't an animal being made ready for the spit, but a person, bound and gagged. Long hair fluttered about the captive's head—a woman.

A violent shiver rolled through her, leaving a trail of prickles along her arms. With a jerk of the reins, Celia slowed her plodding horse to a near standstill. Were they kidnapping a woman?

The short man leapt into the saddle of a nearby horse and nodded at Daniel, who'd entered the circle of campfire light. "Don't do her major harm. Boss only wants her shaken up for her husband's benefit."

The voice of the tiny man sounded familiar, but the only man she knew that size was her father's old foreman, Tom Passey.

She pulled her nag sideways into the hanging branches of a willow. If he caught a glimpse of her, would he rat her out to the marshal?

No. If he tattled on her, she'd snitch on him.

But didn't Tom work for the mayor now?

Mayor McGill already owned more cattle than anyone else, did he really need more?

She shook her head in disgust. Could Mr. Whitsett and the marshal be shady, too?

No, the marshal couldn't be. He was too much of a stickler for rule-following.

After slipping from her saddle, she tied her horse to a tree near the fire.

The short cowboy yanked on his horse's reins, and the poor animal fought against the bit as he made the small horse turn sharply. "Then again, no reason not to have some fun with her. Just don't leave marks." He thundered away in the direction of town, the man's teensy legs bouncing against his horse's ribs.

With her thumbs tucked into her pockets, Celia looked surreptitiously at the woman hunched near the campfire's glow, then moseyed over to the riverside where Daniel was arguing with Rufus.

"She can't see me, or she'll turn me in." Daniel's whisper hissed like the green branches Guy was throwing into the flames.

"She knows me. Her, too." He jerked his thumb toward Celia. "Goes to church with her folks."

Celia stopped beside Daniel and squinted in an attempt to see through the blurry darkness obscuring the woman. The hostage's hair fell in a curtain around her bowed head.

Guy spat on the ground as he moseyed over. "With it being nearly the new moon and two of the ranch hands feverish, there's no better time for cutting out so many head. Boss expects us to round up the cattle tonight."

"How does he expect us to do two jobs at once?" Rufus growled, and his hand shot out and gripped Celia's wrist. She jerked her arm, but he held tightly. "Daniel still hangs around about town, but you don't. Won't matter if the woman knows who you are if you ain't intending to go back."

Celia wet her lips and stared at the captive. "Who is she?"

"Leah Whitsett," Daniel answered.

Celia's lungs sucked in a quick, short breath. "Whatever could she have done?"

"Doesn't matter. Boss's orders." Rufus's hand tightened around her. "But I can't be taking care of no woman when there's a bigger job to do."

Celia's breathing grew shallow. She didn't want to go home. But as sure as sagebrush covered Wyoming, Leah would inform the marshal where she was the minute she returned to Armelle.

Guy stepped closer. "Why don't we just leave her here? She can't go nowhere."

"Because someone could follow Passey's tracks." Rufus shook his head. "Naw, we take her with. Rough her up and drop her at that abandoned farm north of the county line tomorrow. By the time she stumbles into town, we'll be well on our way to Helena."

"Helena?" Daniel whined. "You expect us to go all the way there and back?"

Rufus and Guy exchanged guarded looks.

Daniel crossed his arms. "I'm not helping unless I get paid up front."

"We don't need no whiny kid to deal with on top of this. Go home." Guy snarled. "And if you don't want to find yourself ground into mincemeat, you keep things to yourself."

Daniel tried to stare the older man down, but his gaze eventually dropped to the dirt at his feet. He turned to Celia. "Let's go."

She bit her lip and sized up the filthy men cloaked in their usual skunk-like aroma. Her memory burned with overheard snippets of the men's conversation while they'd separated silt from sand. Talk like she'd never heard about what happened between a man and a woman in houses of ill repute.

Last week, she hadn't even known what those houses along the tracks were.

Did Tom's comment of having fun with Leah mean what she thought it meant?

Guy tapped his foot impatiently. "If you keep your mouth shut, the woman won't recognize you with your short hair and pants."

Celia fingered the hacked lock tickling her ear. Rufus had seemed to lose interest in her when she'd drastically changed her appearance, but Leah was beautiful, well-formed, and defenseless. Just last week, this woman had hugged her and told her she loved her, despite the fact she'd done nothing worthy of the woman's affection.

Could she live with herself if she left Leah alone with these two?

But if they released her as Tom had told them to, why didn't the mayor expect the Whitsetts to press charges? Surely Leah had recognized Tom, and if not, describing him would easily lead to his arrest, for who else was that short and wore such a fancy getup?

Something didn't add up. Celia scratched her head, scraping loose a disgusting layer of caked dirt. "I'll stay."

Her presence would hopefully ensure Leah was left with nothing more than bumps and bruises.

"Then let's go." Rufus slapped his cowboy hat against his leg before jamming it on his head. "Guy, throw the woman over the mule and tie the lead to Celia's saddle."

Daniel took hold of her wrist. "Staying ain't smart. Get out while the gettin's good."

Daniel hadn't proved himself to be the friend she'd thought he was, though it was nice to know he cared a little. "Leah being here gives me no choice. I don't want to go home, but I can't stay with Rufus and Guy forever." One day, she'd gain back Rufus's attention by growing up a little too much. "Helena's as good a place as any."

"Don't say I didn't warn you. Cattle drives aren't a jolly picnic."

She pulled her wrist from Daniel's grasp and crossed her arms to keep them from shaking. Now that the reality of leaving home was sinking in, she couldn't fathom never seeing Ma or Spencer again—she'd even miss the marshal a little.

Daniel mounted his horse and turned his gelding toward Armelle.

Celia sniffed and wiped her nose against her sleeve. Closing her eyes, she willed herself not to get back on her horse and follow after Daniel. She couldn't leave Leah alone. Perhaps if she kept her identity concealed, once they let Leah go, she could sneak back into town and let someone know where they'd dropped her off without getting caught.

Guy walked over to Leah and pulled her to stand. "Soon, it'll be just you and me, darling."

Leah turned her face from his, pushing against him with her bound wrists.

Daniel's silhouette faded into the horizon.

He'd actually, truly left.

Swoony smiles were good for nothing.

Guy hoisted Leah onto his shoulder, slung her across his mule, then patted Leah's rump before bending to tie her ankles and wrists beneath the animal's belly.

Celia's heart chugged at a terrible speed. Maybe she should race after Daniel.

Guy tipped Leah's face up and licked his lips. "As soon as we get the cattle rounded up, we'll have some fun."

He dropped her head, and Leah didn't so much as whimper, though she was holding her head at an awkward angle since her arms were too close together to lie flat.

The men chortled, and Rufus slapped Guy's back as he talked loudly to Leah about their "fun" plans for her.

Celia's cheeks burned hotter than a dozen campfires.

She couldn't stay with these men—she had to leave —tonight.

But not without Leah. She couldn't live with herself if she abandoned one of the few nice adults she knew to these guys.

But how would she get away? If these ruffians caught her, things would be worse—so much worse.

Leah turned her head toward Guy as he finished tightening her knots. "Please, don't do this." Her whisper-soft voice trembled. "You don't need to do this."

Celia closed her eyes. That tiny bedroom back at the marshal's hadn't been so bad after all.

Bryant's hand trembled on the doorknob to his house. No light escaped from around the door, and the crypt-like stillness hadn't changed from the last time he'd been here, just hours ago.

A cricket hidden somewhere behind the cold cook stove chirped its annoying nighttime song. "Leah?"

No answer.

He lighted the lantern and checked every room, even peering under beds and behind furniture this time. Ridiculous to think his wife would be under any of them, but if she wasn't here and she wasn't at his daughter and son-in-law's...

He'd visited them first, but he hadn't told Ava her mother was missing. Their daughter was too close to giving birth to frighten her. Jennie's special boarding school was too far away to visit without Leah talking to him first. And he'd dropped by the houses of their friends, mentioning Leah had thought about visiting them today, though she'd never said such a thing.

No trace of her.

This morning, all she'd discussed with him was what she was planning for supper. But the kitchen hadn't even been cleaned up after lunch.

The only other place he could think Leah might be was with McGill, but the man couldn't be that dastardly.

She could be dead.

He needed help. Needed it now.

He left his house and nearly ran five blocks to pound on the Hendrixes' back door.

Annie opened the door, her eyes bloodshot and underscored with sleepless bags. Her shoulders deflated upon seeing him.

She'd probably hoped Celia was the one knocking.

The girl had been gone for days, which wasn't too surprising; the little vixen was as hot-headed as they came.

Leah, however, wouldn't so much as change the supper menu without asking him if he minded.

He swiped off his hat and held it in front of him. "Have you seen my wife?"

The last time he'd been by, Annie had been gone, likely searching for her girl.

She shook her head.

Telling her of Leah's disappearance would only add to her worry, but he had to tell someone—had to get help. "Is Jake home?"

"Yes." Jacob stepped around her and opened the door wider. "Let the man come in, Anne."

She stepped back, and Jacob lifted an eyebrow. "What brings you here so late?"

Bryant stepped into the cozy warmth of their kitchen. "Leah didn't make me supper."

"Did you not deserve food?"

Jacob's sarcasm wasn't funny in the least tonight.

"No." His throat went dry, but he scratched out some words. "She's missing and..."

Jacob's eyes lost their twinkle. "Let's look around town, shall we?" He grabbed his coat and then cupped Annie's chin. "Please get some sleep."

At their tender kiss, Bryant turned on his heel. He'd wait for Jacob on the porch.

A few moments later, the door clicked shut behind him, and Jacob came near, tugging on his jacket. "When did you last see her?"

"This morning. That's all I know."

"Did she find out about your gambling?"

Bryant shook his head. Even if she had, she'd not leave without telling him.

"Surely, someone's seen her." Jacob led him toward the livery where they saddled their horses.

His friend's silence confirmed every fear piercing his heart. Leah wouldn't be gone unless something terrible had happened —even Jacob knew that.

Once atop his horse, Jacob pointed to the right side of Main Street. "You go north. I'll go south. We'll stop at any house you have connections with, meet up on the other side of town."

An hour later, Bryant rode up to Jacob's mare grazing in the deep shadows at the edge of town. "Learn anything?"

"Nobody's seen her since this morning. You?"

Bryant tried not to let the churning in his gut overwhelm him. "Same."

"You don't think someone would want to hurt her?" Jacob gathered Duchess's reins and remounted.

"Leah doesn't have a single enemy."

"But you?"

McGill. Would the bully sink so low as to kidnap his wife to prod him into doing what he refused to do? His fingernails clawed into his hat brim. "Perhaps I do know where she is."

McGill had to have her—what else could explain her disappearance?

Jacob's horse stomped impatiently. "Where?"

Bryant looked out toward the dark shadow that indicated the ridge. McGill could have her stashed anywhere.

Should he tell Jacob?

If his friend hadn't been able to catch the rustlers or find Celia, how likely would he be able to find Leah?

And if Jacob learned about why McGill might've kidnapped Leah, he was enough of a stickler to put him and McGill both behind bars. And if their boss had no incentive to bring back his wife...

"I'll let you know if she's not back by tomorrow."

"What?" Jacob spit the words as if Bryant were mentally incompetent.

He shouldn't have gotten Jacob involved. "I can get her back."

"Bryant."

"Thank you for helping, but I'll take care of it now." He let out a slow breath, trying to keep himself from turning his horse immediately and galloping across town to McGill's mansion. He wouldn't do so until Jacob was well out of sight and couldn't follow.

His friend's mare pranced around as a pack of coyotes yipped from somewhere near the ridge as Jacob stared at Bryant as if he'd gone mad.

He blew out a long, steady breath to keep his heart from racing any faster. "Trust me."

"I suppose you're going to be as closed-mouthed about this as you were about your gambling?"

At Bryant's nod, Jacob sighed loudly. "I guess all I can do is pray for you then."

"Thanks, we'll need it."

More than you know.

CHAPTER FORTY

"Water. Can I have water?" Leah pushed her head off the mule's ribcage.

Celia pulled down the brim of her hat and opened her canteen. She lifted Leah's head for a drink, careful not to look her in the eye. Was it possible to get her mother's friend home without revealing who she was?

Water dribbled out of Leah's mouth. She seemed to be having difficulty swallowing upside down. "Can I get down?"

In the distance, the lowing of disturbed cattle indicated the men were still busy. They'd said they'd come back after rounding up the beeves and Celia was to follow them to the hidden valley where they rebranded the ill-gotten animals.

Yesterday, she'd been hoptoad mad about them not wanting her help, but now, all she could think about was washing her hands clean of this. If only they were farther away so she could be certain they'd not notice her stealing off with Leah.

"Please?" The older woman's voice was soft, but not scared or whiny.

If she worked quickly and kept her face turned, hopefully she could keep Leah from getting a good look at her. Untying the knots, Celia loosened the ropes enough to slide her charge onto the ground.

"Thank you." Leah groaned and pushed herself upright, struggling to do so since she was still bound hand and foot.

Celia grunted before tipping her canteen against Leah's mouth, careful to keep slightly behind her.

The woman managed several messy gulps before shaking her head. "Thank you, no more." She turned her head, trying to see over her shoulder. "You should go back home, dear."

Backing away, Celia held her breath. Had the dim starlight been enough to give her identity away?

"Can you speak, young man?"

Celia let out the breath she'd held.

"Young man" was good. Real good.

After moving to the side about ten paces to the closest tree, Celia sat down, spreading her legs out most unladylike and leaned against the trunk in the self-assured manner Daniel always assumed.

"Are you from around here?" Leah wriggled her legs out from under her. "Could you get a message to my husband?"

If they could escape tonight, there'd be no need for messages. But if they didn't ... Celia squirmed.

They wouldn't hurt Leah too badly, right? Tom had told them not to leave bruises.

But then, why would Leah be allowed to go home when Tom had made no attempt to hide his identity?

"Please?" Leah's quiet plea unnerved her.

Celia worked her voice to come out as low as possible. "No." Her voice still sounded juvenile, but at least more like a boy's than her own. She grabbed the canteen and guzzled.

"Do you have a home? I'm sure I could find you one. Or you could stay with my husband and me. You can leave this mess behind and have a home with people who care for you."

Choking on her water, Celia coughed until she could breathe normally again. Had Leah truly offered such a thing?

Her size might indicate she wasn't full grown, but she was in cahoots with the woman's kidnappers. "Are you serious?" Her voice had started high on the first word, but she'd quickly deepened her tone.

"Thank you, Jesus," Leah whispered. "Celia."

Celia punched her fist into the dirt beside her. So much for the disguise.

"Honey, I'm so happy you're all right." Leah let out a sigh.

How could the woman sound so happy when she was hogtied and awaiting torture at the hands of two awful men?

"What is wrong with you?" Celia crawled over, whispering. "You've been kidnapped! They plan to hurt you, and I'm not talking about just punching you in the gut a time or two." Celia tried to dampen the high-pitched astonishment in her voice so as not to attract the men's attention. "And yet, you're glad I'm all right?"

"Tell me they haven't hurt you."

"They haven't." Not yet, anyway. "But they're going to hurt you." Celia spit to rid herself of the foul taste in her mouth.

"I know."

She'd said that as if Celia had only informed her that the sun would rise tomorrow.

Bryant had carefully picked his way across town in hopes of not being spotted riding toward McGill's residence.

After pounding on his boss's large imported front door, he took a step back and checked the windows for flickering light. None.

How dare McGill sleep tucked under his quilts as if not expecting Bryant to confront him the second he discerned the reason behind Leah's disappearance.

He poised to knock again, but the door opened before him.

A solitary flame illumined a thin, old man wearing a sleeping hat.

Before Harrison, the mayor's butler, could speak, Bryant sidestepped him into the foyer. "Where's McGill?"

"The mayor retired to his room hours ago." Harrison's voice crackled with sleep and annoyance. "If you don't mind, sir, kindly step out of the house and wait until morn." He opened the entry door wider and gestured toward the street.

"McGill!" Bryant strode to the banister and shouted up the massive, shadowy staircase. "Conrad, so help me, get your cowardly self down here!"

"I say, sir." The butler stepped onto the first stair and spread out his arms, looming over his unwelcomed guest. "Leave now, or I'll call the marshal."

"Don't bother with the marshal, Harrison." McGill's wheezy voice called from the blackness. "Bryant, for Pete's sake, go home. Nothing is so urgent you can't talk with me in the morning."

"Now. We'll talk now." He pushed past Harrison and took three steps at once. "I'll drag you down if I have to."

"Hold your horses, and I'll be down in a minute." The boards above squeaked under the mayor's heavy tread.

"This way, sir." The butler stepped in front of him and pointed to the room at the bottom of the staircase.

Bryant stared at the elderly man, whose wrinkled, imperious face looked haggard in the light of the lantern he carried.

He let go of the railing and stomped down the stairs toward the room Harrison indicated. The butler shouldn't be a witness to the upcoming conversation, so wherever he wanted to stuff him was fine.

The room smelled of leather and cherry tobacco.

Harrison lit a lamp.

In light of the bookshelves, gargantuan desk, and high-backed wing chairs, it seemed he was in McGill's study. "Tell your boss to be down in two minutes or I'll make him come down."

Harrison nodded as if he'd requested something as mundane as tea and exited.

Bryant paced. Should he punch McGill in the face the moment he walked in, or talk first, then punch him?

Lantern light grew brighter on the other side of the door until McGill stepped in, shutting the door behind him. "This is highly irregular, Whitsett."

"Where's my wife?" Bryant took a step toward him, his fists raised.

As if his guest had only stopped in to chat, McGill sauntered to his side of the desk and sat on its edge, putting space between them. "A strange question to be asking me in the middle of the night. How should I know?"

"You know." Bryant's words rumbled through his clenched teeth. But he lowered his fists—for now. He couldn't kill the man before finding out where he'd taken his wife.

"Perhaps." He selected a pipe from a rack sitting on a bookshelf and knocked the tobacco remnants from its bowl. "I'm assuming if you know why she's gone, you also know what I want."

"I told you, no more." Bryant seethed as McGill took his time filling his pipe. How could he have known that his first win at cards would eventually force him into begging for his wife's life?

What a fool he'd been. He should've told her everything from the beginning. She would've likely forgiven him seventy times seven—she was nearly a verifiable saint.

Now she might reap the consequences for each and every sin he'd committed, unless he could placate McGill. "My wife—"

"Is fine, I'm sure." A spark of fire scraped into life at the end of a match. "And she'll continue to be fine—as long as you're cooperative." McGill puffed, turning his tobacco a deep red.

"I'm through with you." Bryant swiped a stack of books off the desk and rounded the corner.

"I wouldn't touch me if I were you." McGill didn't shrink, didn't move. "I know what you want to know."

He blew a puff of smoke out of his nose slowly, as if they were doing nothing more than discussing the price of beef.

Looking for something to smash, Bryant knocked over an elaborate globe from its pedestal stand. The heavy ball thumped onto the plush carpet and rolled under a chair. He growled at the fact it remained intact. "Tell me now or so help me God..."

McGill yawned. "I'll tell you tomorrow after you've done your job."

"Stealing land for you isn't my job."

"It is unless you want to confess your sins, which I wouldn't advise." McGill's pipe tobacco glowed bright red again. "One more paper is all it'll take." He leaned forward and pointed at Bryant with his pipe stem. "You'll get your wife back, a poor man will be unburdened from land he cannot handle, and I'll sell the property to the city once I'm through. Maybe even throw it in with the deal I'll give Hendrix on his ranch. We'll all end up happy."

"But then there'll be another record you'll want me to falsify."

McGill shrugged.

Bryant growled and took a step toward the mayor.

"Of course, if you choose not to help me, your wife may never return."

Bryant stopped mid-stride.

"You do have that option if you really want it."

Bryant stared out the dark window, unable to see the land surrounding town for lack of moonlight. What choice did he have?

McGill owned hundreds, no thousands, of acres surrounding Armelle. Leah could be anywhere.

If he didn't do McGill's bidding, he might never find where his boss had tucked her away.

What was one more doctored ledger?

Spineless acts of deception had endangered her; one last one could bring her back.

"You love that wife of yours rather imprudently, but I'm not complaining. Otherwise, why care about a silly gambling debt? You lost your girl's tuition, sure, but taking a sabbatical from school never hurt anyone. It wouldn't have hurt Jennie. Schooling won't change the fact she's blind."

Bryant grabbed a newspaper off the man's desk, rolled it up, and strangled it. How he'd rather have his boss's flesh crumpling beneath his fingers. But finding his wife was more important. "I'll be in the office at the crack of dawn, and I want my wife home by noon."

"I don't see why that can't happen. You follow through. I'll follow through."

Bryant stormed out of the house and slammed the front door as hard as he could, hoping it cracked off its fancy hinges.

He'd go home, but he wouldn't sleep. A few hours remained before sunrise, and he'd spend it packing. When Leah returned, he'd hire a wagon and drive to meet his youngest daughter in Ohio. If only they'd not have to leave his oldest daughter behind.

But he'd no longer allow Conrad McGill to have any power over him.

Celia gaped at Leah. "You're all right with them hurting you?"

The woman shrugged as if being hogtied and awaiting torture was a normal affair for the housewives of Armelle. "No, but I'm relieved to finally know what's going on."

Celia's heart fluttered. How did any of this make Leah feel better?

She'd thought running away from Ma and the marshal and all their rules would've made her happy, but misery as thick as the night weighed upon her.

Yet this woman, whose world was about to be destroyed, sat calmly, as if she were here to watch the sun rise over the ridge and nothing more. "How can you possibly be relieved?"

"Because I have an idea of what's wrong with Bryant now."

Celia couldn't help but scrunch her face. Leah's good news was learning that her husband had problems? "How so?"

Leah's head twisted in an attempt to look in Celia's direction. "My husband hasn't been acting right lately. Always jumpy, constantly belittling my compliments, angry, melancholy—"

"But I've never seen him out here."

"Mr. Passey is McGill's man now, right?"

"Yes." Tom's name being uttered aloud made her want to spit. She'd actually thought the double-crosser was a cowboy worth looking up to when he'd let her tag along when he'd worked for her parents.

Leah squirmed, obviously in pain from the way the ropes held her hands behind her back. "I heard him say his boss is trying to get my husband to cooperate by dragging me out here. Seems the mayor has something on Bryant. I'm not sure what, but my husband must be refusing to do something he's decided isn't right. But he's definitely mixed up in something he shouldn't be, which explains a lot of his behaviors."

Knowing her husband was a cheat somehow didn't make what they faced any less scary. "Do you think they'll actually let you go?"

She nodded slightly. "I'm guessing my husband is in so deep that talking will hurt us both. They must figure we won't retaliate since they've not hidden their identities. Though they could just be the sloppiest criminals in the territory."

"I'm afraid of what they'll do to you. Roughing someone up can mean different things." Celia shivered. "And these men, with the way they talk about women ... what they've done at those buildings near the tracks—"

"Hush, child." Leah's voice sounded upset for the first time. "I'm sorry you've heard such talk."

"What does it matter?" Celia waved her hands in the air. "They might do those same things to you." She jumped up from the ground and paced. "I'm no match for two men. So how do I get you home without getting caught? My horse and your mule can't outrun a snail."

Leah scooted across the stubbly grasses. "Celia, don't you put yourself in danger."

"I already have." Tears piled up, but she didn't bother to wipe them away. "They might hurt you real bad, and if I don't help them, they might do the same to me." Her breathing spun out of control, and she collapsed to the ground. "I don't know what to do."

"Celia, darling, calm yourself." Leah attempted to scoot closer. "McGill intends little harm to come to me."

Why would a tied-up woman try to comfort her? "Do you truly believe that?"

The older woman sighed and tipped her head back and Celia looked up to see whatever had captured her attention. The twinkling stars seemed peaceful—so very different from Celia's guts twisting inside her.

The lowing of cows and the rustlers' hushed commands grew closer.

Finally, Leah turned to Celia. "I could be mistaken, but I feel as if something is going to go terribly wrong, no matter what we do." Leah's shuddering breath held no hint of tears.

Celia grabbed Leah's shoulders. "Then why aren't you afraid?"

When she didn't answer, Celia crawled behind Leah and started tugging on the knots anchoring her wrists together. If this woman wasn't afraid, she ought to be.

She was plenty afraid for them both.

"Help me figure out a way to get us home." She leaned over to bite at a stubborn knot.

"We can certainly try." Leah wriggled her wrists against her bonds. "But we reap what we sow, and I think Bryant will reap more than he ever imagined."

Celia spit out torn rope fiber. "You didn't sow any of this."

"No." She breathed in deeply. "Leave off with the knots, darling. They're coming back."

Already? Celia's innards danced. "But I haven't even got them loose."

"Don't let them see you trying to help me." Leah's voice was sharper than she'd ever heard from this kind woman.

Celia scooted away from Leah, whose chest rose and fell three times slower than hers did.

"Tell my husband to read my diary." Leah sniffed. "And that I love him. That I still love him, no matter what happens."

"You're just giving up?" Celia whispered. Was this woman not afraid of death—or worse?

Celia barely kept herself rooted to the ground instead of rushing at the men while screaming for help at the top of her lungs.

Because no one would hear.

No one could help.

Rufus's tall form appeared in front of them, backlit by the rosy pink of the morning sun just below the horizon. He rubbed his hands together. "It's time for some fun."

CHAPTER FORTY-ONE

Despite her shaky legs, Celia shoved her way between Rufus and Leah, spreading her arms out wide. “Don’t touch her. Let me do it.”

Rufus’s leer transformed into a scowl. “Do what?”

“I’ll rough her up.” Celia tried to give her voice a sinister edge despite her wavering vocal cords.

Rufus erupted into laughter. “Sure, kid.”

“No, I mean it.” She’d have to punch Leah or something. Her stomach rolled just thinking about hitting the nicest woman in town, but if she beat Leah up, then Rufus and Guy wouldn’t have reason to, right? She’d have to wallop her good to convince them.

She put her fists on her hips. “I think it’d be fun. Boss said we’re only supposed to hurt her a little. I’m too small to do more than that.”

Rufus stroked his jaw, his lower lip protruding. “I guess there ain’t no harm in letting you have at her.”

Guy’s mare trotted away from the nearby herd, and he stopped next to Rufus. “Are you going to grab her or what? We haven’t got all night.”

Rufus was still rubbing his scruffy face. "Celia here wants to pummel the lady for us."

"What?" Guy glared down at her. "We aren't playing games."

"I don't know." Rufus shrugged. "Think it might be fun to watch."

Guy snapped his horse's head to force his mount to walk closer to the women. "Well then, get on with it, girl."

Celia's body trembled, and her teeth ground together so hard her jaw ached, but she forced the corners of her mouth upward. "Good." She turned to Leah, whose face looked no more frightened than before.

Leah frowned. "Don't do this."

Celia took three deep breaths to calm herself. She could do this. She could save Leah from worse. "I'll do what I want, lady." She mouthed the word *sorry*, though Leah had already bowed her head, her lips moving rapidly.

Good thing she had a real good reason to hit Leah. Striking a praying woman had to be lower than low.

She pulled her arm back and swung her fist, making contact between Leah's left eye and ear.

Sparks jolted from her wrist up into her shoulder. "Ow!"

Leah groaned and Celia clamped her hand to her chest. Her thumb pulsed in torment.

The two men hooted with laughter.

"Just grab the woman, Rufus."

"No, wait!" Celia bit her lip against the pain. "I'm not done yet."

"You probably hurt yourself more than you hurt her with that pitiful swing."

"If you don't give me a chance, I can't learn how, now can I?" Celia held up her throbbing fist. "So tell me how I'm supposed to hit her without hurting myself."

"For one," Rufus snorted, "take your thumb out from inside your fingers."

Celia repositioned her pulsing thumb and brandished her fist.

He sighed. "And then wrap it around the front or you're liable to break it off."

She wrapped her thumb around her fingertips, and at his nod, whirled back around.

Leah was still mouthing silent prayers.

"Let's try this again, shall we?" Celia growled menacingly, closed her eyes, and swung. She hit soft flesh, the pain in her hand not as bad this time, though it still smarted.

Leah fell onto her side and groaned. "Father, forgive her."

Celia wanted forgiveness, yes, but she didn't deserve it. Especially if she couldn't keep Rufus from doing what he wanted with a woman who'd rather kiss a fly than smack it.

Though tears blinded her aim, she took another swing, and another.

"All right. Enough." Guy slid off his saddle, stalked over, and pushed her aside. "That was pathetic."

"But—" Her voice held a whine she wished she could snatch back.

"Our turn now." Rufus rubbed his hands together.

Guy hoisted Leah onto his shoulder.

Her body flopped like a green corn husk doll.

"Wait!" Celia blinked repeatedly as she forged forward. "Wait, I can do more."

Leah's head lifted off Guy's back, the pale morning light sparkling upon her damp eyelashes. "No more, Celia. Thank you."

"What did you say, woman?" Guy dropped his burden onto the ground. With both hands on his hips, he glared down at her. "'Thank you'?"

When she didn't respond, he kicked her.

She groaned and curled up on her side.

Guy clamped his gaze onto Celia. "Why is she thanking you?"

"I don't know." Celia put out her hands. "Maybe for not hitting her hard enough? Let me try again."

"You had your chance." Guy turned back to the woman at his feet.

"Lord, save us from evil," Leah prayed aloud while sniffing, probably from the blood running from her nose. "Let us throw ourselves upon your mercy, for we are all sinners—"

He shoved her with his foot. "Stop sniveling."

"May we seek your will, not our own. Let us turn from our wicked ways before—"

Guy kicked Leah in the ribcage.

"Father, help Celia—"

Guy kicked her again.

And again.

Leah let out only the slightest hint of a moan as he continued, and continued...

"Stop!" Celia ran over and yanked on his arm.

"Get off me, brat!"

"No." She pulled with all her might, but his foul, stinking body wouldn't budge.

"Stop, you two." Rufus's voice was low, intense. "We need to move farther away from the—"

Guy hollered from the bite Celia inflicted upon the soft flesh of his arm. He tried to yank away, but she held on, attempting to sink her teeth down to the bone.

"Rufus, you lazy lout, get this she-cat off me." He cursed and punched at her head. One of his glancing blows detached her.

Her backside met the ground with a hard thump. She slammed the flat of her foot against his shin, knocking him forward.

Arms flailing, he fell on top of her.

Celia growled as a bellow rang out from the nearby calves.

Guy popped up on all fours, but didn't move away fast enough to keep her from pulling the revolver from his holster, and in the same instant, the gun kicked with a loud bang, and an explosion of dirt and sharp rocks near Guy's cowboy boots hit her in the face. The gun slid from her frozen fingers, the scent of gunpowder burning her nose.

A frightened uproar rose from the cattle now hastily scattering in every direction.

"Now, you've done it." Guy called Celia his favorite foul word as he scrambled up, then grabbed for his horse's reins as the mare reared up and pawed the air in fright.

A wild-eyed calf ran straight for Celia, and she rolled sideways.

The calf's front hoof grazed her in the back. "Oof." She scrambled across the grass in the direction of a willow tree as the ground shook with the pounding of a hundred hooves.

She hadn't meant to pull the trigger.

A soft body hit her as several steer ran past, almost knocking her to the ground.

Guy hooted and hollered atop his horse, firing his other six-shooter at the ground near the front, trying to turn the stampede. "Get 'em going in the right direction!"

Rufus raced his buckskin toward the opposite edge of the panicking herd.

And Leah was lying somewhere amid the chaos.

Celia hugged the north side of the tree as tight as she could, squeezing her eyes against all thought until the thundering of the cattle grew faint and the dust settled.

She peered around the tree to find both men had disappeared with the herd. There'd be no reason for them to come back.

With how Leah had been left out there, she was likely far more "roughed up" than any of them had ever intended.

And that was only if...

She swallowed hard.

"Leah?" she whispered as she looked out over the trampled grasses.

No answer. No call for help.

And there, in the dirt twenty yards away, lay Leah, a crumpled heap.

"Leah!" A sob wrenched through her, but she punched herself in the gut to stop it. What right did she have to cry over anything!

Oh God, I wanted to save her!

Scrambling toward her, Celia fixed her gaze on Leah's still form, looking for any sign of movement. She rolled Leah over and with trembling fingers traced a hoof mark near the woman's collarbone. "Leah?" Her voice barely sounded above the crickets that had restarted their night time chorus. She picked up Leah's hand, as heavy as a brick. "Leah!"

She shook the woman's shoulders, but the weight of her resisted the shaking.

Her head rolled limply to the side.

"No." Her strangled whisper burned her throat and something banded her lungs together, stealing her breath. What had she done? What had she done!

All she'd wanted was to be free to do as she pleased, but if she took Leah's body back to town...

She hugged herself, and a cold shiver jolted through her as an image of her father, dead and bloody with frightened, unseeing eyes flashed before her.

Hanging her head between her knees, she sucked in big gulps of air. She'd tried to bury that image. Nothing could be worse than seeing one's own father's mangled remains over and over again.

But what if she'd never seen his body? What if she'd had to wonder her whole life whether or not he lived?

With her dirty sleeve, Celia wiped her damp face, then looked to her horse.

The animal chomped the grass hanging from its mouth as if nothing out of the ordinary had happened.

She could sneak onto the train, find somewhere else to live—

Father, help Celia.

She curled her fists.

How could she even think of abandoning the woman who'd used her last prayers on her?

Father, help Celia.

Leah's plea had been in vain.

God wouldn't bother to help a murderer.

A moan.

Celia's heart jumped into her throat. She flattened herself against Leah, pressing an ear to her chest.

Was Leah breathing?

Or had the groan been her own, loosed amid the sobs wracking her body that were as out of control as the stampede she'd caused?

CHAPTER FORTY-TWO

Jacob groaned, rolled over, and draped his arm across Annie's soft body. Except she felt too soft. He opened his right eye. Not Annie—Annie's pillow.

A burning, sugary smell accosted his nose.

The sun wasn't even up, yet she was downstairs baking.

He rolled onto his back and stared at the ceiling.

Celia's disappearance had kept Annie awake, agitated, and restless most every night. Though he wished she had no reason to cry, at least he now had the privilege of holding her when those tears stole her sleep.

He pushed himself upright and scooted to the edge of the bed to pull on his trousers. Outside the window, the deep reds, oranges, and purples of the rising sun over the wide plains shouted of God's magnificent glory and caused him to stop and simply watch.

Once the fiery colors succumbed to blue, he finished dressing and moved to the window.

He scanned what land he could see beyond town, the rolling plains that smacked into mountains. Was Celia out there somewhere or long gone?

She may not have cared a whit for him, but he'd do anything to have her back. And not just because it would bring Annie comfort, but because Celia was his daughter too, no matter whose blood ran through her veins.

And what about Leah? Was she out there as well? Surely not. If Bryant had thought so, he'd have asked him to help scour the countryside—even if he had proven himself rather ineffectual at finding people lately.

Last night, he'd had a hard time falling asleep knowing something was going on between Bryant and Leah. The only reason he could conjure up for her disappearance was that she'd learned of Bryant's gambling and had left him.

Leah leaving her husband felt like the last thing on this planet that would happen, but then, Bryant hadn't been acting lately like the man he'd known so well for so many years either. Perhaps Leah had decided to jolt him into realizing what all he could lose if he didn't straighten up.

Jacob crossed to Spencer's room and peeked around the open door. The boy lay on the floor surrounded by an army of lead soldiers. Though Spencer was certainly upset over his sister's disappearance, he wasn't having as hard a time as his mother was going on about life.

"I see you're already busy this morning."

"Yep. Got some rustlers trapped over there in the Hole in the Wall." He pointed to several books he'd propped up on the floor, creating imaginary cliffs and valleys. "We're going to flush them out."

Jacob chuckled. "If you succeed, let me know how so I can pass the information on to the marshal in Johnson County."

Spencer nodded, his furrowed brow serious.

As Jacob clomped down the stairs, the funny burning smell grew stronger and stranger. Not exactly the smell of overdone sweets.

Annie was slouched over the kitchen table, cradling her head in her arms. A plum cake sat before her with pools of hot wax spread over its top. One lone flame held tenaciously to the single remaining candle wick.

He grabbed a chair, sat beside his wife, and placed a hand on her back.

She faced him, her eyes cloudy. "Today would've been his birthday."

"Gregory's?" He counted the pooled candles. Five.

"No." She returned her bleary gaze back to the cake. "Jack's."

The flame gave out one last flicker before leaving behind a wisp of white smoke.

She'd yet to talk to him about any of the children she'd buried on her ranch. "He'd be five today?"

"Three." She dipped her finger into the hardening wax. "I put a candle in for each of them: Gregory, Catherine, Jack, Augustus—" She gulped. "And Celia."

He scooted closer to wrap his arms around her, and she went limp in his embrace.

He couldn't fathom her pain.

Though he hoped their daughter wasn't dead, he wouldn't chastise his wife for mourning her disappearance along with the rest. "Celia could come home any minute, love."

"But you've heard nothing, found nothing."

"That doesn't necessarily mean bad news." He pulled her onto his lap.

She didn't turn toward him. Instead, she fiddled with the cake pan, running her index finger along its rim. "But there's no hope of you tracking her down, right? If she doesn't choose to come back on her own..."

He shook his head with a sigh. Armelle needed a more skilled lawman for marshal. He'd only ever succeeded at handing out sidewalk fines and corralling wandering livestock.

But finding Celia or the rustlers? Stopping the clothesline thief? Figuring out why his gut insisted Annie's land had been stolen despite contrary evidence? Those he failed at with aplomb.

He pursed his lips and rested his chin atop Annie's head. "I wish I was a good enough marshal to bring her back."

"You've done your best."

"Not enough."

"But it's what's important. Even if you had another job, that's all you could do."

"Would you have a problem with me getting another job?"

"No, but while we pray about it, your best is all God asks of you, so I can't ask for anything more—whether you find Celia or not." She sniffed, and her breathing grew shaky again.

Holding her tight, he watched the five wax spots harden atop the cake while listening to Spencer shuffle about in his room overhead.

After the grandfather clock chimed the hour, he took in a deep breath. "Do we eat the cake?"

She shrugged.

She'd made the cake and lit the candles, but what sort of birthday celebration had no song?

He began singing in a low, rumbly voice, "Many Happy Returns of the Day," but the third stanza clogged his throat as Annie's tears slowly wetted his shirtsleeve.

But if 'midst the greeting there's one that we miss,
And that one was the dearest of all,
'Tis then we feel lone in a moment like this,
When our loudly hailed birthday shall fall.
What would we not give if the hours could restore,
That dear form that is far, far away...

His voice petered out.

What indeed would they not give to have Celia back? He squeezed Annie tighter, and she wiped her face against his shirt.

He restarted the song, humming it this time around.

After the last note, Annie pushed herself away from his chest though not out of his arms. "Thank you," she whispered.

She gave him a tight, sad smile, then slipped off his lap and headed to the parlor. She swiveled the rocking chair to face the front window where she'd taken up praying this past week.

He glanced at the cake but buttered bread for his breakfast instead. He was glad they were on better terms, even if they weren't as carefree as he'd hoped they'd be once they declared their love for each other. But from what he'd heard, grief was a difficult thing to get through even for the strongest of couples.

Lord, if you would, bring Celia back or help me find the rustlers so I can have more time to search for her.

He'd asked every farmer and rancher in the area to keep an eye out, but he'd basically given up gaining information that way. If they had seen her the day or two after her disappearance, they would've already let him know.

So either someone was hiding her or she'd left town.

Of course, she could be camping somewhere, but if she was, she had more stubborn willfulness than he'd counted on.

So he'd gone back to tracking the rustlers. And last night, he'd stumbled upon some out-of-place tracks, but it had been too late to investigate. Hopefully, today would be the day he'd haul them in.

If I catch them, the glory will belong to you alone since it's apparent I can't bring them in.

And though Annie's convinced me you require no more than my best, please allow me to do more than that. Help me bring about justice, along with peace, for both the town and my wife.

Celia slid off her tired nag between Leah's house and the tall wooden fence that screened the side yard from the Whitsetts' neighbors'.

Her horse sidestepped, and she placed a hand against Leah to keep her from falling to the ground.

Only a miracle would explain how she'd not been spotted coming through town with a woman slumped over her horse. And of course, it was certainly a miracle that Leah hadn't been trampled flat.

Then again, since the doctor hadn't answered her knock, what good were miracles if Leah died anyway?

She slid the woman down from the saddle and pressed a hand against her chest. The weak beat and expansion of her chest persisted.

Swallowing hard, Celia vehemently swiped the tears sliding down her cheeks. She hadn't time to sit here and cry.

She got up and took one step toward the back door before freezing, her body shaking with the urge to run. Would to God she could just leave Leah here, let Bryant discover her on his own, and escape the consequences.

If only she hadn't fought Guy, none of this would have happened.

Looking back at Leah, she tried to absorb the courage the older woman had shown earlier while at the mercy of pitiless men.

She hadn't panicked, hadn't cried, hadn't groveled. Only worried about her friend's daughter and Bryant.

Anxious about everyone but herself.

Celia pushed off the ground and hugged herself tight. When was the last time she'd been concerned about anyone other than herself?

She could start by getting Leah's husband out here. He might know who she could fetch for help since the doctor wasn't around—that was, if Bryant didn't kill her before she could fetch anyone. For after seeing what she'd done to his poor wife, how could he not want to strangle her?

Though the distance to the Whitsetts' front door was short,

every step took an eternity—and yet, she faced the brass knocker all too soon.

She picked up the heavy metal and let it drop.

With the first knock out of the way, she grabbed the knocker again and rapped it several times, much harder. The thumping echoed throughout the quiet neighborhood and a dog barked somewhere down the street.

She looked over her shoulder. People would soon be bustling about, and her feet begged to turn tail and run. She grabbed the railing to anchor herself.

The filmy curtain covering the window beside the door fluttered, and Bryant's sleep deprived eyes appeared behind the glass.

Celia steeled herself.

The door opened, and Bryant leaned heavily against the jamb, as if he too hadn't slept. "What can I do for you, lad? It's quite early."

"I'm Celia." She tugged on a piece of short-cropped hair, ashamed at the game of dress up she'd played.

He threw open the door and grabbed both of her shoulders. "Do your parents know where you are?"

"No, I—"

He spun her around toward the street. "Why'd you come here then? Your mother's worried sick."

He all but pushed her down the porch stairs.

"Wait." Celia dug in her heels. How easy it would be to go home and let him find Leah on his own. But the truth wouldn't take long to figure out even if she did. "Your wife—" Dizziness overcame her, and she plopped down on the bottom stair, hitting the edge and slipping onto the sidewalk.

The pain in her backside barely registered over the cramping in her chest.

He kneeled in front of her. "You know something about Leah?" His strangled whisper held too much hope. She might be alive, but with her injuries...

The lump in her throat was too thick for words to break through. She coughed and choked against it, trying to pull air into her lungs, but at least managed a nod.

"Where is she?" The panic behind his words turned his question into a yelp.

"She's—" She swallowed against the bile creeping up her throat.

His fingernails crimped painfully deep into her upper arm as he pulled her to stand.

She couldn't force her gaze up to meet his. "I was trying to save her, truly I was. It's my fault she's..." Her breaths came out in pants. "She's..." She ground her teeth together and glanced at him.

He took a step closer, his bloodshot eyes wide, his pupils twitching. "She's what?"

His shout made her throbbing head pang.

"She'd hurt real bad," she whispered. "I don't know how much time she has left."

"W—what?" His face blanked, and his skin lost its color. He breathed unsteadily and shook his head like a madman. "Take me to her."

The anger and disbelief contorting his face right now would not match the fury he'd feel at the first glimpse of his wife's battered body.

If his rage got the best of him, he'd probably break her neck.

She forced her feet forward, bracing for the moment he learned what she'd done.

I hope he kills me quick, though it's less than I deserve.

CHAPTER FORTY-THREE

In the rocking chair beside Annie, Jacob hadn't done much but watch the sun slowly rise above the horizon outside the window while holding her hand. He needed to get to work, but hadn't been able to leave her praying alone.

Please God, please bring Celia home today.

If God didn't, what else could he do? He'd already arranged to have Nolan and a few other men help him search over the weekend, but if they turned up nothing...

A rap at the back door startled him, and he pushed himself from his chair. Hopefully whoever knocked hadn't come to visit.

When Jacob opened the door, Bryant stood upon the porch with his hat in his hands and a young man behind him. Both looked as grim as his wife, despite the soft morning light illuminating their faces.

The lad lifted his heavily-lashed eyelids, meeting Jacob's gaze.

Not a boy!

"Celia!" He pushed Bryant aside and smashed her shorn head up against his chest.

Never had God answered his prayer so quickly! God's presence overwhelmed him with dizziness. Or maybe he was just lightheaded with the shock of her return.

She stepped back, her fists gripping the front of her over-large shirt, her head bent like a beaten dog.

So she expected a reprimand? She'd certainly have one, but not now. He cupped her cheeks with his hands. "I'm so glad you're home."

Annie.

He staggered back into the kitchen, pulling Celia with him. "Anne!"

His wisp of a wife walked around the corner, brow quizzical, and then her face lit. Her arms flung open, and she rushed to her daughter. "Darling, where have you been? I've missed you so!"

Celia's arms hung limp at her sides as her mother crushed her into an embrace. Both had tears trailing down their faces, but their expressions were completely different.

Was the girl that unhappy to be home?

"How could you have done this to me?" Annie pushed Celia away from her, but kept a hold of the girl's shoulders. "You are not allowed to leave this house ever again."

She pulled Celia back into her arms. "I'm so happy you're back."

Remembering his manners, Jacob turned to Bryant who was sitting in a chair near the door, his hat between his knees, tears traveling down his cheeks.

Jacob frowned at his crying friend. He'd never once seen Bryant cry tears of joy. Not at his oldest daughter's wedding or when she'd announced his first grandchild was on its way.

He'd certainly not do so bringing Celia home.

"What are you wearing?" Annie's happy scolding continued unabated. "And what did you do to your hair?"

Jacob dragged a chair next to his somber best friend and waited, for something told him these two were about to steal away Annie's joy.

"Celia!" Spencer's footsteps pounded as he ran down the stairs, his bubbly voice interrupting his mother's chiding, "Why are you dressed like a boy?"

"We're going upstairs to fix that right now." Annie placed her hand on Celia's back, and the threesome tromped upstairs.

Spencer's babble mixed in with Annie's one-sided conversation. "If your grandmother could see you, she'd fall over in shock. Why she'd..."

Bryant wiped at his cheeks, then crushed and re-crushed his hat. He rubbed his eyelids several times before he looked up, his face wan, eyes fatigued.

Jacob braced himself.

"Leah's home."

That sentence should've brought a wellspring of elation, but the crack in Bryant's voice dampened all positive emotion.

Had Leah come home only to tell him she was leaving him for good? Surely Leah would give Bryant a chance. She was the most patient person he'd ever known.

"Celia brought her back." Bryant's words were all but a whisper. "But she might not live past this evening."

Jacob gripped the arms of his chair. "What?"

His friend shook his head and swallowed several times. "The doc sent me away, while he's ... while he's..." Bryant looked positively green. "Don't let Celia blame herself; the real culprit is McGill." He choked on his breath, as if his lungs were seizing. "And me."

His hat fell to the floor and he dug his hands into his hair. "It's my fault. All my fault."

Jacob sat uncomfortably as the man sobbed like a child.

How were any of them to blame for anything?

Bryant pulled in mighty gulps of air, working to suppress his hysterics. Finally, his mouth tightened into a thin line, and he turned his head to stare at the wall. "I did what I did to keep from hurting her." A twisted smile disfigured his lips as his voice croaked out. "I suppose this is what I get for defying God."

"But you said she *might* not live—which means she could."

He looked up with vacant eyes. "I wouldn't deserve such a miracle."

"God doesn't care if you deserve anything. He loves freely. You just have to ask for it." When Bryant just stared at him without blinking, Jacob scooted closer. "Just ask for it."

Bryant lowered his gaze to the floor and ran a shaking hand through his hair. "But there'd be no reason to if I hadn't started gambling two years ago. Made good money too." His sickly smile drooped. "Until, of course, I lost every cent. Including the savings we set aside for Jennie's tuition. I couldn't face her or Leah, couldn't tell them she'd have to stay home for a few years."

"Bryant, it doesn't matter what you've done. Leah and Jennie love you. They might be disappointed, but—"

"You think Jennie will still love me when she finds out that not only am I the reason she can't go back to school but I'm also why she no longer has a mother?"

"We'll pray that doesn't come to pass, but you've yet to tell me what happened."

"McGill is what happened." He huffed a derisive laugh. "I asked him to cover my debts, but his help came with more strings attached than I'd bet on. I should've just admitted to Leah what I'd done, but my pride ... Do you know how hard it is for a man to admit to his failures when his wife exclaims his virtues to everyone every chance she gets?"

Bryant didn't wait for his answer. "McGill's a smooth talker. He said we were doing people a favor, making the inevitable pass quicker, saving them from losing what dignity they had left—"

Bryant stopped dead in his tracks. "He had me doctor the county tax list so we could repossess land."

Jacob's eyes closed. Why had he not pushed his friend harder to confess what was eating at him these past few months? "How does this tie into Celia and Leah's disappearance?"

Bryant grimaced. "Though I paid my debt, McGill wanted me to continue covering for him to keep my gambling and involvement a secret. I've helped him seize three properties so far." He folded his arms and looked at the floor. "Including Annie's."

Jacob pressed his lips together to keep from bursting. A part of him wanted to run to Annie and inform her they could get her land back, but the misery on Bryant's face and the knowledge that Leah's life hung in the balance kept him rooted to his chair.

Bryant resumed his pacing. "You didn't tell me who you were marrying, remember?" He stopped. "But then, that doesn't matter. I couldn't stop the repossession unless I confessed." His deadpan laughter made Jacob cringe. "I always found it odd how my girls, when they were little, told such outrageous lies to cover for something insignificant. How stupid."

A light tread behind them interrupted Bryant's confession.

Celia, now dressed in a yellow shirtwaist and navy skirt, hesitantly stepped into the room.

Annie followed, her face blank. "Are you saying my Gregory had no gambling debts?"

"Correct." Bryant croaked. "And ... and you need to look into his death. Though I've no proof, I know of several properties McGill had an interest in where the owners died, unexpectedly."

Annie slowly lowered herself into a chair.

Jacob gestured for Spencer, who was standing in the stairwell's shadows, to head back up. "Why don't you go play with your soldiers, son?"

"Yes, Pa." The boy's feet moved like molasses, but he did as bidden.

"I'm very sorry." Bryant talked with his eyes close. "Though I'm sure my saying so helps not a whit."

"How did Leah get involved? What's wrong with her?"

Bryant stared blankly at his hands.

"I can explain." Celia's voice came out soft and raspy. "I've been running around with Daniel like you told me not to." She took a seat in the chair next to Jacob, but slid it back a ways as if needing to put space between them. "He told me about some men hiring workers. I was going to be so smart and make my own money, live under my own rules." She hugged herself. "But I was stupid. Stupid, stupid."

"Hush." Annie wrapped her arm around Celia's shoulders.

Surprisingly, the girl didn't shrug off her mother's touch. "We were just panning for gold. Nothing criminal. But last night, they decided the timing was good for cattle rustling."

Jacob sat up straighter. All the things he hadn't been able to solve seemed to be coming together.

"Tom Passey came out with a tied-up woman Rufus and Guy were supposed to rough up," She glanced at Bryant who only stared at her, "to teach her husband a lesson."

"Tom?" Annie's brow furrowed. "He's the rustlers' ring leader?"

"No, the mayor is." Celia stared at the table's top.

Jacob turned his gaze toward Bryant.

"I didn't know that. But a couple days ago, I refused to doctor another tax entry for McGill." Bryant's monotone voice filled the room. "I tried to convince him we'd get caught doing this too many times. Told him to find another way to get the land his men said contained gold."

Annie's hand covered her mouth. "Does my land have gold on it?"

Bryant nodded. "He's been on the lookout for alluvial deposits."

"What happened to Leah?" Jacob clasped Celia's shoulder.

"I ... I couldn't let them hurt her. I'd heard things..." Celia played with a discarded napkin. "Things they did to the women at the brothels."

Jacob stopped himself from digging his fingers into Celia's shoulder. When he got hold of them...

"I tried to get the men to agree to let me be the one to rough Leah up." She shot a tortured glance at Bryant. "But they laughed at me—" Celia's voice cut off. Her face twitched for a moment, but she continued, "When they carried her away, I fought them."

She strangled the small linen square in her hands. "I thought it would be smart to grab Guy's gun, but somehow I pulled the trigger."

Sound emptied from the room like the color that had drained from Celia's face.

The tall case clock in the parlor chimed the half hour.

Celia closed her eyes, and Jacob feared she'd pass out.

"I started a stampede," she whispered as she clenched the table's edge. "Leah was tied up. She couldn't run." Her rough-shorn head dropped onto the table and her arms came up to hide herself from view. Gut-wrenching, muffled sobs reverberated against the wood.

Annie tried shushing her and smoothing down her daughter's hair, but Celia's weeping only grew louder.

Jacob clasped his daughter's quaking shoulder. "Where did you last see these men?"

She turned her damp face to the side. "Somewhere northwest of our old property by Sullivan's Pass. They're on their way to Helena."

If he could gather up some men within the hour, they might be able to catch them. But how could he leave Celia and Bryant at a time like this?

But if he didn't, how many might suffer if these men were allowed to escape the law?

Jacob strode toward the shelf where he emptied his pockets and stored his weapons at night. He looked at Bryant as he strapped on his gun belt. "I'm afraid I have to go if I have any chance of catching them. If you tell me what you know about their whereabouts, McGill, everything—the judge might be lenient."

"If Leah dies, I deserve to hang." Bryant didn't so much as flinch. "If it weren't for my girls, I think I'd ask for it."

"Stop thinking like that." He turned to Celia. "Where is she?"

"We found the doc, but she's in bad shape. Though he was surprised she escaped with as little damage as she did, he's still not sure she'll wake up. Bryant was being..." She glanced across the room at Bryant with a look that was both sorry and fearful.

"You can't have a raving lunatic around while you're performing surgery, apparently," Bryant said in a monotone.

Jacob looked at the clock. He ought to lock Bryant up, but precious minutes were slipping away. "Do I need to put you in jail, or can I trust you to stay put?"

Bryant stood. "I'll be outside the doc's until he lets me back in."

"You disappear and I won't be able to help you much."

Bryant nodded and slogged out the door.

Jacob gestured at Celia. "Go to your room and stay."

Without protest, Celia turned for the stairs.

With tears in her eyes, Annie watched her daughter until she disappeared. "It'll be a long time before she sees she's not at fault."

Jacob paused in the middle of stuffing himself into his coat. He couldn't let her believe Celia had no culpability, no matter how much it might comfort her at present. "I'm sorry, love. But she was likely caught up in enough criminal activity I'll be bringing her before a judge as well."

Annie shot him a wounded glance.

"Her part in what happened to Leah was accidental—I have no doubt—but she'll have to answer for her involvement with McGill's hired men."

Annie only stared at him, her body so tense, she was surely working hard not to cry.

He pulled her to stand and held her tight, nestling his cheek against her soft hair. "Rejoice over your daughter's return, but don't quit praying. God can use terrible mistakes for good. Pray Leah won't die, and if she does, that her death won't be in vain."

Her eyes turned watery.

Squeezing the thought of Leah possibly leaving them all behind from his mind to deal with when he returned, Jacob rubbed Annie's back until she breathed more evenly. "I'm sure you can find ways to help them while I'm gone. Hold Leah's hand, make Bryant eat. But I have to go if I have any chance of bringing in the men who did this to her."

He pressed a kiss against her forehead then stepped away.

She snagged him back, pressing a desperate kiss to his lips.

As much as he wanted to stay and hold her, enjoying the affection she was just now offering so freely, the rustlers were getting away.

He broke away. "I'll be back."

"Please," Annie whispered against his lips. "Please come back to me."

CHAPTER FORTY-FOUR

Jacob tried to rub the bleariness from his eyes as he sat behind his desk, but the cell bars still danced, just like the semi-elated swirling still humming inside him.

After so many months of chasing them, he'd nabbed the rustlers three mornings ago as easily as if he'd walked into the mercantile and ordered them from the back. A few hours of following their trail from where the stampede had occurred, and he and his four men had rounded up the rustlers along with their ill-gotten gain.

Though hauling in McGill and Passey had proved no laughing matter, Guy and Rufus had squealed all the way home like the wee little pig, making the arrests fairly routine.

Now if only he could get some rest after four days of little sleep, he'd truly feel accomplished, but Tom Passey's snoring echoed off every last bit of metal in the room.

Though the morning was half past, his prisoners had gone back to sleep, which was fine with him, considering the only other thing they did between courtroom visits was fight.

Since Tom's snoring wasn't as bad as an all-out brawl, he'd

have to grin and bear it. Though for a man no taller than larkspur, his throaty rasps sure rivaled a bison's bellow.

McGill, Rufus, and Guy were all lying on their cots with their pillows bunched over their heads. The only one up was Bryant, who was locked in a separate cell for his protection. He'd been standing by his small barred window, blankly staring into the alleyway, since before first light.

Leah's life still hung on a precipice, but once he'd returned to town, he'd had to lock up Bryant. Was doing so cruel?

And yet, with the way the cattlemen were out for blood after hearing about the city corruption, Bryant wasn't safe outside these walls.

Jacob pressed against the pulsing at his temples. Of course, Tom's racket was cruel and unusual punishment of another sort.

As much as these men might deserve such, he couldn't take any more.

Stepping out onto the porch, he held his hand up to block the sun and see down the crowded street.

The sidewalks were teeming with vendors preparing for tomorrow's sentencing, vying for the best spots to sell to the wagons full of people they hoped would arrive soon.

He couldn't stop the county folk from coming in to see if the town's mayor would swing from a noose, but it tore at his gut that people would travel in hopes of watching someone's death or profiting from those who'd come for such a purpose.

It was too soon for Nolan to be headed over to relieve him, but hopefully he'd arrive early and save him from succumbing to madness.

A thump sounded from within the jail cells and he turned to look through the doorway.

"Wake up, you lout!"

Tom stuffed the pillow Rufus had thrown at him behind his head and settled back to snoring.

Rufus groaned and slumped back onto his cot.

Jacob couldn't take it. He marched back inside, grabbed a tin cup, and struck it against the bars. "Wake up."

Rufus kicked Tom's cot's leg, and the rickety bed collapsed.

"Why you—"

"Hey! Don't you touch him, Tom." If they argued much more, he might have to lock himself away for assault. "Leave him be, Rufus. Or I'll put you both back in handcuffs."

McGill's cot bowed under his weight as he sat up. His eyes were bloodshot and droopy, but he still managed to send Jacob a hate-filled glare.

His boss had spent his entire first day behind bars threatening him, but had held his tongue after a group of cattlemen had tried to break in and pull him out for an immediate hanging.

Jacob had barred the door, shouting above the mob to reassure everyone the judge would see to the rustlers in due time, but that hadn't appeased them. Fortunately, several men of integrity had come to encourage the riled-up cattlemen to let the Lord have his vengeance. They'd also periodically relieved Jacob from his constant vigil in protecting McGill from his enemies.

But even with their help, he hadn't been home for more than a few hours these last three days.

"When is that old biddy coming with lunch?" Rufus stood staring at him from behind the bars as if he were in charge.

"Sometime today, I'm sure. I still have coffee if you'd like."

The man retrieved his mug, and Jacob poured him some before sidling over to Bryant's cell. "Want a drink?"

Bryant shook his head.

The man hadn't said a word to him in three days, not that he blamed him. Talking in front of McGill and his associates would only rile up the men more.

If everyone wasn't so intent on turning everything into a reason for fisticuffs, he'd let Bryant out to talk with him on the porch, but he wasn't about to do anything to incite the cattlemen's ire either. Though they'd soon owe Bryant for the charges sticking to McGill, they weren't in the best of moods and might take out their frustration on any prisoner within their grasp.

A light knock rattled the front door.

"Finally." Guy stood and stretched. "I need something in my stomach before I slam these two idiots' heads together."

The smell of baked ham caused Jacob's stomach to rumble as he opened the door.

His lips drew tight at the sight of the old "biddy" who stood outside. Gwen was the farthest thing from old. Thankfully the few times she'd come by to see her father, she'd not tried to flirt. A welcome relief. "Come in, Miss McGill. The men are certainly ready for their meals. Is Mrs. Tate all right?"

"Her arthritis was acting up, so I volunteered to bring lunch."

Gwen? Volunteer?

She shot a glance at her father. "I hope I can still be of assistance despite my connections."

McGill hmphed and turned his back on his daughter.

At Jacob's nod, she passed by and served the men ham, beans, and crackers.

Almost as soon as she handed the plates through the bars, they were licked clean, except for her father's and Bryant's.

She lingered in front of Bryant's cell. "I called on the doc on the way over. I'm afraid there hasn't been much change."

Bryant looked up at her for a second before turning to stare back out the window. That he'd even reacted showed he'd been glad to know it.

Jacob stepped closer. "Thank you for the update, Miss McGill."

She turned toward him and placed a plate on the office desk, decked out with extra food, which Mrs. Tate had never done. "You have to be starving as well. I've fresh butter and bread—"

Tom rattled the bars. "I didn't get any bread and butter."

She planted a hand on her hip. "And do you deserve any of what you got?"

Jacob huffed. She'd make a good schoolteacher. Too bad she'd likely turn back into a flirt once things settled down.

"He can have my food." Jacob slid his plate away. "I'll be eating at home soon enough."

Gwen frowned, but marched his lunch over to Tom's awaiting hand.

The scruffy cowboy caught her by the wrist and licked his lips. "I bet this don't taste nearly as good as you'd—"

"Unhand her." Jacob stalked over to the cell, but with a crash of a fist, McGill had laid Tom flat before he'd even realized his boss had moved.

Rufus and Guy chortled, and Jacob gave McGill the eye, not that he'd punish the man.

And with Tom out cold, well, things might be a bit quieter around here—for a few minutes anyway.

"Did you hurt yourself?" Gwen reached through the bars toward her father, but McGill ignored her and returned to his cot.

Why was McGill intent on rebuffing his daughter?

"Why don't we go outside and let him alone? Mrs. Tate can retrieve the dirty dishes when she comes by to deliver supper and lectures." He offered Gwen his arm, and after one last glance at her father, she took it.

The nose-tickling, pollen-laden summer breeze hit them full force as Jacob escorted her outside. "I'm sorry your father is acting as if his being behind bars is your fault."

She released his arm and jammed her hands on her hips. "Oh, but it is."

"How's that?"

"Those notes you've been finding under your door these past several months—?"

"You're my tipster?"

A smile of pride licked at her lips. "I knew you'd figure things out with a little help."

But he hadn't. However, admitting that wouldn't change anything.

"Well, I'm ... obliged." His muscles tightened. Surely this wasn't some ploy to get on his good side and ruin his marriage. "But why?"

She shrugged and looked ... embarrassed?

"I had an idea of what he was up to, but no proof. Without my brother here, you were my only hope of setting things right."

She turned away, the tilt of her chin less proud than usual. "Though I know God says to love my father, he's not exactly easy to live with, so I feared confronting him. And Daddy was finding it a bit too amusing that you were so befuddled. Of course, he had the advantage of being able to order you around and know everywhere you went. I knew if he caught me talking to you, he'd start watching me like a hawk. So since he has little patience with my flirting, I figured I could cover up any trips to your office as vain attempts to flatter you, and he'd think little of it."

"So this whole time...?"

She blushed a little. "I'm sure your wife hates me, but once I started the ruse, I had to keep up appearances lest anyone inform him I acted one way while he was around and another when he wasn't."

He sighed overly loud, the relief too big to keep in.

Gwen ducked her head in that flirty feminine way she had, but this time, her eyes were more serious and contrite than he'd ever seen. "Have you given any thought to replacing my father? I'm afraid Armelle will need a new mayor soon."

"I figure there's no need to be discussing who might replace him until after the sentencing." McGill should be found guilty, but one could never tell. "Besides, I'm not the one who decides such things."

"No, I'm talking about you replacing him, Marshal. Now

that you've rounded up the rustlers and exposed the county's corruption, you'd easily win the mayoral position. And I can help. I know how to campaign—"

"Thank you, but no." Though he likely could win, he planned to shuck his duties to the city the first chance he got.

"But there isn't another man as honest and good and—"

"Excuse me." Jacob stepped away and flagged down Nolan, who seemed to have realized he'd want to be relieved earlier than he'd requested. "I appreciate your recommendation, Miss McGill, but I'm not interested." Even if he was, Annie would likely prefer he choose another campaign manager, even if Gwen's past flirting had all been a farce.

Gwen's smile dimmed a little. "If you ever change your mind, I'm willing to help."

"Thank you."

Nolan tipped his hat to Gwen as she took her leave and pulled his horse to a stop. "Never seen this town so busy." The man who might have been his right-hand man, if not for how busy he was improving his father's ranch and a missing a leg, wiped his sleeve against his sweaty forehead.

"I wish there wasn't a reason for it."

"Ah, but we're all breathing a sigh of relief for what you've done. Here's hoping there aren't any more of them and we'll be months, or even years, free from rustlers."

Frank Dent crossed the street, frowning at Nolan as he came closer. "Was I not the one scheduled to relieve you this afternoon?"

Jacob frowned at Frank. Ugh, he'd probably told him to come in today. "No. I'm sorry you came all this way. I guess my lack of sleep mixed me up."

Frank shrugged and looked to Nolan. "Since you live closer to town, you mind switching?"

Nolan turned and surveyed the crowd. "I don't mind. Though I'm not looking forward to beating back the crowd for some food, had my hopes on some of Mrs. Tate's sweet potato pie."

As much as Jacob had looked forward to a quiet hour with his wife and children, the price of food at the hotel had likely doubled. "Mrs. Tate wasn't delivering today, but why don't you join me for lunch? I'm sure Annie will have plenty."

The man's face brightened. "I haven't had anything since breakfast."

"Then it's settled." He handed Frank the keys. "Watch Bryant for me, will ya? I'm afraid he's ... feeling like he's not worth much to this world anymore."

Nolan nodded solemnly. "I fear I know that feeling all too well."

Jacob gripped his shoulder. "And as you know, that's hogwash. This world doesn't need to lose a fine man like you or the man Bryant can be."

After some quick instructions for Frank, Jacob turned to find Nolan had already started hobbling down the street. "You planning to eat everything before I get there?"

Pivoting, Nolan walked backward rubbing his hands. "I don't stand idly by if there's a lady's home cooking to be had."

He knew the look Nolan sported only too well—eating beans every day of the year was no laughing matter.

Jacob picked up his pace, his steps light despite the hours of sleep he'd lost. His days of cold bean eating were over. Life was so much better with a good wife, beautiful children, a hot supper every night, and soon, a ranch.

Once Jacob caught up, Nolan turned to him. "Hope Celia gets off easy."

The spring in his step went flat. "Don't know if I want her to get off easy." She needed to face the consequences or else she might turn out worse. "But I do hope the judge is at least fair."

"Right, right."

Talking over the details of the case, they made their way to his house, then tromped up the back stairs together.

When he opened the door, smells not entirely familiar wafted out, but they were still good enough to make his stomach growl.

Annie bustled about in the kitchen alone.

Too bad he'd had to bring Nolan along, for her slender frame called to his arms. How long had it been since he'd held her without her being in tears?

She turned and brightened for a second, but her smile dimmed upon seeing Nolan.

Seems he hadn't been the only one hoping to find themselves alone. Thankfully she recovered quickly since he wouldn't want Nolan to feel the least bit slighted.

"Anne, I hope I wasn't out of line inviting Nolan to lunch." Jacob pointed Nolan toward a seat.

At Annie's welcoming nod, Nolan took off his hat and lowered himself into the chair a mite awkwardly considering his wooden leg. "I can't tell you how nice a woman's home-cooked meal sounds when you're a confirmed old bachelor like myself."

Jacob rolled his eyes. Nolan was quite a bit younger than he was.

Annie's mouth twitched a little. "I'm not sure ... I mean, I hope you'll enjoy what I've prepared. It's not the usual fare."

She ladled out a few bowls, spilling some with her unsteady hand.

What was she worried about? "I'm sure whatever you made will be wonderful."

She slid a strange looking concoction in front of them and bit her lip. "It's oyster soup."

Nolan blanched.

Perhaps the 'ol bachelor' was wishing he hadn't accepted the lunch invitation so eagerly.

The man recovered nicely and unfolded his napkin. "I'm sure it will be heavenly, ma'am."

Jacob reached for his spoon while Annie stared at him like a girl awaiting approval.

He took a taste—not bad. Though nothing he was keen on having again.

Annie hovered as he took another bite. "Do you like it? I've never made it before. Never even thought to. Or wanted to. But then, I've always just cooked plain fare—which is good, of course—but that's when things were different, and I wanted to try something fancy, to ... well, it doesn't exactly matter what anybody else thinks about my cooking, now does it?"

What on earth had her so flustered? And why did it matter what people thought about her making oyster soup?

"So what do you think?"

Didn't she just say she didn't care about anyone's opinion? "Uh, it's the best oyster soup I've ever had."

Her face lit and she folded her hands against her chest. "Do you think so?"

"Yes." He'd eat oyster soup every day if he could put that look on her face more often.

Nolan grabbed a biscuit and swiped the edges of his bowl with it. "I agree."

The man had finished already?

Perhaps salt might help.

Celia came in from the parlor, dressed in her Sunday finest, short hair slicked back, and sporting dark circles under her eyes. She'd been spending every night with Leah to help the doctor and his wife catch up on sleep considering they had several patients keeping them busy.

Jacob pulled out the chair beside him, and she slunk over and dropped into the seat.

"You'll get through this," he whispered with a hand to her shoulder, but she didn't look up to see his smile.

Nolan wiped his mouth and leaned back in his chair. "I suppose you'll be headed straight to the courthouse here soon?"

Annie stiffened as she ladled out soup for Celia.

Nolan slid his empty bowl toward her for a second helping. "Bet you're happy your late husband's name has been cleared.

It's hard to grow up with a good-for-nothing daddy." He crossed his arms over his chest and gave a sharp nod. "But then, my father didn't turn out so bad for having one. Though you never can tell."

If he could've reached, Jacob would've kicked him under the table. He'd yet to tell Annie about what he'd learned this morning.

Seemed he'd been wrong to have discussed the case with Nolan on the way over.

Spencer walked in from the parlor straight toward Nolan. "Does what you just said mean my pa didn't kill nobody?"

"That's right—"

Jacob cleared his throat.

Thankfully Nolan looked abashed and went back to shoveling in his soup.

Spencer's gaze fixed on their guest. "How'd you know that?"

"Spencer, have a seat."

Jacob's heart lightened when he obeyed.

No matter what, this boy would grow up fine. But still, not all the details were fit to tell a seven-year-old. "This morning, one of the rustlers confessed that your pa caught them panning for gold in your river without permission. Seems they got into an argument and Passey shot him. They tried to cover up the crime by framing your father by murdering another man to make the story believable."

Spencer's lower lip worked. "But why would they do that?"

How could he explain such evil when he didn't understand it himself? "Some people are bad deep inside, and without God's direction in their lives, they can justify anything. But in truth, I don't know."

All sounds of clattering silverware and movement in the kitchen had ceased.

Annie was hunched over near the sink, clearly trying to hold back emotion.

Celia had grown paler than milk, and Spencer's unshed tears glistened on his lower lashes.

Nolan stood abruptly. "I better go relieve Frank."

Spencer's gaze followed the man until he disappeared out the door, and then he popped out of his chair and slammed into Jacob's chest. The boy's sunshine leaked out in an onslaught of tears.

Annie walked over and hugged the boy's head, and Jacob hooked an arm around her to bring her close.

She slipped down onto her knees, letting him hold her as she dissolved into tears as well.

His heart broke over their pain, yet still managed to overflow with joy that he could hold them and call them his own.

Gregory's tragedy had become his blessing.

He wouldn't ever take it for granted.

CHAPTER FORTY-FIVE

Annie pulled a handkerchief from her pocket and wiped her face to keep from wetting Jacob's shirt any further.

How embarrassing to have dissolved into tears with Mr. Key here. She sniffed and looked around to find that the man had disappeared. What must he think of her?

Then again, she'd resolved not to care about others' opinions any longer.

Mother had said proper ladies died out West, and perhaps they did.

Or perhaps they just became more real.

Spencer was using Jacob's shirt sleeve to dry his tears, so she handed him her spare handkerchief.

Celia had somehow been pulled into Jacob's embrace, and though stiff, she at least hadn't pushed away.

Jacob's arm pulled Annie in tighter. How loath she was to move. She may have been crying for Gregory, but all of them together in Jacob's embrace just felt right—like home.

But Celia might not be here to love on tomorrow. Annie tightened her stomach to keep from launching into tears anew.

God alone knew what would happen, and she'd have to trust Him to give both her and Celia the strength to endure.

She reached across Spencer and clasped Celia's hand. "You sure you don't want to eat something before we leave? You'll hold up better with food in your stomach."

"Why does it matter?"

"Well, you might faint—"

"I won't faint." Celia straightened, a flash of fight in her eyes.

Good. She'd need some fire to get through today. She'd never seen Celia as placid and hopeless as she'd been since bringing Leah home.

Annie retracted her hand and enfolded Spencer in her arms instead of the daughter she longed to embrace.

The clock chimed one.

Jacob's compassionate eyes glued to Celia. "It's time to go, darling." His bass voice barely sounded above a whisper.

Was there a man better than Jacob, who loved her willful, headstrong girl as if she were his own?

Celia stood without a glance at either of them and preceded them through the door.

"Do I have to go?" Spencer pulled away and looked at Jacob.

"Joe's ma said you can drop by any time you want."

"Can I go now?"

"Give your ma a kiss first."

Spencer gave her a quick squeeze before shuffling outside.

Jacob reached for Annie's hand, but thankfully said nothing. She likely couldn't talk if her life depended on it. He placed a kiss against her hairline and braced her about the shoulders as they walked out to follow Celia.

Her daughter was already navigating the abnormally busy street as if none of the commotion affected her.

Having never lived in town, Annie hadn't experienced the hoopla of a court trial. Wyoming judges rarely sentenced anyone to hang, and only in cases of murder. But with the shepherd's death, and now Gregory's, to be accounted for, there'd probably be more county folk coming in for the sentencing who'd find the gruesome possibility a draw worthy of a holiday.

Annie glued her gaze on the ground as they shuffled along the dusty road, relying on Jacob's arm and her prayers to keep her upright. Her daughter wouldn't hang, she was fairly certain of that, even if Leah died and the charges for her death were added to the long list the court was dealing with. But right now, she couldn't look at the people who might have come to see her daughter die for sport.

Inside City Hall, Daniel sat on a bench in the hallway next to his father, his hands stuffed into his pockets, and Timothy leaned against the wall beside him, head hung. Annie gripped Jacob's arm, thankful he'd convinced the judge to hold a private trial and sentencing for the children before the men's.

Jacob ushered the families into an office where Judge Macrow sat behind a large desk, flipping through a book while smoking a pipe.

The three young adults sat in the chairs directly across from him while their parents quietly amassed behind them.

Timothy's twin toddler brothers hid behind their mother's skirts. Had Annie known Mrs. O'Conner would bring her children, she'd have asked Joe's parents to watch them along with Spencer, but Judge Macrow cleared his throat. Too late to suggest that now.

"I'm assuming everyone who needs to be here is present?" Directing his question to Jacob, Judge Macrow set down his pipe.

Annie forced herself to let go of Jacob's arm. He wasn't merely Celia's stepfather, but also a lawman with duties. He couldn't stay with her no matter how desperately she wanted to cling to him.

"Yes, everyone is assembled." Jacob helped her sit before moving to the front of the room. He'd be in charge of enforcing whatever sentence the judge assigned Celia and the boys. Hopefully her daughter wouldn't hold that against him.

Praying under her breath, Annie kept her focus on Celia, who sat as still as stone.

"I'll make this short. No need to keep anyone in agony longer than necessary." The judge unfolded a paper and put on his spectacles. "Timothy O'Conner?"

"Yes, sir." The boy stared at his lap.

"Since you and the other minors in this case were unaware that the river section you were panning was not on your employers' land, I find no reason for you to be punished. As to you not telling anyone about the possibility of attempted rustling, I hear you have a prized horse you could auction to pay a fine. The county will accept the proceeds of your sale for restitution. From now on, I expect you to report any criminal activity you hear of as a responsible young adult should, even if doing so may cause friends to suffer the consequences of their actions."

Mrs. O'Conner sighed as if a thousand weights had lifted, and Timothy, though visibly distraught over the loss of his horse, slumped with relief.

"With any luck, you've at least learned that keeping company with the wrong people can lead to your destruction."

Annie's heart lightened. Perhaps Jacob's prediction of a light sentence would come true despite her worst imaginings.

"As for Daniel Crawford and Celia Gephart, you both willfully disobeyed your parents and the laws of this territory. As I can only assign sentences in light of the law, I've taken into account your naiveté, foolhardiness, and lack of premeditation, and have determined to simply make you pay back the county for the shenanigans, vandalism, and sorrow you've heaped upon its citizens. You'll report to Marshal Hendrix, who has agreed to mete out your punishment, and work under his supervision until you've helped every citizen meet Armelle's sidewalk code. If he finds you reluctant to attend to your employment, you will become a resident of the county jail until you have had a change of heart." He leaned forward in his chair and looked between the two young folks in front of him. "Do you understand?"

Daniel uttered, "Yes, sir," and Celia mouthed the same.

"Then so be it." Judge Macrow stood and nodded to Jacob. "I'll see you tomorrow."

Annie closed her eyes.

Thank you, Lord, for delivering my daughter from jail time.

She made her way to Celia on shaky legs and hugged her. "This is good news."

"It won't make up for what I've done." Celia's voice didn't so much as fluctuate.

"It won't, of course, but all you can do is choose what you do next, and choose right."

Her shoulders scrunched up in a shrug. "Won't change anything." She tried to pull away. "I need to get back to Mrs. Whitsett."

The Crawfords filed out around them, but Annie kept a hold of her daughter until Celia finally stopped trying to follow them out the door. "You're right; nothing that's happened can be changed. Lately, I've let fretting over my past decisions steal my joy and rob me of making better choices moving forward. I don't want you to do that too."

"It's not as if you've killed anyone," Celia muttered.

She shook her daughter a little. "Neither have you. Even if Leah doesn't survive, you tried your best to save her. What matters now, is what you choose to do in the next hour, what you choose to do tomorrow. If your past decisions didn't get you where you wanted to be, figure out what decisions will. Beating yourself up over the past won't change a thing."

Annie looked over Celia's head to where Jacob was standing quietly by the judge's vacated desk. "I wasted so much time dwelling on things I had no control over that I treated the piece of heaven God gave us as if he were of little consequence. I chose misery when I could've been comforted."

She let go of Celia's hand and turned toward Jacob. "I chose to question your love, instead of simply loving you back. When I think of what I prayed for … Well, God gave me more than I ever asked for when He gave us you."

Jacob crossed over to her before the last words had even exited her mouth and wrapped his arms around them both. "And I'd given up on God ever gifting me a family, but I'm so glad He finally did."

He swallowed noisily near her ear, and she wriggled her arms around him to hold him back.

His voice seemed to be having difficulty un-lodging itself from his throat. "I—I'm sorry for all the times I've been impatient. For if you loved Gregory half as much as I love you..."

His voice did catch then, and he hugged her tighter.

She likely had loved Gregory as much as Jacob thought she did. But she'd been wrong to think she couldn't begin to love Jacob until her previous love had faded away.

She pressed closer and let herself breathe him in.

Thank you, God, for both the loves you gave me.

CHAPTER FORTY-SIX

Jacob helped Nolan push through the crowd at the courthouse with McGill, Bryant, and rustlers in tow. He frowned at the baker sending his children around with platters of pastries, taking advantage of the circus-like atmosphere as they all awaited the outcome of the trial.

A skirmish to his left sent his hand to his gun.

"Get off me, you oaf!"

"If your wide hide wasn't blocking my view!"

The area cattlemen, who'd never cottoned well to McGill's successes, were not at all in a Christ-like mood this morning.

Last night, he'd had to settle a drunken brawl over who McGill had undermined the most, and the losers had slept off their spirits in his one remaining jail cell.

And with all the pickpockets taking advantage of the crowd, he'd had to appoint a few men to keep watch around the clock.

He shook his head and squeezed Bryant's shoulder as they made their way up the courthouse stairs for the second time today. Hopefully they'd be able to maintain order once the ruling was announced. If the more aggressive cattlemen didn't agree with the judge, they might attempt to hang the prisoners themselves.

Though most considered Leah's injuries punishment enough for Bryant, Jacob tried not to hope too much for a light sentence. Though the judge had been quite fair with the children, his facial expression hadn't softened while listening to the witnesses attesting to Bryant's character during the trial.

The courthouse buzzed with noise and swishing fans.

People jostled Jacob's prisoners, and he glared at each in warning—though they probably couldn't help it since there was hardly room to stand. Jacob swiped at his damp hairline and tried not to be agitated by the amount of people pressing close.

Ahead, McGill sneered at the crowd as he was forced through by Frank Dent. Some spectators shrank away, but a few who'd been repeatedly fined for insufficient upkeep of their sidewalks found it amusing to see the mayor cuffed.

After leading his charges up front, Jacob took a wide-legged stance behind the defendants with Nolan and Frank flanking him, creating a barrier from the attendees.

The standing-room-only crowd parted for the judge.

Once the room quieted, Jacob found Annie's concerned face in the crowd near the windows. He nodded at her, and she nodded back, her eyes ashine with ... what? Pride?

Though catching the rustlers was more Gwen's, Celia's, and God's doing, he couldn't help but puff his chest a bit.

A lazy half smile perked her lips, and her eyes ran down the length of him.

He frowned and peeked down at his clothing to make sure everything was where it ought to be. When he glanced back, a flounce of blue feathers passed between him and his wife.

The fluff in Gwen's fancy hat flurried as she weaved her way toward her father.

The animosity McGill maintained toward his daughter electrified the air around them, yet Gwen stopped to stand behind him.

"Come to order, please." The judge stood near the table at the front. The stirring of the crowd quieted, but the amount of shuffling that came with a room packed full of people made silence impossible.

"Be seated."

Wood creaked up front where there were chairs, adding to the muted hubbub for an instant.

Judge Macrow pulled a small stack of papers from his satchel, and the increase in murmuring while he did so made him scan the crowd with narrowed eyes. He closed his satchel and laid the papers to the side. "I'll make this quick. I have to be on my way within the hour."

Bryant hung his head, and the desire to grip his friend's shoulder made Jacob fidget, but he kept both hands behind his back.

"Defendants, please rise." Judge Macrow adjusted his spectacles. "Concerning Rufus Salazar and Guy Harding, guilty on all charges, sentenced to five years in the Wyoming Territorial Prison. Conrad McGill, guilty on all charges, thirty years in Wyoming Territorial Prison."

A sweeping of satisfied male grunts circled the room.

A man near the front tipped his head back and sighed with happy exaggeration.

Gwen's feathers didn't so much as bob.

"Tom Passey, on account of all charges including two counts of murder—hanged at the neck until dead."

Jacob swallowed hard as the heightened buzz around the room pierced through his skull.

"I'll appeal."

"I expected so." Judge Macrow looked out over the crowd. "He has the right to appeal. There will be no vigilante shenanigans to bring about his sentence before he can take advantage of all that the law allows. Not unless someone is eager to face me at trial next week."

Once he seemed satisfied that the county folk would heed his warning, he flipped a paper and picked up another. "As for Bryant Whitsett. In light of his cooperation and McGill's being his superior creating an imbalance of power, six months in the Wyoming Territorial Prison."

"Thank the Lord," Ava breathed.

Jacob turned and nodded at Bryant's eldest daughter sitting directly behind them. She was due to have her baby any day now. He'd tried to convince her to stay home, worried about how today's verdict coupled with her mother's precarious position might affect her, but she'd insisted on attending.

He'd hoped Bryant could serve his time in the county jail so Leah could visit him if she recovered, but he couldn't argue against such a lean sentence.

"Marshal, I'll leave you to arrange for their accommodations. Court is adjourned."

The crowd erupted with talk and movement.

Stepping around Bryant's seat, Jacob grasped the man's arm and put his mouth near his ear. "Say your goodbyes to your daughter before I have to put you in the prison coach. I'm not sure you'll get another chance." Unfortunately, they would have no time to see Leah before they had to leave.

Jacob walked Bryant over to Ava, who hugged him as tight as her extended abdomen would allow.

He then gave orders to Nolan and Frank for escorting the remaining prisoners outside and returned to Bryant.

His friend's glassy eyes didn't seem focused. "What did the doctor say this morning?"

Jacob's throat clogged. He'd already informed Bryant twice today. "It's still possible she might not make it—but then, he's just figuring that using medical knowledge. We've got prayers at our disposal." He clasped his friend's shoulder and started him through the crowd. "And if, God forbid, she doesn't make it, don't you forget about Jennie and Ava. They need you."

Bryant barely nodded—whether he did so out of real conviction or not, Jacob couldn't tell.

Nolan limped back through the crowd. "Are you ready to go? Frank already has the other four secured in the coach."

Jacob grabbed Bryant by the elbow to escort him as one would a prisoner. "We're coming."

Outside, Annie stood beside the coach, her eyes beseeching. They'd said their goodbyes earlier after visiting Leah, knowing he'd likely be leaving immediately after the ruling, but it seemed that hadn't been enough.

He passed Bryant off to Frank. "If you would excuse me a minute."

Jacob pulled Annie back behind the coach and wrapped her in his arms. "How am I going to leave you?"

"You have to do your job." She tried to smile, but failed. "We'll manage."

"I don't know if I can." He dipped his head, placing his forehead against hers.

"While you're gone, we'll get the ranch ready—"

"Don't bother yourself with moving back."

Her brows scrunched. "You don't want the ranch?"

"Not as much as I want you."

She closed her eyes and he let his gaze linger over every freckle and eyelash.

"There's no need to wear yourself out moving boxes and furniture without me. Just be waiting when I come back."

"Marshal?"

Nolan's question was an unfortunate reminder of how little time they'd had together this week.

"I'm coming." Though he likely hadn't said it loud enough for Nolan to hear, he forced himself to step away from his wife.

"Wire me the moment you know when you'll arrive home." Annie squeezed his hand. "I'll be waiting."

He held on for a moment longer. "Nothing could please me more."

CHAPTER FORTY-SEVEN

Annie dumped the dirt she'd swept off her cabin floor over the porch railing and inhaled clean, country air. The place looked as if she'd never left.

Except for Jacob's favorite rocking chair in the parlor corner, his rifles above the mantel, and his dishes stuffed inside her cabinets. Though he'd told her not to worry about moving back while he was away, she'd wanted things to be ready for him to relax after such an unpleasant task as escorting his best friend to prison.

And of course, she wasn't at all the same woman who'd left this place only a handful of months ago. A different ring encircled her finger, and a new love grew in her heart.

Her breathing hitched every time she glanced at the clock. She'd be back in Jacob's arms again come dusk if the stage was on time.

Spencer's gentle murmurs sounded from the porch's edge, where he'd curled up near a batch of new kittens, trying to coax the mama out with some pork fat.

Annie checked her timepiece again. "It's time to head into town. Why don't you grab the linens and hop into the wagon?"

Without complaint, Spencer scrambled up and ran to grab the basket she'd set on the porch earlier.

Though the laundress's hand had healed, Corinne was still behind at the laundry. Celia was too glued to Leah's side to be of much help to the young woman, so Annie had volunteered to take care of Doc Ellis's sheets and bandages.

Thankfully Leah had managed to stay awake for a few consecutive hours yesterday, so the doctor expected her to survive—she would face limitations, but she'd be alive.

However, that hadn't convinced Celia to come home and rest any.

"Can I bring these?" Spencer held out an armful of bloodwort. The pungent plants' tightly-bunched white flowers weren't pretty enough to call attention away from the fact they were wilting from being picked earlier in the day.

Annie fluffed his hair. "I'm sure Leah will enjoy them, but I don't think she needs so many." Though if Spencer insisted on bringing them all, the doctor could dry some for good purpose.

"I'm giving most of them to Celia. She'll need flowers to go in all those vases at Mrs. Whitsett's house. Her flowers are probably all dead by now."

"Good thinking." Whenever the doctor's wife had sent Celia away to rest, she'd chosen to unpack the boxes Bryant had thrown together the night of the stampede instead. "Did you get your bedroll?"

Jacob would likely be exhausted after his travels, so they'd decided to stay in town tonight though his house was practically empty now.

Spencer helped her put everything into the wagon, and Annie happily listened to his chatter on the drive into town.

At Doc Ellis's, Spencer ran into the side office without even so much as a knock.

Annie scurried in after him, and the door swung shut loudly behind her. Spencer was nowhere to be seen. She tossed an apologetic look toward the white-haired doctor. "I'm sorry if—"

"Mama! She's awake!"

Well, if Leah hadn't been awake a second ago, she was now.

The doctor inclined his head toward the front patient room. "She's been trying to stay up long enough to see you."

Annie fought back the warmth in her eyes. Just days ago, the doctor wasn't sure Leah would ever awaken again. Stepping into the plain white room, she smiled at her friend despite wanting to wince at the discoloration and ugly stitches marring Leah's face. Celia was sitting quietly in a straight-back chair beside the bed, an open book in her lap.

"Annie." Leah's voice sounded gritty and painful. But at least she had a voice. With the damage done, the doctor hadn't been sure she'd speak again.

Giving her a bright smile, Annie took Leah's extended hand and sat on the empty chair beside her while Spencer tried to stuff handfuls of bloodwort around the lifeless coneflowers he'd brought in a few days ago.

"As happy as I am that you stayed awake to see me, you should be sleeping as much as you can. We'll have plenty of days to talk." She squeezed Leah's hand and closed her eyes. *God, may it truly be so.*

"Don't worry. I'm fine." The gravel in her voice, the circles under her eyes, and the deep bruising indicated otherwise. "I've been talking to Celia for an hour now, though she's been insisting I rest my voice."

"As you should."

"But our talk's too important."

"Oh?" Annie looked across at Celia, who was staring at the wall.

"She seems to think she can't be forgiven."

Celia did look at Annie then. "She says she doesn't want me to move in with her and help while Bryant's away. Says I have duties with you."

Yesterday, she'd asked about helping Leah while she recovered—one of the first unselfish requests she'd made in a long time—and Annie had thought it a good idea.

She turned to Leah. "She has my permission to do so. We can handle things without her." Since Celia hadn't helped around the house in quite some time, she knew that for certain.

She'd also insisted on regularly checking up on her daughter to make sure she wasn't being a burden rather than a help—but with her daughter's recent behavior, she wasn't much worried.

"But she doesn't need to be helping me in a misguided attempt to earn my forgiveness." Leah's expression remained extraordinarily calm despite how long it took her to push those words out of her ravaged throat.

Celia shrugged. "I don't deserve forgiveness. Not even if I clean your house every day for the rest of my life."

Leah opened her mouth but the sound that came out was nothing more than a rasp. Then she started to cough and nearly choked.

Moving quickly to prop her up on pillows, Annie helped Leah sit up farther as Celia fetched a glass of water.

"It's not that I don't want her help." Leah stopped to wheeze a bit and reposition herself to look at Annie. "But it's more important that she's not doing it to punish herself."

Annie looked between the two. "I take it you've told my daughter she's forgiven, but she has no plans to forgive herself?"

Leah's head bobbed wearily. "I know how it feels—"

"No, you don't," Celia interrupted. "You've not almost killed someone. You've not acted in such a way that your family can barely stand to be around you."

She popped out of her chair as if discovering it was made of nails and headed toward the small curtained window that looked out into the alleyway. "There's nothing I could ever do to deserve your forgiveness."

"Forgiveness is a gift, Celia." Annie rose slowly from her chair and directed Spencer out of the room before crossing over to her daughter. "You're clearly sorry for what you've done, you seem to want to change your ways, and you're helping here as best you can. Beyond that, what do you think you must do?"

"More than that."

"Rejecting forgiveness only keeps a relationship broken."

"I deserve it."

"Like you deserve God's wrath?"

Her daughter stiffened and her face went blank. "Yeah. I deserve God's wrath, too."

"Honey." Annie tried to duck to look into her daughter's eyes, but Celia only turned her head farther away. "All of us have wronged God. No matter how hard we work to be better, no matter how many good deeds we pile up—what we've done has to be accounted for."

Her daughter's body didn't even soften.

"But Jesus offers forgiveness, and so does Leah. If you don't accept it, who are you hurting? Them or you?"

"She shouldn't—" Celia cut herself off with a vehement head shake.

"I'm sorry I've been badly modeling lately how one should accept a gift freely offered. I certainly didn't do anything to deserve how Jacob treats us. I wasn't even able to give him what I'd promised—until now anyway. But what good would it do us for me not to accept his love? What good will it do either you or Leah to refuse her forgiveness? What good does it do anybody to reject God's offer to save? Jacob nor Leah nor God feel vindicated when we choose to suffer by refusing their gifts."

A tear rolled soundlessly down Celia's cheek. "But I'm responsible."

A soft rumbling behind them interrupted the silence. Annie turned to see Leah's bruised face slack with sleep. "You may be. But Leah isn't holding it against you. She's offering you a rare gift to drop your guilt and be friends."

Celia fidgeted while frowning out the window. "Just like Jacob treats me like a daughter though I refuse to listen to anything he says?"

"Yes, just like that. We didn't earn such love, now did we?"

She drooped a little. "When I came home with Leah..." She sniffled. "He didn't lecture me. Just hugged me and told me he loved me. And I think he actually does, and so, I can't exactly hate him anymore."

"Good. And why don't you work on letting him into your heart too? He won't ever take the place of your pa, but he can be a pa to you in his own way."

Doctor Ellis stepped into the room and looked toward his patient. "Why don't you two have a seat in the waiting room with Spencer? I'd like to be sure Mrs. Whitsett rests as long as possible."

"Of course." Annie held out her arm for Celia to join her on the way out.

Mrs. Ellis stopped in front of them with a pile of dirty sheets in her arms. "Celia, honey, go home and get some rest. Howard isn't as worried about Mrs. Whitsett now, and I don't think you've slept anywhere but a chair these last three days. With the other patients gone, we'll be able to attend her just fine."

"But if—"

"If things change, we'll let you know." The woman's grandmotherly smile was softer than any smile the townsfolk had given Celia in quite a while.

Annie let out a long breath. If others were seeing the change in her daughter, perhaps the change would be permanent.

But if her daughter wasn't staying with Leah tonight, where would she stay?

Annie pulled out her timepiece as they walked out of the doctor's with Spencer. "We should be able to get back to the ranch in time to grab your bedding and return before the stage comes, if we hurry." Oh why had she moved everything back already? She'd not thought this through.

"Aw." Spencer's upper lip arched up to the side. "Do we really have to drive all the way there and back again?"

"Perhaps you two would rather stay at the cabin?" She

looked at Celia. Her daughter could certainly watch Spencer, but she had to be certain she'd take on the responsibility.

Celia raised a shoulder in a half-hearted shrug. "We don't need to go back at all. I can stay at the Whitsetts'. I—I do believe that Leah forgives me, but she still needs someone to help her. And I think it should be me."

She squeezed Celia's hand, thankful her girl wanted to help with no prodding. "I suppose that could work."

"Can I sleep there too?" Spencer bounced out in front of them. "I don't want to sleep on the floor."

"I don't think—"

"It's fine, Ma." Celia nodded matter-of-factly, as if she'd matured ten years in the last ten days. "He can come with me."

"Now, Spencer—"

"Mrs. Whitsett told me I could come over any time I want, remember?"

She pulled his wiggly form closer. "Yes, but you'll have to do what Celia tells you to." That was a command she'd not have thought she'd utter a few weeks ago. "We want to make sure Leah is coming back to an orderly house."

"I'll put away all the toys I get out. They only have a trunkful."

"We'll be fine, Ma." Celia stepped over to put her arm around her brother. "You can go … welcome Jacob home. I know I haven't been acting right toward him lately, and I know he didn't marry you to take Daddy's place—I just..." She dropped her head to look at her feet.

"You missed your father. It's understandable."

"But it's not like Jacob had anything to do with his death. If he'd had the chance to save him, he would've."

Annie smiled, her eyes watering up. "Yes, he'd sacrifice a lot for our best."

"So what are you standing around here for? Go find him and have a nice night without us." She turned Spencer by the shoulders and prodded him toward the wagon. "Get your stuff so we can go."

After saying goodbye to them both, Annie watched Celia walk away with her arm around Spencer.

Lord, I'm sorry for being angry at you for letting her run away. Though I'm so terribly sorry Leah endured what she did, if that was how you chose to turn my girl around, I'll praise you for it. Help her accept both yours and Leah's forgiveness so she can give you her best from here on out.

And may you help me give Jacob my best too.

She glanced about the near-empty street and wiped her palms against her skirts.

Tonight's plans were a blank now. With no children to attend to, no packing to be done, and a husband she couldn't wait to see returning in just a few hours...

Her stomach flip-flopped at just the mere thought of being able to touch him again.

She'd told him she'd be waiting at the depot, but perhaps she could do better.

Stretching his arms and legs in anticipation of getting out of the coach, Jacob stared out the window where the edge of Armelle had just appeared on the dusky horizon.

No one walking on Main Street looked like Annie.

Oh, how he'd missed her.

He didn't envy Bryant the months separated from his wife with only his guilt to keep him company.

The man had slumped onto his cot the moment he'd stepped inside his cell, not even responding to Jacob's last goodbye.

Hopefully, the telegram with the doctor's more positive prognosis had reached Bryant by now. Annie's telegram from last night about Leah's improving condition had certainly made his chest lighten. Surely after some days of thanking God for sparing his wife, Bryant would buck up.

Lord, keep him safe and sane.

The rattling stagecoach slowed, and Jacob braced for the stop, frowning at not seeing Annie near the depot.

Last night, he could barely stand the thought of being trapped in this thing another day, but since he'd already wired her of his expected arrival, he'd forced himself back on board.

When the vehicle finally stopped, he couldn't help but groan in anticipation of being freed from this contraption.

He nodded toward Frank on the opposite side of the coach. "Thank you for your assistance. I couldn't have done this without you."

"Not a problem." The middle-aged man put his hat on and practically jumped out the door, clearly as eager to be free of this cage as he was. "I'll come by in the morning if you'd like."

"No need." Jacob winced as his sleepy leg protested the weight he placed on it. "I don't intend to go in early, and I've got Nolan. I'm sure you have plenty to see to at your place."

"See you later then." Frank tipped his hat, collected his things, and headed for the livery.

Jacob grabbed his own bag, thanked the driver, and watched Frank walk down the road.

He nodded at two passersby who'd acknowledged his return, but soon found himself alone on the street.

The smile he'd been sporting died away.

Annie hadn't promised to be waiting the very moment he set foot upon the dirt.

And it was late, and she did have children to tend.

"Marshal!"

He turned to watch Nolan ride up at a clipped pace, cheerfully flagging him with a hat in his hand.

As much as he probably ought to be informed of what happened during his absence, he'd hoped not to deal with work until tomorrow.

"Welcome back!" Nolan reached down for a handshake. "Your wife's wagon is at your house. Figured with how she moved everything to the ranch while you were gone, you might be intending to head straight out, but she probably wouldn't fuss if you stopped by to help her pack the last of it."

Jacob nodded, trying not to appear as if Nolan's information was new. "Of course."

She'd already moved most everything?

And why would she have come into town but not be at the depot? He consulted his timepiece. Exactly eight o'clock. Had the telegraphing office bungled his message?

"You all right?"

Jacob shook his head. Somehow he'd forgotten Nolan was still there. His mouth twitched a little as he tried to form a reply. "Sure. Fine. I'm just tired."

Perhaps she'd lost track of time.

"Good. I'll see you tomorrow then." Nolan disappeared back down the road.

Jacob closed his mind off to the sudden thought that Annie's ranch was worth more to her than him and put one foot in front of the other. He'd known her ranch was important, for she'd married a stranger to save it.

But she'd also told him she loved him. Maybe not as much as she loved her ranch, but love it was, he was sure of it.

He sighed and switched his bag from one hand to the other. Just because she was being practical—coming into town to pick him up along with hauling the rest of their things back to the ranch—didn't mean she wouldn't be happy to see him.

He was no longer in love alone, but perhaps more romance and wooing were necessary so he wouldn't be the only one counting down the minutes while they were apart.

Up ahead, Annie's wagon was indeed parked in the churchyard near his house, but her horse wasn't hitched to it and the wagon bed appeared empty. He frowned at the house's dark windows as he approached his front door.

Had she walked to meet him at the station and passed by unnoticed?

He tried the knob. Unlocked. He opened the door. "Annie?"

His voice bounced around the empty room. Nothing left but the big rug on the floor.

Nolan hadn't been kidding. She'd dragged everything out already.

Though he'd wanted to own a ranch for as long as he remembered, the bareness of the place where he'd spent his first days as husband and father...

Well, he hadn't expected to miss this house, but it seemed he would.

"Jacob, is that you?" Her voice was faint as it traveled from beyond the stairwell.

Though she'd not met him at the station, that didn't mean he couldn't sweep her off her feet the moment he saw her. "Coming."

At the top of the stairs, he peeped into the kids' rooms. Also empty.

She hadn't wasted any time. What did she have left for them to take back?

At the threshold to his room, he stepped inside and took his fill of Annie's profile silhouetted against the window. Slim and fit and all his.

"Hello." Shadows obscured her face, but the warmth in her voice made his worries melt away.

But instead of coming to meet him, she pushed up the window sash, letting in the cool evening air.

This room wasn't bare. His bed still remained along with the big oak wardrobe.

The breeze ruffled the curtain and the strangest screech started, slowly transforming into a bad impression of a musical note.

He groaned. "If anything could ruin a homecoming—"

"Give Joe a chance." She smiled as she walked toward him. "He's been practicing."

Why would listening to that boy ruin perfectly good music put such a smile on her face?

Though an instrument was in the process of being murdered outside, the moment she stepped into his arms, his ears were inclined to forgive.

He pressed a kiss against the top of her head and spoke into her sweet-smelling hair. "Let's run away before he ruins the night."

"Shhh, listen." She backed up to place a finger across his lips, which he immediately kissed.

Though perhaps the heady feeling of her skin against his was turning his brain into mush, Joe seemed to be making actual, recognizable sounds.

At the end of what seemed like an interminable measure of something resembling a song, another violin joined in. Joe's teacher? Then a harmonica entered into the congealing melody.

Nolan was the only harmonica player he knew and ... was that a banjo? "Would that be Mrs. Tate's son?"

She smiled. "Know anyone else who can play one?"

He shook his head.

So this is why she hadn't come to meet him. And yet... "If Ivan's out there, Mrs. Tate likely knows about this serenade. Somehow, I doubt dragging her son out to play for us will make the old woman's estimation of you go up."

She shrugged. "You're probably right, but I don't care anymore."

She raised up to give him a kiss, and he couldn't help but return it with more fervor than was likely appropriate with people only a few feet outside their window.

Though Annie's intoxicating lips were busy sending every thought flying from his head, the song outside formed into a recognizable melody despite Joe's screeching in the midst of it.

He pulled back. "Is this, 'When the Corn is Waving, Annie Dear'?"

He'd never been one to sing this song much, but he might have do so more often now.

"Yes." Annie ran her hand up his arm and onto his shoulder. "Mind if we dance?"

"As long as you promise this dance ends with more kisses than I got after the last two."

She hummed. "I think I can assure you of a little more than that."

How could a man care a whit about dancing after such a promise? "Just a little, eh?"

Her grin was wickedly adorable, and he pulled her against him.

The first night they'd danced to Joe's violin definitely had not ended as he'd hoped, but this night sure would.

She laid her head on his shoulder and he started to sing along with the lazy beats of the verse:

When the corn is waving, Annie dear, oh! meet me by the stile,
To hear thy gentle voice again, and greet thy winning smile;
The moon will be at full, love, the stars will brightly gleam;
Oh! come, my queen of night, love, and grace the beauteous scene.

His voice failed him for a moment and he pressed his lips against her hairline as they swayed. "The whole time I was away, I couldn't wait to hear your voice or see your smile, so when you weren't there to greet me when I got off the stage, I got jealous."

"Jealous?"

"Nolan stopped to tell me you'd moved everything to the

ranch. I started worrying you might never want me more than your land."

She pulled back to stare up at him. "I thought you wanted the ranch? If you'd rather we buy land that would feel more like yours, we can. You're more important than a piece of property—though I'd want to put something into the deed about being able to attend the graves."

The song outside the window ended in a plaintive chord and he nuzzled her ear. "Don't worry about it. Wherever you are is home enough for me." He kissed the freckle at the corner of her eye and then the one below that.

"I'm sorry I didn't meet you at the station. I was late getting everything set."

The vibrations of her words buzzed against his lips as he trailed kisses down her neck.

"Our plans changed last minute, so I had to come up with a new one."

Leaving off with the kisses, he cupped her face, and couldn't help but smile at every adorable inch of her. "Please tell me this plan doesn't involve us picking up the children and driving out to the ranch."

"No, we're staying right here."

"So you're mine for the night?"

"And every night."

Just as Jacob leaned down to kiss her for all she was worth, the band outside started up again.

He growled and tipped his head toward the window. "And how do we make them go away?"

"Drop the sash and extinguish the light."

Without another word, he closed the window and blanketed them in darkness.

And though it seemed he hadn't been the only one counting down the minutes until his return, wooing and romancing his bride was certainly no hardship.

No hardship at all.

I hope you enjoyed *Romancing the Bride*! If you did, please take a moment to share with others. You can do so by posting an honest review wherever you purchased this book and also on Goodreads.

[Please note that an e-reader may ask you to rate a novel after the last page, but that won't show up on their site. That rating helps them recommend other stories you might enjoy.]

Also consider mentioning *Romancing the Bride* on social media, especially where you talk about reading! Word of mouth is the number one reason people pick up unfamiliar books, so I'd love for your help in getting the word out. Every review and mention helps!

I'm currently writing more stories in the *Frontier Vows* series. In the meantime, if you'd like to read another marriage of convenience story by me, check out *A Bride for Keeps* in my *Unexpected Brides* series.

To keep up to date with my book releases and special announcements, subscribe to my newsletter at melissajagears.com

ACKNOWLEDGMENTS

Books are such enormous things, not only do they span many, many pages, but sometimes many, many years. I wrote this book in 2010, and my old Scribes 203 group helped me revise my way through it when it was in its infant stages. It certainly needed a lot of help at the time! Thanks to Anne Greene, Glenn Haggerty, and Naomi Rawlings for working with me back when I was still struggling to find myself as a writer while also learning how to write around a newborn.

Eight years later and after a massive rewrite, I had the privilege of getting help from fellow authors Naomi Rawlings (I forced the poor woman to read this again) and Myra Johnson. Plus my beta readers Iola Goulton, Cara Grandle, Hannah Gridley, Sarah Keimeg, Stephanie McCall, Amy Parker, Karen Riekeman, and Anne-Marie Turenne lent a hand in helping make this story into what it is now.

Thank you Najla Qamber for your artistic expertise with this novel's cover. It makes me happy just looking at it.

Thanks to my agent, Natasha Kern, for your encouragement and belief in me.

My family, as always, sacrifices a lot to have a writer in their midst. I'm rather astounded that they're proud of me for every new release knowing how often I'm zoned out while working on a story and shoving things to the back burner to meet deadlines. Thanks for your support.

And of course, I pray that these works are acceptable to God, for it is the talent He laid in me that makes this possible.

ABOUT THE AUTHOR

Much to her introverted self's delight, award-winning writer Melissa Jagears hardly needs to leave home to be a homeschooling mother and novelist. She lives in Kansas with her husband and three children and can be found online at Facebook, Bookbub, Pinterest, Goodreads, and melissajagears.com. Feel free to drop her a note at author@melissajagears.com, or you can find her current mailing address and an updated list of her books on her website.

To keep up to date with Melissa's news and book releases, subscribe to her newsletter at melissajagears.com

facebook.com/melissajagearsauthor
amazon.com/author/melissajagears
bookbub.com/authors/melissa-jagears
goodreads.com/Melissa_Jagears
twitter.com/MelissaJagears
pinterest.com/melissajagears

Published by Utmost Publishing
www.utmostpublishing.com

Printed in the United States of America

Library of Congress Cataloging-in-Publication Data

Names: Jagears, Melissa.
Title: Romancing the bride / Melissa Jagears
Description: Wichita, KS: Utmost Pub., 2018. | Series: Frontier Vows
Identifiers: LCCN 2018910819 | ISBN 9781948678032 (pbk.) | ISBN 9781948678025 (ebk.)
LC record available at https://lccn.loc.gov/2018910819

The song excerpt in chapter 2 is *The Sparrow on the Tree* by Alfred S. Gatty
The song excerpt in chapter 23 is *In the Evening by the Moonlight* by James A. Bland
The song excerpt in chapter 26 is *For the Beauty of the Earth* by Folliott S. Pierpoint
The song excerpt in chapter 42 is *Many Happy Returns of the Day* by Eliza Cook and John Blockley
The song excerpt in chapter 47 is *When the Corn is Waving, Annie Dear* by Charles Blamphin

COPYRIGHT

Cover design © Qamber Designs and Media
Author represented by Natasha Kern Literary Agency